# THE PEOPLE'S REPUBLIC OF ABSURDIA

or

*BLIGHTY: THE STATE WE'RE IN*

by

## ED SPENCER

SIGMUND FRAUD BOOKS™
SFB001

Published by **SIGMUND FRAUD BOOKS™**
London & Norfolk
sigmundfraudbooks.com
if you need a word > info@sigmundfraudbooks.com

*BRUTALIST WRITING, LAUGHING LIKE A SCREWDRIVER*

ISBN-13: 978-1-911403-00-5

Cover design by Josh Tinsley

Typeset by **THE BARN**
North Walsham Road, Suffield, Norfolk, NR11 7AJ

British Library Cataloguing in Public Data.
A catalogue record for this book is available at the British Library.

## About the author

Ed is something of a nomad. Having attended eight different schools he's travelled extensively during his 36 years, doing all he can to avoid a 9-5 job. He's long since thought life is a black comedy. Whisky, coffee and ale are important.

Ed has had stories published on EtherBooks, been short-listed for the Unbound Press Flash Fiction Award, co-founded a political zine and written for numerous publications including Artrocker magazine. *The People's Republic of Absurdia* is his first novel.

# Praise for
## *The People's Republic of Absurdia*

"He captures the truth of the times very well" – Arthur Riotus, *Well Thumbed (The Second Hand Porn Mag)*

"In light of widespread dismay at the way we're run, this novel is for anyone that thinks the government is just taking the piss" – Terrance Gonzo, Activist

"Spencer has a rare brilliance for making stuff up" – Halton Pickles, Author of *My Mother Was A Vegetarian In A Tribe Of Cannibals*

"This book rejuvenated my interest in contemporary fiction" – Jez Thorburn, Political Leader

"Well what can I say? It's, er... Interesting?" – Jasper Ranjitsini, Entrepreneur & Coloniser

"This novel is like the Monster Raving Loony Party...with ideas. If we're not careful, this will be our future" – Rosette Tokelove, Author of *I've Never Been Wrong Yet*

"I've just never liked disabled people" – Gideon Oxform, Chancellor of the Exchequer

*To Guy*

# THE PEOPLE'S REPUBLIC OF ABSURDIA

## CONTENTS

# 1

# GOTCHA!

FRED HAD SPENT the late afternoon and early evening electronically thumbing through *Citizens' Accounts*. He was looking for a loner, someone who drank a lot, someone at the fringes of society who would embrace this rare opportunity. He was certain any number of people in Hellevue would be grateful for it, but he needed someone with a bit of personality, someone whose apparently new and radical approach to life would truly inspire.

He had got as far as *Life Administration* Group Four and still only had a handful of possibilities, none of whom had really whet the proverbial. He scrolled down the page, hoping for inspiration.

*Payne, Kevin* – Priest. Recently branded *Disruptive Dogmatic*. Required to take courses to escape trappings of fantasy and whimsy. Three Social Behavioural Points. Threat to have rations cut. Definitely more like it, thought Fred. Could play well as a reformed character.

*Peacock, Anthony* – Unable to verify Citizen's whereabouts 19:54-22:37, June $6^{th}$ and 07:30-09:02, June $8^{th}$. Incomplete Environmental Footprint. Two Social Behavioural Points. Required to attend interview to explain actions.

Probably the Scanners not working properly in Hellevue. Pass.

*Peel, Joseph* – Failed to attend Community Athletics event on Life Admin Group Designated Activity Day. Two Social Behavioural Points. Rations cut for one week.

Not exactly the arch maverick I'm looking for.

*Pierce, Michael* – Arrested for smoking within half a mile of a Primary School. Three Social Behavioural Points.

Better, but...

Fred was just starting to lose a bit of heart, which was rare for him. His ideas always worked and this one was arguably among his best. But he needed to find his man. Pausing to finish the last mouthful of beer from his bottle, Fred thought he might go home for the evening. Get back on it in the morning. Maybe ring Denise tonight and unwind.

Just ten more minutes he told himself.

*Pope, Robert* – Divorced. Financial problems. *Misaligned.* Current Abode: *LifeManagement4Life.* Maxed out on Social Behavioural Points. Crimes include...

As Fred took in the Citizens' data his brain experienced a sensation akin to watching fruit line up in a slot machine. My God, he thought, I've found him! This man, this Robert Pope, seemed to be something of an outsider, from the northern nation no less. Had been in London only six months. He was unemployed, lived in social housing, received rations and spent all his benefits on tobacco and alcohol. *And* he was currently enjoying a bit of modern medicine at a *LifeManagement4Life* Institute. A *Misaligned.* Though he frequented pubs he did not seem to entertain guests at his abode. Of course, with the SwipeScanners in Hellevue not functioning (had they ever?) a full map of this particular Citizen's movements was hard to acquire. However, Fred felt he knew enough. This was a man who ticked all the boxes. This was a man whose charge sheet read like the calling card of a deviant, a man either unable or unwilling to participate in the new society.

In his head office at the *Citizens' Announcements Unit* Fred dialled the personal number of Dr Zini. He always enjoyed talking to the doctor, the flirty old thing. Never consummated that particular relationship but he certainly relished coming up with Health Policy with her. She was wild!

"Good evening, Doctor. And how are you?"

"Oh very well, thank you Frederick darling. It's been a while since we chatted."

"You know how it is, Doc. But you are always on my mind, naturally."

"You are too kind. So to what do I owe the pleasure?"

"I'm calling about one of your patients. A Robert Pope."

"Oh yes?"

"Yes. I need him. For a little project."

"How intriguing."

"Yes."

"I see. Well, he needs to complete a few more realignment modules before he's ready to be released. Are you thinking of a temporary loan or would he be out indefinitely? He's quite an angry man."

"Well Doctor, it would be a permanent assignment. With your blessing, naturally. Regarding his anger, that's the point really. Though I'm sure you've done some sterling work already."

"Will he like what you've got in store for him?"

"Has he liked everything so far?"

Silence from Zini's end.

"I think that's your answer. But there are rewards in my little scheme. And I need someone with a bit of fire in his belly. It'll make the whole thing work that much better."

"Well I'll need a week or so but after that-"

"Perfect. Thank you Doctor. Speak soon."

The timespan was exactly what Fred needed. He had a few other things to sort too, not least the arrangements for Republic Day. But he was more interested in what would be happening in the celebration's immediate aftermath. Quite a few people's worlds were going to be turned upside down. No change there then, thought Fred, as he poured himself a little whisky.

As he washed the fine Scotch round his mouth - a fitting drink given the land of Pope's birth - Fred toasted the ease with which his latest ruse was coming together. He smiled. He lived for pleasure and his life pleased him greatly. He was one of the lucky ones who knew what he wanted and, more importantly, how to get it. Never from his mouth, *if I knew then what I know now*. He was delighted with everything he had achieved so far. Undoubtedly he was ahead of events. He was shaping them, after all.

## 2

## *LIFEMANAGEMENT4LIFE*

PONTIFF LAY NAKED on his bed. The Time Indicator, or *clock*, as such things had been known in the past, indicated he needed to get to breakfast. Attendance was compulsory.

On cue, a light tinkling of piano began over the speakers. This was the Sonic Technicians' idea of a nice alarm call but it was entirely unnecessary. Every *Misaligned* in here would already be awake given the punishment for missing an appointment.

As the first forays of a summer morn lapped his face, Pontiff rubbed his bald head and yawned. He bathed a moment in the warming rays and tried to ready himself for another day. After a couple of seconds he reached onto the floor to locate his white briefs and white t-shirt, and levered himself out of bed. He clothed and set about his morning routine: fifty sit-ups followed by fifty-press ups followed by fifty sit-ups, followed by ten pull-ups on the metal curtain rail that surrounded his single bed. He was a man of medium height and well-set build, and needed to keep his strength up in this place.

At the small sink in the corner of his three-by-three metre cell Pontiff splashed some water on his face and head and took in his reflection. He was lightly tanned, a surprising skin tone given the land of his birth, and the scars of battle were evident. He had felt the full force of the People's Republic of Britannia on an almost daily basis at Life Camp – and indeed for some time before that – and staring into his own green eyes he felt every minute of his forty-three years.

For three months this place had been his home, just one of the many centres brought in to aid those that could not cope with the rigours of the improved, modern life. Many in here had been interred a lot longer. Many had become so institutionalised they felt they would never be able to live outside the parameters of *LifeManagement4Life*, the prospect of returning to society to fend for themselves filling them with dread.

As he did every morning Pontiff looked out across the playing fields to the perimeter fence. Standing a mere thirty metres high with a subsidiary bulwark beyond, it was peopled with the requisite armed Blackguard and had all the allure of a Cold War-era Berlin Wall. Scanning the horizon, Pontiff's eyes came to the entrance arch of the mammoth gated complex and the start of that long gravel drive, the approach to the imposing white grandeur of *LifeManagement4Life*. The flag of the republic billowed delicately in the breeze. A poor mock-up of the Japanese imperial standard, the red sun spouted alternate red, white and blue rays, the colours of the old Union Jack.

Pontiff rubbed his bald head again, gave it a robust itch, and leant across his bed. From a small table he picked up his *LifeManagement-4Life* booklet – *A Guide for the Misaligned*. He looked over his timetable to see which of the lessons, field activities or role-plays he had in store today, or which of the daily chores he was to complete to ensure he (like every *Misaligned*) understood that a clean and tidy home made for a clean and tidy mind. There was a relentless obligation to always be somewhere, always doing something. *Letter Posting Best Practice* awaited him before lunch. Today's bonus? An assessment-cum-presentation, and a key moment in demonstrating his realignment. Then, later in the day, he... He didn't want to look. He knew what else was coming. Modern medicine beggared belief.

From atop the dresser on the window-side of his bed, Pontiff grabbed his Life Camp uniform and donned the all-in-one linen suit and regulation moccasins. Both white, naturally, like everything else in here. The Liberal Compassionates felt white best evoked feelings of purity, of goodness, of transparency.

"Not to mention a little slice of heavenly godliness," Dr Zini had added. "It will help you realign."

Pontiff left his room to passages teaming with anxious *Misaligneds*, all dressed in white, all trying not to be late for breakfast.

5

"What a fucken shit show," he muttered, following the throng through the curved corridors. There were no corners, no hard edges. Anything as abrupt as a right-angle might upset the balance of a *Misaligned*.

Hoisted on the parabolic walls were holographic screens upon which the camp's leader, Dr Zini, would appear to pump out mantras, advice, timetable amendments and any other messages she might have. These screens were also used to play images from the recent past, of the millions that had met their ghastly demise at the hands of *Plasticitis*, of toothless, ill and washed out people sobbing into the body bags of their loved ones, of the time of great fatigue, of people shuffling through life amidst pollution and disease, of the outgoing government dripping with the carnal goo of sleaze, energy sources all but vanquished, when many, if not most, had slipped into poverty. These images were reminders of why life had had to change, reminders of what had led everyone to where they were now, reminders of the importance of *Easification-Facilitation*. Nobody spoke.

*"Misaligned, time to meal-on, time to meal-on. Misaligned, time to..."*

As the droning tones of the Sonic Technicians filled the corridors Pontiff remembered he was due to mentor today. A new intake was arriving after lunch and Dr Zini had decided to see how he would react to some responsibility. He laughed in anticipation.

A series of long benches filled the cafeteria, and enough room to accommodate the two hundred or so campers that lived here. Sunlight flooded in from the adjacent playing field and Pontiff found an unoccupied bench at which to sit. He perched on the end, struggling down a piece of toast and a cup of tea, a numb sickness disallowing hunger. He was relieved to be unaccompanied. The fact that many *Misaligneds* seemed to reserve a special anxiety about his presence was a blessed break from the mania that characterised his spell detained at the President's pleasure.

On a bench close by were the remedial diners – *Misaligned* that had not yet been cleared to use forks at dinner times. They had to be segregated. Health and Safety. Incredibly some had failed the *Cutlery Usage Test* more than once.

6

"Morning," said a female voice.

Pontiff didn't have to look to see who it was.

"Awright," he responded as Susan sat opposite him.

"Still popular, I see."

"Oh aye."

Pontiff looked up and, as ever, felt slashed by that arctic gaze. Such piercing blue eyes. Susan was somewhere in her mid-twenties, tough-looking and slender and though her beauty had not been entirely washed out of her, life seemed to be taking its toll. Pontiff noticed her shoulder-length brown locks had gone.

"You've hud a haircut," he said. "Very chic."

"They said a cropped look would make me more appealing to you."

"Fuck me, Susan, it's first thing in the fucken mornen!"

"It's a joke!"

"Aye, well dinnae joke about it. No that."

He hated it when Susan made light of the horror of what was expected of them. He feared her troubled mind didn't understand the gravity of what she said. He had come to regard her as somewhere between a daughter and a sister and the only thing he had was to try to keep her safe. Alas she was not as strong as the first impression he had had of her. They ate in silence.

"I had my test yesterday," offered Susan.

"Oh aye. An you got away wi jus huvven a haircut, eh?"

"I scored very highly."

Christ, she seems genuinely pleased.

"Did you do anything good last night?" Susan asked.

"Did I dae anyhen good? In here?"

"Alright, alright, no need for the tone!" Susan replied, slurping on her porridge.

"Do you have tae dae that?"

"Jesus! Who pinched your prick this morning, moody!"

"Oh well sorry for killen ya buzz."

"Oh come on. Don't be like that. Ask me what I did."

Given Susan's spritely mood Pontiff feared they'd upped the dose. Sometimes she was virtually mute at breakfast. She had been at Life Camp for just under a year, sent for realignment for a crazy passage of

7

behaviour that had seen her try to visit her aunt two days before her *Designated Family Day*. The next day she had attempted to board the Monorail on her no-travel day. It was because of this *free spirit* she had been paired with Pontiff.

"So what did you dae last night?"

"Had my group's mantra chant."

"Oh Jesus," groaned Pontiff.

"No! It was good!"

"Good?"

"Yeah. The theme was *too much thought leads to numbness of emotion.*"

"Jesus fucking Christ."

"Oh! He's off again!"

Pontiff looked to the ceiling and clenched his teeth. All he asked for was a couple of minutes at the start of each day to acclimatise.

Soon the bench started to fill up, and there was great excitement. A group of experienced *Misaligned* were approaching realignment. Having excelled at a number of tasks five of them had a *Controlled Leisure Excursion* that evening – a constituent part of every *Misaligned's Realignment Programme* – and in plain terms, a trip to the pub. Pontiff watched on with a mixture of jealousy, mirth and unease.

"It's gonna be amazing!" said a young man Pontiff found excruciatingly eager. "We're gonna be treated like celebrities!"

"Now Jack. You know we don't worship celebrities these days."

Pontiff turned to the green-clad man who had made this comment, a man he had taken a dislike to the moment he had met him – Technician Peter, the smug, scrawny, ferret-like specimen with the intellectual acumen of a serial killer. *The Ratman.* It was interacting with this character that Pontiff perhaps detested most of all about his interminable stay at Shrink Clink.

"Sorry, Technician Peter," said Jack. "I'm just so excited!"

"Me too!" said Meredith, a twitchy middle-aged woman seated next to Pontiff. They had enrolled on the same day and she disgusted him terribly with her inability to eat with her mouth closed.

Surely they had to sort that out before they released her back into the wild, thought Pontiff.

He pitied whoever'd been partnered with *her* for *Instinctive Joy*.

"You can imagine how this'll play out," Pontiff said to Susan. "They'll be flippen out and have to be tranquilised before they even leave the grounds. An if th'actually get tae the boozer they'll all start fainten left, right and fucken centre, gan tae shock at the sight of normal people."

"Your negativity knows no bounds does it, Mr Pope?" said the Ratman.

"Oh Technician Peter, you're talken tae me. What a delight. All I can say is good luck."

"Luck doesn't enter into it but thank you for your concern."

"Don't mention it."

The Ratman turned away to address his group but Pontiff stopped listening. His heart was pounding. The sickness was welling up inside again, a feeling only ameliorated by drink. He'd been forced to cease intake of alcohol at the *LifeManagement4Life* Institute and it had had a profound effect on his psyche. Three months without booze – the clarity wasn't appealing. The elixir combination of tobacco and alcohol allowed Pontiff temporary detachment from the absurd cruelty of new Britannia and was the one aspect of normal life (whatever that meant now) he most missed. How much longer could he go without a drink? He thought he'd kept himself remarkably together given its absence. But again the question came – for how much longer? The one hope he held onto during his stay-without-end was a *Controlled Leisure Excursion* but he knew it unlikely he would be granted a stab at this task given he had not performed with his *IJP*.

Though it had been difficult to be an honest smoker-drinker for some time, many commonplace habits and desires of the people were now deemed incongruous to their collective safety. Pontiff knew things were going wrong when jelly babies were banned because they promoted cannibalism.

Seeing Pontiff's discomfort Susan reached across the table and took his hands in hers.

"You know, Pont, I'm a lot happier for knowing you. I feel a lot healthier now."

"Aye well less no get carried away while we're all still in here, eh?"

"Well if we *are* going to get out, it might be wise to-"

"No!" shouted Pontiff, pulling his hand away. "We've been through this!"

"Anyone would think you don't find me attractive."

"Stop it! Fuck's sake."

"Does my new hair not do it for you?" asked Susan with a smile.

"That's enough!" shouted Pontiff again, getting up. "Jesus I need a fucken cigarette."

"Oh dear, Mr Pope. We are in a state this morning," said the Ratman, his attention diverted from a chat with another table. "And still intent on contaminating your lungs?"

"At least when I contaminate ma lungs I take full responsibility for it. An that's a fucken rarity these days."

"Aren't you supposed to have given up by now?"

"Well the fact that you and the Government want me tae stop is reason enough tae carry on, tae fight the political ethos of the People's Republic of Britannia that simultaneously treats everyone like naughty schoolchildren and terrorists. What a country, eh? Revolven around the idea that everyone's incapable of self-determination and needs rescuen from themselves."

"Well we are right in most cases, wouldn't you agree?" countered the Ratman, nearing Pontiff.

"Well to be honest it's a real chicken and egg sit'eeation, Technician Peter. We've bred a nation of idiots, only comfortable when they're conformen to crazy levels of control. They're either too scared or too stupid tae think for themselves."

"Well I think *you think* too much. I've been watching you this morning. I knew I was right. You two," the Ratman said, pointing his claw-like finger at Pontiff and Susan, "have such passion together, such chemistry. Is today the day, Mr Pope, Miss Baxter?"

*"Time to Meal-Off! Time to Meal-Off!"*

"Well," said the Ratman with a smile, "no doubt we shall find out later. But come now, you've heard the Sonic Technicians. You best get to class. And you especially better hurry, Miss Baxter. You're expected on the Athletics track shortly and that's a trek in itself. But Mr Pope will see you later, when you have some free time before our session."

*Free time* was an odd phrase, thought Pontiff. The cost varied but there was always a cost.

"See you at lunch, Pont," said Susan as she left the table.

"Aye."

"I see the way you look at her, Mr Pope," said the Ratman as Pontiff watched Susan leave the canteen. "Quite something, isn't she? Come. Let us walk together. We are going to the same place after all."

In his mind Pontiff played out his fist colliding with the Ratman's jaw. What difference would it make if he attacked? He doubted he would ever get out of this place anyway. He ambled to the canteen exit, his daydream taking on a particularly pleasing hue – the Ratman's nose rearranged all over his face – when, without warning, he was knocked to the floor. A young man of about twenty – a fellow *Misaligned* – had run straight into him trying to evade the clutches of a pair of Life Technicians both dressed in the requisite green. He landed on top of Pontiff and was screaming and pleading as he was hoisted to his feet.

"No! I don't want it! No! Please! I want my own face! I want my own face!"

"Come on now, don't be a silly boy," said one of the Life Technicians, restraining him. "It's for the best."

As he uttered these words the other Life Technician eased a syringe into his arm.

"That's better, isn't it? It'll make you all nice and calm for your surgery."

The young man withered and melted, and was placed in a wheelchair.

"So what are you doing now, Technician Georgia?" asked the Ratman.

"Well Technician Peter, as per your instructions he will be taken to solitary confinement and be provided with the necessary nudging to undergo this critical part of his realignment."

"Good, Technician Georgia. You are having an excellent first week. You are undoubtedly one of my top students."

"Oh thank you, Technician Peter. I'm learning so much."

"Good. Well don't let me detain you. Keep up the good work."

"Thank you, Technician Peter."

Pontiff watched this unfold lying on the floor. He felt numb and a little sad to be so normalised to this type of occurrence.

There had been many new and wonderful ideas put into practice by President Hair's coalition of Liberal Compassionates and Neo-Luddites but the preposterous malignance of *Pretty-Making* had taken things to a new level.

Despite banning publications like *Cosmo* for the negative imagery they forced down people's throats (not to mention the pollution they caused) *and* dubbing advertising 'institutional violence', President Hair, or somebody in his office, had come up with the idea that *a pretty face is a happy soul*. Wanting to make everyone as equal as possible (amongst the common folk at least) Hair, or somebody in his office, had decided on a quite revolutionary scheme to improve personal happiness.

All *Misaligneds* were required to undertake a beauty test in which a whole host of attributes were analysed and discussed by a panel of Holistic Medicine Technicians. If you failed, under the knife you went. It was a rather literal take on the remit to restructure each person's life. If anyone refused their voluntary-compulsory surgery they were sent to solitary confinement, to rooms with wall-to-wall mirrors and huge speakers piping through messages telling them how ugly and disgusting they were. Distressed and crying people were taken from these mini-detention centres straight to surgery once they had relented. It didn't take long, as you can imagine. That's where the young man was headed.

*"People want to, and should, feel good about themselves,"* reasoned President Hair. *"These measures can only be beneficial in the long run. You'll feel better after surgery. It is obviously making society better and I don't think anyone can argue with that now. After all, a pretty face is a happy soul."*

When people returned to the main *Misaligned* population they were often hard to recognise depending on the severity of their procedure. In some cases only the voice remained of the original person. Pontiff had taken his test the week before. Happily he'd been deemed attractive enough in his own right and was not part of the group liberally and compassionately described as *Fatties* and *Uglies*.

Pontiff remained on the floor watching the last few *Misaligneds* make their way to the exit, going about their business, studiously ignoring what had just transpired.

"Well Mr Pope, I suppose we both better make our way to the entrance hall," said the Ratman. "Dr Zini will be waiting for us. I do hope you will behave a bit better than you have this morning. We wouldn't want to have made a mistake in giving you this opportunity. Dr Zini is trying hard for you. I hope you appreciate that."

\*\*\*

The refreshment area was drawing large crowds and Pontiff stared at the rabble of assorted shapes and faces, young and old, male and female, all still dressed in their own clothes. Pontiff took in the tears, the farting, the general sulphuric odour of nervousness. He remembered his first day – it had been much the same – though there'd also been the whiff of booze emanating from his pores. It had all created quite a heady atmosphere. Chewy almost. At that stage Pontiff had been too pissed to feel perturbed. He'd even found it funny initially. But as that first day wore on and an afternoon hangover started to kick-in, a vague nausea and a strong desire not to be here anymore started to grip him. He remembered pondering trying to escape but with the alcohol starting to wear off and hunger setting in he didn't want to jeopardise his chances of securing a bacon'n'egg roll. And though he had eaten then, his appetite had never really returned.

In a matter of hours he had gone from drinking and talking tactics with the RevKev to being unable to reach satisfactory conclusion at the post office to being bundled away to a *LifeManagement4Life* centre. It had been rather unfortunate timing to be taken into custody just as things were hotting up. In fact, he felt a bit careless to be taken out of the game on the metaphorical eve of action. He wondered how they were getting on out there. He'd heard nothing on the news but then even if it was happening, it wouldn't be reported. And certainly not in here.

Thinking of his comrades Pontiff noticed a curious looking little fellow putting three chocolate bourbons in his pocket while two others battled over who was next with the hot water. People feel they're missing out if they don't get their fair share, whether they want it or not, thought Pontiff, particularly if it's under the banner of *free*.

The biscuit thief had a slight build and nervous disposition, his sharp nose fitting perfectly the eager face. Clapping eyes on this meek little man gave Pontiff the sense the whole *LifeManagement4Life* operation was akin to Crufts – snappy little dogs on a shit assault course.

Pontiff watched Crufts approach the posters that adorned the walls of the entrance hall.

There was:

*Health is Wealth*; *Money can't buy everything, let's aspire to something else; Valuing People; The Great Clean-Up; Don't forget to brush your teeth;* and information on the Life Camp's imminent Republic Day parties. This was nothing new. This type of stuff was rammed down peoples' throats in what was loosely termed the 'real world' as well.

"Fucken absurd, eh?" said Pontiff.

Crufts turned, terror-struck.

"Pontiff," said Pontiff sticking out his hand.

"Oh, er, Clyde, Clyde Trepid" said Crufts, meekly reciprocating. The weakness of the shake made Pontiff want to vomit.

"So Clyde, how you finden it so far? You met your *IJP* yet?"

"My what?"

"Welcome everyone," said Dr Zini. "Welcome to *LifeManagement-4Life*."

The group turned to the doctor who smiled a warm smile. Pontiff estimated she was sixtyish, and certainly still an attractive woman. Like him, she had green eyes though only one was visible, the other concealed behind a black leather eye patch. This in turn was partially covered by grey hair that tumbled down to her elbows. She had an intelligent raunch, was petite and in good shape, with a certain Helen Mirren-ness to her. The enigma as to why she was one eyed had also always given her a certain *je ne sais quoi*.

"Now," continued the doctor, "you are all here, as you know, because you have been diagnosed as *Misaligned*. Some of you are here voluntarily."

This point was still shocking to Pontiff.

"Others have been referred to us because it was in their best interests."

"Why she looken at me?" said Pontiff, nudging Clyde. But Clyde didn't want to know. He didn't want to be caught talking on the first day.

"Here," announced the doctor, "we shall give you instruction that will help you manage your life for the rest of your life. Hence the name."

"And what a good name it is," offered Pontiff, looking at the group and nodding, again nudging Clyde. Clyde looked petrified.

"Thank you, Mr Pope. And maybe this can be our first unofficial lesson. To know when it is appropriate to voice your opinion. This is something you still clearly need to learn." The doctor looked directly at Pontiff as she said this before she smiled, flirtingly, at the rest of the group.

"Once you leave us, you will be ready to reintegrate into society. How long you stay here depends on you. But none of you can now be discharged without the express approval of our panel of Life Technicians. You will be under constant assessment and we will review your continued presence here at regular intervals. The Government cares for your welfare and we, the staff, will all work tirelessly for you. But we need help. Help us help you. Here you will be reminded that nothing in life is smooth except the slippery slope."

The doctor went on to talk about the great strides – always that phrase – that had been made by President Hair and his Liberal Compassionate Government. She reminded the group that they too could experience the positive in the new way of life. And today, in the run up to Republic Day, there was a special treat. President Terry Hair himself. Or rather, a recorded message to be played on the holographic screens. *HairVision!* was a feature of life everywhere and reminded the simple man what was what. The group watched Hair turn and smile, as if a sportsman being introduced on TV from days of yore.

*"Liberal Compassionatism delivers joy to the masses and peace to the good people of this country. We care for you. We know what is best for you. Life's decisions are easier under us. We*

*will improve your life, the complexity of everyday survival tossed aside!*

*"We have the confidence in our conviction to carry out the consensus of change and will continue to meet the challenges for modern Britannia, meeting these challenges with rolled-out, front-end, top-down systems, enabling us to reorder the config-uration of choice. Through reform we will ensure fit for purpose delivery of service!"*

People's lives are hard enough without contaminating their ears listening to that guff, thought Pontiff. To him, the political vernacular was little more than the pseudo-cerebral cousin of footballer chat with all the cosmic revelation of *"Dazza's got the ball in the box and I've got on the end of it,"* as footage showed Dazza getting the ball in the box and the interviewee getting on the end of it.

Apart from the content, it was the sinister visage, the toxic grin, the diabolic eyebrows that were so unnerving. They seemed the embodi-ment of malevolent evil. Also, Pontiff could never trust a man who could fully cross his legs over like a woman. It wasn't right, was it?

Ah yes, he thought, Terry Hair, what a fine charismatic young man, a man who claimed to possess *a clear idea of what the country wants*, a man who spoke in a *I'm a reasonable guy* kind of way, a man of principal. Of that, Hair was, as is the political vogue, *absolutely clear*. His best friends had been bankers, lawyers, the leaders of multinational conglomerates, Arabic dictators. It was all absolutely clear. Until the now infamous Liberal Compassionate Party conference, that is, and a most dramatic political volte-face. As Hair read out the speech that changed everything for everyone, Pontiff recalled how even some LibCom high rankers had looked shocked. Especially Heath Cliffe, the finance man. It almost seemed as though Hair had come up with it at the last minute. And what about his wife, Sherry? *Cruella Deville*. At her happiest speaking at charity events. Or when she got the pay cheque afterwards. Terry and Sherry, thought Pontiff. Good Lord.

"Now let me make this clear," Dr Zini intoned, soothingly, "at the moment all smokers will be permitted to smoke. We are well aware-"

A match scraped and popped. Rings of smoke filled the air.

"Mr Pope, please will you extinguish that cigarette."

"I thought-" all innocent.

"Mr Pope," again soothing yet firm.

"Where shall I-?"

An ashtray materialised from nowhere, thrust into his hand by the Ratman.

"Oh, thanks. Thanks very much," said Pontiff, stubbing out the cigarette. "Where shall I-"

The ashtray was promptly snatched off him and dispatched.

"He's very efficient."

Don't try me, said the Ratman with his eyes.

"Mr Pope, if I may continue."

"Of course, Doctor."

"Thank you and thank you also for another lesson." She turned to the group, calmly and pleasantly. "I think Mr Pope is really taking his mentoring position seriously by showing you all how not to do things. How very thoughtful. I will have to give him his reward later. Now, as I was saying. We are all aware that coming here may cause a certain amount of emotional upheaval and for a bedding-in period, you will be permitted to smoke." She looked at Pontiff. "In designated areas." A pause. "Ultimately, it is our aim, and soon will be yours too, that the habit is kicked. There will be designated smoking times, and there will be ten such times throughout the day. You may not smoke outside of these times. This will also provide all smokers with company as you will congregate in the smoking area. We believe, rather, we know, through literally months of experience, that ten smoking times are ample and sufficient."

While a Life Technician escorted the smokers to the designated area Dr Zini addressed the other half of the group, those that were uninitiated in the splendour of nicotine.

"So," she began, smiling a sweet smile. "I trust you are all settling in, even if it has only been a couple of hours. We are all aware, as are you, of the problems you have experienced living among others and adjusting to the demands of our modern, improved way of life. Here at *LifeManagement* we believe in a holistic approach to care and rehabilitation." She started to walk amongst the group, touching shoulders, smiling as she floated through.

"One of our beliefs we have cultivated here is that experience enriches the soul."

A few of the assembled nodded their agreement.

"As we know, an ideal of our Government is to facilitate, and that is one of our remits. So," and with that she pulled a hemp purse from her white apron, held together with a thread made of natural fibres. In a show of mock rebellion she untied the packet and tossed the thread to the ground. She then pulled a thin sheet of foil from the pouch, screwed it up and again threw it to the ground, smiling at her enraptured audience as she did so.

"Now," she said, "I'm going to join you, so you won't be alone."

There was disbelief as she started passing round cigarettes to the group of worried faces, who received them completely dumbfounded. A weaponed guard produced a black lighter and started to ignite each individual's cigarette.

"What, you want us to smoke them?" came a quiet voice.

"That's right, Clyde. Breathe in that new experience."

There was a cacophony of spluttering, wheezing and a haze of smoke. Clyde was looking doubtful at the object in his left hand, letting it smoke in front of him, holding it between thumb and forefinger.

"I don't want to, Doctor."

"But it's a new experience for you. And that enriches the soul." She walked towards him. "Look, I'll do it with you," and she inhaled, seductively so, thought Pontiff.

"Come on Clyde... For me?" She lowered her head slightly to look straight into his eyes.

"Dirty bitch," Pontiff whispered to himself, in a state of semi-awe. The doctor seemed younger in these moments with an easy, elegant feminine charm. She looked smaller, though no less authoritative. She was compelling in her playful, girl-like manner and succeeded in teasing and tempting Clyde into trying smoking.

"Well done," she said, with a ruffle of Clyde's hair. He wasn't convinced.

"But the important thing is that you tried. Your life is now fuller."

At that, a girl emptied her stomach, a sort of carrot-tomato compote, all over the white floor. Pontiff laughed loudly.

"Bravo!" he shouted before two sets of black-gloved hands seized him and dragged him out of the entrance hall.

"I do hope you will be this exuberant later," said the Ratman as Pontiff was restrained on the floor by two Blackguard. "By rights I should tranquilise you for your performance this morning but I have a feeling that a man like you will perform if your blood is up."

"Oh Technician Peter, you misunderstand. I was jus tryna be supportive, tae be the best mentor I can be."

"And the smoking, Mr Pope?"

"I dae ma best thinken when I smoke."

"If you persist with this behaviour you will have all the thinking time you want in solitary confinement. See you after lunch."

The Ratman and his assorted cohorts departed. Soon after, the new intake filed past.

"Good luck Clyde, ya wee bass!" shouted Pontiff, still laid out on the floor.

Clyde looked at Pontiff briefly before quickening his pace.

The mentoring had gone well.

\*\*\*

*"Misaligned, time to meal-on. You are important. Life is worthwhile. You must integrate. You must eat together. Commune and improve. Commune and improve. Time to meal-on, time to..."*

Pontiff had been enjoying a nap in his room until this interruption jolted him awake. For once he actually felt quite hungry, his appetite not compromised by the Sonic Technicians' quasi-American-cum-Management speak.

All in all it had been a particularly galling morning. After his swiftly aborted mentoring, Pontiff had been returned to his standard timetable and, as expected, called to the front of class to demonstrate *best practice* when posting letters and generally how to conduct oneself at the post office. He had had to talk through where he had gone wrong in the past as though confessing in an AA meeting while the rest of the group were encouraged to applaud once he had made his confession and completed the task to a good level. This was part of a wider module in Pontiff's realignment – *The Importance of the Life Administration Directive*, of *Easification-Facilitation*.

The *Life Administration Directive* had been one of the first acts of the Liberal Compassionate government, its aim – to provide the necessary provisions for all people and prevent any further deterioration to the environment.

But first things first. Before anything else had happened in *The Great Clean-Up* of the country and most people's favourite bit – the apportioning of blame (including but not limited to: bankers in stocks, big business nationalised, the Royals dethroned, gated communities with private militias broken up, the 1%'s assets seized to fund the rebirth of the nation) – the scourge of poverty had had to be addressed. But this wasn't as easy as it sounded. You couldn't just go round dumping rations on communities. No no. It had to be properly organised. The country had to be simplified. *Easified.*

The easifying of existence began with the whole country being divided region by region, city by city, area by area, into alphabetical groups (Surnames A-E was *Life Administration* Group 1 and so on). Then, to ensure the smooth running of *Life Administration* another new government body was set up – The National Identity Proof Scheme Department (NIPSD). This department assessed each individual before providing the relevant benefits. To that end, each Citizen had to set up a *Citizen's Account* and prove the specifics of their case before they could receive their rations, healthcare and housing.

In order to receive the most bespoke care and benefits, all past afflictions, psychological traumas and abuses had to be confessed. Indeed, every aspect of a Citizen's existence had to be divulged. All social media posts, *likes*, comments, email correspondence, phone records, texts and internet browsing history were combed to corroborate the information each Citizen had provided – and to weed out those with questionable pasts. Many a low-level facilitator was adjudged an arch criminal for selling an eighth of hash here and there. The plethora of personal details held by various private agencies and companies and state-run departments were also collected. Details of every app you'd ever used were gathered and if details emerged of, say, an STD, then your interactions on dating apps were looked at to see who your sexual cohorts had been and then they in turn were checked out and so on. Only once this process was complete was a NIPSD card issued and benefits able to be enjoyed.

In the past such cards had been threatened for reasons ranging from international terrorism to identity theft. Finally, they'd been brought in to set up an elaborate dole.

Granted, a version of the NHS had been brought back after a previous government had privatised it – along with everything else – but Pontiff lamented the day he'd set up his *Citizen's Account*. He knew at the time it was a mechanism through which more control could be exercised on the people, the scope of the scheme widened in response to each perceived emergency. What else they were going to do with all this data wasn't clear. But they had it. As Pontiff often noted, the Facebook age had fucked us all.

Now, without these cards, you didn't exist, you couldn't live. Every *Life Transaction* required them. Wages and benefits were paid onto them, travel was only possible by paying with them, picking up rations, purchasing food, having a drink at the pub, entrance to buildings, exit from buildings, *everything* required these cards. Problems were endless. There were stories of people coming home to find their entire block of flats locked because the central NIPSD engine room was on the blink. They'd have to sleep huddled together in doorways, made homeless by the Government. One time Pontiff had gone three days without being able to buy food because his NIPSD card hadn't been updated with his wages. Sometimes people were overpaid and made to pay it all back, whether they had the means or not.

The other function of *Life Administration* Groups was to determine what day of the week each Citizen was to carry out a task or directive designed to protect the environment or improve social cohesion.

Examples included – *Designated Family Day, Designated Non-Travel Day, Designated Dry Day, Designated Activity Day, Designated Letter Posting Day* – all *"necessary regulation as the environment has been trampled on and it is imperative to step lightly."* Attempting a task on the wrong day or ignoring a directive (boarding the Monorail on your *Life Administration Group's Designated Non-Travel Day,* for example) resulted in accruing Social Behavioural Points.

Pontiff's little episode at the post office had been the last in a long list of *Life Administration* misdemeanours though it was a mystery two Social Behavioural Points showing up on his *Citizen's Account* that fateful morn that had propelled him into incarceration. Despite the system having the propensity to go awry, and the very real prospect of wrong information finding its way into your data, NIPSD evidence was 100% irrefutable. Falling foul of the scheme had become known colloquially as being 'nipped' or 'nipsd', and Pontiff had certainly felt the pinch.

He finished his lunch quickly and it was then that things went from bad to indescribable.

The incident in question began like every other interaction between the Ratman and his two most reluctant charges. He met them, as always, in the Cell of Intimacy. The room contained a round bed, mirrored walls and ceiling, and a small fridge full of oysters.

"Good afternoon you two. Are you going to be good little children today and perform for me?"

"Not on your fucken life," responded Pontiff.

"I have to say we are all getting a little sick of your intransigence," said the Ratman. He was flanked by his usual phalanx of Blackguard, dressed, as ever, in their usual get up of black military gear, small firearms and red berets. Today there were six in attendance instead of the usual two.

"Well let me say, dearest Technician Peter, I'm getten a little sick of your presence in ma life. In fact, I have a wee theory of m'own about *you*. I think you're a fucken pervert. Am I close?"

"Mr Pope, while you are undoubtedly a prodigiously talented comedian, you are spectacularly unwell. You would do well to follow the instruction given to you to ensure you do not suffer a further deterioration to your already compromised health."

"Technician Peter, please go away. We were huvven a nice conversation til you lot turned up."

"Conversation? You are not required to talk, you are required to perform! Am I going to have to show you how to do this?"

Pontiff laughed. "Oh, that's class. What are you gonnae do? Get a blow-up doll and talk us through the birds and the bees?"

The Ratman smiled a brief smile and reached into his briefcase, removing a small card and a document.

"Do you know what this is?"

"It looks like a bitta paper and a NIPSD card."

"With your name on it."

"So it is."

"Would you like to be able to use this card again, Mr Pope. Mmm?"

The Ratman waited for Pontiff to respond. Pontiff said nothing.

"I suspect you do."

Again Pontiff declined to respond.

The Ratman put Pontiff's NIPSD card back into the briefcase and turned his attention to the paper.

"Do you remember what you wrote for your last essay, Mr Pope?"

Pontiff shook his head.

"Nah."

"Allow me to remind you then."

"Please do go on."

The Ratman began to read aloud:

**"I think Life Administration is tremendously important for this country. My only reservation is that it doesn't go far enough. I, for one, would greatly appreciate lessons on how to tie my shoelaces as well as some guidance as to the correct method for picking up crockery. I have smashed so many plates, you wouldn't believe! Also, I feel the country as a whole would benefit massively from NIPSD SwipeScanners being installed in Toilet Facility Chambers so that there is a record of bowel movements for every Citizen. I have no doubt that social harmony would improve if everyone knew what time everyone else was taking a shit."**

Pontiff nodded and mmmed.

"I have to say Mr Pope, I'm very concerned about your anger and deep self-loathing. You seem to be in a state of permanent, smirking annoyance."

"I thought that essay was ma best effort yet."

"Mr Pope, very soon that sarcastic tone will desert you and you will confront the reasons you are here. As you are unable to care for yourself, I am responsible for your care. You will be realigned. Susan," continued the Ratman, suddenly distracted. "Put that cigarette out. You know you can't smoke in here."

Susan took a last drag and extinguished her cigarette against the wall.

"Well that's just lovely isn't it? Would you do that at home?"

"Yeah," she responded, giving a 'fuck-you-and-all-you-stand-for' smile.

"I do rather fear Mr Pope has had a negative influence on you, Miss Baxter. You've always performed in the past. Why not now?"

Silence.

"Well. Despite your attitude today and how you have both behaved these last few weeks, you are still the perfect partners to help each other overcome your blockages. You have been alienated from your instincts. It is the root cause of all your problems."

"As I've said before, Technician Peter, it's ma natural instincts that have landed me in here."

"We are looking for intimacy, not insolence, Mr Pope," said the Ratman.

He turned and motioned to the Blackguard behind him. Three of the six approached Pontiff matter-of-factly and restrained him. The other three guards approached Susan and restrained her.

The Ratman approached Susan now too.

"Why must you force our hand in such a way?" he said, returning his gaze to Pontiff and unzipping his fly. "You leave me no choice, Mr Pope."

"What the fuck?"

"Get your hands off me!" yelled Susan.

The Ratman turned back.

"Hold her."

He ripped Susan's linen suit to her waist and began.

"This. Is. How. You. Get. Intimate," words in rhythm with the thrusts.

Pontiff tried to wrestle free of the Blackguard and went to call out, but his mouth was covered. After a short while, the Ratman shuddered. He paused before withdrawing. He then zipped-up his fly and patted Susan on the bottom, licking a bead of sweat from his upper lip. After limbering his head and shoulders like an athlete about to take on the long jump, he turned to Pontiff.

"That, Mr Pope, was very avoidable, but you wouldn't listen, would you? Be in no doubt that this was your fault. You are making us do your work."

The Ratman mopped his brow and blew out his cheeks.

"I do hope you will listen in future. Both of you. I think you'll both enjoy it once you get started. We're not asking for much after all. Just a bit of dogturtling."

"Yeah, come on Pope. Just slip her the loveturtle," chimed in a guard.

The Ratman put his gleaming face next to Susan's. She was still gagged by a black-clad hand.

"I think you may have enjoyed that a little bit already," he said. He grinned, purulent cheeks and rodent dentures on display. "OK, guards, you can release them."

Susan remained motionless. Pontiff was momentarily frozen in revulsion too, but he soon sparked into action, his right fist making favourable contact with the Ratman's face. He rained down a few more blows but his fightback, though virulent, was short-lived. Not for the first time in his recent history Pontiff was outnumbered.

Having been sent to the floor, the Ratman staggered to his feet. He dabbed at his lip.

"Oh dear, Mr Pope, we are aggressive today, aren't we? Perhaps we need a little chat with the doctor, mmm?"

After the Blackguard had given Pontiff a thorough and physical reminder of his responsibilities, he was dragged through the camp in full view of his fellow *Misaligneds*. They distanced themselves from the scene. Those that still had ambitions in the outside world did not want to do anything that might impede the speed at which they would be permitted to leave. Any comment or wrong glance would no doubt lead to repercussion.

Carried like a coffin, Pontiff's head banged into the door of the *Life-Management4Life: Management Office*, his elbow smashing the door-frame. The impact made the window shake and the neatly rolled Venetian Blinds suffered a violent rattle.

Everything in the office was white save for the large wooden table, a chair either side – the doctor's leather and comfortable, the patient's rigid metal. Dr Zini rose in the surrounds of the reassuring whiteness to greet Pontiff.

"Oh dear. Not more trouble from Mr Pope was it, guards?"

"Fraid so, Doctor. He attacked all of us this time."

Pontiff swallowed back some blood and tried to focus with his one open eye. He couldn't stand up on his own given that he'd taken about as much as a man could take, and was handcuffed to boot. This was certainly a very liberal and compassionate way to break his will.

"You're not ignoring me are you Mr. Pope?" asked the doctor.

Pontiff, slumped forward, again propped up by hands under his armpits. He could not make his mouth respond.

"Oh dear. OK, thank you guards. Leave him with me."

The Guards seated Pontiff, fastening one of his arms and both his legs to the chair.

"We know how you work, Pope" said one. "You better behave in here or you'll have me to answer to."

The Ratman and the guards shuffled out, leaving the schoolmistress with her charge. She raised her eyebrows at Pontiff and gave him an I-told-you-so smile.

Pontiff sat, his one open eye fixed on the doctor, lip bloodied, elbow throbbing.

"You are a mess, aren't you?"

With that she slapped him.

"Naughty boy. Time to learn some manners."

Pontiff's head rung, his eyes crossed momentarily.

"I did warn you not too long ago that if you darkened my door again a different phase of medicine may be required. I even tried giving you some responsibility with the mentoring scheme, but that only seemed to make your behaviour worse. Why do you keep sabotaging yourself? Clearly you need re-educating."

Zini leaned on her desk and lit two cigarettes. She approached Pontiff, bent down and popped one in his mouth.

"Now, what was it this time?"

Pontiff said nothing.

26

"Let me ask you a different question, then. Do you think you are making progress? Because I think I can say your case may need quite a bit of time. We are here to help you, remember. And you are a particularly troubled soul, Mr Pope."

He couldn't argue with that.

"Robert," continued the doctor, in softer tones, "do you not think that all this reticence to co-operate creates barriers, barriers that obstruct you from relating to your fellow man? Does this not in turn permeate all your relationships and create this pent-up aggression that, to name but two examples, erupted so violently at the post office and now again this afternoon? Do you actually want to leave *LifeManagement*, Robert?"

Pontiff's only response was dropping his cigarette butt to the floor.

Zini sighed through her nose.

"You know, your reticence does nothing to help you. A strong person is someone who can curb his natural will to destruction and rein in some of his vices. And that's what we're trying to teach peo-"

"I just seen a rape!" shouted Pontiff. A new horror swept through him, evinced by saying out loud what he had witnessed.

Zini tutted and shook her head.

"You are in more trouble than we first thought. It is indeed unfortunate that you, how can I put it, *misconstrue*, what you have seen. It appears that in addition to your general intransigence, your mind cannot process what your eyes see. It is clear you are deluded, as well as ill. I think you've lied so much to yourself that you've started to believe the lies."

Pontiff's head slumped and bounced as though falling asleep on a train. Zini got up from her seat and removed a bottle from the cabinet behind her. A whisky bottle. Pontiff's heart started to beat faster. I will not accept that, he promised himself. Not like this. Zini poured two whiskies. She sipped from hers before placing it on the table. She then opened Pontiff's free hand and closed it shut around the other glass. He wanted to reject but his desire was greater. Three months without the warming burn of equanimity weighed heavy. He knocked it back, but as the booze began its gracious slide, unease swam with it.

The doctor refilled the glass, smiled and touched his leg.

"That's better isn't it?"

Zini sat on her desk, pulling her chair in front so her legs were exposed as they rested on it. Pontiff had again finished his whisky yet perspective remained elusive.

"We are trying to help you," continued the doctor. "It is evident you have this internal congestion. Your mind is telling you that you have seen a rape. But that is wrong. We are engaged in facilitation. It will have done Miss Baxter no harm. Now what we are-"

"Are you fucken serious?"

"Mr Pope, I really don't think there's any need for such linguistic dexterity."

"Do you approve of what that Ratfuck did today?"

"Approved, Mr Pope, approved? Good Lord."

Zini laughed before her smile collapsed abruptly. Pontiff felt he had spied the Beast in that moment.

"You don't think Technician Peter comes up with all this theory on his own, do you? Good grief."

The doctor rose from the table, walked slowly to the damaged man before her. She placed both hands on his cheeks and gently lifted his head by his sweaty face. Pontiff's eyes, like his mind, were unable to focus as Zini lent in and whispered, "I ordered it."

# 3
# SECULAR JIHAD

FROM HIS L-SHAPED, six-man sofa on the top floor of a tall, three-storey former brewery, Fred sipped at a coffee and looked out of his vast window onto the grandeur of River Drive. It was a bright, sunny late morning and near the river bank a small platoon of Environment Technicians wearing Bio-Hazard suits and helmets were dealing with an outbreak of *Plasticitis* effluent. Given the health threat it was advisable to stay inside until it was contained.

The day's sunlight bathed the open-plan flat and seemed to create yet more space already afforded by the high ceilings. Fred drank in the warmth of the sun, its presence most welcome given that a rather insistent hangover had accompanied his waking.

Not that he'd struggled with getting up. He was always out the bedclothes with a zeal that had long since deserted many of his countrymen.

On the wall a huge screen played celebratory scenes from the day-before's first anniversary of the Republic, and reminded Fred of the cause of his throbbing head. Next to the main screen were a series of smaller screens controlled from a panel embedded in the wooden table in front of the sofa. From here, Fred had access to the myriad CCTV cameras around the capital.

There were a smattering of books in a bookcase behind the sofa while a large desk faced the window, and an antique, wooden record player stood below the screens. The kitchen and dining area, replete with walk-in fridge and every modern accoutrement de cuisine, lay to the left of the sofa.

"Do you want any more coffee, babe?" said Denise, the flowing blonde hair of the President's secretary the first part Fred saw of her as she emerged from the fridge.

"No, I'm good," responded Fred, watching Denise walk to the window wearing only his shirt from the previous night's Republic Gala. It fell off her left shoulder as she turned to him, her movement unleashing a sunbeam directly into his eyes.

"How long did they say it'd be?"

"Won't be long now," Fred responded, shielding himself from the light with his hands.

"So we've got a little bit of time then?" said Denise, climbing onto the sofa. She began crawling towards Fred and he watched as his shirt rode up her body, hung tantalisingly from two buttons. She started to kiss him on his neck, her hands moving towards his lap. As he turned to meet her mouth his new phone started vibrating on the table. Fred let it ring out but it started up again immediately. Again he let it ring out and again it started up immediately.

"Oh for f-" said Denise into Fred's tongue. His phone buzzed for the fifth and sixth times. "You better get that."

"I'll deal with it in a minute," Fred responded, pulling Denise back to him.

"A minute? Is that all?"

"Figuratively speaking."

Despite the incessant buzzing and vibrating of his phone Fred felt that rebuffing the advances of a beautiful woman seemed careless in the extreme. Whatever government business required his attention could wait. Hardly anything moved without his say-so anyway. He saw to the task at hand.

After mutual satisfaction Fred reached for his buzzing phone. It was the latest model off the production line and he had received it just a few weeks before, a twenty-fifth birthday present. Though the environment had to be protected – manufacture was illegal for the common Citizen and anyone engaged in acts of such industry, no matter how small, was taken away, never to return – a special branch of Signor Oli Garqi's workforce developed telecoms for the elite on a regular basis. For now, Fred was rather fond of his new device.

30

"Hello," he said, a light smack on his rear accompanying his standing. "What?... Oh Christ... No, we don't want to see him. It's not the first time is it? Just sack him... No. We better replace him with one of their lot. Keep the special relationship ticking over. Honestly, some of these ministers. They get a new smartphone and they go absolutely mad... Exactly... Yeah, if you can get hold of Martin and can understand the lisp ask him who he wants to put up for promotion. If not, get in touch with Nicola... Yep. See you in a bit."

"Somebody's celebrations go a bit too far?" asked Denise. "Reinhart, by any chance?"

Fred nodded.

Samuel Reinhart, the Minister for Gender Equality, a married man of decent vintage, had been forcibly removed from a strip-club for lewd behaviour whilst severely intoxicated.

"Well he was well on his way at the Gala last night," said Denise as she returned two coffee cups to the kitchen.

"And he wasn't the only one, was he?" responded Fred. "El Presidente was hardly in fine fettle."

"No but Sherry was! She tried to kiss me in the Ladies."

"Is that a euphemism?"

"It's not the first time she's tried something. And Zini! Bloody hell. With that young Blackguard."

"Yeah," said Fred, laughing. "It was certainly some night."

The Reinhart episode brought to mind the first ministerial casualty of the Liberal Compassionates' tenure, Graham Calloway. He'd made some pretty eye-watering remarks about gender regarding insertion and consent, although it was a cat-impersonation on national television that had finally precipitated his departure, some fiasco involving lapping at an imaginary saucer on one of Garqi's reality shows.

President Hair's push to be *whiter than white* had meant a new code of conduct: *The Public Accountability Directive.*

This edict demanded that:

*Those in the public eye set an example of decent behaviour to the rest of the country.*

It was the Glasnost to befit the Perestroika. Calloway was told his actions were incongruous with his position, and was cut loose. He had

31

avoided incarceration though, a fate that befell many sportsmen and women guilty of advertising soft drinks, fast food and alcohol.

At least this type of story didn't find its way into the papers anymore. Think I'll file this Reinhart fandango under *lessons will be learnt*, thought Fred, pondering also options for promotion. He knew President Hair would oppose the advancement of any more Neo-Luddites but what Fred wanted he usually got.

Hair had never been entirely sure of his *liaison politique* with his coalition partners. It infuriated him how difficult they were to get hold of. They certainly lacked a contemporary sense of efficiency, and with the exception of Reinhart (who seemed to have ditched all his principals since coming to power), they possessed no phones, computers or any other communication technology, preferring instead an elaborate message relay system involving many comrades. They advocated the end of lawnmowers – the gardener's oppressor. *"A man should be able to work free from the shackles of machinery!"* they cried, though the gardeners in question found them quite liberating. But getting the Neo-Luddites on board – and in particular their leader, Militant Martin – had been the clincher in getting into power. It was he who had coined the phrase *the end of the era of gadgetry*, a phrase Fred rather liked, and a phrase that had rather set the tone for his project.

"I'm not looking forward to the mountain of post-Republic Day admin I'll be doing for His Royal President," said Denise finding her shoes under the lounge table.

"I'll tell him to go easy," said Fred.

"I should think so too," said Denise giving Fred a lingering kiss. "Right, I'm going for a shower. Tell me when it's safe for us to leave."

"Sure thing, babe," he responded.

Denise walked past him and gave his derriere a quick squeeze. He watched her enter the bathroom, a facility with every type of comfort, the key features being the free standing bath and a shower with a head the size of a dustbin lid.

Not for the first time today Fred's phone buzzed. It was his deputy at the CAU (*Citizens' Announcements Unit*, more colloquially known as *The Cow*). She had an important query regarding a policy announcement.

Fred was being asked to rubber stamp –

*"Following the death of a man in his forties, dressed in a Superman outfit, capes are now to be banned. This is the best option going forward."*

Apparently some fool had leapt from his window dressed in this heroic garb. The idea of an accidental death had been brushed aside by the Investigative Unit in charge of this sort of thing. They had reached a verdict of death by suicide and so now the two, capes and suicide, were inextricably linked and it was decided that for the people's safety, capes would be banned.

"In addition sir, we suggest a ban on all fancy dress outfits to follow. We believe there is a real issue of identity crisis at work here."

Fred laughed inwardly at the culture he had inculcated. "Indeed," he responded. "Release this immediately and add – *Why do these people want to pretend to be something they are not? We must help them confront who they are. We must be tough on identity crises, tough on the causes of identity crises."*

"Very good sir."

Fred hung up the phone and sauntered to the master bedroom. He used the other bedroom as an occasional office or, more usually, his female guests used it as a dressing room. Both were replete with super king-size beds and walk-in wardrobes.

In his own room's wardrobe Fred surveyed his choices, the rows of sharply-cut handmade suits of every imaginable colour and design, all meticulously arranged, and the huge array of clothes for every occasion. There were roughly forty pairs of shoes. Today he would wear his favourite brown lace-up brogues, freshly polished. Selecting a suit and shirt he put the garments on the bed. He clothed, and beheld himself in the full length mirror. Svelte and a little over six foot with a complexion that alluded to a foreign lineage, Fred had a distinguished and handsome look. He looked like someone you would like. He looked like someone built for success. It's probably what had taken him so far, so quickly.

Fred had always harboured a strong desire to become involved in the machinery of government. Not for any ideological end you understand. He hadn't gone into politics to eradicate inequality, for example

– though given his own background that would have been a reasonable assumption. No. Fred's only loyalty in life was to having fun, to mischief. He wanted to see how far he could get, and moreover, what he could get away with (not unlike most politicians). That his wild practical joke had had the whiff of sense, of *justice*, even, had made it all the more plausible.

For Fred, the opportunity, timing and execution could not have been better. He knew a people as disillusioned, tired and ill as the Britons of those recent times were ripe for the taking; that if he could penetrate the corridors of power, the collective state of inertia could afford him *carte blanche* to reshape the country. And how right he had been. He had reorganised the very texture of lives on a hitherto unimagined scale. Just to see if he could.

Advising a delusional drug-addled President who trusted him implicitly was like having his own toy and whatever whim or flight of fancy Fred dreamed up he could make happen. Thanks to Fred, the age of Consumerism – golden to some, a stain of regret and shame for others – was over. Thanks to Fred, *Life Administration* and NIPSD had revolutionised existence. *Easification-Facilitation*. Fred still laughed about that now. How could anyone have taken that seriously? He felt immense pride at the level of absurdity he had influenced. It was all more fun than he had hoped. As head of *The Cow* Fred liked to think of himself as the Goebbels of the LibCom regime, the government joke writer. He had great fun feeding lines to President Hair, often wilfully ridiculous. The funniest thing was that people had taken and continued to take his every word seriously. Coming up with the *LifeManagement-4Life* mantras and *HairVision!* had been particularly enjoyable.

Tying his tie, Fred's phone beeped. He looked at the message.

**"River Drive Plasticitis outbreak neutralised. Safe to leave."**

Fred smiled again, not at the speed with which the situation had been resolved – he expected that – but because every outbreak of *Plasticitis* effluent reminded him that the advent of this deadly plague had been crucial in getting him to where he craved to be.

It was watching Militant Martin on TV that night almost two years ago that Fred's idea had begun to slot into place.

He remembered the leader of the Neo-Luddites, puce with rage, arguing that for as long as anyone could remember an overriding idea had prevailed; that only newness could mark out a culture, a society, *a way of living*, as civilised; that it was so ingrained in the people to *upgrade* every six months some believed it to be a natural state. Certainly Fred did. But the rabid lust for the newest gadget that had reigned so supreme for so long, built on the possibility of selling the perfect life, had delivered anything but. People had gone on and on about climate change until they were blue in the face but in reality there was now a concern more pressing than the great feared-for tidal wave due any moment.

Martin fumed that everywhere you looked were reminders of the decadence of the age. All over the country huge piles of phones, laptops, kettles, computer consoles, disposable contact lenses, disposable lighters, plastic cutlery, last season's trainers, sweat-shop t-shirts, toasters, external hard-drives, plastic packaging, bubblewrap, eBook readers, plastic bottles, bottle tops, branded plastic bags, electric bottle openers, memory sticks, plasma tellies and any number of other device, appliance, gimcrack and bibelot adorned the landscape. There were old cars with a thirst for petrol that could never be sated again, fallen power lines, filth and debris everywhere, the waste from a million corporate events, the split black bin liners of rampant domestic refuse.

And the forests? Sold off and turned into vast dumping grounds. And as the people had become evermore at pains to find new junkyards to discard their unwanted, out of date *objets d'amour*, the earth was dug full of great pits for this refuse, this consumerist expectorate. Plastic effluent began to seep through the soil and land accompanied by a grotesque miasma leaching illness into the bodies of the populace.

The plague had become so widespread any policy could be justified by its continued presence. It was possible *Plasticitis* had even affected the genetic make-up of the people. It was still too early to tell. Not even *The Great Clean-Up* could fully solve the issue.

When such outbreaks occurred (as they did regularly) the response was supposed to be rapid (as it had been in this case) but there was something of a post code lottery involved. An early missive Fred had penned for *The Cow* spelled out that –

*"Unfortunately there just aren't always the resources to add-ress every situation immediately. The Liberal Compassionate Party care deeply for your wellbeing and safety. Stay indoors until Environment Technicians can arrive."*

Fred knew in some cases people waited up to three days, house-bound in the interim. This disparity was undoubtedly a contributing factor to the dissention that was now re-emerging. Just as Fred had known it would.

It was time for President Hair to discover what the Government would be doing to tackle this dissention and Fred had something quite special up his sleeve. In fact, his sleeves were bulging. He removed a thin document from his cherished briefcase, the one relic he had of his father. He looked at the document for a moment, slightly in awe of the courage of those behind it. Can't wait to see the old dog's reaction to this! he thought. He popped the document back inside his briefcase, delight and excitement coursing through him. Fred had been looking forward to this day for some time. Not only would Prez Tez be in for a bit of a shock, finally Robert Pope would begin his special role.

"Denise!" shouted Fred, walking out to the lounge. "We're good to go."

"K!"

As Denise emerged from the second bedroom Fred grabbed a handful of jelly babies from the bowl on the coffee table, and they headed out.

\*\*\*

Fred smiled at everyone as he entered Buckingham Palace, greeted in turn with well wishes and general enquiries about his health. He strode with purpose, his every step met with awe, this tall, slender, good-looking, brown-skinned man, who was well-heeled to boot.

Despite his earlier exertions Fred elected to take the stairs, one of the very few permitted access to the sleeping quarters of the Palace. He approached a door and knocked.

On the other side of the door, in salubrious surrounds, a woman nudged her lover awake.

"Hello Mr President."

They rubbed noses as was their wont.

"So great not to be common any more, isn't it darling?" she said.

Before the President could answer there was another knock at the door.

"Enter!" cried the woman.

Upon hearing this command, Fred did just that.

"Good afternoon Mr President, First Lady," he said. "I trust you slept well and are ready for the next chapter in salvaging the country?"

"Hello Fred," mumbled Hair.

"Hello Frederick," said Sherry, smiling eyes only for him.

She was wearing a tight fitting black robe. She looks good, thought Fred. He took the President's wife's hand and kissed it, maintaining eye contact while he did so. Sherry didn't think she'd ever met so dashing and debonair man in her life. He looked vibrant. Her husband looked strung out.

"You are a vision as always."

Sherry giggled.

"Oh stop it Fred. You've no chance. You know I've only eyes for one man."

"Quite right too. And what a man he is."

But the President didn't notice this flirtatious interplay. He was troubled.

"I can never get this right," he said, fumbling with his tie, "and it needs to look just so."

"Indeed it does," Fred responded, coming to his leader's aid. "There you go. Perfect."

"Thank you Fred," said the leader, smiling affectionately. "God I feel terrible. I need a drink."

Sherry was quick to accommodate.

"What would you like dearest heart?" she said, still glowing from her exchange with Fred.

"Whisky. Make it a large one with lots of ice."

Sherry was quite taken aback by the abrupt tone. She rather liked it.

"Coming up," she said, kissing her husband's neck. "Fred?"

"Yes please, First Lady."

As Sherry winked at him, Fred turned to the President.

"Yes sir, that was some party, wasn't it? Hair of the dog – if you'll excuse the pun – should get us going."

With his back to his wife at the drinks cabinet, Hair nodded, said nothing, rubbed his eyes and head. Fred, sat directly in front of the President, watched Sherry slowly rolling up her robe and sucking her finger.

"Er, sir, if I may, can I use the-?" Fred motioned towards the bathroom.

"Of course, Fred, you needn't ask."

"It's always better to be polite, Mr President."

Fred mouthed 'naughty' at Sherry before entering the Presidential khazi. It was a fair size, containing a Jacuzzi and shower, and a bizarrely enormous toilet. After he had spent his penny, Fred flushed, a luxury not available to most.

Upon re-entering the Premier's chamber, he saw Hair open a hatch and remove bountiful portions of bacon, egg, mushrooms, beans, fresh coffee, muffins and a selection of juices. Hair tucked in, while a sleepy Sherry pushed her food round her plate.

"I told those idiots down there that I want Muesli and Grapefruit. Why won't they listen?"

"I'll have a word," said Fred.

Hair ladled a spoonful of beans towards his mouth. Half fell on the floor, the rest he gorged on.

"Republic Day was a disaster," he said, expelling a beany-mush.

Oh God, he's not still going on about this is he? thought Fred. No wonder Sherry's so sick of him.

The anniversary of the accession of The United Kingdom to People's Republic of Britannia had indeed been a muted affair. For many hours after the celebrations President Hair had been sat in his study here in the Palace drinking away his gloom, remote control in hand, watching footage of the recent ceremony over and over again, flitting between obsessively rewinding and viewing the footage and staring vacantly into the middle distance, asking anyone nearby if it looked as bad as it felt.

Again, Hair pressed play and a close-up of his grinning mug filled the screen.

God he looks gaunt! thought Fred. Garqi did a number on him there, didn't he?

Indeed. Signor Oli Garqi – head honcho of MediaCorp International and whose donations to the Liberal Compassionate Party had bought unilateral media control – had explained to Hair that he would appear more empathetic, more able to relate to the Citizenry if his appearance reflected the austerity of the times. Fred glanced at the leader sat next to him. Doesn't look much better now, he thought.

Hair was fixated on the screen as he watched himself come out to a lukewarm reception.

*"All hail the President, leader of the People's Republic of Britannia!"*

The LibCom flag-wavers had been there but that was about it. And as Fred watched more closely, he could see the leader say through smiling teeth – *Where the fuck is everyone?*

Hair shook his head in disbelief as he watched himself speak the announcement Fred had prepared for him.

*"Now that we as a nation have finally moved on from an era of preposterous tradition, we can celebrate, united together, the freest we have ever been, the undue privilege afforded the Royals and CEO's of Big Business removed forever."*

"Oh it looks terrible," said Hair. Again.

"As I've told you President," said Fred, texting one of his new girls, not looking up, "don't worry. It looked different on the news. The re-shoot was amazing and demonstrated a unified response of support and adulation. Remember, we have skilled cameramen and the high-lights programme looked spectacular, edited complete with footage of teeming Monorails and grinning public."

"I just can't help thinking that it went out live," Hair whispered.

"Oh darling, come on. It looked better than you think," said Sherry. "How about another drink?"

She took Hair's glass from him, not waiting for him to respond.

"Fred, how about you?"

"If you're offering," responded Fred, looking up momentarily.

That's not all, darling, her eyes seemed to say.

"I can't believe people weren't there!" said Hair, suddenly animated. "Why didn't the Public Harmony Unit do their job properly? They should've been letting it known in no uncertain terms that each Citizen's presence was required!"

"All I can say sir is that lessons will be learnt," Fred responded, finally putting down his phone and looking at the President. "We have launched a review of best practice immediately."

"After what you promised me as well."

"Sir all I can say is there was a communication breakdown. I can't apologise enough."

"Honestly Fred, they can't even be bothered to come and show their appreciation. After all I've done."

"I know, I know."

"Are we in control here? Why was there no-one there? And I'm convinced Cliffe is up to something."

Heath Cliffe, a thorough if uninspiring operator, was the man in charge of the country's finances. Though he had developed the concept of Liberal Compassionatism it had been agreed he would have a more secondary role to the charismatic Hair – albeit that charisma was now on the wane. Since then of course, Fred had rebranded the party somewhat and found Cliffe easy to side-step, believing him not to have the gumption to destabilise the LibCom ship.

"Oh it's a lot of piss and wind where he's concerned President. He hasn't the balls to try anything. I wouldn't worry about him."

Hair nodded unconvincingly and picked up a muffin. Another emotional dip was imminent.

Fred was well versed in the President's propensity for wild swings in humour – he was responsible for most of them, after all – but he hadn't seen Hair this uncomfortable since the start of his project, when he had put it to Hair that adopting the policies of the Neo-Luddites would win a landslide. When Fred mooted that *Plasticitis* was the result of a pyramid of wealth built on the sinking, contaminated sands of a throwaway culture perpetrated by banks and big business, and that electoral success lay in bringing them to book, Hair's eyes had glazed over. And when Fred put it to Hair that years of tax evasion and bonuses and a desire to own as much wealth and property as possible had driven the country into the dirt, that seizing their assets would fund the rebirth of the nation, Hair had been more than a little squeamish about the prospect of crucifying old friends.

But when Fred put it to him that he could be the people's saviour, that, dare he think it, he could be their Messiah, Hair had nodded. Yes, he knew it was true. He had always known it was true. He just needed reminding.

Well, thought Fred, reaching into his briefcase, this'll shake his belief in that.

"There is perhaps something you should see sir," he said, handing Hair a thin, crumpled booklet.

"What is it?" Hair asked through a mouthful of muffin.

As the President scanned over the document incredulity took hold of him, the last morsels of muffin falling to the floor, panic spreading to his eyes.

The face of it had changed – the production values representing the limitations of the times – but the bold black letters etched onto a white background showed **KARMATARMAK** had made its return!

"I thought these fuckers were no longer operational!" Hair cried. "Where did this come from? How did it get here?"

"It appears they have been dropped all over the Central and North Districts. There's no reason to believe this current crop emanates from anywhere other than Hellevue. Despite the considerable success we had in arresting vendors of the publication last time they tried something, and many contributors, we never did find the top brass, nor find out where it had its headquarters, even in its legal days."

Until he had received an email out of the blue about four months ago, Fred had assumed **KARMATARMAK** was finished as well. Surely no-one would dare carry on after the last crackdown. In fact, he had wondered if anyone connected with it was still alive.

Hair picked up the copy of the zine – which comprised four sheets of A4 folded into a sixteen sided A5 document – and began reading the words of the editor, *Herr Enigma.*

**"We were promised a green revolution. And what did this revolution bring us? Exactly what we had before,**

**just with different faces. Hair says: 'These are com-
plicated and trying times, to hinder the Government is a
treasonable offence.' I would suggest reasonable.**

**"As we witness a year of the Republic, of eighteen
months of Liberal Compassionate rule, I call on all of you
to take part in mass acts of civil disobedience and to take
to the streets again. Yes, the road to sedition, we must
travel it! Disrupt the *Life Administration Directive*, board
the Monorail on your no-travel days. We need one last
push to overthrow these thieves of liberty!**

**"We do not make this make this call to arms lightly – I
am all but aware of the terrible suffering after we last
published. But we must do something, otherwise there
will be no end to the horror and our country will be
irrevocably damaged, future generations born into ever-
expanding tyranny. Love to all who love freedom."**

"Didn't think they could still write over there in that cesspool!"
raged Hair.

"Well it appears they can," responded Sherry as she wiped bean
juice spray from her arm. "And with no shortage of lyrical prowess."

The persistence of this **KARMATARMAK** greatly irked Hair. Being a
vainglorious character – thereby upholding the political tradition – he
wanted to be liked by all.

"Have the PHU uncovered anything?" he asked, sending bits of
sausage spiralling through the air, impatient for answers. He fixated
on a cartoon of himself, *The Joker*.

"In terms of identities, it's early days, sir. We only started enquiries
last night. We are-"

"Last night? Why wasn't I told?"

"I didn't want to disturb you sir. It was your special night. But as I
say, we are questioning people as we speak. Tonight we will go to the
terror district and commence operation *Hellevue Harmony*."

"What about CCTV footage from when the zine was being delivered? Have you looked through that?"

"Of course, sir. But they were very well disguised."

"Why didn't the Blackguard stop them at the time?"

"We're looking into that, sir."

Hair slumped forward, disconsolate.

Sherry looked at Fred, mouthed 'I want you.' Fred wagged his finger at her.

"Sir," he said, snapping his vision away from the leader's wife. He tipped the remnants of a wrap onto the table. "Here. This will help with policy development."

He chopped at the powder in front of him and handed the mirror to Hair. Hair brightened, nodded girlishly.

He'll have to stop crossing his legs like that, thought Fred. People don't trust a man who can cross his legs all the way over. And neither should they.

Hair snorted and snorted again.

"One for you, First Lady," said Fred, giving a mock bow with a rolling hand. "I know what you lawyers are like."

"Oh, that," said Sherry pulling her eyes away from the ice bucket to see Fred chopping on a mirror. "Yeah go on then. Thank you, my Liege."

She handed her men their drinks.

"This governing thing certainly suits us."

It certainly does, thought Fred, hardening at the prospect of some more time alone with the President's wife. He basked in this thought, sipping at his whisky, watching Sherry drape herself over the country's premier.

"What an outrage!" shouted Hair, suddenly indignant after his granular intake. "I bloody well saved this country, practically single-handedly, and this is the thanks I get! And this isn't the first time they've attacked me either, is it? No. What did they write when I first came to power, before we illegalised them onto the Un-British list?"

"I don't recall President."

"Is *he* in there, Fred?"

"Who, sir?"

"You know."

"Oh. *Ockham*, sir?"

"Yes, *Ockham*."

"Er yes, sir, he is." Fred picked up the zine from the table.

**"The Grinning Idiot of Salvation..."**

Egg flew out of Hair's mouth in a flurry of mucussy babbling.

"I've a good mind to go down there myself and tell these people exactly what I think! Denigrating the country like this! And *Ockham*. Hasn't even got the decency to show his face! What I wouldn't give for ten minutes alone with this character!"

Fred started again.

**"The Grinning Idiot of Salvation cancelled our voices to *protect the environment*, emoting on the specifics of our times. The very action of creating led to all our problems, he claimed.**

**"Yet this is a debate the Dear Old Saviour deliberately misrepresents. In truth it isn't the action of creating he wants to prohibit, but the disparaging content. The Cultural Revolution has banned new books, film, music, art... And us. Well we're still here. They used violence but they never caught us and now we will rise again! It is time to launch a campaign of unceasing secular jihad!"**

"Secular jihad!" bleated Hair. "Cultural Revolution! All these so-called writers and artists! Why don't they get a proper job! I was a rock star when I was younger but I realised I had to grow out of it!"

From time to time Hair would throw his toys out of his pram and have a hissy fit because he'd never made it onto the stage at Glastonbury. It was why he had swallowed with such gusto the idea of what was now colloquially dubbed the Cultural Revolution, thought Fred. Sour grapes. He continued.

**"We've all heard about the autonomous tribal zones throughout the country. The rest of us should follow. We must end the horror of *New Democracy*. Liberty for the United Kingdom!"**

"Oh, I've heard enough!" cried the President. "It makes me quite mad. Where does this bastard get off? That's incitement to riot! I mean it's bad enough to attack the Government and me, personally, but democracy? Well, that's just going too far."

"I quite agree sir," said Fred.

"What fools!" exclaimed the President. "What absolute, bloody...."

Hair slumped into his chair. He looked distraught.

"What am I gonna do, Fred?"

More panic and confusion engulfed the leader's face as he again nuzzled the mirror.

"Now President, don't you worry about that. The PHU are a very well trained and highly motivated bunch who hate all things literary or seditious. They'll close down anything they come across, arrest anyone contravening Public Safety Directives. They live for it."

"And there's no sign of revolution?"

"Good grief no," laughed Fred. "Of course, the problem doesn't go away when we arrest this scum. New terrorists are always waiting to fill any void. Anyway, we'll get em all, eh?" said Fred, slapping the leader on the side of his left arm. Hair nodded, uncertain. "Let's not get depressed. Good work is being done, progress is being made and you, President, *you*, are transforming the country. You're doing a fantastic job."

This drew a smile from the leader like a smitten daughter for her father.

"You think so, Fred?"

Fred nodded.

"Well, yes, yes I am," said a now buoyed Hair. "And no two-bit parasite in some rag is gonna sway me from my destiny!"

"That's the spirit."

"Yes," said Hair, "my people," then softer, "my people...." He looked up at Fred. "The only mistake I make is not listening to myself enough. I know I'm right but sometimes I just don't have the courage of my convictions."

"Come sir, we all wobble from time to time."

"That's right darling, you're doing fantastically," agreed Sherry, rubbing Hair's back, pulling a 'yawn' face at Fred.

"You will need to make a statement though, sir," said Fred.

"Can't you get someone else to do it?"

"It'll be better if it comes from you, sir. You are the President, after all. Your car is waiting."

Reluctantly Hair stood up, turned to Sherry and kissed her passionlessly before turning to the door. As her husband looked away, Sherry looked up at his young companion and blew a kiss. Fred doffed an imaginary cap, bowing ever so slightly. Sherry smiled, gave a flirtatious wave. Fred was having too much fun. He waved back, regally. Tart, he thought to himself. I like tarts.

Then Sherry, louder, evidently for her husband's benefit, "Bye Frederick."

"Bye First Lady."

Having given Hair a statement to read and assuring him that the *Hellevue Harmony* campaign would get underway forthwith, Fred bid a temporary *au revoir* to Hair. Though the President had wanted his confidante near him, Fred had declined. He was fastidious about not making public appearances. He had no intention of alerting a wider audience to his influence. His reasoning to Hair was that he didn't want to detract from the premier's limelight. As ever, Fred had the President just where he wanted him.

So what next? thought Fred. To flush out all those who may be *inclined* to get involved in revolution Fred had contacted NIPSD HQ and instructed all *Citizens' Accounts* Technicians to focus on analysing the Social Media output and internet usage of Hellevue residents. In the main only those employed by the Government and the elite used computers these days but by looking at historical evidence – all the data had been gathered just after the LibComs came to power – the Government could get an indication of the *likely* characters. The slightest whiff and a Citizen was to be detained. Irrespective, the Blackguard and Public Harmony Unit had orders to arrest five per cent of the men of Hellevue later that night. Fred then planned to announce significant arrests through *The Cow*, to announce **KARMATARMAK** terrorists had been brought in, whether true or not. This, he had assured Hair, would lead them to the ringleaders.

And this all meant Fred had now arrived at the auspicious moment to release his story to *warm the hearts of the nation*, to show the great strides being made by the Government in Hellevue. Now that terrorism was back, it was time to launch Robert Pope into stardom. To do this he would need the help of his old friend and employer, Signor Oli Garqi, the sole foreigner in the LibCom operation. Foreigners were something of a rarity these days and though the world had de-globalised and international ties were virtually non-existent, a few people did still maintain international links, media moguls being the most preeminent of this group, topping even governments. It was thanks to Fred that Garqi had been brought in. And it was thanks to Garqi that the LibComs had had the funding to win the election. Fred loved the poetry of funding a Green-Commie revolution with the ill-gotten gains of an Italian media mogul.

After unfavourable coverage of phone-hacking at one of his papers in Italy and the imprisonment of one of his editors, Garqi was finally run out of his home country for fraud. Two things amazed Fred about this. Number one, that Garqi hadn't been able to buy himself out of it. Second, Fred thought it pretty incredible that anyone had been charged with fraud over there. Knowing the Italian wanted to relocate his base and extend his vast media empire into Britain, Fred had come up with a plan. As his influence over Hair had grown, Fred offered Hair and the LibComs the chance for an injection of cash. As long as there was something in return. Garqi was brought in as a donor at first, with a tacit promise he could dismantle the BBC.

Official line had been that MediaCorp International had taken over the running of the BBC to make it more competitive, and that current independent channels would cease broadcasting due to the pollution they caused. In the early days there had been a bit of a walk out as the pro-government agenda was gradually imposed, departing employees speaking out about the tinkering with a story here and there. But the voids were easily filled due to the surfeit of unemployed journalists, which included, in no particular order, careerists and apolitical types and those that could put aside their ideology to secure a fairly decent standard of living. It wasn't hard to *look the other way* if it meant a bit more domestic comfort. This was known as *doing an Eriksson*, either accepting money to turn a blind eye, as here, or selling yourself to the highest bidder. It was named after a philandering football coach from yesteryear.

In addition, all newspapers had been ordered to dismantle and hand over their resources to the Government. (Fred concocted this as revenge for an exposé on expenses. It was unanimously agreed by the newly seated LibComs). Because of the limited resources and the potential for pollution, only one broadsheet and one tabloid were permitted, both established out of the ashes of those that had disbanded. They were: *The Daily Sentinel* – the broadsheet, and *The Daily Rumour* – the tabloid. Naturally enough, Garqi now had both in his vast international portfolio. Unsurprisingly, more Citizens read *The Rumour* which was useful as the type of story Fred wanted to concoct was tabloid-friendly. Garqi had been very receptive to Fred's idea. He liked it a lot, found it funny. Just say the word, he said. Well *the word* wouldn't be long coming.

The idea to have an inhabitant of Hellevue display loyalty to the Government was undoubtedly a winner. It would change the perception of the district, show that it wasn't just the playground of terrorists. This would make the people of Hellevue feel included. And make the life of Robert Pope rather different.

It had worked well that Zini had required Pope to complete 'a few more realignment modules' before he could be released. Fred had had to wait for the other player anyway – what was her name, ah yes, Clementine Romain – and for the final round of **KARMATARMAK** copies to find their way into the central districts, and most importantly, President Hair's hand. Then the Hellevue raid could start and Fred's news story could come out the next day. Tomorrow.

Fred rummaged in his pocket, found his phone and dialled.

"Hello Frederick, my darling. How are you?" cooed Dr Zini.

"Hello Doctor. A little ropey from last night but other than that, as good as ever."

"Yes. Sorry I had to leave early. That young Blackguard just tickled my fancy!"

"I bet he did, Germolene, I bet he did. Now look, I'd love to chat all day but I'm sure we're both busy. Is he ready yet?"

"Who? Your man Pope? Indeed he is. There's just one more thing he needs to do. As agreed, he'll be out tonight."

"Perfect."

Fred hung up and dialled again. Garqi.

"Freddi dear, ow iz your 'ead?"

"Much better now. You?"

"Oh good, good. Wendi look after me today. But what about dee President? I have concerns about iz 'ealth."

"You're not the only one, Oli."

"Yes, I know. I 'eard a few others ad started talkeen as well. Cliffe and dose Millipede brudders. Just ow ill is e? Is e finished?"

48

"Maybe soon, Oli. But for now, what about our story? Are we ready?"

"Yes we ready, Freddi dear. Are you?"

"Yes I am, Oli. Release the hounds!"

# 4
# WAKEY WAKEY

PONTIFF LAY IN the pitch dark, rather sore. He was trying not to make too much of a movement of his bruised body. The cuffs cut into his wrists and his hands ached, joined in front of his belly button. Through the dark he heard voices and the unmistakable jangle of keys and stomping of boots. The violence-cum-patronisation units had returned.

After much clunking of keys and bolts, the huge metal door – the fourth wall in this thin, rectangular shaped cell – was heaved open. Light flooded in to reveal two Blackguard Pontiff knew rather too well.

"Wakey wakey trouble," said the larger.

"Ooh, he is tough looking, isn't he?" said the smaller "Some of the others I've dealt with don't look like they're up to much, but this one. What a fighter, eh?" He tutted, bit his bottom lip and shook his head. "Come on, up."

Pontiff's neck was stiff with pain. How much more of this was there? His eyes slowly adjusted to the light. With the help of some truncheon-prompting, he raised his battered body.

"Ah for fu-!" he exclaimed as he knocked his elbow. A blood patch grew on the sleeve of his white suit.

"Oh, does your funny bone hurt?" said the first guard, the larger. "Aaah."

"Come on Pope!" shouted the smaller guard.

Pontiff lay unmoved on his concrete slab.

The smaller guard approached him and lifted him up.

"You gonnae take these off?" asked Pontiff, raising his conjoined hands.

"Not until after your consultation, Pope. You need to understand the gravity of your actions. Protocol must be followed. We are to ensure your safe passage to the doctor. To not do this would be a dereliction of duty."

"D'you cunts ever speak English?"

An elbow flashed from the little man, and Pontiff's face was split open. Down he went. Blood oozed and Pontiff pulled his still-tied hands to his face. The larger guard threw him a handkerchief.

"Are you gonna cause us any more trouble, Mr Pope?" he said. "Because there's plenty more where that came from if you're asking!"

Pontiff remained silent.

"I suggest you answer Pope," added the smaller.

After a short pause, having mopped up a bit of blood, Pontiff did answer.

"You'd better take me to the doctor then."

"Good. Now, how's your face?"

"How the-"

A raised eyebrow promised more pain.

"A little sore as it goes," Pontiff conceded, still on the ground.

"Well if you are going to be a naughty boy, we will have to punish you. Any more carry on like this and you'll be in here for longer than you dare dream. Now, we are taking to the doctor and expect you to keep your nose clean. Understood?"

Waiting at the *LifeManagement4Life: Management Office* was Dr Zini. She scanned over her new arrival.

"Ah, Mr Pope," she said, "you're back." The right side of her face scrunched up as she focussed on the specimen before her. "Have you rested well?"

Pontiff nodded.

"Oh aye."

"What's happened to your face?"

"Hud a nose bleed."

Pontiff was forcibly seated in the metal chair. With his hands still shackled, the guards produced a new set of cuffs and Pontiff's right hand was manacled to the right arm of the patient's chair. The old cuffs were then removed and Pontiff's left arm was pulled behind the chair and reattached to its back. Next, his right hand was released from the second set of cuffs and attached at the back of the chair to Pontiff's other hand and the frame.

The doctor nodded at the guards who promptly departed.

Pontiff looked past the doctor to the window, partially obscured as the Venetian blinds were lopsidedly arranged.

Silence.

"So," said Dr Zini as she rose from her cushioned seat. She went to the window and adjusted the blinds so that they were uniformly swept to the top. "Has the thinking time been beneficial to you?"

Pontiff said nothing.

"I see. Well, I know you have this, how shall I put it, injured soul. And I want to help you." She paused momentarily, apparently finding something on the horizon incredibly fascinating. "Do you understand the events of the last week?" she said, still looking out the window. She looked back. "How it has helped Susan?"

Pontiff couldn't fight anymore.

"I understand, Doctor," he responded.

In his recent hours of solitude Pontiff had turned over again and again in his mind how his behaviour that morning and his refusal to play along with the Ratman had resulted in... He couldn't finish the thought. He refreshed his mouth with the Ethiopian level of saliva he had available to him and asked "how's she dae-en?"

Zini scratched the lid of her eye patch. "How's she doing? Why, fine, splendid, yes, very good. She understands." Zini trailed off, looked back out the window. "Cigarette?" she said as she turned.

The doctor approached Pontiff.

"Mr Pope?" she said, leaning in.

Pontiff catgulped the saline sludge in his throat. "Aye, sure."

Zini had hundreds pre-rolled. She produced a pair, lit both, and held one in front of Pontiff. He inhaled a couple of long toots.

"Good," said Zini as she watched him, "good." She breathed in heavily, as though suffering a great burden. "Robert. I think you are nearly ready to leave us."

Of course, thought Pontiff, they're gonnae kill me. What else was left? There wasn't much he hadn't tried.

"But. Due to your absolute refusal to..." the doctor looked for the words in the air, as if trying to breathe them in through her nose, "*connect* with Miss Baxter, I have had to develop an alternative course of rehabilitation." She paused. Pontiff remained motionless. "You know, it would have been nice if you'd been part of the Republic Day celebrations. We had a great time. Susan had a great time," she added, pointedly. "Still. What's done is done."

Zini approached Pontiff with a damp cloth. She smiled at him and began cleaning the blood from his face. When she had finished wiping Pontiff's nose she tossed the cloth to the floor. Suddenly she was sitting on Pontiff's lap, straddling him. Her one eye winked as she moved her curly hair behind her ears. She began stroking Pontiff's bald head. He tried to speak but nothing came out. Horror and disbelief rose in equal measures. He writhed as the doctor started to kiss his neck. She leant back and produced a bottle of whiskeysquash, putting it to his lips. Pontiff refused to swallow, but she rubbed the liquor on his mouth. He noticed its fine quality.

"I've always loved the taste of whiskey on a man's lips, such a virile perfume. And you are ruggedly handsome man. Especially with your bloodied face." She paused, tried to look into Pontiff's eyes as he bowed his head. "Maybe I can be the vehicle to ease your blockage... and you, mine." She unzipped Pontiff's fly and manoeuvred herself on top of him. "Oh yes, I think you can."

Zini started to move slowly, uttering sounds of increasing contentment. She unbuttoned her shirt and pulled Pontiff's face into her breasts. She circled faster and with more vigour. Pontiff was overcome with horror and mounting pleasure. Zini moved with yet more speed, more speed, more speed, before finally, with high register vocal delight, she reached her goal.

Pontiff approached. His very fibre begged him not to but his very essence was spilled. He buried his head into the doctor, shame engulfing him as she unhinged herself from her patient.

"Yes," said Zini, steeping away to fasten her buttons and straighten her garments. "I think that's a lot better, don't you?"

Pontiff kept his head bowed. He feared he would vomit.

Zini looked at him, and smiled.

"Now," she said, her clothes restored to effortlessly impeccable, "I'm going to release you from your cuffs but if you try anything there are six Blackguard out there who will stop at nothing in their pursuit of justice. Do I make myself understood?"

Pontiff acquiesced the subtlest of nods. Zini undid his cuffs, lit two more cigarettes and handed one to him. Pontiff rubbed his wrists and smoked.

"You know, you are very lucky to have been treated here at the mothership, Robert, at the apex of cutting edge medicine."

She looked at Pontiff for his agreement.

"Do you understand what has just happened?"

Pontiff said nothing. That awful numbness returned.

"Tell me what you feel. As a doctor it is important to know my methods work."

Through the numbness Pontiff's main feeling was repulsion. He gulped back bile.

With broken vocals, "that I been..."

He cleared the rattling limpet of phlegm from his throat.

"That you helped ease my blockage."

"Good. Good. I believe you do understand."

The doctor smiled.

"Good."

She let the smile linger before returning to her seat, and nodded and smiled again.

"Well," she said as she reached into her drawer, "I think congratulations are in order, Mr Pope. You have been realigned. You are now ready to reintegrate into society."

Pontiff remained silent as he was handed his NIPSD card.

"I've added a bit of extra cash to your *Citizen's Account* as your Admin Group's Rations Pick-up isn't for a while."

Pontiff studied his NIPSD card intently. He wanted to leave. Desperately. But guilt rose in him. How could he leave Susan in here? But then, what could he do if he stayed?

"You alright there Mr Pope?" asked the doctor, breaking Pontiff's thoughts. "You do not seem too sure. Need we ask you to stay a little while longer?"

He looked up at the doctor, directly into that sole green eye.

"You seem sad to be leaving us," she continued. "Dare I say it, sad to be leaving me?"

The sentiment revolted him. But for these final moments he wanted to maintain a sense of equanimity.

"You know, it's funny, doctor," responded Pontiff, "throughout my life people huv always asked me that. You know, what's wrong, what am I sad about. Must huv a depressive look." He paused. "Nah, I'm ready."

Aye, he thought, ready. But for what? What could possibly come next?

"Good. Well here are some leaflets on how to avoid further realigning. I suggest you read them carefully, or there is the danger you may become a resident here once again. Possibly even permanently. They will give you advice on best practice going forward. The Liberal Compassionate Party cares greatly for your well-being."

They must do, thought Pontiff. Every government office, agency, facility, you-name-it, produced leaflets like this to guide you on *best practice going forward*. Fuck me, he thought, *going forward*, the most vacuous phrase in our evermore spasticated language.

"Something amuse you, Mr Pope?"

"Nahnah."

"Good, good. I am sure you can see the benefit of such literature. We must continue to modernise, after all."

"Absolutely, Doctor."

"So," continued Zini, suddenly jaunty. "What are your plans when you get out?"

Pontiff gave the briefest shake of his head.

"Looking for a job, perhaps? Might be beneficial. In fact, I'll see to it you have an appointment with an Employment Technician in the next week or so."

Oh good, thought Pontiff, a return to the bi-weekly chat that threw up nothing of excitement. Anyway, he had another job to get back to.

"Well then," said Zini, lifting Pontiff from his thoughts, "I suppose the time has come." She reached under her desk. "You'll be needing this, I expect."

She tossed him a rather heavy hemp sack in which Pontiff found his clothes. His dirtied white shirt, his blue t-shirt, the old faded blue jeans ripped at both knees and finally, the old brown and battered lace up brogue boots, topped off with an aged scuff. Also in there, a form in a brown envelope he hadn't been able to post. Finally he could get out of the Shrink Clink uniform.

After he had changed Pontiff followed the doctor out of her office and through the rest of the Life Camp to the main entrance. He stepped up to the door and passed his NIPSD card over the SwipeScanner.

The exit process was supposed to take a couple of seconds but delays were not uncommon if NIPSD HQ was being inundated with Swipe Requests.

"I was right," said the doctor, luxuriating in these last exchanges, "you are ruggedly handsome."

At one time those chocolatey tones had stirred Pontiff. Not now. At least, not in the same way. He remained unmoved, fixing his stare straight ahead.

He thought about asking to see Susan but he knew he'd be refused. Plus, he couldn't face her. He felt too ashamed. Eventually, after an agonising minute and a half, the scanner beeped and Pontiff's photograph materialised on the screen. He looked at this image and saw a rather pleasing if somewhat inaccurate reproduction of his physical appearance – a healthy facsimile that aged Pontiff junior to his forty-three years. An instruction flashed up to place fingertips on screen and eyes up to the iris scanner. Pontiff did as he was bade.

A message appeared.

*"Application to exit Correctional Facility. Environmental Footprint being calculated. Patience, Citizen, is a virtue."*

This was a bizarrely hi-tech process considering the Dark Age existence most people were leading in all other areas of their lives.

*"Individual Carbon Footprint: 2.1"*

Pontiff mentally tutted to himself. What did that even mean?

A new message materialised.

*"Thank you Citizen. The environment has been trampled on and it is imperative to step lightly. You are helping in the drive towards a cleaner, more efficient country."*

This scanning-in made an imprint at NIPSD HQ and the Citizen's movements were recorded. Pontiff imagined little people in isolated booths casting their beady little eyes over NIPSD records and facilitating. He could envisage them there, pouring through CCTV footage and NIPSD imprints to make sure you were where you were supposed to be at the designated time, not creating unnecessary pollution. And then these monitors, in turn, being monitored by other facilitators in booths, and so on, ad nauseam, like some vast Orwellian Russian Doll.

The door buzzed open and Pontiff stepped outside. It was a warm night.

"Good luck Mr Pope," said the doctor, breaking the silence. "I do trust I shall not be seeing you soon."

"So do I, Doctor," replied Pontiff.

Zini handed him what was left of the whiskeysquash bottle and a packet of tobacco.

"If you hurry you'll catch the last Monorail to Hellevue."

It was then that Pontiff was struck by the oddness of the whole thing. Why was he being released in the middle of the night? Why was he being released at all? He again thought of Susan. Was it right to leave? But what could he do? Having seen what these people were capable of he knew he couldn't protect her staying here.

Before he started out down the gravel drive, Pontiff took one last look at the huge pile that would no longer be his home. His eyes settled on the sign emblazoned high on every wall.

## *CLEANING UP THE MIND, BODY AND SOUL OF SOCIETY – RENEWING THE FABRIC OF OUR LIVES!*

That had worked about as well as taking the countryside back, he thought. The abomination of the goings on at *LifeManagement4Life* – what he'd seen, what he'd had to do for his freedom – begged the question in Pontiff's mind as to whether it had been sanctioned directly by the Government or constituted an abuse of power. It didn't matter. Since time immemorial, if government had been anything, it was legalised criminality washed down with a bit of vacuous sloganeering.

He soon reached the entrance arch of *LifeManagement4Life*, passed his NIPSD card over the SwipeScanner, presented fingers and eyes, and stepped out into his freedom. He immediately heard the familiar whirring buzz of the CCTV, and could see the first camera track him, his movements monitored and recorded, until he was picked up by the next camera, positioned on a lamppost less than twenty metres away, and so on, down every road in the land.

Ah yes, thought Pontiff, the CCTV camera, the totem of modern British society, the red phone box of its age.

He started out for the Monorail Station and at the earliest moment tossed the *best practice* leaflets along with the brown envelope into one of the recycling barrels that appeared every couple of blocks. He rolled a cigarette, inhaled deeply and took a glug from the whiskeysquash bottle. He was feeling far sturdier for the alcohol and nicotine coursing through his veins. He wouldn't normally have been so brazen in his public drinking but it was nighttime and he couldn't wait.

The first moment Pontiff had fallen foul of the *Life Administration Directive* had been *Life Administration* Group Three's *Designated Dry Day*. The policing of denying indulgence in alcohol was random, and therefore always worth the risk in Pontiff's view. But one day, carelessly, outside the relative sanctuary of Hellevue, feeing the joyous haze of illicit afternoon booze, Pontiff's mood had been brutally interrupted by two young Blackguard.

*"NIPSD card," said the larger.*

*"Pope, eh? And where have you been?" said the smaller.*

*"I've jus come back fae playen fitbah," drawled Pontiff.*

*"Have you been drinking Mr Pope?"*

And that was that. Out came the breathalyser kits and his NIPSD card was updated on the spot with three Social Behavioural Points. Not fit to walk apparently.

*"Aye, the rules," agreed Pontiff. "Of course. How saved we are, the people of Britannia, by the rules. The rules! What every civilised country needs to stay civil. Everyhen mapped out in the finest detail so as to avoid uncertainty. God forbid people get confused, or have a bitta fun at the wrong time. Christ, your time's no longer free tae organise yourself, is it?"*

*"Well no, we tried that before, didn't we Mr Pope? And practically wrote ourselves off."*

*"Are you really tellen me I'm killen the planet by drinken a pint on a wet Wednesday?"*

*"Not only that, Citizen. Intake must be monitored for your own safety."*

Pontiff remembered being given a few extra Social Behavioural Points for *wilful destruction of the environment* after he had flicked his cigarette butt to the ground. He did so again this evening, and rolled another.

Suddenly he vomited. The image of Zini on top of him, what had precipitated his release, that Susan was now alone, all, *everything*, brought shame to his perpetual nausea. He didn't need any more reason to join the fight, but he had it anyway. And any shred of doubt or apprehension about embarking on the *wilful destruction* of Terry Hair had now fully evaporated.

As a keen student of history – indeed, as a man who had quite a vast and varied knowledge on how human beings had organised themselves through the centuries – Pontiff was not so naive to think that an overthrow of the Government would necessarily lead to immediate freedom. He had always been fairly cynical about revolutions – or more specifically, those that led them – but with all that happened he felt compelled to do something.

Pontiff had not seen the final copy of the new **KARMATARMAK** before he'd been taken into custody, had not even been able to say goodbye. Christ, if they knew I was involved in that they'd've locked me up forever, he thought, thrown away the key! Pontiff wondered whether it had been released yet, whether Godfrey, nom de plume – *Herr Enigma*, the driving force and editor whose private income funded the **KARMATARMAK** enterprise, had been able to raise the capital or even get someone to print it. After the last copy had been released in autumn the year before – before Pontiff had arrived in Hellevue – the fightback had been speedy and deadly. Quite aside from the content of the zine, private manufacture was illegal (save the odd license granted for personal enterprise). As had been hammered home, and shown many a time, anyone threatening the environment with non-state sanctioned use of materials would soon be disappeared. The leadership group of Godfrey, the RevKev (*Cardinal Cad*) and Clem (*Foxhunter*) had not been caught, yet many others had, most of whom were occasional contributors writing about anything other than the crumbling political environment. Fearing they too would be tracked down, Godfrey had ceased all zine activity. He felt huge guilt that so many had disappeared yet he was safe. If a new edition was out now, what would be the response? Either way, Pontiff couldn't wait to renew hostilities against the Government. Though the risk attached to trying to start a revolution was considerable, what choice was there?

# 5
# IT'S IN THE POST

"SO MUCH MORE energy than Terry!" exclaimed Sherry.

"Well he is running the country and must be very tired. I'm just glad I could be of assistance, First Lady."

While President Hair had once revelled in his position of saviour, young Fred was still revelling in all sorts of positions, and on a regular basis. He had always possessed a penchant for the older, flirtatious woman, the advancing vintage serving to imbue the object of his desire with added naughtiness. And the Premier's wife was a salty old sort who was a lot of fun.

Sherry pulled him close to her.

"Ready to go again?"

Jesus Christ, thought Fred, she's got some stamina. But he always had energy for this kind of thing.

"Of course."

He did want to leave himself a bit in the tank, though. He had a lot of thinking to do tonight.

After the act, "My dear First lady, you have worn me out."

"Well, *you* have left me satisfied," responded Sherry. "Unlike that joke of a husband. God, sometimes I... I mean...the man's useless! No...*vitality.*"

Fred knew to expect an outburst like this. It had happened quite a lot recently.

"You saw him today," she said. "God I can't bare his childishness, his *neediness*. All I bloody do is reassure him. He used to be so much more of a man."

Sherry liked decisive, strong men. That's what had drawn her to her husband in the first place. Now. Now, he was different. *Weaker.* That's why she liked Fred and was relieved she could slip out for a while this evening, unnoticed. She also enjoyed the deleterious effect the **KARMATARMAK** zine had on her husband, reserving a special fondness for the section called *Ockham's Razor.*

"Read it to me again," she said, snuggling up to her young beau.

Fred breathed in, and began.

**"Remember The Joker, flanked by that louche missus of his-"**

"Louche missus?" cried Sherry with mock indignation. "How dare they! About right though. Carry on!"

**"Remember The Joker being sworn in as supreme leader, grin morphing into a gurn after a night going hammer and tongs on the power powder? Remember him stood there, nose dripping, declaring: 'We're in this together?'"**

Sherry was laughing.

"Bloody hell!"

**"Well, it's not quite been the case, has it? No, it turns out the pie isn't big enough and there certainly isn't enough filling for you or me. No. We've had the return of... TWO-TIERISM! The governors and the governed. What's worse? This, or the casino-banking era? In an age of desperation and extreme personal difficulty for most of us – literally and metaphorically kept in the dark – government workers are reminded where their bread is buttered."**

"Oh the poor lambs," said Sherry. "It is very funny though. I kind of hope you don't catch him. I wonder what he's like. I'd love to meet him."

"Or her," said Fred. "Remember, we don't know who any of them are."

"Well, I *sense* it is a man."

Fred's phone buzzed. It was Zini.

"Germolene, how are you?"

"Oh fine, Frederick, fine. Look I don't want to keep you. I know it's late."

"Ooh never too late for you, Doctor."

Sherry rolled her eyes, heard Zini laughing.

"Now listen," said Zini. "Your boy has just left."

"Ah. Splendid. You've finally let him go."

"Oh yes, he performed his duties rather well! But anyway, how is my gorgeous brown-skinned beauty? And I don't mean you Fred."

"Oh you disappoint me. I presume, then, it is Ms Romain to whom you refer."

"Indeed."

When Fred had seen the image of Clementine Romain he thought she could have been his sister. He much preferred white women anyway, relieved his mother hadn't put him off.

"Oh she's fine," he said. "Her brief journey from your institute was no problem. Your sedatives were perfect."

"She was only with me a week you know, Fred. After your story has blown over, perhaps you could send her back. She was rather gorgeous."

"Well, we'll see. Night."

Fred had needed two pawns for his newspaper story and yet again, it had been Dr Zini who provided him with the perfect co-combatant.

This Clementine Romain's story was as follows –

Fearing *Plasticitis* was taking grip in her son (all the symptoms were evident – fever, bouts of unconsciousness, hallucinations, blueyblack bruises on the arms and legs, unbearable throat pain when trying to swallow, a phlegmy rasping cough, a sense that limbs and joints were broken) she took him to see the doctor, believing she was entitled to the necessary medicine. Normally this was the case but when the doctor examined her *Citizen's Account* on her NIPSD card, a warning stated there was an outstanding water bill, unpaid and long overdue. Until she paid this she was not entitled to free health care for her child. She had no means to pay the bill and certainly no funds to buy the medication privately. Her son *could* get the medication but if only if he was removed from her custody and taken into care.

This hadn't gone down well. By all accounts this Romain was rather feisty.

"What was the phrase she used again? Ah yes," Fred laughed as he regaled Sherry. "She told Zini that the doctor was *'some cunt comin across like a bearded Switzerland!'* It was when Romain threatened to *"go eccentric and yards 'im up"* that her son was taken off her and she was told she wasn't fit to continue as a parent."

"Will she see the boy again?" asked Sherry, looking at Romain's *Citizen's Account* photo.

"That might be tricky."

"Why?"

"Wait til the morning's paper."

A Hellevue mother was what Fred had been waiting for. That she was of foreign extraction was even better. Racism wasn't dead yet. That was why Fred had had to change *his* surname. To cap it off, she had been at the same Shrink Clink as Pope, though he wouldn't have seen her having been in solitary at the time. But he was out now. And that gave Fred an idea.

"Sherry, before you go, I want to show you something. Give you a brief glimpse of an imminent national celebrity. Load up the CCTV footage of Hellevue Post Office 2309 and select *Drunken Snuff*."

Fred opened his vast fridge and grabbed some beers nestled next to his caviar, pâté and steaks. Yes, it was all coming together superbly. Pope out, Romain in place, the story ready. And now the Hellevue offensive underway and a direct assault on terrorism. That Fred was contributing to the terrorism was neither here nor there.

He turned out the lights, got comfortable with Sherry under the duvet on the sofa, and pressed play.

*THE SCENE – An empty Post Office. In walks a man wearing a dirtied white shirt, a blue t-shirt underneath, some old faded blue jeans ripped at both knees and some brown and battered lace up brogue boots, holes in the boots.*

"Like his style," said Fred. "Same footwear as me."

*Drunk, and holding a brown envelope, the man, Robert Pope, proceeds to the first of the three free clerks. They don't look particularly busy. In fact, it looks like they have little to do except commune with each other. Pope is told to go back and wait at the white line that denotes the place they want people to start queuing. As soon as he has retreated to the white line and an appropriate amount of time has elapsed, illustrating who holds the power in this exchange, the man is waved over. He staggers to the window.*

*"I need tae send this off."*

*"Name."*

*"Robert Pope."*

*"That's P. That's Group Three," replies the young woman behind the screen. She employs the requisite patronising, idiotic tone of those vested with a small degree of power in largely inconsequential settings. "Today's Group Two Postal Day. You'll have to come back tomorrow."*

*And with that, she returns to her conversation with her neighbour.*

*"Ri-ight." Pope pauses. "I huv t'admit I wasnae aware that today is no my designated day. But I dae need tae post this cos if they dinnae receive m'application by tomorrow I'll huv tae wait another month tae re-apply for new threads. As I am sure you're aware. And you need only tae look at me tae see that ma need is great."*

*He steps back, makes 'ta-da hands' at his appearance.*

*"Look, there's nothing I can do for you. Today is not your Postal Day. What you can do is come in tomorrow for me." She pauses. "Can you do that?"*

*"But if I wait til tomorrow, I'll miss this month's deadline."*

*"You will indeed miss this month's deadline. That is correct."*

*"Look. No-one's here. Can you jus add this tae that wee pile behind your left shoulder and help me out?"*

*"You. Are Group Three? Today. Is Group Two Day? As I have explained, it is not permissible for me to accept your letter for posting today. Now. Do you think I can put your letter on that pile?"*

*She turns to her colleagues, wafts her hand under her nose, mouths 'he stinks of booze.'*

*"BUT THERE'S NO FUCKER HERE! JUST PUT THE LETTER ON THE FUCKEN PILE!"*

*"Sir. Please lower your voice and stop swearing. I can't help you if you're swearing."*

She taps a sticker on the glass that separates her and the drunken Pope. It's one that reminds customers that employees have the right to work in an environment free from abuse or the threat of violence.

*"Aye, well, if you weren't such TOTAL DICKS, I might agree!"*

*"Sir. These are not my rules. These are the laws of the land."*

*"Ah come on! This is absurd. There's no-one here!"*

Pope rants on, unaware of three fingers from the three clerks simultaneously pressing panic buttons. Two security guards dressed in black military gear, sporting red berets and firearms come into the fray. The smaller one is about five foot, with squashed in features, all congregated around the mathematical centre of his face. The other is well over six foot with a broad face. They both appear younger than Pope.

*"Is there a problem sir?"* asks the larger of the two.

*"Where the fuck did you gadgies come from?"*

*"Never mind that,"* again from the larger. *"And I remind you not to swear in the shared public domain. Now. What is the problem?"*

*"Basically I need tae post this form off. And as the girl has so eloquently informed me"* – she gives an instantaneous fake smile before collapsing her face into a smirk –*"today is Group Two Postal day. And I, be-en endowed with a surname that starts with P, am in Group Three. So the problem is I've got tae wait till tomorrow which I cannae dae."*

The larger guard motions to speak. Pope carries on, pre-empting him.

*"Look I realise that this constitutes appallen life management skills on ma behalf, but as there's no-one else here I thought it might be OK for her jus tae pop ma form on that wee pile and help m'out."*

The smaller guard gets involved now.

*"Sir, clearly you understand why you cannot post that letter today. Indeed, you realise that your actions, and I'm using your*

words now, constitute appalling life management skills. So
we're asking you nicely to come back tomorrow."

"Yes but if I come back tomorrow-"

Pope stops. He turns to the larger of the guards.

"Did you used tae dae the NIPSD Patrol?"

The large guard shuffles and smiles, proud as if recognised as a
celebrity.

"Yes. Yes, I did," he says.

"You've accosted me before," says Pope.

Suddenly official, "We do not accost, we enquire."

"Aye, well. You're the cunt that nicked me f'drenken."

With that, they're on him. After a brief struggle, the guards have
him face down and handcuffed, making reference to his alcoholic
bouquet.

The gaggle of blond triplet clerks watch this struggle to their
great amusement. As Pope is dragged off, one gives him the
English salute – the reversed victory sign – another mouths
'wanker.' Unable to walk, Pope slumps into the wall.

"Right. We will need to see your NIPSD card."

"Oh aye, of course," responds Pope, having trouble staying upright.

The guards wait. Pope looks at them. He nods his head, puffs
out his cheeks.

"Aye well, my card's in my wallet. Which is in my pocket."

Again, not a flicker from the guards.

"Aye, well ma hands are tied. Literally. So..."

Like that, the guard's hand is in Pope's pockets, ferreting
around, scooping and snatching.

"Pope?" says the small man, before looking up.

"Correct! Jesus, this country's fucken peculiar!"

"What?" barks the larger one.

"Eh?"

"What did you say?"

"What? Oh, I was jus singen to masel."

"Don't play sill buggers with me, Pope."

"Who's playen silly buggers?"

*"Well you better not," says the guard pointing a finger in Pope's face. "Now. What Life Transactions do you have tomorrow?"*

*"Do you need t'ask? Does it not say it on your wee machine?"*

*"I suggest you answer the question."*

*"It's ma Rations Pick-Up."*

*"Well if you want to keep your benefits you'd better stay out of trouble. We are going to mark your card."*

*'Mildly Insolent' flashes up on the screen.*

*Pope laughs.*

*"This is no laughing matter, Pope. You are only one setting away from Directionlessly Deviant. And with your recent past I suggest you keep your nose clean."*

*"What's the worse setten?"*

*"Mr Pope, again you are asking things that are none of your concern."*

*The smaller guard nudges the bigger guard. The bigger guard looks at the pulsing portable NIPSD SwipeScanner. They look at each other. They grin. The smaller one speaks.*

*"Oh dear Mr Pope. Well. In answer to your question. The worst setting is Inclined to Sedition." The guard turns his scanner to reveal the very same words flashing on the screen. "It seems you have hit Detention Level. We will now take you to a LifeManagement4Life centre at which the consequences of your actions will be spelled out to you."*

The ensuing kerfuffle featured Pope react badly to the news that he had maxed out on Social Behavioural Points. After he had head-butted the taller of the two, the cameras cut out.

"And he's your new project, is he?" asked Sherry.

"That's right."

"Well I hope you know what you're doing. He seems a touch unpredictable."

"You think I can't control him? You underestimate me, Sherry."

"What if the Blackguard arrest him? *Hellevue Harmony* is underway now, isn't it?"

"I've given explicit instructions to locate but not arrest him."

"So you're not gonna bring him in if you find him?"

"Ooh no. Where's the fun in that?"

"What if he goes on the run?"

"Well that's fine. It won't have any bearing on the impact of the story. If he doesn't want to be involved, that's up to him. But I don't see that happening."

Fred's phone buzzed. It was Garqi.

"Hello, Freddi dear. You receive my parcel yet?"

"Er, not yet, no. Why? What are you talking about?"

"We've gone off-stone and I av sent you a sneaky peak. I thought courier would be dare by now."

"Ah well, I'm sure it'll be here soon."

"You're confident your man Pope will bite?"

"Jesus! What is this?" responded Fred. "He'll definitely get in touch. He'll be surprised as hell I should think!"

"You theenk he'll get out of Hellevue alive? We done a real number on im, you know."

"Well. We won't have to wait long to find out, I'm sure."

"OK, Freddi. Ciao."

"Ciao."

Sherry looked at her watch. "I best head back to the President now. Or at least be there when he wakes up. I've given him some sleeping powder so he should be out for a while. I just hope I didn't confuse it with other stuff. God knows he's had enough of that. If I have, well, I've got hours of his pathetic shit about the low turnout to look forward to."

She pulled on her tights and was reaching for her earrings.

"So who else are you hooking up with this evening then, young man? Denise?"

"Not tonight, Sherry."

"All the cabinet wanna bone her. She's a pornographic wet dream. You're young, enjoy yourself. God knows I do."

"Don't worry about me," responded Fred.

They both jumped at the sound of the buzzer.

"Ah, that'll be Garqi's man, I expect. I'll come down with you and you can have a quick look."

Fred put a £100 note into the courier's hand and showed Sherry his handiwork, the front page of *The Daily Rumour*.

*"MAN FIRED FOR MASTURBATING AT WORK – CAUGHT ON TOILET CCTV.* Is that the one?" asked Sherry.

"No not that bit! The main article!"

"Oh. *SON DEAD DUE TO PARENTAL NEGLECT"* read Sherry. *"A twenty-six year old Hellevue woman, Clementine Romain, has failed in her duty as a mother, neglecting her terminally ill son, resulting in the little lad's death."*

"And there, look, you see," said Fred. "Damning testimony from our boy, Robert Pope."

# 6

# HELLEVUE

A VAST, GRAVELLY disused no-man's land signposted the borders of Hellevue, acting like a buffer between the district and the rest of the capital. Partially-condemned blocks of flats – homes for scores of people – surrounded mounds of debris and rubble. There were areas cordoned off with warnings of *Plasticitis Effluent Hazard*. In the near distance lay half-built schools and medical centres, aborted housing developments, roads that led nowhere but to dust and decrepitude. Hellevue was almost entirely encased by areas like this and very few outsiders ventured this far. In fact, in the not too distant past, when the district had been left to its own devices, the Government had become more and more remote. A lot of things didn't work round here, and because of the lack of electricity, Hair and the words of the LibComs had rarely been heard. It seemed that although Citizens needed to jump through the odd governmental hoop here and there, whoever was in power did not make much of a difference to them. There was a sense of *do what you like, we'll get on with having some fun*, and to be fair they had made a pretty good fist of dodging the absurdist bullets from the Government. According to the RevKev, his great friend (and saviour, lest Pontiff forget), the simplification of living habits had actually allowed greater freedom to live.

No longer obsessed with traditional home entertainment – video games, DVDs, social networking sites, computer games where you did virtual cooking like flipping pancakes and making stir-fries, whiling away hours on the sofa watching the virtual tennis and darts world championships – a multitude of groups with different concerns and

71

interests had emerged. *The Arty Party* demanded production of books and film be legalised again, something *The Intelligentists* (a meeting of whom Pontiff had attended when he arrived in Hellevue, and where he had first met Godfrey) were very keen on as well. *The Fashionistas*, also known as the *Fashion Brigade*, who had close links to the *Urban Rustics*, weren't interested in all this repression talk. They just wanted access to fabric and material. They held outdoor fashion shows in summer, parading the latest Hemp Design in Recyclo-Chic and their new interpretation of punk fashion. They were adorned in ripped clothes, canvas sewed on old leather, self-cut hair. There were many others and all different types had rubbed along quite happily with each other, free, to a certain extent and for a little while, from the outrageous shackles of modern politics. There was poetry reading, live music, theatre, story-telling, all in dilapidated and disused buildings, on the streets, in people's homes, a word of mouth spreading of ideas that served to bring people closer together. There were streetgigs – huge parties with bonfires as the centrepiece, and an atmosphere of ragged commune, of real warmth and unity between folk despite the destitute nature of their lives.

As **KARMATARMAK** had always striven to be as cultural as it was political there was a listings section for these streetgigs, adverts for actors for new plays, essays reviewing forgotten literary masterpieces, news on book exchanges and spoken word events. In short, whatever a Citizen of Hellevue wanted to talk about, **KARMATARMAK** was the forum. And that is why so many had disappeared in the last crackdown, often whether they had been involved or not. Subsequently, the Citizens of Hellevue had become more subject to the laws of the land. And when the Government decreed they were less than impressed with huge plumes of carbon dioxide being sent up into the atmosphere from the fires at the streetgigs, not to mention the dangers involved – the health and safety implications – they were banned too. Alas, the denizens of Hellevue could do nothing to prevent the NIPSD twitchers spotting smoke on the horizon.

"It proves you can never out-mad the Government," the RevKev had said. "If it seems absurd, it will probably come to pass. The Lib-Coms are doing their damnedest to create a society through legislation and though they want harmony, they don't want too much cohesion. That might spell problems for them."

As the Monorail pootled along, past junk piles and refuse heaps from antiquity (*The Great Clean-Up* had not extended here), Pontiff thought of his sister, nursing sheep somewhere out in the highlands last he heard. She had always said he'd end up in custody. Then again, she always said that everything happened for a reason.

Oh aye? Pontiff would ask. What does putten onion in your salad signify?

No, no, she'd smile, you're being trite.

So if it was only matters of great import that fell under this banner of *everything happens for a reason*, who or what decided? At what critical point did this external force deign that *a,b,c* be put in motion so that at some unknown juncture *x,y,z* would come to pass? For Pontiff, chaos ruled. Things happened, full stop. If you could extract some sort of reasoning, great, but *dinnae fight the trajectory into which life propels you* was probably the best you could do. His sister said it was a semantic difference and Pontiff had met many who shared her philosophy. Despite that, it never ceased to amuse him when people would say in those very knowing, apparently worldly-wise terms that *everything happens for a reason*. Pontiff felt that most people simply couldn't live without there being an explanation for everything. He was sure it was why his sister was religious, why she believed so vehemently in praying.

But if *everything happens for a reason* and God's got a path mapped out for us, what was the point in prayer? Surely it should make no difference. Not unless God's quite indecisive. He's up there, decreeing left, right and centre, and then he starts to get inundated with a load of prayers and says to the Angel Gabriel: *'Ere Gabby, look at all these suggestions. D'ya think these people have a point? Do you think going down that path would be better?'* What does he do, Pontiff would ask, wait for a hundred prayers and then some sort of device goes off alerting him to the fact that a rethink is needed because people down on earth have been on their hands and knees asking him to reconsider? Does he start thinking things like: *'My word, this Robert's popular, isn't he? A hundred and ninety-eight prayers came in for him not to be convicted of that murder he didn't commit. Maybe we should cancel the execution.'* And so the path changes and lucky Robert is saved. On the flip side, he's thinking: *'Oh dear, only six prayers, that's not nearly enough. My original idea stands. Get the guillotine ready.'*

But was there a meaning to all of this? The circumstances of Pontiff's recent past had certainly challenged his formerly unshakeable view. And to such an extent, that he had occasionally found himself sending the odd plea or two heavenward.

As the Monorail arrived at its last stop – Hellevue – Pontiff again wondered why he had been released. It can't have been good behaviour, he thought. He took a swig of the whiskeysquash and put the bottle in his pocket. He wanted to save some for when he got in. It was late, he was tired and he was already a bit drunk. He rolled a cigarette with one hand and followed the thin crowd to the exit. He supposed he felt good to be back.

A large crowd gathered just outside the station and that meant that getting through the SwipeScanner took longer than expected. As Pontiff made it through, he heard screaming and sobbing. And then he saw the body, the battered dead body of a man lying in a pool of blood. Pontiff worked his way through the crowd to get a closer look.

"Oh Christ!" he exclaimed, as he looked at the man's eye sockets. They were empty and his upper limbs stopped at the wrist.

"Did they get his NIPSD card as well?" someone asked.

They were murmurings to the affirmative.

What was evidenced by this murder was a new type of violent robbery, the very poor mutilating the slightly less poor, extracting fingers and eyes along with the NIPSD card to gain access to the deceased's home, eager to top up their ever more meagre rations. NIPSD cards were supposed to *alleviate* the social injustices that led to the desire to rob, maim and kill, thought Pontiff.

An old woman, noticing fresh horror in eyes unaccustomed to such imagery, said to him: "It's desperation that did that. And you almost can't blame em. I've seen three more this week."

Jesus, what district have I come back tae? thought Pontiff, disquieted also by the apparent nonchalance with which the woman had described this gruesome scene.

He was then aware of a hand in his pocket. His whiskeysquash was vacating his person. A fist flew into his face. It momentarily stunned him but Pontiff was battle-hardened. In one movement he grabbed the bottle from the teenager and swung with his left hand to connect with the other assailant. A younger boy went down. The bottle thief ran off and Pontiff walked on. He thought about heading straight to The Forest Arms – the boozer was the one refuge he knew in life and it was where he would likely find his **KARMATARMAK** comrades – but he knew it would be closed by now.

As he carried on his walk the district was remarkably quiet. Jesus Christ, he thought, what a fucken day. Quite a way to greet what they called *freedom*. He got to a few blocks from his house when he saw that the whiskeysquash was running low. He had no cash on him but knew his word was good with his old dreadlocked pal, John Rer.

Rer was the son of Barbadian immigrants, a former candle-maker and largely viewed as a weirdo having become unhinged since his time at a *LifeManagement4Life* Institute. Though self-employed (the pitching process for the private manufacture license had been a bureaucratic nightmare) Rer had been arrested after being discovered working past designated employment hours to complete a large order. The Government felt it imperative Citizens had an appropriate work-life balance so Rer was bundled out of his own office for realignment. Being inside had meant Rer had lost his business and his girlfriend, and was now a virtual recluse who spent his time making whiskeysquash. Pontiff was one of his few friends and Rer was always happy to accommodate with a sample of the latest draught and a chat about music and history. Pontiff was about to see if Rer was still up when he was stopped in his tracks. He thought he was going to vomit his heart out onto the pavement. A tatty poster adorned a low brick wall. It seemed like it had been up there a while.

## CLEMENTINE ROMAIN - ACID CIRCUS SINGER

# MISSING

### TRIBUTE GIG THIS SATURDAY

And scrawled in charcoal on the brick –

### WHeRe Is CLeM?

Next to it was some of her artwork, a signature *Foxhunter*, a cartoon of Hair as *The Joker* wearing a Chairman Mao t-shirt, holding a rod to his own back.

"*Farming will be the chief pursuit of non-urbanised Citizens!*" the speech bubble exclaimed.

It was widely believed that many farmers now had private militias and were refusing to sell their produce. Little wonder there wasn't enough food.

But was Clem's disappearance connected to the zine? Anyone that risked circulating banned literature had to reconcile themselves to the potential consequences. If you had family, children, you didn't get involved. If you were taken in there was no telling what they would do, not only to you, but also your loved ones. Clem had a young son. Where was he? Pontiff immediately turned round. He had to see the Rev and Godfrey tonight.

He had taken barely two steps when his heart again changed direction. A couple of blocks away on a street corner stood what looked like a platoon of Blackguard. Blackguard in Hellevue? They were never present in the district. His heart thudding, Pontiff aborted his journey, resolving to see his comrades the next day. Not fancying being asked questions at this time of night he also eschewed a visit to Rer, and with what whiskeysquash he had left, continued his walk home, panicked by what he'd learned of Clem.

Within minutes Pontiff turned right onto a semi-grassy plot of land. He passed his hands through the long weeds that sprouted between cracks in the concrete and stopped before an inverted L-shaped block of flats. They had been designed as a straight-bottomed horseshoe but the left side had not been built. The two blocks that did stand each comprised three storeys of twenty flats each. Halfway along each floor were the stairwells, with ten flats fore and aft. Pontiff lived on the ground floor next to the stairwell on what would have been the horse-shoe's base, the block straight ahead of him. To the left there was a gap where the final battlement had been intended and then after a little way, and another patch of sorry looking turf and concrete, a raft of far bigger buildings. Directly behind the half-built horseshoe was a high wall, and behind that lay the next residential street. Pontiff walked up to his flat and put the bottle of whiskeysquash on the ground, noticing the SwipeScanner was still out of action. He was relieved that at least this aspect of living in Hellevue was the same.

With regular examination of each Citizen's Environmental Footprint – garnered by the log of buildings you had swiped in and out of – it was almost impossible to avoid the NIPSD twitchers knowing your movements. If you didn't swipe in on arrival somewhere getting back out was impossible as your Environmental Footprint deemed you to be outside and your swipe request was refused. In addition, if your Environmental Footprint showed you had not swiped in anywhere when it had been snowing or raining, for example, you were invited to an interview to clarify where you had been during the inclement weather. Most of the time it made sense to just go along with the whole swipe fiasco.

But in Hellevue, roughly half of the population never had to swipe in and out of their homes due to malfunctioning technology. This gave a freedom of movement not felt in other parts of the capital. This had been particularly useful when organising meetings of the zine, meetings that had taken place mostly in the RevKev's cellar. Though Godfrey's abode was arguably the most pleasant, SwipeScanners were still operable in his part of the district. Pontiff feared that made Godfrey a prime target for the new type of robbery he'd seen at the Monorail station.

Pontiff reached into the front pocket of his faded blue jeans, removed his NIPSD card and positioned it where a conventional lock would be found. He gave it a wiggle and with a bit of a heave, burst his way in. Oh it's nice tae be back, he thought. It's no the biggest, but it means I dinnae huv tae worry about getten on the fucken property ladder. Thank God those soulless days are over.

There had been a time when inflated house prices signified a highly evolved society. Now, the size of any Social Housing was determined by the number of inhabitants. Pontiff's flat was the regulation size for a person living alone. A glorified bedsit, it contained a sofabed on the wooden floor, a small, rickety table, an adjacent bijou kitchenette with linotiling, and a shower-toilet-basin combo dispatched behind a curtain in the corner. Pontiff took a swig from the bottle and put it on the sofa. He flicked the light switch on the wall and a bare, solitary light crackled and shone dimly, swinging in the night. It was always pot luck whether electricity would be available, especially in this part of town. The idea was that a minimal allotment of two hours of electricity was available in every home, to be used at the discretion of the householder. Once the designated amount had been consumed, the *Automatic Shut-off* blocked any further usage. It was rare to get a full two hours as black-outs were frequent.

A healthy settlement of dust covered the room. Pontiff wiped the surface of the sofa and slapped the grey cotton wool-like substance off his hands into the air.

Pulling back the curtain of his bathroom, he looked into the mirror. Staring through the unidentified patches of brown that stained the glass, he saw a washed out face and the physical trauma he had experienced. Now he had new injuries. The cut on his bald head from the punch at the Monorail station was scabbed and gammy and there was a growing jaundice around his eye. The whites of his green eyes were a dull colour, greyed and browned, murky, dirty. His nose throbbed.

Pontiff removed his white shirt and the blue t-shirt under it and looked at his battered torso in the mirror. He reached his hand into his slopping out bucket. A grey film and extinguished insect life had created a rancid meniscus. He wiped it away, washed his hands and tried to clean up the cuts on his eye and elbow. It was futile. The elbow injury was an older one – sustained by his head-first entrance into Zini's office – and all Pontiff succeeded in doing was unleashing a new round of gushing blood. He had one towel with which he used to mop up the blood before he rewrapped his elbow in some material ripped from his t-shirt.

He moved a few inches to his left and unzipped his fly.

"Oh for fuck's-"

A rogue pube was trapped in his japseye and the angle of his piss was directed past the bowl, onto the floor, and onto his feet. Causing himself great pain he temporarily ceased the bladder emptying to release the pube and realign the flight path of his jet. Relief reflowed as he recommenced. Afterwards, he washed his hands again and used the bloody towel to wipe up the spilled urine. Aye life, thought Pontiff, it isnae what I had in mind. Maybe *LifeManagement4Life* had had a few benefits. Round-the-clock electricity, warmth, security, food even.

He rolled a cigarette and took a long drag before he turned to the bottle. He took a big gulp. And another. At least Zini had good taste in whiskey. Pontiff drained more of the viscous golden-brown liquid into his gullet, but the feeling in his liquor-soaked guts as he recalled the man lying in the road, his experiences at the *LifeManagement4Life* Institute – especially what had happened to Susan, and now Clem's disappearance, reminded him you could only ever have a temporary reprieve from the grim surety of life.

He sat down on his two-seater black leather sofa and noticed that previous absent minded pulling at the cover had left parts of the yellow foam exposed. He flicked the switch on the TV. It took a second or two but with an electronic squeal, it burst into action just as the opening chords of the *NewsZeit!* theme tune were starting. Feeling the whiskey-squash stick to the back of his throat Pontiff walked the short distance to his tap. He put a glass under it. Fingers crossed. Relief. Water this time. He sat down again, perching the glass precariously on the small, battered table next to the sofa.

*"Countering the terrorism of* **KARMATARMAK** *is ultimately the reason for the liberation of Hellevue,"* stated the reporter.

Pontiff spat out his whiskey.

*"It looks increasingly like speculation is growing that* **KARMA-TARMAK** *have been recruiting, though rumours of the fact that this is happening are uncorroborated at this moment in time. Also there may be a degree of growing unrest in other areas. Where these areas are is hard to say and it is far too early to draw any real conclusions. But without doubt I can tell you that the situation is critical."*

Holy fucken shit! We got it out! You fucken wonderful bastards!

In that moment Pontiff forgot the pain of his injuries, the pain of the humiliation and the degradation of life under the LibComs and thought only, momentarily, of a future free from this horror.

Alas, reason and reality seeped back into his system as quickly as it had departed.

*Liberation of Hellevue,* he thought.

He remembered the Blackguard he'd seen. He worried for his friends, for himself, for the district, for Clem.

*"There will be a burning of copies in the next few days and anyone found with a* **KARMATARMAK** *after the deadline will be charged under terrorism laws."*

More compulsory requirements were to be added to all *Citizens' Accounts.*

Pontiff didn't quite catch the precise detail. Something about sperm and egg donations being required in order that a full analysis of terrorist families could be carried out.

*"We have examined the evidence and reports from the myriad focus groups that look into this kind of thing and feel it would be a dereliction of duty not to add to the scope of the NIPSD programme. These additions are over and above what records are already held on each Citizen's Account at this moment in time and will make the cards more secure and in turn the lives of ordinary people more secure. It is imperative we do this to curtail terrorism."*

Pontiff's mind reapproached its awnings.

Over *and* above, he thought. *Moment in time.* Aside from anything else, this tautology was hard to bear.

Next on was President Terry Hair.

Christ, he looks strung out, thought Pontiff.

*"These people, though it is indeed charitable to refer to them as such, are trying to destabilise the country, derail YOU, the good Citizens of this land. They are not attacking us in Government, they are attacking YOU, the people. You deserve a peaceful existence, to live your life happily and without torment, to not be fed this bile.*

*"These fools constitute nothing more than a tin-pot organisation whose sole purpose is to destabilise the country and create difficulty for the average person. We will not lose the battle for hearts and minds!"*

Oh God, not that fucken phrase again.

*"Yesterday was a joyous day, a day to reflect on all the progress we've made. But it is important not to be distracted from the job ahead. We have provided health and security and a sense of well-being, something severely missing before we came to power. We have always maintained that that is the right of all not merely the preserve of the few."*

Nice idea, thought Pontiff. Shame it's no worken out. If he starts goen on about the pyramid of wealth again or undue privilege...

*"We've all read the preposterous lies in that two bit rag,* **KARMATARMAK**, *and their conspiracy talk about this so called cessation of liberties. How can we be accused of this? People are freer and more comfortable than they've been for years! They claim we are recreating the two tier society. Ha! We dismantled the two tier society and now everyone is better off. I do not see how people can dispute that. We put the bankers in stocks! We took their assets to pay for the rebirth of this nation!*

*"These mudslingers say our measures are authoritaaa-rian..."*

Hair lingered on that word, delivering it with a quotation finger-spasm.

*"I say to them, do you want anarchy? Which is a stupid question because of course they do! But seriously, joking aside, we are not controoo-lling"* (another finger spasm) *"the people of Britannia as these conspiracy theorists would have it. We are regulating, ensuring people's lives are easier. We are in a tough period of the history of our country, of the planet even, and we will not shy away from the big decisions. The levels of pollution and disease are why what we are doing is so necessary.*

*"The fervent spread of disease and no little shortage of pestilence has rendered the country flabby, dirty and unworkable, like much of the populace. Lives are now, and will continue to be, the hardest for generations. Our nation has been strangled and we need to take measures that will release it from this grip of disease and depression. Lest we forget, the environment has been trampled on and it is imperative to step lightly.*

81

*"It is inevitable that stringent measures are required to keep people, I mean services, in check. It's quite a juggling act, let me tell you, keeping everybody happy in a small, overcrowded country with a rising population and limited resources. But these measures ensure our future prosperity. We know you'll adjust to whatever is thrown at you."*

Hair paused.

*"Not that we're throwing things at you."*

He soothed the situation with one of his grins.

*"Rest assured, I am still hell-bent on outlawing views that conflict with the country's culture of tolerance! Of that, there is no doubt. And let me be clear, I welcome criticism, but not when it is of the vindictive and unhelpful kind.*

*"To the country I say, be in no doubt that these terrorists will be caught. And they will be punished. We will shut them down forever this time. Social dangerousness must come to an end! We need dehystericalisation!*

*"I reserve my final word for the terrorists themselves. We know where you are and we will come for you. Desist from your operations or there will be severe repercussions. Turn yourself in, and we may well afford you some leniency. We know the Hellevue District is your home, in the rundown, ramshackle streets, hiding behind innocents your cowardly game. We've got you once and we'll get you again! And to anyone who thinks they may be inspired to revolt... Well, we will deal with you accordingly.*

*"We have sent in the PHU and the Blackguard. We will stop you. The Government will stop you. Britannia will win!"*

Well, thought Pontiff, as he took a conservative sip from the much depleted whiskeysquash and rolled another cigarette, it's all happenen. It's time tae be as strong as I said I would be.

In its pre-terrorist days, at a time an inalienable right to freedom of expression was taken for granted, the founding members of **KARMA-TARMAK** agreed that their faces would not be known, that they would use pen-names and never reveal their true identity in public. They felt it would add to the punch if they removed all possibility of celebrity. Of course, gaining celebrity for intelligent writing did seem farfetched anyway, but there were no pictures of them in circulation, no prospect of being recognised for this work. And with the way things had gone (and were about to go again by the sounds of it), they were pretty glad of that ethos.

And then he thought of *Ockham*. A writer none of them knew.

*Ockham* had been the cause of some consternation. This writer had arrived after the 2nd edition of **KARMATARMAK** and had maintained total anonymity from the rest of the ziners. The RevKev had never been entirely convinced with this arrangement. He argued the stakes were too high to have a comrade of whom they knew nothing. But *Ockham* kept delivering the goods and that was the only benchmark Godfrey used.

*"What we are doing is illegal!"* screamed the Rev one night. *"And that is the only benchmark the Government uses! Surely it's too risky to maintain links with someone of whom we know nothing. He could be anyone!"*

*"Yes dear boy,"* Godfrey responded calmly, *"but he knows nothing of us either."*

And that thought consoled them all in the days after the first round of Hellevue reprisals. At first they didn't know if this mystery writer had been caught or not, Godfrey unwilling to invite heat by contacting *Ockham* in an agreed area of the dark web. In fact, it hadn't been until four months ago when *Ockham* responded to Godfrey's most recent call for revolution (penned as *Enigma*) that they knew their comrade was still alive.

And now Hellevue was to come under attack again.

Pontiff could imagine Godfrey smiling with relish: *"We've engaged the beast!"*

Well, I hope he's got a plan, thought Pontiff.

*Enigma* and the rest of the ziners had always expected a fightback from the Government. That wasn't difficult to forecast. As such, they had promised they would not release the zine unless they had an army of people ready to fight, willing to follow their words. Without that they were just putting the people of the district at risk again. But as Pontiff thought back to the Monorail murder and the attempt to rob him, he sensed community and common purpose seemed to have been misplaced. This was not the Hellevue he remembered.

As Pontiff went to roll another cigarette, the power cut. It was always best to know where your essentials were to head off the ballache of finding things when the electricity went down. The torch had replaced the mobile phone as the essential item to have on your person, provided you could procure batteries. Maybe I should get intae candlemaking, thought Pontiff as he searched in vain. Mind you, look what happened to poor John Rer.

Accompanied only with his thoughts, Pontiff drank into the dark.

\*\*\*

Pontiff woke, abruptly, banging his elbow, lying in a semi-congealed position. At some stage in the night he had tried to pull out the sofabed but had aborted that after a few unsuccessful efforts.

He ripped his tongue off the roof of his mouth, momentarily gagging on the dry crispness at the back of his throat and slumped his head forward. His eyes were reluctant and as soon as they were slightly ajar, the maximum extension in this torpid state, the stale throb of yesterday's buzz greeted him in the form of a debilitating headache. Water, he needed water. He reached for the wooden table and put what he thought was a true hand in the direction of his glass. Radar a little off, the glass and its liquid content were swept from the table, swiftly followed by the ashtray and its fluffy filth. "Bollocks," he muttered, as a flurry of grey snow engulfed him. He swung himself round, planted his feet on the floor and slumped his head down again.

He picked up the bottle of whiskeysquash and brought it to his lips, but as he was about to drink he started suddenly at a clunk from outside. And another. The sound of the liquid moving in the bottle disallowed Pontiff's hearing. He pulled the bottle away from his lips, suspending it in midair, and squinted his eyes to listen closer. Whatever it was had apparently stopped. He picked up the glass, set it on the table, dropped the last glug of whiskeysquash into it, and like a frog snagging a fly, quaffed the remnants of the bottle. After a quick rub of the face and eyes, Pontiff was ready to try standing. He felt bedraggled.

He felt dirty. He looked out the window and imagined it to be around 3am. He had no watch and the clock had stopped. He decided to have a shower.

The jet of water hit him with surprising yet refreshing vigour. Normally it was like having an incontinent old man pissing on your head, all sprinkly fountain, spray everywhere, no jet. This was bizarrely luxurious. Pontiff lathered himself in soap, enjoying the warmth. He was being lulled into a stupour, feeling humanity returning to his veins, when the shower cut out.

"Ah for f-"

And then the realisation dawned. The four minute shower rule. He got out but as he looked in vain for a flannel to wipe off the soap, the metallic flap of the letterbox alerted him to a presence at his door. What was the meaning of this unlikely intrusion? Naked, pissed, bemused and soapy, and now a visitor at three in the morning. Pontiff thought it was probably a neighbour to see if he had any booze. He knew a few round here had a drinking problem. Who didn't?

Moments later the slamming became a relentless crashing.

"Christ, I'm comen!"

With that the door came off its hinges and in marched four men dressed head-to-toe in black military fatigues, black boots, red berets, sporting black truncheons and brandishing arms. The five now stood cramped in the soapy naked man's flat.

"Mornen" said Pontiff. "Please do come in."

"Pope!" barked the man who seemed to be in charge.

"We're looking for Pope!"

Panic struck. Had they discovered the identity of the **KARMATAR-MAK** terrorists? Were they on to him?

"Are you Pope?" barked the black-clad man again.

Pontiff didn't want to commit to anything at this stage. He was suddenly very aware of his nakedness and felt rather exposed. He really ought to put a towel on.

Regaining equanimity, he asked: "Do you mind if I-"

*"ARE YOU POPE?!"*

"Aye, I am," responded Pontiff calmly.

"We need to see your documents."

"Eh?"

"Your NIPSD card, Mr Pope."

"My NIP-. What the? Christ lads, it's a bit early for all this, isn't it?"

"Mr Pope, assuming you are, you are aware that you are not permitted familiarity with agents of the state. You shall refer to us as Guards. With regards to your question, the NIPSD patrol specifically uses this hour. Even terrorists must sleep. We are here to verify your identity. Now, your NIPSD card."

Terrorists? Oh God, was this it? Did they know?

And Christ, where was the card? As with any dealings with government agencies, as long as you had the right paperwork there was less likely to be a problem. However.

Pontiff staggered and ransacked. All to no avail.

"Hang on, it's just here."

"Mr. Pope, you are aware of the protocol surrounding these enquiries?"

"Er, remind me," said Pontiff, going through his jeans pockets.

"I am duty bound to advise you that you have only ten minutes to find the necessary documentation until you are categorised as suspicious and immediately detained."

"Well how long's it been so far?"

"Six minutes."

"So I'm already a wee bit suspicious, eh?"

Pontiff regretted that immediately, cringeing mentally. That wasn't the type of the thing you wanted to be saying to government officials, particularly when you didn't know the nature of their visit. Pontiff could detect patience being lost by the men before him. He suddenly upped his ante, a not inconsiderable feat considering the hour and his state.

Finally, "Got it! How long was that?"

"Eight minutes and forty three seconds."

The black-bedecked man looked, checked and verified. He handed the card round the group. There was a consensus of nodding. "Thank you Mr. Pope. Now, who else is here?"

"Eh?"

"On the SwipeScanner it is recorded you have a domestic guest."

"Wellass news tae me."

"You're not harbouring literary terrorists are you?"

"Nah! Absolutely not!"

Don't go overboard, Pontiff told himself.

The guards placed his NIPSD card on the SwipeScanner, input *one Citizen*. A red light appeared.

"That's not what it has on your scanner, Pope. Are you lying to us?"

"No. I'm no. Who does it say is here?"

"We ask the questions, Pope."

"I see. Well, I donno what tae say. That thing's no worked for months. Somehen different flashes up every day. I don't know. You're the guys who're supposed tae know about this type of thing."

"Pope, we are going to check your flat. You had better not be telling us porkies."

Pontiff turned round and wondered where exactly they would be checking. What you saw is what there was. There were no hiding places. Still, that didn't stop them. They checked in the bed, under the bed and behind the bathroom curtain, and, well, that was it.

"OK Pope, we've checked your flat and we are satisfied there's no-one else here, although you do live in a sty. But we are a little concerned that the SwipeScanner has been tampered with. That is government property."

"Honestly, lads-"

"Guards."

"Aye right, *guards*. Look, do you mind if I-"

Pontiff went to swipe back his bathroom curtain.

"Pope, where are you going?"

"To get somethen to cover me up, if you don't mind."

"Please, be our guest."

"Oh thank you."

Pontiff grabbed the towel. The guards took in the garment with revulsion, noticing the red of blood and yellow of the urine.

"Now, Mr Pope, did you hear the announcement by our leader?"

"Aye."

"And?"

"And what?"

87

"Do you know anything?"

"About what?"

"About the literary terrorism of the area."

"Nah."

"You haven't heard anything? No matter how minor."

"Nah. I been away."

The guard in possession of Pontiff's card, nodded. He was bearded, friendly-looking, not your average fresh-faced bloodsucker from the middle classes that often peopled this unit.

"That checks out, Sarge," he said.

Pontiff heard tuts and expulsions of airy mirth from the other two guards.

"This is definitely the guy," said one.

Pontiff was instinctively unnerved by that comment.

This guard was your clean-shaven, mean-looking, average fresh-faced bloodsucker from the middle classes that often peopled this unit. President Hair had called for absolute harmony in the interests of securing a better future for all, and part of this was the need to speed up the whole lagging process of punishment and justice. Now, government officials had been given extraordinary levels of jurisdiction, vested with the power of judge, jury and, in some cases, executioner. Those perceived to have had a half-decent education were the ones trusted to make such decisions.

"Where have you been tonight?" Sarge asked.

"Well as I'm sure it says on your wee machine, I was jus released from Shrink Clink."

"What about that murder at the Monorail? Did you see anything?"

"Nah."

"Are you sure? What happened to your face?"

"I fell down the stairs at Shrink Clink."

Sarge stared at Pontiff. Pontiff returned the gaze. He released a slow smile. Sarge picked up the whiskeysquash bottle.

"Have you been purchasing illegal contraband?"

"Nah. That's government-issue booze. Look at the-"

"OK, that'll do, Pope."

Sarge looked back to the Scanner.

"Looks like drinking's got you into trouble in the past, Mr Pope."

"Or was it more..."

"Was it more what, Mr Pope?"

"Er... ma forgetfulness about Life Admin. But I willnae make that mistake again."

"Good. We have trained you well in that case."

"Oh aye."

"So what is the fundamental importance of *Life Administration*, of *Easification-Facilitation*?"

Fucken *Easification-Facilitation*, thought Pontiff, the bane of ma fucken life.

There were so many things to remember. He knew he had to re-count the answers word-for-word.

"To ensure energy usage is conserved, thereby minimisen pollution and saven the environment for future generations."

"And why was it in doubt?"

"What?"

"Our ability to safeguard the planet."

Again Pontiff knew this had to be word-for-word.

"Er, because fu, er-"

"Ye-es"

"The biggest threat to our collective struggle is that after the end of the era of gadgetry, lives did at first seem emptier for some people."

One of the other guards, one of the bloodsuckers, started to input something on screen.

"Er, sorry," said Pontiff, noticing this activity, "that in the early stages of withdrawal lives did at first feel somewhat emptier."

Sarge nodded and smiled.

"And now?"

"Now," continued Pontiff, "Liberal Compassionatism is delivering joy to the masses and peace to the good people of this country."

"What day of the week would be, let's say, your Life Admin Group's Post Office day?" asked another.

Pontiff smiled, momentarily. He had a feeling he would be asked that.

"Well, seen as I'm in Life Admin Group Three, that'd be Thursday."

Again Sarge nodded and smiled.

"Good, Mr Pope. Good. But we are going to caution you for possible tampering with government owned devices."

"What?"

"Be thankful you've got off lightly. We are only cautioning you because there is no name coming up, and that is peculiar. Now, regarding the door, it is your responsibility to get it fixed and after you have done so, send the bill to your local NIPS Department. The paperwork will be phased there."

"And remember," added a bloodsucker, "you must always swipe in and out, and that includes your guests."

"Aye, well it doesnae work."

"Well it is your responsibility to get it fixed," asserted Sarge. "Again, they can help you at NIPSD. Also, you will have to show your card to verify what you have said to us here today. We are inputting what you have told us as well as the time of your appointment. Do you understand everything we've said to you?"

"Aye, I understand everythen you've said but there is just one thing I cannae work out. Why if you're satisfied there's no-one else here do I huv tae go to my local NIPSD office to verify?"

"It's the vagaries of the system Mr Pope, and none of your concern."

"Right."

With that Sarge handed Pontiff his card.

"Good day," he said, and the four trouped out.

"Right-o, cheers lads."

Pontiff staggered back to his bed. His hands shook as he wiped at the now drying soapiness of his body. He needed a drink but the whiskeysquash bottle was empty. He sparked a cigarette and felt steadier. And then he laughed. "Good. Fucking. Christ," he voiced out loud. Evidently they were *not* onto him.

He had a deep drag of his fag and looked at the doorless entrance to his flat. It's like I'm liven in a contemporary cave, he thought. He was about to lie down to try and get some kip when he heard yet more crashing noises. Going to investigate, Pontiff saw that his little interruption appeared to be one of many such visits throughout Hellevue. The courtyard was teaming with Blackguard.

Across the way, on the other part of the 'L', a young couple, half-asleep, were berating each other. A back and forth ensued of 'I haven't bloody got them' and 'You had them last' punctuated at regular intervals by being told how much time they had left before the cuffs would come out. 'How has our son got his card, yet you don't know where ours are?' et cetera.

"Ten minutes! Detention Level!"

And that was that, the couple both had their *Citizens' Accounts* updated immediately with two Social Behavioural points, were reminded that criminality was a dangerous and dead-end street and that really they should think about their responsibility to their son. They were then carted off until proof of identity could be confirmed, their young son placed in a neighbour's care.

Protocol was –

if NIPSD cards could not be located, detention occurred until ten *other* people with up-to-date NIPSD cards came to vouch for you.

Note of caution –

if you were a part of a group of *vouchees* whose number didn't reach ten, needless to say that didn't look good for you either. It was all very Sharia rape law.

As Pontiff looked into the middle distance he saw a mass of white vans and huge numbers of the men of Hellevue being bundled away.

# 7
# FRED'S METEORIC RISE

FRED WAS WORKING from home this morning, on the sofa, under his duvet, tapping away at his laptop. Reports had come from the Blackguard that Pope's whereabouts had been verified. Now it was waiting time. How would this Pope react to the sobriquet Fred had given him? He felt certain it would be entertaining.

In the meantime Fred kept himself amused working on some new *Cow* output. He looked at what he'd written.

*"TOO MUCH THOUGHT LEADS TO GROSS INACTION"*

He was pretty happy with that.

He was also toying with the idea of a new National Alarm Call. 7:30 every morning. Would certainly promote unity, though implementing it may be tricky. Electric shocks in bed? A new Snooze Patrol Unit? He'd have to discuss it with the wonks in Garqi's lab.

As he worked, Fred half-watched, half-listened to the frothy debate about the return of literary terrorism on Garqi's mid-morning current affairs show. The reporter was sounding as absurd as ever.

*"On a scale of one to ten Jeremy, I'd say it was a nine."*

In the studio Militant Martin, the leader of the Neo-Luddites, was agitating. He was a slight man, bespectacled and spotty, and his unfortunate lisp served to make him more combative.

It had always amused Fred that one of the things that most irked this curious little cove was that for some reason the richer society had become, the more advertising space we had had to pay for.

*"Materialithm had to end. Thum people had never even theen the thea! They thought of it only ath thum thort of vatht bin! It*

*wath right to put natural health above financial wealth. Black-*
*berrieth are fruith again! Lath Vegath to infinity ith what we*
*would have had if we'd let conthumerithm continue!"*

As Militant Martin vented full fury he waved a copy of **KARMATAR-
MAK** around. He's slightly missing the point, thought Fred. This isn't
about the restoration of consumerism. But then Martin often did miss
the point. The man was berserk. Fred did retain a certain fondness for
him though, as his wild pronouncements and Fred's own meteoric rise
were inextricably linked. Equally synonymous with Fred's power grab
was **KARMATARMAK**, it had to be said.

Having finessed his creative mind studying Politics, Psychology and
Sociology at Cambridge (alongside performing with Footlights, film-
making, novel-writing, and general womanising) Fred landed a job at
Garqi's MediaCorp International. His application for the role had had
the usual questions.

*Name. Age. Gender. Sexual Orientation. Experience. Religious*
*Orientation. Favourite colour. Tobacco Intake. Number of Sex-*
*ual Partners.*

Hoping to high step his way to the front of the queue, and doubting
the quota of *Homosexual Sikh* had been filled, he answered accordingly. In the end he decided against turning up to his interview in a
pink turban.

Fred was employed as a roving reporter and occasional columnist,
doing investigative stuff and opinion pieces for the website. It was doing an article on what was then a new zine, **KARMATARMAK**, that he
met Terry Hair for the first time. Immediately Hair fell for him. I know
a star when I see one, thought Hair. It takes one to know one, after all.
He loved Fred's wit, his intelligence. In truth, he felt a little bit in awe
of what he thought a demonic intellect and was so taken with Fred, he
said – "the Liberal Compassionate Party could use someone like you."

This intrigued Fred. He knew the Liberal Compassionates were
struggling. They'd been out of power for some time. But he wasn't sure
they were the key to his plans. He parked the offer and followed up his
intrigue in **KARMATARMAK** with a telephone call to the editor, *Herr*
*Enigma*. Fred was drawn to the idea that the ziners kept their identities
secret and was interested in **KARMATARMAK**'s potential power.

That evening Fred wrote the article on **KARMATARMAK** and also bashed out a little piece to submit to *Enigma* using the pen-name, *Ockham*. This piece concerned the issue of the new plague, *Plasticitis*, and what could be done about it. This was in no small part inspired by the news reporting multitudinous deaths ascribed to this new plague and moreover, the apoplectic reaction of Militant Martin. As Fred started to plan his monumental social experiment – an ambitious prank rivalled only by the time Mao Zedong decided he fancied a bit of a stroll – he thought that to be the actual *face* of change seemed a touch uncouth. Needing a puppet through whom he could execute his plan, Fred decided he would take up Hair's offer and arrived at LibCom HQ at the age of twenty-three.

When *Enigma* got in touch to say he loved Fred's article and was so impressed he wanted *Ockham* to do a regular column no less, Fred didn't hesitate. From that moment on he took immense pleasure in dissecting the ineptitude, suppositions and flowery verbiage of government in his section, *Ockham's Razor*. Though he was invited to zine meetings Fred decided he would keep his identity secret, and politely refused to attend.

Also at this time Hair became so taken with Fred's innovative thinking he invited him to join the party's inner sanctum. Unlike most politicians Fred had first-hand experience of living on the breadline and Hair felt intuitively that could help him connect with the masses. For his part, Fred detected a certain ease of malleability in Hair and was more certain than ever he'd found the vehicle to propel himself into power.

Once in this rarefied position Fred began to flex his muscles. He went about it slowly and methodically, perfectly pitching the pace of his operation. Gradually his meetings with Hair became more intimate and it was in the leader's suite on the day of the Party Conference that Fred made his final move. At the last Hair had wavered slightly, but Fred guided him through.

*"You can fix everything sir," said Fred, as the low autumnal Blackpool sun gleamed through the window of the budget hotel room. He always thought this a beautiful time of year. Colours so vivid.*

*"Yes, you're right Fred."*

*"But the only way is with this new strategy."*

*Hair looked blankly, eyes glazed over.*

*"Sir, we've been through this. Every generation thinks they are getting it right; that relentless progress is being made, but now there is an acceptance that things need to change, that we need to live differently. You can lead that change. You can be the change."*

*Hair looked pensive, uncertain.*

*"Sir, why is the country sliding to oblivion?"*

*Hair remained silent.*

*"What is the cause of this plastics plague? This Plasticitis? Who is responsible for this waste? This disease?"*

*"Er, well, er-"*

*"The answer is Big Business. The answer is the bankers. **They** have created a pyramid of wealth and **they** are at its narrow apex. The poor live in abject pestilence, the rich in unstinting immodesty – a garlanded few with militias that have super- seded the police force. Naturally the horror of Plasticitis doesn't affect them, does it? It's something for the underclass to deal with. And if any of the underclass dare to vault their walls to try and acquire something as outrageous as food they are picked off, packed up and given their last rights – a final insult given that 'rights' have become somewhat of an elastic concept. We must cease the religion of ownership. If money can't buy everything, maybe we will aspire to something else! Maybe we will have equality! How many more must die before we take action?"*

To be true, none of this troubled Fred unduly. But it *was* the angle to exploit for electoral success.

*"But I have always backed Big Business and the perpetual manufacture and purchase of God-knows-what as a way of lub- ricating the economy,"* argued Hair. *"And a good economy is the height of civilisation. There must be something left to privatise. Or why not just bail out the banks again and get them to lend more?"*

"Is it not this lust for ownership and economic growth that has led to this disease and death? Bail out the banks? Allow Big Business to continue to regulate itself? No sir, they can't be trusted! You must promise to bring to book those responsible for the dramatic downturn in our quality of living, for public health having reached a low more akin to the Dark Ages!"

"But I am a man of principal. How can I change overnight the direction of my political beliefs?"

"You can shake off the cynics who accuse you of betraying your ideology. Yes, your political life has hitherto been based in a different **kind** of ideology. But to be based in something is to be mired in something."

"You're right, the country's in danger. We need a new approach. What did you call it again Fred?"

"Health is Wealth."

"Yes, Health is Wealth. And what's our slogan?"

"Money can't buy everything, let's aspire to something else."

"Yes, yes. God you're so right. Honestly Fred, I can fix everything, I know I can. It may sound delusional, but it's not. I and I alone possess a clear idea of what Britain wants. I can save this country! I can save the world!"

"Of course it's not delusional," Fred responded, calmly squeezing the leader's shoulders. He then reached into his cherished briefcase and handed Hair a small bundle of papers, the final piece in his well thought-out jigsaw.

"What is it?" asked Hair.

"In a manner of speaking, sir, it is your victory speech; a promise to restore the nation to former glories. Now repeat after me. The country needs rescuing..."

"The country needs rescuing."

"And rescued you will be..."

"And rescued you will be..."

"If you vote for me..."

"If you vote for me."

"You need a catchphrase as well, sir. Something reassuring and strong. Try, of that there is no doubt."

*"Of that, there is no doubt."*

*"Good."*

*Hair mouthed this mantra a few times before turning to his most trusted ally.*

*"And this will work, will it?"*

*"Sir, people will swallow this shit. They'll lap it up."*

Either that, or they won't take the blindest bit of notice, thought Fred, laughing to himself as he sent out Hair with the speech that detailed the new direction for the party. Heath Cliffe's face was a picture!

Having masterminded the election victory and the ensuing absurdity of the *end of the era of gadgetry*, Fred saw no reason to cease contributing to **KARMATARMAK**. Maintaining his anonymity with his pen-name *Ockham*, Fred attacked the very laws he devised. In effect, he was having a slanging match with himself, a pamphlet war, aiming most of *Ockham's* ire at President Hair.

Could life be any more delicious?

And while the green agenda had got Fred into power he didn't concern himself with that stuff much these days. And now, if not entirely persona non grata in the coalition, Martin had certainly been sidelined somewhat. The Neo-Luddites had always been the junior partner, brought on board to give the environmental agenda aspect of the new LibComs approach a touch of propriety. Once in power, they had been given microscopic roles – measuring contamination in the animal kingdom, prosecuting non-recyclers. The real government work was being done a long way from their meddling hands.

He probably lives in incredible austerity, laughed Fred.

In Martin's ever-diminishing *Environment Now!* section in today's *Daily Rumour* (a column in the press was a cornerstone of the coalition agreement), there was a sea toxicity update detailing how during the *era of gadgetry* great containers of consumerist waste had been bundled into the waters surrounding the UK (as it was then known). Some of these containers of detritus had not been sealed properly and as a result, swathes of marine life had vanished, murdered by this synthetic excrement. The report documented the extinction of another seven species. This was another of Martin's hot topics, something he shoehorned into every debate.

Fred continued to flick through the paper. There was the usual poll conducted by his own *Citizens' Announcements Unit*. The Government currently had an approval rating of 96%. Not quite a hundred but very high. Made it seem as though it could have been a real poll. There were more stories on youth stabbings – mostly in Hellevue. There were reminders of the importance of *Life Administration*. There was the usual name-and-shame of Social Behavioural Points. And then finally it was back to the magnificent front page.

As Fred surveyed his work there was reaction on the news from the general public about the story.

*"They're evil in Hellevue. This Pope really is a hero. Taking a stand."*

*"I'd bomb the lot of them. Once Pope's out of course."*

*"I've heard all the mothers are like that in Hellevue. You can't trust 'em. Take all the kids off 'em, that's what I say."*

You're not far from the mark, dear mad old woman, thought Fred. But one thing at a time.

Thinking of Hellevue, Fred turned his mind back to **KARMATAR-MAK**. He wondered how his unknown comrades were faring down there. *Hellevue Harmony* had led to many arrests, though the revolutionary conspirators of **KARMATARMAK** had not been tracked down. *Had* a revolution started down there? If the vox pops Fred had just heard were the benchmark, a coup would stall the moment it left the borders of Hellevue.

About six weeks ago, Fred had heard from *Enigma* that *Phase One* had been a success and that the first wave of copies of the zine had been circulated. After this Fred had heard nothing more. He considered messaging to ask what was going on but knew that if he did he would be making a tacit admission that he did not live in Hellevue. It seemed useful to Fred that *Enigma* believed *Ockham* to live in Hellevue. Fred also felt it was the mark of the man that *Enigma* still hadn't asked his true identity especially with what was happening now, with what Fred had set in motion.

Was Fred putting himself at risk? Would his role be uncovered? He didn't see that happening. His comrades didn't know his true identity any more than he knew theirs, and he had given himself significant protection through the codes, passwords and addresses he had used in correspondence with *Enigma*. Fred knew all **KARMATARMAK** writers changed contact details and contact methods regularly to avoid detection – *Enigma* had insisted on it.

In any case, the Public Harmony Unit had almost entirely ceased investigating electronic correspondence as it was believed the masses no longer engaged in such activity. While still operable – albeit not internationally – the internet was hardly used, what with electricity being at a premium and the cost astronomical. The addiction to instantaneous knowledge was now in virtual quarantine. The glorious age when information was readily available from all over the planet had all but disappeared almost as soon as it had arrived. It had felt normal, quotidian. Now it was seen as a freak moment in history.

Anyway, the Government could pin the *Ockham* thing on anyone. It would be Fred who decided. They could say it was a construct. Anything. But again, it wouldn't get that far. Fred would make sure of that. No. There was no chance of anyone finding out. In fact, with the raid he didn't actually want to flush anyone out. He had a lot of respect for the writers of the zine, especially *Enigma*. Respect, that after everything, they were willing to give it another go.

Fred thought back to that first message four months before. He had deleted all but one of his *Ockham* contact portals and wondered how many more messages hadn't got through.

**"Dear boy, would have liked to get in touch sooner but felt it was too dangerous. For both of us. I need your help. *We need a revolution.*"**

As soon as he had received this, Fred's keen mind had begun whirring. He'd had the forethought of a raid, and what would come after. Ah, he laughed, some things are just meant to be! Why not get involved? Not for one moment did he believe **KARMATARMAK** could inspire a peasants' revolt and topple the Government – nor did he want it to – but it would be fun to write something. Just as the little Hellevue tabloid story had been. On that note, he rang Garqi to congratulate him on a well-executed front page.

"Not at all Freddi dear. Iz all down to your wonderful creative mind."

"Well thank you Oli. And I tell you what, el Presidente won't app-reciate you giving Martin airtime."

Garqi laughed.

"No. I know. But what e gonna do?"

"Indeed. You coming to cabinet later? I've got something planned."

"More creative theenken, Freddi dear. I'll be dare!"

So creative it may be my crowning glory, thought Fred, although there were a few things that would take some beating.

Fred's marquee act had undoubtedly been the creation of the twin pillars of *New Democracy* and the People's Republic, all achieved one spectacular afternoon.

It began with armed Blackguard storming the Commons, pointing guns, swinging batons, throwing a few threats around. Opposition MPs' first reaction had been to stay and protest but after a short conflab they soon felt it best to comply with the Blackguard, certainly safer and less bloody, and what MP worth their salt doesn't have self-preser-vation high up on their agenda?

Reading Fred's script, Hair announced –

*"We have entered a phase of New Democracy, the most efficient system yet that we have developed to serve you, the wonderful people of this country.*

*"I am clear that, ideally, we need opposition. Of course. That is a fundament to traditional democracy. But when this so-called opposition is guilty of immaturity and unhelpful comments, espousing non-sensical drivel intended to ignite riot, they render the system ineffectual. I welcome criticism, but not when it is of the vindictive and unhelpful kind.*

*"In our liberal, compassionate society we simply will not tol-erate negative naysayers whose raison d'être is to disrupt. What we need is constructive discussion not inflammatory rabble rousing that contains no political substance to it wha-tever. For the good of the country they have disbanded."*

And now that they were gone, what difference did it make? Most of the old guard had been steeped in grubby business involving duck islands, moats and lobbying, with resolutions in the chamber often trade-offs, deals and the securing of special interests. It had hardly been a beacon of purity. Either way, some people still had to be in charge and it took a certain brand of sociopath to fill the role. Terry Hair was just the man!

Only minutes after the opposition had been led out of parliament at gunpoint, Blackguard swarmed Buckingham Palace.

Hair's *bons mots* here –

*"For the cleanliness of the type of environment we all want to live in, it is essential to do what we are doing today. The state of our economy determines that we can no longer sustain a monarchy that takes money directly from you, the good people of Britain. The Royals are an impediment to our modern future, the system neither practicable nor just.*

*"I have come here to meet the King personally to ensure a smooth and orderly transition of power. We are not storming the Bastille. We are possessing of class, the like of which those continentals can only dream. Now, let's go and give His Royal Highness a bit of a surprise!"*

Having witnessed what had happened in the Commons, the King put up minimal fuss and he was unceremoniously removed from the Palace.

Of course, as *Ockham*, Fred lambasted this move, calling it a disgrace this nobbling, this ignobling of British tradition.

**"Terry Hair has snorted up the soul of the country with the same ferocity as a banker snorting coke off a whore's tits. Now we live in a Cromwellian nightmare, the country is a poorer place."**

But I am a richer man! thought Fred, and he couldn't wait to see how his next little piece of chicanery was going to play out. I bet Dr Zini's Life Camp wound Pope up a treat!

# 8

# A LOVELY WALK

CREAMY FATIGUE WASHED through Pontiff and his eyes burned and watered. A sticky residue had encrusted in the corners. He'd slept awkwardly on his elbow. The sheets were crumbly with old soap and he blinked, yawned, and looked at the walls. The walls stared back blankly. The room was embossed in a surprising darkness. He lay a while in this dark, a sunless day leading to a grim interior. Renewed liberty had begun with renewed feelings of isolation. Today, though, he would see the old crew. Or at least he hoped so. Would they have survived the night?

A nausea rose. He thought of his ex-wife. He remembered how happy they'd been in the early days, waking up hungover together. Two good people that just couldn't seem to make it work. After Life Camp Pontiff thought it probably wouldn't work with anyone ever again. He prised himself out of bed and wiping and chipping off the rest of the soap, reacquainted himself with yesterday's clothes, every-day's clothes.

A furriness was present in his mouth. He swiped back the bathroom curtain and turned the tap. Nothing. We used to think these things would run forever. Burdened by thirst, he was transported back to moments of tipping unwanted drinks down the sink. He felt the waste keenly at that moment. He scooped out some of the decaying flush water, mixed it with a chunk of rationed *DentSoap* – which had hardened considerably – and did his best to clean his mouth. He splashed more water over his neck and under his pits, and winced again as he jarred old wounds.

As he reached for his boots Pontiff noticed a letter had been placed on the ground next to his broken door. He tore it open and groaned. It was a Social Obligation Appointment reminder, informing him he was required to head off to Coordination Centre 79F for an employment consultation at midday today. Marvellous. But what time was it now? He looked out the window. Nine-thirty, he surmised. He was pretty good at guessing the time as he'd been without a timepiece for so long. As Pontiff tied his bootlaces he wondered why this appointment had not shown up on any of the SwipeScanners yesterday. And why hadn't Zini told him last night?

The last letter he'd received of this ilk was one to remind him he had missed *Non-Familial Syncretization*. Having no family did not negate a requirement for Pontiff to participate in some way in *Designated Family Day*. *Non-Familial Syncretization* gave each family-less Citizen a support network.

Pontiff had always found that an odd term, a rather business-like way of referring to loved ones. And so, by virtue of the alphabet, he had a cobbled support group aligned to him. Sitting round like schoolchildren and hugging and making cakes was not particularly amenable to Pontiff but one absence had clocked up two Social Behavioural Points with a further point to cover the cost of the letter. And despite having his Social Behavioural score reset after leaving *LifeManagement4Life*, Pontiff was going to have to be diligent and attend. Recent leavers had only six points to play with for six months before a full complement of twelve was awarded to their *Citizen's Account*.

Pontiff staggered to his broken door and stepped outside into an overcast, melancholic day. He was about to set off when he heard clunking on the metal steps and looking up he saw two men in black suits carrying a body bag down the stairs. It seemed they had taken the body from the flat above Pontiff. He had never known his neighbour that well, just that he was an old man and that he'd had his cat taken off him because smokers weren't allowed to have pets. What next? Smokers can't be parents? But at least he was a decent vintage, thought Pontiff, unlike some of these poor bastards. And at least this meant there was no housing shortage. In fact, it was probably a struggle to fill all these homes, if you could call them such a thing.

He was then aware a handful of people had stopped at his doorway. He had been unable to re-hinge the entrance to his abode.

"Awright, get an eyeful, why don't ya?" he called out.

He thought that would prompt them to disperse. They did, gradually, a few of them shaking their heads. He was sure he heard one of them say "is that really him?"

As the crowd dispersed a young man with two bags walked past Pontiff, up the steps and into the recently vacated flat above. While the outgoing tenant was off to meet his maker, they'd had a quick turnaround and got someone else in. I suppose I should applaud their efficiency, thought Pontiff. He propped up his door, giving it the closet approximation to 'locked' he could manage, and strode off. They can have what they want, he thought, more in reference to the possible larceny of the light-fingered Blackguard than his neighbours.

As Pontiff strolled through the district heading straight to the Rev-Kev's house, moving at quite a pace in a bid to clear his head, he saw kids on bikes doing tricks, some attempting more ambitious stunts on the railings, painted once in yellow, now crisped, chipped and metallic. He was reassured to see that the few CCTV cameras that did have a home in the district were still non-operational and seemed to quite forget about his pressing engagement.

Thinking of the furious zipping of body bags Pontiff was armed with the thought that as natural causes would probably kill him soon enough, why not start the day with a fry-up. Aye, a nice spot of sausage-induced bowel cancer followed by a ciggie. After all, Zini had given him some extra money to play with. Then reality struck. He had to find out the time.

Everyone he asked had no watch. Or watches that had given up. A few people had refused even to talk to him. Some looked at him with genuine venom. It was odd. Hellevue was normally so friendly. But then things had clearly changed in the district if the bloodbath at the Monorail station was anything to go by.

The streets were still far quieter than usual on Pontiff's brief constitutional. A few media people were here, a few more body bags, a smattering of Blackguard, but by and large the people of Hellevue seemed to be engaged in some sort of passive resistance en masse. The Forest

Arms was still closed. A temporary arrangement? There didn't seem to be any representation of **KT** or revolution, either vocal or physical. Were they scared? In hiding? Planning? Biding their time? Had some been taken in the night? Pontiff prayed – *prayed* – that that had not happened to his comrades.

Towards the centre of Hellevue, things changed. There was action galore. Blackguard were everywhere, stopping and searching the few that were out and about. In fact, because they outnumbered the normal folk on the street, many of the patrols looked bored out of their minds. And Pontiff could imagine why. They wanted aggro and violence. They wanted to teach people the hard way they were liberal, compassionate people. For once the Government was staying true to its word. Helle-vue was coming under attack.

One guy wearing an old, tattered t-shirt emblazoned with *Sex Ins-tructor: First Lesson Free,* had been stopped for chucking an apple core into a hedge and was now being reprimanded for littering. He was warned as to his future conduct and had two Social Behavioural points added to his NIPSD card.

"Surely you should approve," he argued. "Doesn't it do more good in the hedge than in the incinerator? Returning it to nature and all that."

The Blackguard nodded, and gave him a further two points for insubordination. There were sites like this all over Hellevue and many more arrests.

It wasn't long before Pontiff was asked to present his NIPSD card and go through the usual q'n'a – where he was going, why, whether he'd bought **KARMATARMAK** before, if he knew where it was sold, if he knew any contributors. Pontiff said he hadn't and didn't. For once, it was all quite painless. Indeed, Pontiff's questioner gave him a knowing smile and a pat on the arm. This was all very strange. He also informed Pontiff of the time. He was going to be late. Pontiff immediately changed direction and headed away from the Rev's. Though he needed to know what was happening with the zine, and more importantly with Clem, he had to crack on. He could not afford to miss this appointment.

Pontiff was filled with hunger as he hurried past various eating establishments, the bevy of closed fast food chains. There were only sit-in places now. No longer did the people have the option of take away meals encased in polystyrene, paper and plastic bags, with added plastic fork and thirty napkins. *On the go* living had ended. The Citizenry had accepted, by and large, that it wasn't too time consuming to wash up glasses and mugs rather than simply discard a plastic cup after one usage. No longer were individual UHT milks and plastic stirrers available, the life expectancy of which had been a matter of seconds as they too were given to become obsolete after a moment's dip in hot liquid. The practice of individually shrink-wrapping carrots had been consigned to history. Aside from cutting down on unnecessary waste, the idea was that people sat down, took a moment, communed at the dinner table, had proper breaks. All well and good, except that life was too hard to relax these days.

In theory at least, Pontiff supported the idea of *the end of the era of gadgetry*, the idea that the beings known previously as consumers found their lives no less worth living with the overhaul of existence, that there was not a decline in civilisation. Or at least, it wasn't for those reasons.

The narcissism of gadget use had always irked Pontiff. The way people would check their phones or take a call mid-conversation as though what was incoming was more important, even in intimate situations. His ex-wife used to do that. After twelve years it became maddening though Pontiff always enjoyed reminding her that despite the onset of personalised gadgets into every corner of existence we all still took a shit on the same toilet seat.

His real bête-noire, though, was people talking in cinemas or fiddling with their laptops, phones, cameras and the like while the film was on. At least that was an impossibility these days. Pontiff was all up for those fuckers getting the Walter Wolfgang treatment. And who decided popcorn was suitable cinema food?

As he carried on towards the Monorail station, Pontiff was vaguely aware of some distant abuse in his general direction. He thought nothing of it. He thought nothing of the kids playing, of the sun hitting the roof of the newsagent, of the crowd that had gathered there.

Then he saw the front page of *The Daily Rumour*.

"Motherfucking Christ!"

As those next to him shrank away, a stranglehold of nausea gripped Pontiff as he read what was in front of him.

### SON DEAD DUE TO PARENTAL NEGLECT

*"A twenty-six year old Hellevue woman, Clementine Romain, has failed in her duty as a mother, neglecting her terminally ill son, resulting in the little lad's death."*

It got worse.

It said a certain Robert Pope, no less, the... what the fuck ONE TIME LOVER of Clementine Romain, had been quoted as saying:

*"I knew she was an alcoholic and neglectful mother. We hud many chats. Eventually, she broke down. She confessed. She couldnae take the pain any more. I think she felt better getten it off her chest. I couldnae huv lived with masel if I'd no said what I knew. It wasn't right. A little boy hud died. I didnae care what the neighbours said. They wanted tae close ranks, keep it hush hush. I hud tae act. I think the influence of that Karmatarmak has brought the district into disrepute. If I hudnae hud life skills trainen and been realigned, my good citizenship may not huv come to the fore. They do such great work at LifeManagement-4Life."*

Mmm, I see, thought Pontiff. This *was* interesting. What the fucking hell was this? And they've quoted me phonetically. Nice touch.

He turned to page two and saw a photograph of himself, taken from his *Citizen's Account*. A government spokesman mused:

*"This is an example of the hard work still left to do. Of course, it does rather imply the terrorists are killing their own now, which can only be a good thing! The actions of this Pope confirm all is not lost in Hellevue. Indeed, our recent work there may well save that district from internal combustion."*

Terrorists killing their own? What? The wee man cannae be dead, can he? And why am I involved?

Finally, there was the considered view of the editor, Piers Mormon:

*"Today, The Rumour praises Robert Pope, who risked the scorn of his community and cries of betrayal to do what he knew was right.*

"Today, The Rumour calls on the Government to reward a modern Britannian. The Hellevue Hero."

Now Pontiff understood the distant abuse he'd just received. Jesus, he thought, I'm fucked. *The Hellevue Hero*. Pontiff had a feeling that might stick. Life certainly was not what he had in mind. But it felt totally in keeping with the events of his life *at this moment in time*. He thought of his sister's words again. *Everything happens for a reason*. Christ I'd like to know it!

# 9
# NEWS

FRED LOOKED AT his watch. It was time to go and prep the old dog. He picked up his car keys and briefcase, placing into it a sauna-like contraption, and made his way downstairs. He was about to leave his block of flats when he noticed a letter. He recognised the writing immediately. It was from his aunt, his mother's sister. Bloody country people, thought Fred, why don't they use the phones I got them? Then again...

When he had come into office Fred had provided a new home for his mother and aunt – far and away the stand out one on the street. His mother's only gripe was that there was a Libyan couple a few doors down. She didn't think it right that two women shared a bed.

But now, unruliness was afoot in the boonies. His mother had been the victim of an arson attack – maybe the Libyans – and was currently in hospital with severe breathing difficulties and minor burns. The reasoning seemed to be it was known she had a son in government. This was worrying. Recently there had been anecdotal evidence that the countryside was becoming a sequence of nation states. Fred was heading out to his grace-and-favour pad late this very afternoon and this gave him pause for thought.

Though what his aunt had written would conventionally be termed *bad news*, this family business was a real drag for Fred. Especially when he considered himself his father's son. He still felt it a slight betrayal (albeit necessary) to have adopted his mother's surname *McVelly* rather than use his father's *Singh*. Fred hadn't seen his father since he had left his pregnant mother when Fred was just two years old. The sudden departure put a severe strain on his mother and she miscarried a while later. While she struggled to raise her only son, every day a constant battle to feed and clothe them, Fred's father went to Brazil and was now one of the millions of Brits stranded abroad since the aviation industry had become permanently grounded. But Fred never held it against him. Apart from having ambitions to travel himself, it instilled in Fred his guiding principal. *Personal responsibility*, he thought, *to thine own self be true.*

Fred knew he had inherited his intelligence from his father and he was grateful for that. He'd also inherited his father's dark skin and his mother would often tell him he was the son of a pirate. Or had she meant pilot? Caring though she was, she annoyed Fred intensely with her malapropisms.

*"I know you're a real technophobe with all your gadgets,"* she would say, or complain that a day out had been *'a damp squid.'* When she found herself increasingly shut out of Fred's life, she tried to remind him of the good job she had done as a mother. *"I never battered an eyelid when you would get in at all hours, Frederick. I never asked you for pacific details!"* Each one was like a stabbing pain into his intellect. Why *did* his father marry her? The fact still amazed Fred.

But though his father was absent Fred never felt abandoned. He was always self-contained, even at a very young age. School came easy for him and through various enterprises he'd built up quite a bit of capital by the time he'd got to university – mostly from low-level drug dealing and the very many tips from his time as a barman, the older female punters especially generous. Often at university he found that he didn't need money.

Fred felt it quite an achievement to be so successful after being brought up by his mother and aunt. But his childhood *had* provided him with the ammunition for his next big policy announcement and that would be happening in a few hours at Cabinet. Ah yes, he remembered, getting his phone out, best tell them all they'll be needed for a slightly later sitting.

Having sent messages to the relevant parties, he looked back to his aunt's letter.

*"I know you've never loved us as much as we love you–"*

Oh Ker-rist, thought Fred.

*"but we're so proud of everything you've achieved. We may not be as articulated as you–"*

Oh bloody'ell, if she mentions how they all felt the day I left for St Pancreas...

*"but we are your family. Your mother needs you. You're her only son. Please visit her. She is desperate to see you."*

Fred didn't appreciate what he viewed as the worst kind of emotional blackmail. And that's what had swung it for him. Plus he had one of each waiting for him, a blonde and a brunette, and the prospect of a *ménage a trois a la campagne* with those two hotties was far more amenable than weak tea and bad food with the rellies. Fred tapped out a response. These people will use the technology I've given them!

**"Can't make it this week auntie,"** he texted.

**"Busy with Republic Anniversary celebrations. The country needs me. Give mum a kiss from me x**
**p.s. I'm sure she'll be fine!"**

Fred wired some money, got in his car and drove to the Palace.

\*\*\*

At the Monorail station:

*"BE MORE EXTERNAL. BE LESS TIMID. HELP YOURSELF AND YOU WILL BECOME LESS NUMB"* wafted over the speakers.

Eventually it was Pontiff's turn at the Transit SwipeScanner. He stepped up and swiped his NIPSD card hoping his only task today was attending the job centre. If something else had been lined up for him, which was not inconceivable, it would pay to adhere to it.

*"Welcome back to society, Realigned. And good luck!"*

*"The LibComs care greatly for your wellbeing..."*

*"Hellevue Life Admin Group Three Jobcentre Day today. Hellevue Life Admin Group Three Designated Family Day next Friday."*

It started to beep.

***"WARNING."***

*"Citizen must attend Non-Familial Syncretization Day!"*
***"WARNING."***
*"Citizen must attend Non-Familial Syncretization Day!"*

It beeped a bit more before Pontiff removed his card, catching the end of a nearby conversation.

"That zine has done too much damage already. They release it and where's the protection, eh? I just hope the LUK can do something. I don't know about revolution but I just want Hellevue back."

Her companion responded but the sound of the arriving Monorail train rendered it inaudible to Pontiff. L-U-K? What was that?

The door opened and Pontiff stepped on, feeling the low murmuring vibrations of conversation, cramped by the parsimonious dimensions. The transit was comprised mainly of moulded plastic. The carriages were cylindrical, tube-like, claustrophobic, the ceilings low. There were fleeting views of the urban landscape illiberally sliced through each paltry portal. There was barely enough space to rest hands on the fun-size tables. The whole set-up exuded inadequate function. CCTV cameras buzzed eight to a carriage.

There was a sign –

*Toilets out of order. We're sorry for any inconvenience that may*
*be caused. The LibComs care greatly for your wellbeing.*

They never think to drop the price when things aren't working properly, do they?

In the station, a whole host of Citizens had swarmed into the Transit SwipeScanner area. The passage was clogged as each person had to board one at a time. There was the inevitable delay in setting off. Eventually, the Monorail train screech-fizzed into motion.

A faint smell of sweating refuse and the sound of people wheezing pervaded the carriage. Another tough day for the people of Britannia, it seemed. Maybe they're all off to the pub, thought Pontiff, eager to spend what little money they have on escaping the tragedies of life. That was nothing new but the people did look sadder than usual these days. In truth, it was probably in the Government's interest that people had a refuge from the quiet swelling of insanity they had to navigate on a daily basis. That said, if you quit the booze you were still required to go to your local one day a week in order to *better relax and commune with your fellow man.* Alcoholics and teetotallers were exempt from drinking but attendance was compulsory nonetheless.

I could dae wi'a drink masel, thought Pontiff, as thoughts of Clem's disappearance and his new predicament occupied his brain. People were recognising him, nudging each other. When Pontiff met the gaze of any onlooker they quickly averted theirs. He was relieved for his minacious appearance.

The sound of rustling paper suddenly disturbed him. He looked to his right. A woman was reading *The Daily Rumour.* Abruptly, she got up, leaving the paper on the seat. As she brushed past she swept it back to the front page. An awful reminder. Pontiff picked up the paper, turned to page seven and tucked the front page round the back so nobody could see a comparison between a photo and the real thing.

## "GUNMAN GOES ON RAMPAGE IN SCHOOL – LESSONS WILL BE LEARNT"

*Lessons will be learnt,* eh? More platitudes. It's all you ever heard. *We'll learn from this. We'll grow as people.* Monorail over-budget? Lessons will be learnt. Thirty-eight people killed by gas explosion? Lessons will be learnt. And now... *Gunman goes on rampage.* It was no longer acceptable just to call an occurrence a *tragedy.* Somebody had to be responsible. And not just the gunman. That wasn't good enough. There always had to be some systemic failure to blame.

It didn't take long to travel the two stops. And, as ever with modern Britannia, it didn't take long for the mind to boggle yet further.

"It's like I've always *said sweetheart?*" said a young man to his girlfriend. "A mantra loses its oomph *if you say it too much?*"

There it is again, thought Pontiff, having alighted the Monorail, another example of the cancerous disease that has leeched into every corner of the language. The statement-as-*question?* had always been attributed to over exposure to Australioamerican culture but Pontiff maintained the misplaced question mark – and the attendant intonation – was the legacy of the text message.

He looked to where the couple fixed their gaze. A new *Cow* billboard had been erected at the station.

### *"TOO MUCH THOUGHT LEADS TO GROSS INACTION"*

"Je-sus fucking Christ."

The young couple turned askance at Pontiff's reaction, the boy-friend putting his arm around his companion. They edged forward, trying to get to the exit that little bit quicker. Pontiff edged right behind them. He could detect a nervousness in them, in no small part due to his *just-released-from-bird* look. Aside from his compromised attire and battered physical appearance, he'd had to rip off the other sleeve of his blue t-shirt to wrap around his relentlessly bleeding elbow. He had cracked lips, a swollen nose, a black eye, some blood on his teeth. The couple edged further forward, nudging a man in a suit. He turned, disapprovingly, and shot a look like he'd smelled a bad fish.

Just round the corner from the station lay Coordination Centre 79F – a six-storey white edifice, quite at odds with the other buildings on the street which stood, just, greyed and dirtied. Naturally there was a sign.

## *VALUING PEOPLE –*
## *LIVES SIMPLER, EASIER,*
## *MORE MANAGEABLE, MORE FREE*

A lengthy queue snaked all the way back onto the road.

My God, thought Pontiff, this is gonnae take ages.

A few people pointed at him, there were whispers.

Fucken bangen. I'm a fully fledged celebrity.

## 10

# LEVELS OF UNDERSTANDING

FRED AND HAIR had made their way through the Palace's labyrinthine passages to the leader's main office and were preparing for the hastily arranged cabinet meeting. While looking over some statistics and images from the Department of Health Fred had received a memo from Martin requesting extra funding to do some fieldwork. Fred wasn't sure why this had turned up on his desk and forwarded the memo onto Heath Cliffe, suggesting the Finance Minister permit it. *It'll keep him out of the way*, wrote Fred. He wasn't surprised he'd heard nothing back.

"I'm determined to go further Fred," said Hair, "to do more for this country. Despite what those **KARMATARMAK** ignorants say."

He hoovered up another line. "We need more reform and I can do it." Another snort. He touched his middle finger to his nose before examining it for residue. "I'm saving this country."

"I know sir, I know. That will be your legacy."

Fred knew Hair's legacy would probably be something quite different as he watched the President look over the documents in front of him.

"There really aren't enough resources to go around are there, Fred? We shouldn't be trying to keep people alive when there isn't enough space. There's barely enough air to breathe!"

"I know sir, but I tell you what, with everyone looking emaciated we should set up some vast modelling agency."

They laughed, Hair's face impressed with a strange demonic contortion.

115

"Seriously though, sir," said Fred, "your legacy is shaping up pretty nicely. The *Hellevue Hero* story has been an unqualified success. Garqi's had to print more copies. This front page will probably win an award!"

But Hair was back on edge.

Yes the media had reported the great strides being made but for all that he felt, he was losing grip slightly. He was obsessed with people's perception of him, as preoccupied as ever with the cut of *Ockham's* words. He was also still buzzing in anxiety about the low turnout at Republic Day and remained convinced that that bastard of a Finance Minister, Cliffe, was up to something.

"Tell me, Fred, have we got any leads on the whereabouts and identity of this *Ockham*?"

Fred rolled that over in his mind.

If you only knew, he thought smilingly.

"Not yet, sir. But to be honest, if you are to take greater control of the country as a whole, indeed to track down this foul traitor, *Ockham*, you need to understand the enemy."

There was a blank expression from Hair.

"What do you mean?

"Here, try this," said Fred, removing the sauna-like contraption from his father's briefcase.

"What is it?" asked Hair.

"*Zondyke Plethora*. A drug from Hellevue. If you are to understand them sir, you need to be on their level. It will also help with policy development."

Hair positioned his head above the makeshift sauna. There was a grey block of ash on a plastic dish at the bottom, about two inches wide. Coming in from the side of the device was a small tube which hovered above the ash. Fred motioned Hair to put his head into the contraption and then placed a towel over him. Fred tipped red powder into the tube and it started a slow sizzle as it made contact with the ash. Fred then removed the tube and inserted a stopper in its place.

"Just breathe normally sir. It will be hot at first and you must keep your eyes closed. It'll take a couple of minutes to get full and then a further minute or so to work its magic."

Hair saw himself on a throne, witch-like characters floated around him, streets of grinning people, vivid, almost blinding sunlight.

"My goodness Fred, this is brilliant."

The he vomited, violently.

"Don't worry President, you won't feel sick for long. And you are one step closer to destroying them!"

\*\*\*

After about half an hour, Pontiff found himself at the entrance.

*"Application to enter NIPSD Facility. Environmental Footprint being calculated. Patience, Citizen, is a virtue."*

*"Individual Carbon Footprint: 0.9"*

*"Thank you Citizen. You are helping in the drive towards a cleaner, more efficient country. Enter, enjoy your day. Be aware of your unit intake."*

The door buzzed and Pontiff was granted entry.

"Name's Pope. I've get an appointment apparently."

"Ah Mr Pope," said the Administration Technician, taking in Pontiff's bloody features and looking at him nervously. "Yes, please, have a seat. Unfortunately we're a bit behind schedule. But we shouldn't be long."

Pontiff walked to a spare seat in the huge waiting area where bored people with no hope of a job sat waiting to jump through the relevant hoop. Twas ever thus at the job centre.

There was an array of posters. In one, a smiling Employment Technician held a jar.

*Our staff carry spittle kits so they can submit spittle for DNA testing.*

There was also –

## HEALTH IS WEALTH

And –

*The Great Clean-Up: Truly achieving the Big Society!*

And –

Money can't buy everything. Let's aspire to something else.

And finally, a huge holographic screen.

A version of President Terry Hair turned and smiled.

*"The lights have gone out but I can make bulbs glow anew!"*

And then it played again. And again. And again.

Pontiff was about to tell a member of staff the video was on the blink when he saw the couple he had seen outside the Monorail. Expressions of mild horror filled their faces as they spotted him. The only available seats were directly in front of Pontiff. They contemplated standing by the door but you were liable for such a long wait that without a chair it became unbearable.

They sat down opposite Pontiff. He smiled at each of them as they did so.

Minutes ticked by, fidgety ennui grew.

Pontiff looked on as a rather chubby man explained his predicament to his Employment Technician. He couldn't work as fast as the other employees at his job, was therefore largely ineffective, and now faced the cull.

"I have a co-ordination disability," he complained.

"Well you can't do the job then can you, you cunt?"

"Mr Pope, is it?"

"Aye," said Pontiff, laughing to himself.

"Just to let you know, you're next in the queue. It'll be about another ten minutes."

"Oh. Thank you."

The couple had been silent for some time, not making eye contact with Pontiff, but quietly the girlfriend began to speak.

"I didn't tell you. My cousin's gotta go Shrink Clink."

Pontiff's ears pricked up.

"Really?" responded her fella.

"Yeah, sfor the best though. She's crazed these days! First she smashed all her RecycloWare at her Rations Pick-Up, then she complained the portions were too small! Can you believe it? Honestly I think it might do her some good."

"Well she never was one for respecting authority, was she?"

The girlfriend nodded.

"So what do you want to do this Saturday?" asked the boyfriend.

"Well it's my neighbour's kid's birthday party. Don't worry you don't have to come! And then I'm free."

She paused, before adding, "I do miss Saturday afternoons at Ikea. All those lovely things, the mugs, the lamps, the cutlery. It was so exciting when a new store opened."

"I know, I know."

Grand openings? thought Pontiff. Christ. Thankfully they'd been a thing of the past for some time now, banned because people couldn't be trusted not to arrive tooled up on Black Friday. I blame the parents, he thought. Each generation seemed to be more vacuous than the last. What hope was there if the parents didn't even know who Winston Churchill was? *Not* the first black President of America, as he had had to say more than once.

The girlfriend played with her hair, looked out the window.

"You know it's actually a good thing they *stopped Facebook*? I used so much electricity on it I hardly ever had enough left to cook with."

"Aye, well it's fucken Facebook that's got us an your cousin in this mess," said Pontiff leaning on his good elbow.

The young woman didn't know what to say. She looked to her boyfriend. He looked like he wanted to say something but Pontiff's insistent eyes scared him. His girlfriend nudged him, motioned with her head.

"Are you gonna let him get away with that?" she whispered.

"Get away wi'what?" asked Pontiff.

The girlfriend nudged her man again. He gulped.

"Look," said Pontiff, leaning forward, "people like you need tae wake up tae yourselves. It's people like you who laid the foundations for the sit'eeation we all now find ourselves in, right, incluten your cousin."

"What on-"

"Look, people, *like you*, supplied personal information to all and sundry for years. You mighta thought publishen microscopic detail about your lives on the internet was a habit of seemenly no great import, that it was all about friendship, sharen and networken or that booken a holiday with a company and allowen them access to your Facebook log-in details just made it easier, but what it did was give all sorts o' corporations, consortiums, fucken you name it, little snippets about everyone. And now where is all this information, eh?"

Nothing.

"I'll tell you where. In the careful hands of the fucken Liberal Compassionate Government. Wi'all these disparate strands be-en brought together, quite a pretty picture they're able tae paint of each Citizen now, aren't they? Do you really think they're ensuren our carbon neutrality and the preservation of the environment by storen information about our medical conditions and sexual preference on our *Citizens' Accounts*? Cos that's what people were putten on their fucken Facebooks!"

"Come on, let's move," said the boyfriend.

He got up. His girlfriend got up. Both their legs rubbed against Pontiff's knees. With difficulty they squeezed past him and stood by the door before the Administration Technician shooed them back as they were getting in the way of the new arrivals.

Aye, thought Pontiff as he watched them come back and stand a safe distance from him, that says it all. Despite the advances of Government further into our lives, many believe it's all for the best, while others are as indifferent as they ever were and ever will be.

How had they not seen that Hair was the worst kind of opportunist? One minute he's voting *for* the forest sell-off, the next, fuelled by an apparent new and genuine concern for the environment, he's shacked up in a coalition with an extremist green party.

At one stage, at the height of his pre-election fame, Hair had even starred in an advert endorsing a new social networking site. Just months later his Government began retrospectively prosecuting Citizens for crimes against the environment using photographic evidence from the very same site. Others were jailed for the charge of *inappropriate behaviour* based on photographs they had published online. Some were jailed for four years for *planning* a riot that never happened. At one stage it was touch and go whether Pontiff would receive rations as his lifestyle did not match up to approved modern standards.

He would like to have been bewildered by the robotic response of many of his compatriots but Pontiff had come to the conclusion that the general public was, by and large, painted with the same brush, sent this way and that by the sweeping of opinion and the latest panic. This time all the *this is the most important election for a generation* guff had probably actually meant something.

It was hard to tell when the nadir had been reached, there had been so many low points. Life and its hitherto intrinsic liberties had not been whisked away like the proverbial tablecloth from under a neatly-arranged china tea set, but tugged ever so gently. So subtle had the movements been that they had evaded the scrutiny of a vast majority of the country. Stealth-like manoeuvring was governmental tradition, an inching here and there from one side replaced, at various intervals, by another lot and their own take on the inching and manoeuvring of government, until finally we'd landed at a government that no longer had the need for stealth.

But, thought Pontiff, *we* have been party to this drizzling away of autonomy for some time, creating an almost moronic adherence to the status quo. Even now there were people like these two for whom the only loss of liberty was an inability to buy home improvement articles at the weekends or *share* what they'd put on their toast at breakfast and how their last shit went. One of the reasons Pontiff had been so glad to join **KARMATARMAK** was that he viewed it as the one beacon of sense left in this mad country, engaged in what might best be termed as resisting modernity, in all its guises. He argued that though the seemingly nonchalant slide to collective idiocy *was* exasperating, it had been a feature of life for so long that not all gripes could be levelled at the LibComs on that front. The country had begun its ride into the sunset of absurdity some time ago.

Is this fucken revolution even gonnae work?

"Mr. Pope, is it?" said a suddenly materialising NIPSD Technician.

Bloody hell, they like to check, don't they?

"Aye, that's right."

"We're ready for you now."

"Great."

Pontiff walked to where he had been pointed.

"Good day Mr Pope," said the Employment Technician looking up, running her eyes over Pontiff in surprise.

"Let's see if we can source you a job."

"You mean find?"

"Sorry?"

"Doesnae matter."

Pontiff had come to this centre a few times before but had never seen this particular Technician. So this was where Deirdre Barlow had ended up.

"Are you alright Mr Pope, you seem distracted."

"Aye, fine," responded Pontiff. "Let's jus get this over and done with."

He handed over his NIPSD card.

"OK," higher pitched, jaunty, ultra-enthusiastic. "So, what are you trained in, if I may ask?"

Deirdre pushed her red rimmed glasses back onto her face.

"I'm a history lecturer as it goes."

"Ah yes, so it says here on your data." Deirdre removed her glasses and looked up. "There's not much call for that type of thing these days. We are trying to train our young people in something they can use in their adult life."

Pontiff remembered the advent of astronomical fees marking the beginning of the end of the traditional university experience. Since then the whole idea of intellect had been thrown out the window. Academia was the preserve of inequitable societies like Ancient Greece so that wouldn't do for those pc-ing their way round Whitehall or Blackhall, or Colour-neutral-hall, or whatever the correct terminology was these days. Christ, what a county we've ended up with, thought Pontiff, the land of the administrator, the bureaucrat, the middle-manager, the idiot. Free thinkers sacrificed for compliant cogs.

Deirdre paused, examining the data on her tiny screen.

"Oh," slightly taken aback. "I see you've been having life skills training. How did that go?"

Pontiff ruminated briefly, and then with gusto –

"Oh aye, it was fucken great. Everyone had to pair up and fuck. And what was that other thing?"

Pontiff looked away touching his hand to his chin in mock remembrance. "Ah yes," he said, pointing, "that was it. If you'd never smoked before, you had tae try it, and if you smoked you had tae quit. What did they say? *"A little of what you love is fine, but there has to be a cut-off point. Here at LifeManagement4Life, we want people to experience new things and learn to love life. We can look after your soul."* So, yeah, if you mean did the life instruction, the excessive regulation and the bizarre medicine do wonders for my soul, then I'd have tae say it was an undiluted success. And now I know. A clean and tidy home makes for a clean and tidy mind."

Finally Deirdre smiled a brief, uncertain smile.

"Ah, well, good, yes, erm, I've heard they do great work there."

As expected, there were no jobs for Pontiff and he was furnished with the usual benefit monies. Given that his Rations Pick-Up was still five days away they gave him a bit extra to buy some food. With housing and sustenance paid for, his disposable income could be used almost exclusively for smoking and boozing. No everythen's goen against me, he thought.

"Now, Mr Pope, you are aware that in order to continue to receive benefit you must offer yourself as a useful tool to the land. I see you haven't been on refuse duty for a while. Can we pencil you in for next Monday?"

"Huv you got a pencil?"

"It's just a phrase we use, Mr Pope, it means-"

"I know what it means."

"Right." She paused. "So, shall I *ink* it in?"

"You can dae whatever you like I imagine. We are creatures of consciousness and conscience, are we no?"

Pause.

"Indeed, now, can I just swipe your card to update it with everything we've said today?"

"Wi'everythen we've said?"

"Yes. Transcription of these appointments is vital to improve our services at the point of need."

"Great."

The Technician swiped but nothing came up. She rubbed it on her leg. She rubbed it on her sleeve. Nothing.

"Oh, well this is all very embarrassing," she tittered nervously.

"Yes, isn't it?"

She tried again. Again nothing.

"I'm afraid to say Mr Pope that a transcription will not be available to you, or us, for this appointment. If you wish to complain, I can give you the num-"

"I dinnae wantae complain. I *do* want tae make sure my benefits are on there, though. I dinnae want tae starve or be locked out of my home like those other poor bastards I heard about. Or be maimed, or even murdered for that matter."

"Oh come now, Mr Pope, those things don't happen. It's just tittle tattle and hearsay."

"Aye right," said Pontiff as he stood up. He needed to make a phone call.

Outside he picked up his pace and made his way to the nearest Public Comms Centre. Here, as a way of promoting civic unity, there were free calls to national media outlets. Primarily it was a way of informing on anyone *who you believe to be living amorally, immorally, or just plain wrong. Anyone at odds with the ethos of harmony (CAU)*. In the true spirit of Snitch-Britannia Terry Hair was at pains to instil, any friend of Government would receive extra food allowance in reward for their community spirit as they were the type of person *moulding the country in the manner both you and I want* (Terry Hair).

Pontiff pressed his NIPSD card onto the scanner.

*"Application to make free PCC call. Patience, Citizen, is a virtue."*

There was the usual rigmarole with eyes and fingertips. Finally he got through to *The Daily Rumour*.

"I'm the gadgie you quoted in the papers."

"One moment."

There was an insubstantial pause.

"Ah Mr Pope, we thought you might call. How about you come to dinner this evening with the editor Piers Mormon, and proprietor Signor Garqi, say seven o'clock?"

"What time is it now?"

"Just after four."

"Fine. See you later."

## 11

# THE CABINET

HAIR WAS MAKING notes in his armchair. He had decided to write his memoirs, working title – *The Journey*. He had recovered from his *Zondyke Plethora* episode and come round inspired, *enlightened*.

Fred's phone buzzed. He feared it would be his aunt. It was a text from Garqi.

**"Your man Pope coming for dinner. 7pm. Shall I tell Cook you will be coming too?"**

Fred was delighted. That hadn't taken long at all! But he was torn. Though he wanted to meet this Pope character face-to-face, he had a rendezvous in the country with two of his girls. Pope can wait, he reasoned. He'll be with us now anyway.

**"Not tonight Oli. But great work. I look forward to your feed-back."**

As he put his phone away Fred detected a presence at the door. He looked up to see Denise. She blew him a kiss. Fred caught the kiss mid-air, placed his hands down his trousers. Denise ooed, mouthed *later*. Then louder, "sir, the cabinet have arrived."

"Right, thank you Denise," said Hair, not looking up as he finished writing a sentence.

"Another little tickle before you face the twats?" asked Fred as his eyes followed Denise's majestic figure out of the room.

"Go on then. I don't really need to concentrate with them. They never say anything of import anyway."

"Too true," responded Fred.

"How do I look?" asked Hair, eyes dilating furiously from the nasal input.

Like a fucking maniac, thought Fred.

"Just great President, just great."

And with that Hair strode off down the hall. Fred followed after.

"Are you alright sir?"

"Yes, yes, of course. I just feel there's a little bit of hostility from those fuckers these days, particularly Heath."

"Not at all, sir. They're all right behind you."

It was always like this, Hair needing a bit of ego massage. Hair stopped just before entering Cabinet. He turned to Fred and hugged him.

"It really is great to have you with me you know, Fred."

"The pleasure is all mine, President. Now go get em."

Hair felt emboldened, on top of the world, medicined to the eyeballs. He entered the room the former monarch had used to receive high-ranking dignitaries, and acknowledged the gathered with his usual grin.

Entering after Hair, Fred was greeted, as always, with the scowl of Heath Cliffe, the number-cruncher. Fred was well aware that he was mistrusted and that his conversations with the leader were frowned upon for their recondite nature. Cliffe was the one for whom Fred's presence caused most displeasure. Jealousy and discontent emanated from him. He still craved the leadership desperately but though fiercely intelligent, he was easy to wind up, not possessing of the necessary aesthetic for the top job nor the easy style with which Hair had won over the electorate. Cliffe was scruffy, looked in perpetual need of a haircut and espoused a schoolboy dribbliness. Worst though, was his unsightly sucking-in mid-sentence, an almost panicky gasping for air, a hoovering-in of his bottom lip.

"Heath," said Fred as he plonked down on the sofa next to him. His problem is he doesn't look like he was conceived in love, thought Fred. How negative the man's demeanour is. No wonder he's not the leader. Maybe if he developed a sense of humour...

The room was set up in the usual way, two huge sofas flanking Hair's armchair. On the other side of Cliffe were his two key allies, two brothers, the Milipedes, or Siamese, as Fred called them. They were a bit older than Fred, though hardly worldly-wise. Political geeks. The elder held bananas strangely and his face reminded Fred of fish fingers. The younger of the two spoke as if with a mouthful of porridge.

On the other sofa sat Nicola Clegg, the deputy leader of the Neo-Luddites. She was a mousey looking woman. Her job was to take the minutes. She fastidiously insisted upon using pen and paper.

"Thought you'd probably write in blood," said Garqi, who sat next to her. "Or dee juice of fallen fruit."

Next to Garqi and his balding yet somewhat gelled pate were a smattering of *Hairies*, no-mark yes men and women, and a few other token Neo-Luddites.

"Now," said Hair, sniffing, "let us begin. We need to enter the next phase of governance and ensure the hard work we have already put in does not go to waste. Especially with events of the last few days. First though, I'd like to say a big thank you to Heath who has done an excellent job number-crunching."

Hair gave off a big jolly teethy grin.

I hate that big jolly teethy grin, thought the number-cruncher. Why must he belittle me so?

"He's put in a fantastic effort to ensure all the numbers add up and we've delivered the fourth phase of the Monorail system only slightly over-budget."

As Cliffe sucked in, ready to extol, Hair moved quickly on.

"Now, on to the important stuff. To say I'm perturbed by the reapp-earance of **KARMATARMAK** would be an understatement. The cheek of these people. And especially *now* as the country celebrates a year of the Republic. Do you think they were involved in the low crowds? I take it we are all in agreement that we need to do more to stop these fucks once and for all. This *Ockham* character is particularly scathing."

"Quite right, Mr President," interjected Fred. "He is a literary terr-orist."

"And Oli," said Hair, "why did we have that moronic Martin on the telly earlier?"

Garqi apologised with a smile.

"He should leave the TV stuff to me! He's the junior partner in this coalition."

Garqi nudged Nicola who was writing furiously.

"Where is he anyway?" demanded Hair.

"A key species of worm is threatened," responded Nicola, agitated but meek. "He is doing some fieldwork."

"He's what?" shouted Hair. "Never mind!" He dabbed his nose and picked up a copy of **KARMATARMAK**. "This is the enemy. This is what threatens us, what threatens the people of this land. We must silence them. By any means possible."

There was a shiver from some of the assembled. Even now, thought Fred, some of these fools still had the cosy idea that the LibComs were a party of justice and goodness. Especially the Neo-Luddites.

Ha! You left your morals at the door when you signed up with us!

"I mean, how do they circulate it?" demanded Hair.

"Perhaps we need a recruitment drive" said Garqi in his slow, deliberate Neapolitan tones. "More people out lookeen for dese shits."

"Yes, Oli, what a good idea," agreed Hair, eyes widening.

"Er (*suck-in*), we don't really have much cash to play with (*suck-in*)," said Cliffe. "As I was trying to say-"

"Well make some available, Heath! Oli's right. We need to get on the offensive again!"

"But some of our programmes are already running out of cash (*suck-in*). And Republic Day proved to be very expensive."

"Look, what is more important, eh? Feeding a few more mouths or ensuring that civic harmony is maintained? If we don't get hold of these people, we won't be in a position to help others!"

Cliffe remained unconvinced, simmering in his default setting of moody dejection.

Why can he never see? thought Hair.

"It's for the greater good, Heath. I thought that was one of your guiding principles!"

Nothing.

"Look, we're gonna have a bloody revolution on our hands if we're not careful! And I do mean bloody. Is that what you want?"

"Eh!" said Garqi, holding his hands up. "How much you need? Eh? Don' worry. I give you dis."

There was a brief a pause.

"OK," said Heath.

"Buu-ut," continued Garqi. There was always a 'but' with Garqi.

"Remember ow I said eet would be better to make eelectricity more widely available? So audiences for my programmes will grow and we can spread our beliefs?"

There were some nods.

"So?" smiled Garqi.

"Deal! Three hours for everyone from now on," said Hair. Cliffe went to protest, Hair ploughed on. "I can't believe these... Read this. It's absurd!"

The leader handed a copy of **KARMATARMAK** to Nicola. She looked uncertain.

"Read it out, Nicola, for Christ's sake. Don't just sit there!"

"Are you sure? It does have the capacity to make you a bit upset."

"Of course I'm sure. Read!"

So mousey Nicola started to read.

**"Our Terry is very persuasive. He is always at pains to point out the benefit to us of his every move."**

"Well that bit's alright," said Hair.

**"In another life he might have been an actor. That's the level of charisma we're dealing with here."**

Nicola paused. "Shall I con-"

"Yes Nicola!"

"Right, sorry, I-"

"Get on with it!"

**"He probably charms himself. And who could resist? With a fanfare of delight and nationwide glut of expectation, Terry Hair was sworn in as the new leader, the new exulted one.**

**"He told the country that he lived for reform. He lived *to* reform. That he craved the moniker of *Radical.* Great cheers went up through the land as he made promise after promise. The nation warmed to him like a dog to its master, the collective tail wagging and countrywide drool emanating from the land's singular mouth. This new brand of thorough, one-size-fits-all political morality, this modern take on modernisation, THIS was the rescue mission the nation had been praying for!"**

"Are they being sarcastic?" asked Hair.

No-one answered.

"Fred?"

"I wouldn't like to say sir," he replied, noticing Cliffe hide a smirk.

"I bet they are, the bastards! How have they not been shut down? What else do these feral beasts say?"

"Er, Something about Liberty for the United Kingdom?" said Nicola.

"Liberty for the United Kingdom!" screamed Hair. "This *Ockham* always fucking goes on about Liberty for the United Kingdom!"

"And the horror of *New Democracy*, sir," added Fred.

"I know! I mean I bloody well explained all this already, didn't I? Which part of *New Democracy* do they not understand? Britain is undoubtedly a better country with me, *us*, at the helm! This thing," Hair grabbed the copy of **KARMATARMAK** from Nicola and began waving it, "will be destroyed. To do that, we're gonna put even more force into Hellevue and reacquaint ourselves with the lowlifes peddling this porn. We will close them down once and for all!"

"Well sir, if I may?"

"What? What is it Fred?"

"Well, we must be mindful of a few points. To be honest, searching through Hellevue for *Ockham* will be harder than trying to locate him in an underground tunnel in Afghanistan. If we want to achieve all that we want to achieve for this country, if your legacy is to be what we both know it should be, we have to put our resources elsewhere."

"But I –"

"Sir, what the low crowds on Republic Day show is that Hellevue isn't the only problem area."

Hair winced at the mention of low crowds. Fred could see Cliffe suppressing another smirk.

"It is prudent," Fred continued, "to try and make inroads in other dissenting areas. And I'm not just talking about urban districts. Unfortunately, **KARMATARMAK** is correct in its assertions that rural tribalism is increasing." Fred thought of his mother. "These areas have followed to a tee the drive to live smaller and become self-sufficient and as such are becoming less and less integrated. The recent food shortages are only going to get worse."

Fred didn't blame the farming Citizens for their reticence in providing food for the drug-addled urbanites.

"But how *do* they know all this?" demanded Hair. "It's never reported!"

"Which is why we must strike them down before it is common knowledge sir."

Garqi nodded.

"Look, we just don't have the manpower to fight on all these fronts. In Hellevue we've had the all-important show of strength. We have arrested five per cent of the males as we said we would. And now we are interviewing them. If we find more information we will act on it. But the assault on Hellevue has been successful. We may not need to pursue **KARMATARMAK** any further. I feel sure they will be out of action. The Government has imposed itself and we've found nothing. There is no revolution. We needn't worry. We won't make strides elsewhere unless we leave Hellevue now."

"But we're still no nearer to uncovering the identity of the terrorists!" shouted Hair. "And in particular, *Ockham*."

"The PHU has made exceptional progress on a number of accounts," Fred replied. "Admittedly, the group behind **KARMATARMAK** remains elusive but the key thing now, President, is that with this show of strength I am utterly convinced they will cease their activities. Our story," Fred nodded to Garqi "shows we're winning the battle for hearts and minds in Hellevue. The district's not going to be a problem now."

"Where is he anyway? (*suck-in*) This Pope?" asked Cliffe.

Fred went to respond but Garqi put his hand out.

"Eath. E come to see me later. Eet eez all under control."

With another hand gesture Garqi motioned for Fred to carry on.

"Thank you, Oli. Realistically we need to be addressing other areas. There could well be a sense of revolution elsewhere. Fortifying the boundaries of London is key. *The Rurals* are probably too localised out there to mount an attack but still. As long as they get nowhere near London, we'll be fine. So it is best to be prudent."

"But as I have just mentioned (*suck-in*), we don't have enough money."

"Exactly Cliffe and that's exactly the premise I've been working on. Rest assured, I've got an absolute belter of a plan for Hellevue – indeed everywhere – and it won't cost half as much as an assault from the Blackguard."

"Well, I think it'd be far better to stay in Hellevue (*suck-in*)."

"I thought you said we didn't have enough cash, Heath," said Fred.

"Yes Heath" interjected Hair, and then with an attempt at a conciliatory tone, "just... be quiet for a moment and let Fred finish. Go on, Fred."

"Thank you sir. The problem in this country is sub-standard parenting." I should know, thought Fred. "If we really want to alleviate criminality, terrorism and benefit bludgers, we need to breed out the undesirable."

Nicola gasped. Garqi grinned.

"Go on Fred," said Hair.

"The fabric of society needs to be stitched together if we are to ensure that every child has the right start in life. Bad starts equal bad endings. And that's why we have these deranged terrorists. That is our duty, is it not?"

"But I thought that's why we brought in *Designated Family Day*."

"Oh be quiet Nickoola, let eem finish," said Garqi.

"Well you are right Nicola. We did bring in *Designated Family Day*. But that does not go far enough. Aside from anything else, do we really want parents who fill up their baby's bottle with cola? Do we really want the type of parent who gives birth then vacates the hospital every hour on the hour for a quick cigarette while their newly delivered progeny lay crying and wailing? Do we want another Karen Matthews? Another Baby P? The answer is no, we do not."

"What are you suggesting?"

"Well," said Fred, reaching into his briefcase and retrieving some documents. "Allow me to outline my proposals."

## 12

# A PEOPLE UNITED

OUTSIDE THE PUBLIC Comms Centre, the ubiquitous CCTV awaited Pontiff. Also waiting for him – the unrelenting grimness of modern day Britannia.

There was no real distinction between pavement and road. The denizens of the area were largely on foot, scurrying and weaving between horse and carts, bikes, others peddling furiously on cycle-rickshaws – gruelling employ when navigating this scrum of directionless people. The only permitted motorised transport were emergency service vehicles, Blackguard vans and those that ferried around top ranking government officials, which whizzed through occasionally. Most people had stopped using cars prior to the personal ownership ban as the cost of fuel had escalated so much. Most people had enough on their plate trying to get enough on their plate, let alone worrying about petrol.

Citizens were, by and large, kitted out in the same clothes – state-issued chinos and black shoes with a choice of shirt colour for the men, flat shoes and a summer dress with a choice of colour for the women.

I musta gone inside at the turn of the season, thought Pontiff.

Clothes, at first a luxury, then for centuries a norm, were now regarded as a symptom of the people's unnatural desires that were killing the planet. Now, it was incumbent upon each Citizen to demonstrate that he or she truly needed new items, that their clothes were in serious disrepair and it was not merely a whim of fashion. Pontiff had never secured that appointment.

It was funny to think of the seemingly arbitrary way things were allowed or not, he thought. Clutching a water bottle used to be the

133

height of sophistication. Now you'd be laughed at for being some sort of materialistic caveman.

As Pontiff continued, he walked past long since closed internet cafes, the odd pub, some fruit and veg stalls, cycle repair shops, rickshaw repair shops and clothes repair shops. Most of the buildings were state-owned – alcohol shops, government recruitment centres, health centres – not that they were all they were cracked up to be. There were lengthy queues at hospitals and doctors' surgeries. Getting appointments was a Kafka-esque farce. Incongruously the national bank – *The Britannic Co-op* was owned by a foreigner – Signor Oli Garqi, as was the *Britannic People's Loans Company*. There were big queues there too. It was doubtful many would have their applications approved.

But what does that greasy cockerel Chirac lookalike want wi'me? thought Pontiff, as he ambled along. He didn't have time to walk back to Hellevue nor did he feel like a burning a significant part of his funds on making the journey to and fro by Monorail. But he did want to get back to set the record straight. What would his allies at **KARMATARMAK** think now he'd been outed as a traitor and a pervert? And what of Clem? Was she safe? And *dead* son?

Pontiff went to the nearest government alcohol shop and bought the cheapest big bottle he could find. Now he just needed somewhere to drink it. As he traversed the streets, he took a few hits. It made him feel at least partially restored. A few more gulps stiffened him further until he walked past a park or *Designated Green Area* as they were now known.

The People's Abode Law – an attempt to reverse the catastrophic decision to sell off all woods and forests – had created more green spaces for the populace. For now, it looked a little bald but with time would no doubt illuminate with its vast shrubbery. But there was another striking detail about this park, in all new parks, commissioned by the PAL. No benches.

### POLITE NOTICE – NO LITTERING. NO LOITERING.
### THE LIBCOMS CARE FOR YOUR WELLBEING.

Pontiff took clandestine swigs from his bottle as he walked past the people's abode people were debarred from using.

He then saw a mass of Citizens congregating in front of a building and a sign above the huge shutters that remained bolted to the concrete yard in front of it. The slogan was a trifle misleading, the lofty ambition not quite being delivered on. This was a Rations Pick-Up Centre.

### *A COMMON GOAL FOR A PEOPLE UNITED – PRIVATE ENTERPRISE IN STATE HANDS ENSURING A SLICE OF PIE FOR EVERYONE!*

"Fuck me! We been waitin ere two hours!" shouted a young mother. "Come on! Open up. We're ungry!"

The problem – a glitch with NIPSD. *Life Administration* Group Two had been misinformed that their Rations Pick-up Day had changed. Or wait, no. It was that Life Admin Group Three's Day had been changed and *they* hadn't been informed. Ah no, it was that the workers had taken the day off after the Republic Day celebrations.

"Apparently they're all too hungover to come and open up," a partially inebriated man said to Pontiff.

Whatever it was, none of the hungry throng were getting any closer to getting their bellies filled. The sun was beating down and bonhomie was just starting to be replaced by restlessness. Anger seeped insidiously into the collective mass.

"We're not prepared to be denied today. It's *Meat Day,*" said another man who swigged at a whiskeysquash bottle and handed it to Pontiff. *Meat Day* only came round once a month. You could buy meat at any time but the expense precluded most from that luxury.

"Cheers mate," said Pontiff, focussing to swallow the burn of the liquid. He handed back the man's booze and offered him some of his bottle. It was marginally better.

All around were people, *hungry people*, clutching their Recyclo-Ware – government-issue hemp bags, jars and bottles, the standard receptacles for rations. As it was prohibitively expensive to replace these items, a great deal of care was taken in their upkeep. Chants were breaking out, drinking was rife.

The crowd was huge and Pontiff found himself firmly ensconced in the middle of the scrum. Blackguard circled all around the periphery. He knew they would have their breathalyzer kits on them but whiskeysquash bottles were passed freely throughout the crowd. Everyone seemed to be indulging. Was this the first open sign of dissent?

There was then an uneasy quiet, a sense that something grotesque may be about to happen. And sure enough....

Suddenly a great surge went through the crowd and ugly scenes broke out, like watching a humanitarian disaster on the TV from yesteryear. Every day was a humanitarian disaster in Blighty. All sorts of objects started fizzing through the air as people, *hungry* people, carted themselves around like composite parts of a mass whirling dervish. As fighting broke out between protesters, Blackguard waded in brandishing weapons. Some on horseback charged through, clubbing protesters as they made their gallop.

I gottae get outta this, thought Pontiff.

So soon out of incarceration, he couldn't afford to get involved with this violent outpouring of emotion. That would hardly demonstrate he was realigned. His name, face, identity and habits had been flagged up as *Inclined to Sedition* and he knew it was preferable to go hungry than be a criminal.

"Do yourself a favour and move on, or you'll be in trouble!" shouted a Blackguard.

"Oh yeah? We're exercising our right of freedom of speech!"

Freedom of speech? Pontiff laughed to himself as a jam jar smashed into his face.

"I suggest you pipe down!"

"What are you gonna do? Arrest me for talking?"

Yes they were.

Feeling blood dripping from his head, Pontiff tried to battle his way out. The blue t-shirt material he used to wrap around his bleeding elbow was flapping free and dollops of claret coloured his permanently dirtied white shirt. His battered brogue boots were now replete with a healthy smattering of blood, not all his. People charged in different directions, punches were thrown, smashed glass covered the floor.

It reminded Pontiff of the independence riots in Scotland a few years before. Or how a week prior to that he'd brought a few of his old students down to a demonstration in London. A police chief was being honoured for services to communities just months after a foreign worker had been gunned down on the Public Transport System. Of course now, from the humble beginnings of killing unarmed foreigners underground, the police and Blackguard did it out in the open, on the streets, often bagging a few indigenous into the bargain as well.

Pontiff could see some of the protesters trying to force the shutters of the Rations Pick-Up Centre. Others had fled into the park. The crowd was dispersing.

At the moment his group of students had split up on that day out in London, Pontiff had managed to snake his way through the crowd and escape. Miraculously he never received an invitation to come down to the police station to explain himself. Pontiff thought it would have been a matter of time before he was tracked down through CCTV. But he never was. Despite the surveillance society, a healthy slice of incompetence stood in the way of total totalitarianism. Doubtless someone had forgotten to put a video in the machine.

At one time, protesting had been the right of every Citizen. Now some sort of application was necessary. It was rarely approved. If it was, it was so watered down, with the sting so much removed that it was reduced to mere ornament. They take the romance out of everything, thought Pontiff. They'd done it to busking some years before.

But now, it seemed, protests were back. Those caught would undoubtedly feel the wrath of the People's Republic of Britannia, but maybe others would be inspired to revolt. Maybe the change was coming.

# 13
# MODERNISING

FRED WAS PRETTY sure he had remembered everything. He'd come up with the idea a week or so ago, between receiving female guests. It had been triggered by the whole Clementine Romain story. His proposals would herald the birth of a new government agency, the Parental Suitability Unit.

As he spoke Nicola looked disbelievingly around the room, searching for those who also opposed this barbarism. Had someone shared her worries it wouldn't have mattered. The only opinions worth anything in here were those of Garqi, Fred and Hair, the latter gazing with great admiration at this young genius.

"All pregnancies will be registered with the PSU," said Fred. "Then, a team of specially-trained moralists will weigh up the relative pros and cons of allowing the subject of their assessment the right not only to bring a child into the world, but also whether they can be trusted with the raising of that child. If the prospective parent is deemed suitable, permissible, generally OK, then that'll be the end of it, and a license to raise the child of your loins will be granted. The thing is, you need a license to fish, you used to need a license to drive, you even need a license to watch television, so why not a license for parenting? The whole licensing business is completely topsy-turvy."

"And what happens if the parent-to-be is deemed unsuitable?" asked the younger Milipede, Porridgemouth.

"Ah," answered Fred, "well then two courses of action are available to the PSU. The first potential outcome is that the pregnancy is permitted but after birth, the baby is put up for adoption. The child would then be placed in a new state-of-the-art government orphanage and wait to be familified."

"And the other?"

"The alternative is termination. But this will only happen if the adoption rate of newly-orphaned babies drops, and there's an excess backlog of unclaimed children."

Nicola gasped. "This is gruesome!"

"Not at all," retorted Fred. "This is merely extending the basic tenet of Liberal Compassionatism; from saving incompetent people from themselves, to saving children from incompetent parents. Come on Nicola. Curbs on the type of person that can be a parent? That's what most of the country wants! Think of Clementine Romain. She's the most recent in a long line of cases. Remember, we are the modernising party and we are not afraid to make the necessary reforms that ensure the future prosperity of this country."

Fred knew Hair would go for that. The President liked to divide everything along the lines of tradition being associated with backwardness, and reform and modernising being the ethos to apply to every aspect of life.

"Regulating the rate of childbirth will enable us to regulate resources as well, the paucity of which does undoubtedly lead to terrorism, as my graph shows."

"This is not what we came into government to be," said Nicola as she flicked through the document.

"Oh Nee-kool-aah darleen," patronised Garqi, "you are so out of touch. Eet eez like dat time you recommended dat police and secoority personnel use fluffy handcuffs to detain suspects and not dee metal ones because eet was against deir human rights. We need affirmative action."

Nicola looked down, petrified. Cliffe, as ever, looked constipated and uncomfortable, his strange plastic smile, scabbarded.

"But you're suggesting social cleansing," said Nicola, eyes still at the floor.

"Yes. But in a good way. We are Liberal and Compassionate are we not?"

Hair was convinced.

"You're right Fred, of course. We can stop the steady flow of terrorists and idiots into our society by controlling the type of people being born. We'll introduce a set of guidelines surrounding procreation, something the people of this country enjoy rather too much if you ask me, especially the young. Nicola, do you really want youth stabbings to escalate? For these people to have children to stab others? For more rags like this" – he picked up the **KARMATARMAK** – "poisoning the minds of our people?"

"This is some sort of quasi-Cantonese approach to child birth to stop the country breeding beyond its means!"

"Thank you," Fred responded. "And before you ask, yes, as liberal and compassionate leaders we will ensure social status is the benchmark in deciding the quantity of children permitted."

"What about the right, not to mention the need, of a child to be with his or her family and to know who they are?" argued Nicola. "Furthermore, do you really believe that having a child languishing in a glorified orphanage is better than the parental home?"

"Almost certainly in a good deal of cases," said Fred. "But that is the type of decision that will be taken by the PSU. I must say though that removing a child from a climate of potential abuse, ill health, a diet of cheeseburgers and lollies, not to mention a chronic lack of aspiration can only be beneficial. That's why they become terrorists. We can pilot the scheme in Hellevue alongside the other activities that will be tackling the area's degradation. It can be the policy that marks the second year of the People's Republic of Britannia, and President Hair's glorious tenure!"

"I don't think you can say with any great conviction that they will be removing the child from abuse." cried Nicola, who was conscious no-one else was fighting her corner. "It'll be more like out of the frying pan and into the fire!"

"Oh look," said Fred, "let's not have a catfight about who's most at fault for the abuse of minors. This is why most people are so disillusioned with your politics, Nicola, why no-one took you lot seriously til you joined us. But most importantly, surely the children we help will have a clearer idea of what they are capable of rather than having to settle for what they are born into. Therefore I think I can say with some confidence, they will have greater opportunity to mould their identity however they see fit. In these *glorified orphanages* as you rather injudiciously put it, these children will have access to a decent education in a loving and healthy environment. I thought you lot, as a protest party, would be right behind this. Better future for all and all that. If you can't see that, you're contributing to the ills of this country."

"How dare you! And how you dare you set such a dangerous precedent in which all morality descends from Number Ten!"

Bit late for that love, thought Fred.

"Er," stumbled Cliffe, "(*suck-in*) we're actually at Buck-"

"To do nothing to save these children, or rather unborn children, would also be dangerous for the fabric of our society," continued Fred. "You've seen where the status quo has led us."

"And what of those that are terminated? Where is the moral legitimacy for state-enforced abortion? Where does that fit in with the ethos of salvation?"

"Clearly you're not familiar with Utilitarianism, Nicola!" cried Fred. "This is a perfect example of the weakness that has bedevilled you and your backward party for years!"

"This is a disgrace! This is vile politics. A form of class-cleansing!"

"Look, this is a delicate issue that you clearly do not understand."

"I do understand it. I understand it as evil of the highest order!"

"Calm down dear," said Garqi.

"It is precisely this kind of nit-picking that has rendered you out of touch, Nicola," continued Fred.

"Perhaps it's time to hang up your boots, Nikki," said Hair.

"What?"

Garqi started to chuckle.

Hair nodded like a parent to a child and then, in a whisper, "It's time."

Instantaneously, four armed Blackguard entered the room.

In shock, Nicola was led out of the room, and out of a job.

"Right," said Hair "any of you other Neo-Luddites got anything to say?"

Silence.

"OK then," said Hair, straightening his tie.

Cliffe had been pondering, or was in need of a shit, it was hard to tell, but he asked one of his questions now. He was always one for logistics.

"Do we not need to present some real detailed analysis as to why we will be carrying out these operations (*suck-in*)?"

Hair sighed. "Look Heath, we just assure the public that there is justification. That's all there is to it. What do they know anyway? We don't need to get bogged down in the minutiae of the scheme. People just aren't interested in all the whys and wherefores."

Cliffe looked nonplussed.

He's always such a stickler, thought Hair.

"C'mon," continued the President, "I know the people of this country. I listen to rock music. Used to *play* rock music."

He paused, looked at Cliffe.

"Look, if it means that much to you, we'll say something about responding to the growing levels of crime in our society, that this is in direct response to literary terrorism. You know, the usual thing, this is an issue of modernity, not liberty, something like that."

"I suppose we could refer to it as a response to literary terrorism, yes," agreed Cliffe, sombrely.

"Whatever you want Heath, but we have to do something or we'll have bloody anarchy on our hands." Hair paused. "OK. Payrise? Let's have a show of hands. So that's one, two, three... Heath?"

Cliffe pretended he didn't want it but up came his hand.

"Well that's everyone...OK, done," said Hair. "Now, let's sort the finances for the PSU. Heath?"

The Finance Minister stared deathlike, sullen, dribbly. He noticed Fred smiling at him. This young, good-looking little upstart seemed grotesquely self-confident. That's why Cliffe was so intimidated by him. And he'd never forgiven Fred for the change in policy at Conference. Fred laughed to himself. Another victory.

And anyway, the finances chat had only been for Cliffe's benefit. Garqi had already moved a bit of money and the first wave of PSU operatives were heading into Hellevue at that very moment. Meanwhile, the Blackguard were coming the other way having already been informed to wind up their operation.

After Cliffe left in haste with the Milipedes, everyone else started filing out. Fred was about to leave Hair to his counsel when his phone started buzzing incessantly.

"Riot at ration's centre just outside Hellevue," flashed up on the screen.

"Christ," said Fred, plugging his phone into the Video Wall.

"What is it?" asked a panicked Hair

"This."

Fred pressed play to show footage from the riot.

"Oh my God," said Hair, slumping into his arm chair. "Oh my God. But... There hasn't been an occurrence like this for, well...how long, Fred?"

"The best part of a year, sir."

Fred trawled through the footage before stopping in amazement.

"Holy fuck! Pope!" Fred laughed as he watched the jar crash into Pontiff's face. "Oh he'll lap up what we've got in store for him!"

The video cut and a new message appeared on the wall. Fred's girls were waiting outside.

# 14
# MEDIACORP INTERNATIONAL

AT JUST AFTER seven o'clock, Pontiff approached the vast skyscraper of MediaCorp International HQ, rather worse for wear. A glamorous couple left the building and held the door open for him. He shuffled in.

There was a smattering of people milling about in the lobby, news presenters, a few politicians, the odd footballer, a few Blackguard here and there. This was one of those businesses permitted more than just two hours of electricity. Here, Garqi's British Empire was stationed.

There were only two television channels in Blighty these days – MCIBBC1 and MCIBBC2. These two channels had initially only broadcast from 6pm til midnight but Garqi had persuaded the cabinet to extend these hours. MCIBBC1 was dedicated to entertainment, MCI-BBC2 dedicated to news, current affairs and sports. Licenses for different time slots were granted to different production companies, all of whom had Garqi as nominal head. Of course those that were offered first dibs were the connected ones who had prospered under the old arrangement, the old society, the ones who had peopled the new revolution. Garqi also controlled the Britannic Internet Service Provider. Not much of a take-up there these days but it couldn't hurt to have that power.

*The Daily Sentinel* and *The Daily Rumour* also had their offices in this building and the receptionist pointed Pontiff in the direction of the appropriate lift for the latter.

Feeling a little wobbly, Pontiff entered. He still ached from where he had taken the miscreant jam jar above the left eye during the riot and the rips in both knees had been lengthened by the day's violence.

"Hello sir," greeted the security guard.

He was thin with trousers that were too big for his scrawny legs and a white shirt that bagged out from underneath a beige waistcoat. He looked pleasant.

"How are we this evening?"

The guard held his smile as Pontiff looked at the name badge. *Nathan-Ian*.

"Well Na-. Sorry. You get a double-barrelled first name?"

"That's right sir."

"Jesus Christ."

"That's double-barrelled too, sir."

"Aye," laughed Pontiff. "Anyway, *Nathan-Ian*. In response tae your question, I'm drunk, an yet still in a lotta pain."

"Oh I'm sorry to hear that sir."

"Aye, well it's no your fault. Anyway, I dinnae ken which floor I need. I'm here tae see-"

"Oh I know who you are here to see, sir. Mr Mormon's office is on the top floor. Have a good evening."

"Aye. Cheers, *Nathan-Ian*. You too."

The editor of *The Daily Rumour*, Piers Mormon and the owner, Signor Oli Garqi, were enjoying some wine when their slightly unsteady guest announced his arrival with the ping of the lift.

"Ah, Mr Po-, Jesus, are you alright?" enquired Mormon. "Are you ill? What happened to your face?"

"I'm actually looken better than I was. But thanks for the welcome."

"Oh. Need we ask more?" probed Mormon, whose weak moon face seemed to Pontiff the embodiment of inconsequentia.

"Nah," responded Pontiff.

"I see." Mormon paused. "Well, Mr Pope, I am the editor at here at *The Rumour* and this is our owner, Signor Garqi."

"Mr Pope, nice to meet you."

Garqi was studiously grand, the paragon of quiet elegance. He extended his hand.

You smirken slimed hair bastard, thought Pontiff.

"Would you like a drink?" asked Garqi.

"Aye."

The Italian filled a glass and handed it to Pontiff, who turned to the huge window to take in the view. This was a part of town that had benefitted from *The Great Clean-Up*. Pontiff gawped at the sparse, clinical Kubrik-esque images of the urban landscape, cleaner yes, but deadened. He knew that when the sun went down many of the buildings would be shrouded in total darkness and that it was fair to assume any building with continuous energy housed workers engaged in government activity. Canary Wharf loomed in the late evening sun, illuminated from within.

Pontiff had drained his glass and it was refilled by Garqi who slimed another smarmy smile.

Mormon approached. "You like the wine, I see."

"Aye, it's awright."

"According to your *Beverage Behaviour* on your *Citizen's Account*, you are more of a Guinness and whisky man. Is that not the case?"

"Somehen like that, aye." Pontiff finished his second glass of wine. "Mind if I smoke?"

"Please, be our guest," said Garqi, pulling a lighter from his pocket.

Pontiff leant in, his hands touching the Italian's as he shielded the flame. He nodded a thanks with his eyes.

"So is this from your homeland then, Signor Garqi?" asked Pontiff, lifting his glass.

The Italian laughed. "Good Lord no. Importeen eez extremely problematic dese days. No, eet's English actually. Dis new ot climate eez wonderful for dee grapes of Cornwall. As a lover of Celtic drinks eet does not trouble you to poison your palate wid suntheen English?"

"The Cornish are Celts."

Again, the Italian laughed.

"Intelligent and a way wid words. Perhaps you should offer eem a job, Piers."

"Well, its words we wish to discuss so that seems fitting, doesn't it?"

"Indeed." responded Garqi, inquiring with silent eyes whether the Scotsman's just drained glass needed another top-up. Pontiff held out the vessel. The Italian filled it. Garqi then removed another bottle from the box on the floor and started to open it. "But please, let us sit."

The three sat down at one end of a large conference table. It was covered in every imaginable cuisine of luxury – cold meats, canapés, lobster, prawns, fresh salad.

"I'm fucken starven," said Pontiff, putting out his cigarette.

"Ah. Dee linguist iz ungry eh? Well eat den! Dis iz a dinner iz eet not?"

Settling down to such a fine platter of food, Pontiff felt a tinge of joy. He'd not seen anything like it in, well, how long? The food was delicious. He did have a momentary pause for the people, the hungry people, he'd seen today, but those thoughts vanished down his gullet with fine sea food and wine.

He had pondered how he was going to handle all this. He'd settled on a game-plan of calm, to see if he could get some information on the whereabouts of Clem. And find out why he'd been chosen. As he ate, he surveyed the room. Scattered about the rest of the offices were sofas, little desks, telephones, screens with CCTV access, plasma televisions. All-in-all a chamber of comfort and power.

"I see you enjoy dee food," said Garqi. "Good."

"Mr Pope, there's something we want to show you," said Mormon, wiping his mouth on a napkin.

He handed Pontiff a piece of paper.

"Read it if you would please."

There was a short interlude of silence as Pontiff scanned over the page.

"Out loud."

Pontiff stopped, looked up at Mormon, rattled the paper, cleared his throat and began.

### "FOCUS ON THE HELLEVUE HERO – SELECTED QUOTES"

Pontiff looked at his two hosts before continuing.

*"In truth, Hellevue is loyal to the Government. That zine – I'm not even going to use the name – deliberately misrepresents the greatness of the area. I don't need to tell you that the conditions they report are a wee bit overplayed! Austerity – or rather efficiency – will make the area – the country – great again."*

*"There a few rogue characters that run the zine – and one or two got to that young Clementine Romain. She was a good woman turned bad."*

*"That zine are trying to brainwash the young. The Blackguard are protecting them."*

"Ooh, dat's very good. Evocative," ventured the Italian.

"It is *some* story, isn't it Signor Garqi?"

"Eet certainly eez, Mr Mormon."

Pontiff looked left to right as his hosts continued addressing each other like teachers in front of a pupil. He lit another cigarette.

"Is it something we'd be interested in following up, do you think, Signor Garqi?"

"Undoubtedly, Mr Mormon."

"A weekly column?"

"Maybe a daily thought?" mused Garqi. "Yes Mr Pope, eet's good of you to come. We should thank you for your comments."

He passed some chocolate truffles round.

"Elpeen us report dee great strides being made. Ensureen dee safety of our youngest and most vulnerable."

"That's right," agreed Mormon. "Showing all is not lost in Hellevue. Here."

He handed Pontiff another bit of paper. It was a feature about the district, full of quotes from residents who had apparently been only too happy to be questioned. The conclusion was clear. **KARMATARMAK** enjoyed no significant support and there was relief the Blackguard had arrived to sort them out.

"Yes, Mr Pope," continued Mormon, "you are showing how the Government have turned it around, that decency isn't dead in the terror heartlands. Some of the parents in there aren't fit-for-purpose! And that is why what you have done is so wonderful. You saved her son from domestic abuse."

"So he's still alive?"

Mormon and Garqi exchanged a look. Another smile oozed out of Garqi's mouth, parting his lips.

"Where have you taken them?" asked Pontiff, caressing the inside of his left cheek with his tongue as he put the document on the table.

Garqi feigned being taken aback.

"I'm sorry Mr Pope, I don't quite follow."

He looked up from his pouring wine into Mormon's glass.

"Why are you so anxious to know?"

Pontiff said nothing, drank more wine.

"Am I right in infereen you actually knew Ms Romain?"

Garqi threw a surprised smile at Mormon. The slow deliberate Neapolitan tones were just starting to prickle the Scotsman.

"Why have you chosen me?"

"Chosen you!" laughed Garqi. "We did not *choose* you, Mr Pope."

"I must admit," said Mormon, "at first, I was a bit surprised a man like you would agree to talk to the press. But then I suppose in everyone's life, even the unemployed and useless, there comes a time when a sense of civic duty takes over."

"But to do dat about someone you actually knew?" added Garqi. "Wow."

History was always written by the winners, thought Pontiff. Like many things, truth was an elastic concept.

"Of course, you should be rewarded for seein dee light."

"Yes indeed, Mr Pope. And our offer of this new role at the paper could elevate you out of your current situ in life, couldn't it? A situ that is less than desirable, is that not the case?"

"My sit'eeation is no gonnae improve with what you're sayen thasforshir." Pontiff paused for another gulp of wine. "But there'll be enough that'll know the truth, that'll see through all this."

"Oh dear. Oh dear, oh dear," said Garqi. "Dis eez a shame. Dee thing eez Robert, may I call you Robert?" He didn't wait for a response. "Dee theeng eez, whether you like eet or not, dee truth, *our* truth," he motioned at himself and Mormon, before pointing to Pontiff as well, "eez common knowledge. Throughout dee country. Now. You have a choice. Two choices. And one eez much, much better dan dee udder. Dee whole country has read dee incredibly tragic story about dee death of a young boy, essentially at dee ands of eez mother."

"That didn't happen."

"Yes, Mr Pope, eet did. Eet did because we say eet did. And do you know who told us?" Garqi nodded and smiled. "Dat's right Robert,

149

you." He paused. "Do you think you can return to your district now? Do you think your people will welcome you, a traitor? Anyway, your district is implodeen."

On the wall a plasma screen eased down and the evening news was beamed straight into the dinner party.

*"VIOLENCE IN HELLEVUE –*

*RIOT MAKES IT IMPOSSIBLE TO HAND OUT RATIONS!"*

*"Here we see images of violence from the inhabitants of the undesirable district of Hellevue."*

*"We are not here to hurt normal, law abiding Citizens,"* said one Guard. *"We want to put an end to their misery. It was only those whose actions added to the misery that needed to be removed. For everyone's safety."*

*"You can see aerial footage of the riot from our ZeitCopter on our website, those of you that have access to that,"* said the newsreader. *"Coming up later, our in-hospital cameras will follow the operation of a rioter. Will they save him? Should they save him?"*

No matter how long TV had been this way, the reportage was still troubling. Pontiff noticed some of the footage looked surprisingly old, archive-like. It was all very nicely edited. It included footage of the riot at the Rations Pick-Up, though that hadn't been in Hellevue. There were reports of arrests and some obviously constructed images of Blackguard handing out rations.

"Look how little everyone has," said Mormon. "Look at what you've got tonight. This could be the norm for you. Do you really want to go back to that?"

"Look at dem!" cried Garqi. "Dey are fighteen demselves!" He started laughing. Mormon followed suit.

"Way I see it, people are fighten back," said Pontiff. "This is the start. The beginnen of your end."

"Oh. You support a revolution, do you?" asked Garqi.

"I didnae say that. I jus said your days are numbered."

"Oh my days are numbered?" Garqi violently jabbed himself in the chest with his right forefinger. "My days, Mr Pope?" The Italian leant back, composed himself. He licked his lips and lit a cigar. "Mr Pope, look at dee fuckeen state of you. You are a mess. Your brain is a mess. Now think, *remember*. Dee woman, Clementine, was given medication for her son but because of er poor parenteen, she failed to administer eet and dee child died. Eet was er fault."

Pontiff shook his head.

"Mr Pope, let me ask you a question because obviously you knew Ms Romain. What exactly did dee child murderer tell you?"

"What?"

"You 'eard me. What did dat foul bitch say to you, mm? Because I find eet difficult to think dat a man of your intelligence would be so easily taken een. You can't honestly believe dee rants of an alcoholic and neglectful mother? A mother so uncareen she allowed er son to die."

"If what you are saying *now* is true," added Mormon, "why aren't her neighbours, friends and family up in arms? I think you've reached the point of no return in your own head and you're believing your own delusions."

Pontiff thought her friends probably were up in arms. He needed to get back.

"And when's the next story comen out?" he asked.

"Tomorrow," responded Mormon.

"Wonderful. I'll look forward tae that."

"Eet certainly eez, how you say, a belter, isn't eet?" responded the Italian with a nod of approval.

"An what if I don't agree?" said Pontiff, lighting another cigarette.

Garqi quattro-tutted. And then calmly, softly, "I don't think you'll choose dat course of action, Mr Pope. You seem an intelligent man. Dis eez a great story. And you are a national hero. Doeen your civic duty, calleen in dee police. And you shall be rewarded for your actions, oh yes. We have prepared a little ceremony tomorrow, all in your honour. Think of dee glory."

"Well, you've planned this well, haven't you?"

"Planned? Come Mr Pope, what do you take us for? We have no control over events, as you know."

"Aye, of course. You report."

"So?" enquired Mormon.

A burning sensation crept up Pontiff's face. His head felt like the final stage of a Champagne cork's journey to popping. He stood up and moved away from the table.

"Don't get wound up, Robert," patronised Mormon as he stood up too. He reached a hand to the shoulder of his guest. "This story is what the country needs."

Pontiff shrugged him off.

"Dis eez a respectable paper, Mr. Pope," said Garqi as he walked towards Pontiff. "We are not in dee business of unnecessarily disparageen Citizens. Dis eez an example of dee strides bein made by Mr Hair. A man from Hellevue chooseen to support dee Government over one of his own? Dis eez a story to cheer dee hearts of dee nation!"

Ah, thought Pontiff, as he started to sway, vision blurring round the edges, the coup de grace.

He exhaled deeply, drained his glass. Garqi refilled it and then his own.

"Do you want to cause unrest, Mr Po-"

Pontiff charged into Garqi, bundling him across the table. He held the Italian by the throat with his left hand and drew back his other to strike. But before he could rain down a punch on that slimy head an empty bottle smashed over *his* head and not for the first time today, Pontiff fell to the floor with blood gushing from his cranium.

Garqi got off the table, straightened his tie, and ran both hands delicately over his slicked, heavily gelled wisps of hair. He looked at the prostrate Pontiff, smiled and shook his head. Calmly pressing the sole of his left shoe into Pontiff's still-burning cigarette, Garqi leant down and lifted Pontiff up by the collar so he was making eye contact, and spat in Pontiff's face. Like all these media types, he lacked a certain degree of class. Pontiff just about managed to open his eyes and mouth, but it was weakened somewhat by the aggregation of blows he'd received in his recent past.

"My my, we are aggressive aren't we?" said the Italian. "I thought we were goeen to have a nice meeteen, a civilised dinner."

"Indeed," added Mormon. "I thought you'd come to meet the men who've put you on the map. This is a funny way to say thank you, wouldn't you say, *Pon-tiff*?"

The Italian chuckled. "Clever nickname." Then agitated, "Pope! Here are your choices! Either you take credit for being a hero, for doeen what you thought was right and your life will be projected on an upward curve, or... Well, do I need to spell out dee 'or'? What would you rather av, eh, *Pon-tiff*? Life, comfort? Or miserable pain? How much longer can you cope on dee breadline? A man with your intake. Come on, don't be a silly boy. You know what makes sense. What about your NIPSD points, eh? Dee way you're goeen eet won't be long til we av to detain you again for your own safety!"

"I think what Signor Garqi is saying is right," said Mormon. "It is clear from tonight's little performance you drink too much. You must have got yourself arrested, what, four times before you were sent to Shrink Clink? Informing on Romain might be the most intelligent thing you've done. But at least you've not lost your bite. That's a good thing I suppose. If you could just learn to channel this energy you might get on the road to recovery."

The pain in Pontiff's head was verging on the unbearable. He wiped the spit from his face and using all the energy he had left, mustered the strength for a couple of choice words from his position on the ground.

"I'm gonnae fucken take you down, you greasy piece o'shite."

The Italian smiled. "Oh dear. Oh deary me. Do not be so stupid. Do you not know who I am, what I can provide?" Garqi touched his hands to his lip tentatively. "Why do you insist on dee ardest route?"

"Get tae fuck."

This displeased the Italian greatly. You can't say that type of thing to a Mediterranean man and expect to get away with it. "I don't think so, Mr. Pope." With a sharp volley to Pontiff's belly Garqi launched into that custom known commonly as a kicking.

After quite considerable exertion, the Italian relented. He calmed himself. "Why do you hate your country?" He grabbed Pontiff's head and ripped it skywards. "Eh? Eet eez not too late for us to tweak our little tale ever so slightly. Perhaps dee mother had an accomplice? Do you want to be associated with a murderer? Do you want to go to jail?" He then softened, stroked Pontiff's head. "Or do you want a better life, a *simpler* life?"

Pontiff couldn't respond. He'd passed out.

Mormon pressed a buzzer and gave instructions.

Two security guards materialised, and dragged Pontiff from the scene.

"Well?" said Mormon addressing a perspiring Garqi.

"He'd be a fool not to go along wid eet," said Garqi, recoiffing his gelled pate. "I'm sure eet will be fine. Little rewards keep people in check. Eet's never failed before. I'm sure e won't want to test dee alternative."

## 15
# THE COUNTRYSIDE

SINCE WINNING THE election there had been many moments of genius. Being able to lord it over those hypocrites he'd met at university had been especially satisfying for Fred, the organically aware children of bankers who liked fruit juices and frappes in nice fancy plastic cups with the plastic globe on the top, replete with plastic, decorative straw, who bought branded bags of sushi encased in plastic, eaten with plastic spoon, who committed the lot to the refuse of history on a daily basis; the same people who were owners of multiple properties, who had bought and bought with impunity and left over a quarter of the populace homeless. Houses had stood empty during the week whilst the indigenous folk lived in tents, or in some cases, under no cover at all. Those that did have brick shelter had often had an entire family in one room. The empty homes were then filled at weekends by the arriving 4by4er's who wondered why they were so poorly received. These people had felt the bite of the land-grab.

In the carve-up that occurred after the LibCom-NeoLuddite Government took over, Fred had inherited a grace-and-favour country pile – all part of the smashing of the pyramid of wealth. A number of properties had been available and were divvied out to high-rankers in government, the Blackguard, PHU, the media, and the myriad other state agencies. A lot of this hierarchy had their second homes clustered together in elite communities.

These areas were well guarded but Fred had eschewed them. Though generally the elite holidayed at different times there had recently been a spate of Republic Day parties for the new Aristocracy, many still ongoing. Fred didn't want work-chat over the privet hedge with various agency leaders. He wanted something more secluded, just for him and his girls and good times. Fred's chosen property was in a part of the country that had avoided becoming a refuse site or being concreted over like a lot of the island. There wasn't much other habitat around, a few villages but they were a couple miles from the house. Despite its remoteness, it was still protected, Blackguard platoons guarding it in shift. The previous owner had been a Godfrey Golightly. Fred had been a number of times with his girls but hadn't visited for a while. Friends? He didn't really have them.

It was approaching seven o'clock. The girls had drunk a lot of sparkling Cornish wine and were now snoozing in the back of the car. They had taken it in turns to sit in the front with Fred. Some pleasuring had occurred. Fred especially liked that driving at high speeds, powdering his nose at the same time, but as he had drunk more than usual he was also feeling a little woozy.

As Fred drove up to the brick gates everything seemed normal. The barracks on each side both had a Blackguard, though they appeared to have dispensed with their berets. Upon closer inspection Fred saw they were not wearing standard-issue fatigues.

He buzzed a switch and his window eased downwards. He had his NIPSD card ready but on the fence where there used to be a scanner hung only exposed wires. Fred went to present his NIPSD card anyway but was waved through. This was odd. He didn't recognise either of these two and normally, even if it was a guard he recognised, Fred had to present his card – as did his guests.

The drive was long and winding and as soon as Fred turned the final curve, past a huge fifteen foot high hedge, his heart started to beat faster. Lights were on in the house and there were revellers in the circular parking area that surrounded the fountain. Some were splashing about in the water. And was that fancy dress they were wearing? Fred reached for his gun.

As the car crunched up the gravel, there was cheering.

"He's arrived! He's arrived!" cried one.

"Where d'you get this little beauty?" cried another, pointing at Fred's car.

Hannah stirred, sleepily, rubbing her eyes.

"What's going on Fred?"

"I don't know."

Three men dressed as animals approached the car. They were banging on the bonnet, squealing, hooting. They were covered in food.

"Alan, Alan!" they shouted. "Get in there before they waste everything. We've prepared a huge banquet in lieu of your decision to join us. But you know what us country folk are like. I know you're the guest of honour but hurry!"

Alan? Guest of honour? Joining who?

"Who are those little treats? Are they for us?" said another, staring like a savage at the girls. They opened the doors.

"Who are they Fred?" shouted Becca.

"Fred?" asked one of the revellers. "Why you calling him Fred?"

Just then there was the sound of more tyre crunching on gravel.

That'll be Alan, thought Fred. Oh Christ.

"Close the door Hannah!" he shouted, as Becca was bundled out the car.

"What about Becca?" cried Hannah. "Aaaaagh!"

An arrow had plunged into her arm. It had come from the roof dispatched by someone dressed in a cow outfit.

Then someone shot an airgun, the pellet smashing into the window, covering Fred's face in glass. Fred didn't hang about. He floored it. Sorry Becca, he thought, as she was forced inside. Hannah was screaming.

"Close the door Hannah!"

Fred scraped past the huge hedge in the middle of the drive. Alan's car had pulled over and was trying to block him. Fred wound round the corner, Hannah bleeding, him bleeding. At the gate, the Blackguard opened fire. He crashed through them, knocking one down, smashed through the gate, and sped off.

"Fred! I need a doctor! I need to get this arrow out!"

"I know Hannah, but not here. It's too dangerous."

"But it hurts!"

"I know, I know. I'll find somewhere where we can pull over but we need to get out of here!"

As he drove off, Fred thought back to Alan's car. It was white. A state-owned car. Who was Alan? A local Blackguard chief? Fred already knew of the autonomous zones – but in inconsequential places like Northamptonshire or Hull. But here as well? Maybe we are actually losing grip, he thought. And not only are we losing areas but people are deserting!

His phone started buzzing.

"Oh Christ! What now? Yes?" he shouted, answering.

"Freddi! Dis guy eez your selection for dee *Hellevue Hero*? E does not seem as malleable as you suggested! Bastard tried to kill me!"

Christ, thought Fred, what's gone wrong now?

"What are you talking about Oli? What's happened?"

"What's appened? I've gone ten rounds wid dee prick, dat's what's appened! Your man eez quite a fighter let me tell you, Frederick. E may be an alcoholic but e doesn't strike me as dee desperate man you portrayed to us. I don't think dis eez going to be as straightforward as you led us to believe. You should have done your research better. You should have told me e was a nutter!"

"I am as surprised as you at his actions, Oli."

That wasn't strictly true. Footage from Pontiff's arrest at the post office had given Fred a little glimpse into the soul of the man. And now this. Fred rather liked this Pope character. Liked his steel. Still, who *would* turn their back on this offer?

"It is most unusual, would you not agree, for a Citizen given the opportunity to improve their life to throw it back so spectacularly in our face? When has our offer of a better life never been taken?"

"Dat's what *I* said!"

"OK well, keep him there. I'll pop over in the morning and we'll sort it all out then. Let him sleep it off in the meantime. To be honest Oli, I'm not having the greatest night myself."

Hannah was moaning again.

"What is dat noise, Freddi?"

"My night."

"Are you OK?"

"Fine, Oli, fine. I'll ring you tomorrow."

Fred hung up and called to Hannah in the backseat.

"Sweetheart. Are you OK?"

"No I'm fucking not, Fred! What the fuck? Aaaagh. It hurts!"

"OK baby, I'm gonna get you to hospital. Just hang on."

The backseat was covered in blood and Hannah was in considerable pain yet Fred couldn't help but think of this Pope character. His first thoughts had been that Pope was essentially an angry old soak, a lost cause that had been to *LifeManagement4Life*. Slowly, though, that was changing. Even now, Pope was fighting back, refusing to be drawn in. This was interesting. This Pope seemed to be a man with honour, credibility, dignity even. Those were long since departed traits of modern Britannians. Let's see how he fares in the cold light of day, thought Fred. That will be the mark of the man. Still, I wonder. I can't imagine him behaving himself at the ceremony. But the prospect of meeting this man, the object of his little game, was incredibly exciting. Fred pondered going straight round there. But what would be the point? Pope would probably be comatose and it wasn't like he was going anywhere. He also needed to get Hannah to a doctor and get home after his ordeal. Fred was starting to believe the only safe place left was London.

# 16

# INSTINCTIVE JOY

*"POPE! YOU'RE GONNA have to learn pretty quickly that you cannot speak whenever you want to!"*

*The veins on the side of the Ratman's head bulged like an excited penis, his face pulsed a deep crimson.*

*I have a theory on you, you know!" he barked.*

*"Oh aye?"*

*"When was your last copulation?"*

*"Excuse me?" Pontiff responded, slipping out of the Blackguard's grip.*

*"Last copulation?"*

*"Wha-"*

*"Just answer the question, Mr. Pope."*

*"I'm no answeren that."*

*"Suit yourself. You will in time. For now, we'll assume that my hunch is correct."*

*After inspecting the Scotsman for a matter of minutes, the Ratman believed Pontiff to have had no carnal knowledge of a member of either sex for the best part of three years.*

*"Well, you don't mess about do ya?" Pontiff laughed. "I certainly haven't had any dalliance with my fellow man, thasforshir."*

*"Pope, I don't believe you have even kissed a girl in the time span I talk of."*

*"What's the matter Pope, taking your nickname a bit too seriously, eh? Taken a vow of celibacy?"*

*"Oh very drole, Guard."*

*"Well?"*

*"Well what?"*

*"Is the Technician correct in his diagnosis?"*

*"Lemme ask you somehen. What the fuck is it with the get-up you guys wear? I mean you're wearen Greens, Technician Peter, and I've got no beef wi'at. But, Guard, your outfit is hardly in keepen with all this 'relax, Zen will soon be yours' stuff, is it? The Gestapo look isn't all that welcomen. I do like the berets though. I may be misaligned but I still know chic."*

*"Mr Pope,"* interrupted the Ratman, *"I realise that at the moment you are not aware of all the problems you have. It's only your first day after all. But you will listen to us, obey us, and, as I'm sure you would agree, a certain amount of respect for our expertise is necessary. Now, we're going to introduce you to someone."*

*"What, now? How exciten."*

*"Someone who we believe can help you overcome this...this blockage."*

*"Blockage?"*

*"You have been alienated from your instinct. It is the root cause of all your problems."*

*"Yes, you are to be re-introduced to your natural instincts,"* chimed in the guard.

*"It's ma natural instincts that have landed me in here! And I dinnae think I've finished ma induction yet, so..."*

*"Never mind that Pope!"*

*"Alright. Suit yourself. Who ma gonnae huv the pleasure of meeten?"*

*"A young woman,"* responded the Ratman.

*"Oh aye?"*

*"Yes, she will be your IJP."*

*"IJP?"*

*"Instinctive Joy Partner!"* bleated the guard.

*"Proceed to the Cell of Intimacy!"* exclaimed the Ratman.

*"Cell of Intimacy?"*

*A slap on the head from the guard's black-clad hand ceased Pontiff's mirth.*

*"Intimacy, Mr Pope, not insolence," said the Ratman.*

*"So I'm supposed tae get intimate with my IJP?" asked Pontiff, rubbing his head.*

*The Ratman nodded.*

*"And what if I cannae get intimate with my IJP?"*

*"You will."*

*"Oh aye? Whatya gonnae do? Force us at gunpoint?"*

*"Mr Pope, very soon the humour will disappear. That sarcastic tone will desert you and you will confront the reasons why you are here. We are responsible for your care and as you are unable to care for yourself, we will let all this behaviour go. But I assure you, it will change. You will be regenerated."*

*They escorted Pontiff through the Life Camp, past the Pretty-Making Lab, through the corridor that housed the Tutor Rooms and finally arrived at one of the very many Cells of Intimacy.*

*"Susan," said the Ratman, "how many times? You know you can't smoke in here."*

*Susan took a last drag and flicked the butt towards the new arrivals.*

*Ah, a woman after my own heart, thought Pontiff.*

*"We've brought someone to see you," continued the Ratman.*

*"Oh how lovely."*

*Susan looked at Pontiff – the first of many times he would feel that slashing gaze.*

*The Ratman divulged what he expected.*

*"To start with, a little bit of progress will be fine. We will return shortly so you've got some time to chat and learn about each other. When we come back we will expect you to have made some headway."*

*"Headway?" asked Pontiff.*

*"Relax Mr Pope. I'm talking of a kiss, perhaps."*

*With that, the Ratman and the guard trouped out.*

*Pontiff began to look around at the decor: a round bed, mirrored walls and ceiling, a small fridge containing oysters. Silence.*

*Susan lit up another cigarette.*

*"Want one?" she asked.*

*"Aye, cheers."*

*She lit another and handed it to Pontiff. He sucked in hard, his morning buoyancy replaced by a sense of impending doom. When the day had begun Pontiff was all strapped in for revolution. Now he was incarcerated at a macabre love motel.*

*"So how long you been here?" he asked.*

*"A year. You?"*

*"About two hours."*

*Susan smiled. "So you've been fast-tracked?"*

*"Aye, somethen like that."*

*They both smoked on in silence.*

*"Er... so.... why are y'in here?" asked Pontiff.*

*"Ah you know, the usual, disobeying the Life Admin Directive. Then got diagnosed with depression. The doctor said they used to prescribe medication to all and sundry but they got so slap-happy they are now of the opinion that rehabilitation is better than creating a nation of controlled-substance addicts."*

*"Aye, aye."*

*Pontiff paused, sucking in support from the nicotine.*

*"So, how does all this work?"*

*"Well once we've become intimate, and the technicians are satisfied that we've enjoyed it, one part of our rehabilitation is complete and we are moved on."*

*"And how do we convince em?"*

*"They say it's all in the performance."*

*"Performance?"*

*Susan nodded.*

*"In front of people?"*

*Pontiff blurted out a short laugh. He steadied himself.*

*"How many people?"*

*"At least two as they have to consult. Sometimes four or five. Sometimes as many as ten if the trainees are in."*

*Susan stubbed out her cigarette in the ashtray. "Look, they're gonna be back any minute," she said. "It's in your interests to just give us a quick smacker, a bitta tongue and then they'll leave you to your own devices for a little while."*

"And what happens if I don't?"

"Great violence," responded Susan.

"Aye, I might have guessed."

"God, it's not that awful proposition, is it?" said Susan laughing.

"No, not at all, not at all. It's jus you seem very calm."

*Pontiff was churning inside.*

"You get used to it. Every day feels more similar than the last." She paused. "You're not kinky, are you?"

"Er, well, I think that's relative, wouldn't ya say?"

"The last one I had was pretty kinky. He told me that when he was a teenager his favourite wank material was Viz and Eurotrash. Got quite attached to me. Eventually he said – look, I just need to know. Where do I stand?"

*Susan paused, took another drag of her cigarette.*

"So I told him – preferably over there."

*There was a curt knock and the Ratman and two Blackguard swiftly entered.*

"So, are we ready?" asked the Ratman.

"Yes, we're ready" responded Susan. She looked at Pontiff. "Aren't we?"

*Pontiff drew a long breath in through his nose, tilted his back and paused looking skyward for a moment before turning to Susan. He smiled at her, put his hands to her face and gave her a good old fashioned snog.*

"Good, good," enthused the Ratman in a whisper, taking notes. *Releasing himself from Susan's mouth, Pontiff turned to the Technician.*

"Will that do?"

"For now Pope, yes."

"It's Mr Pope."

"Don't ruin all your good work. You've made real progress today. It would be a shame to have to take punitive measures so soon."

\*\*\*

Pontiff woke in horror, temporarily believing himself still to be at Life Camp. He never thought he'd say it about anything, but being cooped up in there was worse than the final days of his marriage. He wondered what Susan was doing this morning. His guilt at leaving returned.

Replacing horror was agony. Pontiff felt bruised, unsure of where he was. Unsure of a good many things. His head was in terrible pain, his nose throbbed, there was a pulsating gash on the back of his head. His elbow was none too clever either, bleeding again. He looked round the room. It was a small office and he was under a blanket on a small sofa. He raised himself gingerly and looked at the table next to him. There was water, painkillers and a handwritten note.

*"Mr Pope, we trust you slept well. At approximately midday we will be escorting you to your ceremony at which you will be formerly presented as the Hellevue Hero. We will return before then to prepare, feed and clothe you. Please relax until we arrive. Mormon."*

How marvellous.

Pontiff looked at the clock in his room. It had just gone seven thirty. He went to the door and peered out. There, snoring away, was a Blackguard. After everything that happened, Pontiff was unwilling to go down the route of government patsy. After a quick assessment and still feeling the benefit of several units of decent booze, Pontiff began to tiptoe past his security. Deciding the lift would create too much commotion he opted for the stairs, descending past a series of sideways glances.

In the lobby Pontiff felt certain he would meet more agents of the state but as he delicately prised open the door to the foyer he saw the door of the ground floor toilet swing and close. Pontiff scurried to the exit, wondering whether Garqi and Mormon had disabled his NIPSD card. He placed it on the SwipeScanner.

*"Application to exit Media Facility. Patience, Citizen, is a virtue."*

Come on, come on!

Nothing was happening. Then the scanner beeped its disapproval.

*"Illegal request. Records state Citizen is already outside."*

What? Ah, for f-

Pontiff tried again. More beeping.

*"Illegal request. Records state Citizen is already outside."*

Pontiff heard distant flushing.

One more time you piece of shit.

Again he swiped. Again, nothing, but just as he was about to dart behind one of the sofas in the entrance hall, a beeping from the scanner told him it was primed for use. Pontiff scanned his irises and verified his fingers.

*"Exit request granted. Appointment at NIPSD required to explain actions. 13th July. 12:30."*

Pontiff was out, spots of blood dripping from his elbow. He was sure his absence would be spotted immediately and knew he would be tracked given that CCTV captured all audio and video of street activity.

Luckily, the streets were reasonably busy and because it was starting to rain, and indeed was a rather chilly morning, many people were breaking into light jogs. Relieved the rain gave him reason to run, Pontiff melted into the crowd. After a couple of minutes he turned into an adjacent street and waited to see if he had been followed. As yet, nothing.

Pontiff's mind was scrambled, his heart thudded. He needed a smoke. He reached into his pocket and found his tobacco. There, miraculously, lay a tattered, pre-wrapped cigarette. Whatever happened next, he could at least have one last suck at the teat of normalcy. He found some matches, removed the cigarette, brought it up to his mouth, and... a raindrop splodged, and the tobacco stick slumped and crumbled in his hand. Oh the distress caused by a damp cigarette.

Pontiff's feeling of unbounded relief at evading the clutches of the Government was quickly vanishing. He scanned over his meagre options. He wasn't particularly convinced any gave him a real choice. He felt fairly sure his best hope of survival was getting out of London. But was that even a possibility? Although the SwipeScanner hadn't suggested it, he was certain his NIPSD card would have been updated to detail that he was highly profitable bounty. He was the *Hellevue Hero*. He was a fugitive from justice, however spurious that justice was, and at the mercy of the Government, or worse, the masses. That meant travel was out. And even if Pontiff could navigate himself out of London, what then? There he would enter the tribal areas where, as legend had it, they had become increasingly feral and didn't take kindly to outsiders. In fact, most Citizens never left the relative security of their own districts for that very reason.

The key thing wasn't any of those things though. If he did flee, he knew he would look guilty of what the paper had accused him. His only real option was to go back to Hellevue, find the RevKev and Godfrey and put the record straight. Also, he couldn't just walk away. He wanted to find Clem. He had to find Clem. Pontiff threw his wet cigarette to the floor and rejoined the main street.

It wasn't long before he came across an absurd yet commonplace spectacle, a spectacle that reminded him of why he had joined the fight against the Government. An elderly gentleman was standing with an empty pint bottle. Two Blackguard, one male, one female, both in their early twenties, had detained him. At least this government has done something for youth unemployment, thought Pontiff. The female officer pressed the man's NIPSD card on her portable SwipeScanner.

"I know you old dears, you coffin dodgers, think that after a certain age you can do whatever you feel like," she said, "but we can't have everyone breaking these laws, laws that are in place to make your life better. *Easification-Facilitation*. The clue's in the name."

"I only wanted a cup of tea," responded the old man.

"Oh, he only wanted a cuppatea," continued the woman. "Isn't that sweet?"

"The voluntary-euthanasia scheme hasn't had the plug pulled yet, you know," said the male officer. "I'm not sure we can really afford you old dears and your pensions, no matter how meagre they are."

"No, nor your wild ways," agreed the female officer.

"Perhaps a bungee jump's the answer."

"Yeah," said the woman, laughing. "Bet you've not tried that before. That might be the best mode of extermination. We want death-contestants to have new experiences just the same as anyone else."

"You'd probably have a heart attack on the way down, wouldn't you?" added the male officer.

"He probably would. Though if he did survive the incredible surge of adrenalin stuttering and staccato-ing through his frail frame, we'd just cut the cord."

They both laughed at that. The man looked petrified. He'd got confused and thought that today was Life Admin Group Four's grocery day. Illegal shopping was the charge. Pontiff felt like introducing himself to these two black-clad law enforcement angels and resolving the situation in no uncertain terms but that was a sure-fire way to head straight back into custody. Sorry old man, he thought, and walked on, the conversation still audible.

"In fact," continued the male guard, "if more of you Citizens that had had a good innings stepped forward, everyone else's meat and potato portions would be slightly more substantial. How would you feel about that, hey? That could be your legacy. Do you want that?"

No response.

"No I don't suppose you do."

"Cor, he's selfish, innit?" said the woman.

"Innit? I suggest you keep your nose clean. What do you reckon, Carla?"

"Communal Litter Picking. And I hope you realise that you are not special and in future need to be better organised." She paused. "Think we'll update you with a couple of Social Behavioural Points, as well."

Behind this little scene, Pontiff spied a screen. *HairVision*!

*"We are all of one consciousness now!"*

The leader cracked one of his grins. He leant forward, a glint in his eye.

*"I can even answer those nagging existential questions!"*

Aye? thought Pontiff, I've got a few. Still, dinnae fight the trajectory into which life propels you. He carried on, passing the Monorail station. It was out of action.

*We apologise for any inconvenience that may be caused by this slight delay.*

Pontiff had no intention of using the Monorail anyway. He knew any Blackguard in attendance would arrest him as soon as the Swipe-Scanner started beeping and the queue stopped moving. A walk it was. It would be a long old trudge back to Hellevue. But he had to be quick.

How long would it be until his absence was noted? He ploughed on but the rain was increasing its summer ferocity. The heavens had opened. It was the start of the June monsoon. Undeterred, Pontiff broke into a light jog, going as fast as his tobaccoed lungs would take him, panting and wheezing.

The urban landscape slowly changed on the way to Hellevue. There was a gradual descent into dereliction, into the forgotten areas in which lived people who could not even claim to be at the margins of society. Once shiny new things were now disused, misappropriated, decrepit. It looked as though there had been an exodus, and this was the return to the ruins after the desertion. Rubbled buildings were uncertain whether they were derelict or desirable. The whole place just looked ill, John Major grey, the most sullen of all shades.

There was residual evidence here of the old Municipal Waste Parks and the now outlawed practice of poorer districts taking waste from the better-off, all for a minor fee. This is where *Plasticitis* first took root, and where the gypsy people still lived, living much the same existence, replete with rag'n'bone carts and cancered children. The only living these folk could drum up was to pick through this rubbish for usable trinkets, something to snack on or perchance something to resell. Despite the promise of restoring health there was little anyone could do to combat the legacy of *Plasticitis*. And despite the promise of more food, passions had dwindled in government to deliver on such pledges. Every day these people lived with the dual horror of going hungry or being exposed to *Plasticitis* effluent.

I expect these poor bastards have get a few existential questions for dear old Mr Hair, thought Pontiff. Aye, an I expect a few people have get a few questions for me back in Hellevue.

Pontiff needed a disguise and began to look around for possible candidates. It was a good thing this was a bleak part of town. He didn't want to turn up in Hellevue in finery. But it *was* a little edgy and he knew if he picked the wrong customer out here he could meet a sticky end. He saw a group of kids. Fagan's Flies. They would often come into town to casually mug people. When Pontiff saw them looking at a paper he didn't think much of it. Most of these kids couldn't read despite the promise of improving education for all.

Pontiff carried on, his eyes searching.

And then. Would you believe it? Pontiff recognised the apologetic body language immediately.

"Clyde! Clyde ya bass!" shouted Pontiff. "Mr fucken Trepid! How are you, my man?"

He put his hand on Clyde's back. Clyde Trepid shuddered. He felt certain he would never encounter this grotesque Scotsman ever again. He felt certain that this Pope would never get out of Life Camp.

"Fuckinell Clyde, they let you out quick!"

## 17
# SPILLED COFFEE

FRED HAD SNOOZED through his alarm for so long he thought it prudent to disable the thing. The insta-coffee machine had gone into overdrive and there was a reddybrown stain on the carpet from the overspill. He felt like booze this morning anyway. His experiences in the countryside had certainly added a new *frisson*, had tested his resolve that he was master of all he surveyed, that everything was a laugh. He'd got in late and though he would recover quickly from his minor injuries septicaemia had been a concern for Hannah. He said he'd go and see her when he got the time. Christ, but how was Becca getting on?

He switched on his phone. It buzzed and beeped with numerous missed calls and messages. Hair, Porridgemouth – he's taking on more responsibility these days, isn't he? – *The Rumour, The Cow*, Sherry, Hair again. In order, Fred listened to some indecipherable whooping and cheering from Hair. *'It's great news'* was all Fred could make out, maybe something about the Neo-Luddites? It was only when Fred heard the soggy, sober tones of Porridgemouth he fully understood.

*"More bad news from the countryside, Mr McVelly. Martin has been brutally and fatally stabbed by what we believe to be a group of tribal farmers. He was remonstrating with them for using homemade pesticide and they took his life. The Neo-Luddites, now led by Clegg, have announced they have formally left the Government."*

Just as Fred was digesting that a message began from a frantic member of the news desk at *The Rumour*. What the -?

Fred didn't know whether to be amused or enraged. How in the hell had Pope managed it?

Suddenly energised, Fred leapt from his bed. He rang Garqi but the Italian's secretary said he was not to be disturbed.

"Well tell him to ring me as soon as he can. It's urgent."

As he hung up the phone, Fred walked into his lounge and pressed a series of buttons on the control panel next to his sofa. First, MCIBBC2 came into life – the late morning news bulletin. Fred then massaged and swivelled the array of apps and buttons he had on his state-of-the-art viewing system, accessing CCTV footage from *Rumour* HQ to watch Pontiff's escape.

On the news, Porridgemouth Milipede was reporting early successes for the PSU. He was hardly the most natural of orators, thought Fred, but here he was again, overtaking his brother.

*"Yesterday was a busy first day and I want to congratulate the PSU Technicians who have carried out their work with efficiency and fairness. What we have seen recently in Hellevue, and I point specifically to the rise of terrorism and damaging pollution of* **KARMATARMAK***, makes this new agency an essential step in the safety of our most vulnerable. And if you look at the specific case of Clementine Romain, it is further proof – if further proof were needed – that the PSU will perform a vital role in our society. It is likely her son's death would have been averted if the PSU had been in place a little earlier.*

*"Now it's time to take stock and prepare to roll this out to the rest of the capital, and indeed the country, and continue our work of keeping the vulnerable safe. We reserve the right to return to Hellevue if we need to. But we will move on from our work there for now. We don't want to be seen to be persecuting the Citizens of the district!"*

Put your teeth back in, Porridgemouth!

Porridgemouth's lips slowly rolled back down, enveloping his equine ivories. A serious blaze returned to his eyes.

*"We have engaged in a proportionate response to what has occurred in Hellevue. What we mustn't forget is that there is a growing rudeness in the young throughout society. A great*

*factor in this is poor parenting and is causing a breakdown in social cohesion, and ultimately terrorism. The PSU will prevent a life of crime, a life of benefit, a life of drugs..."*

Porridgemouth paused, took a long uncomfortable breath –

*"...and degradation, desolation and depravity."*

The teeth popped back out momentarily.

*"However, children themselves do not escape censure. With the BACK DOWN THE MINES WITH YOU campaign, Neo-Victorianism will counter their often reprehensible behaviour. The legal age of criminality will now be 6 years old and children who engage themselves in criminal activity will be removed from their parents' custody, who in turn, will have their parenting license revoked. When we say to a child JUMP, they should be saying HOW HIGH?"*

Clearly no-one thought that sounded facetious, mused Fred.

While he watched this, the second screen showed Pope's journey back to Hellevue.

Fuck me, he's got some balls heading back there!

Fred's admiration was growing for the man. Above anything else, Fred really wanted a chance to meet this robust character.

He watched the CCTV footage, followed Pope's journey on foot and the quite hilarious mugging of a scrawny little man. It looked friendly at first, a bit of conversation. Pope then seemed to make a threat and the small man stripped off, pleading while he did so. He received some ripped jeans that were far too big for him as his part in the exchange. A record of the journey stopped just as Pope got to Hellevue.

Fred cursed the oversight of not fixing the CCTV cameras in Hellevue. A chance had slipped. Still, he thought, all adds to the fun. Reluctantly, he would add *DETAIN IMMEDIATELY* to the Scotsman's *Citizen's Account.* All Blackguard would be alerted.

Fred didn't like to do this to one he admired, but those were the rules, even if it was Fred who was coming up with them. The fact that Pope had absconded filled him with glee. There was, after all, at least one person who hadn't swallowed everything hook, line and sinker. Fred felt a kindred spirit.

He was still going to flush him out though.

Having sent a series of emails Fred was in the middle of making phone calls to various department heads when his laptop pulsed. His aunt had got in touch again.

What now? thought Fred, as he scanned over the message. Oh for the love of God. His aunt and mother were planning a trip to London as part of his mother's convalescence.

They want to come to London to convalesce? Are they mad?

His aunt continued, saying his mum would love to see him and they were disappointed he hadn't pulled some strings for them regarding food and supplies. His aunt had accrued Social Behavioural points for visiting the hospital on the wrong day of the week. She also said, having watched the President, "maybe that will be you one day."

You must be out of your mind if you think I want that job, thought Fred. And now they wanted to stay with him.

**"We won't get in your way, we'll do your housework. You've got a big place, you have room and you must be busy. I think you owe it to your mother. Auntie Jill xxx"**

No chance, thought Fred. I'll deal with that later.

The news was summarising the day's events so far, Clegg's show of strength somewhat rebadged. The Government felt that Martin's death in the countryside signified a dissatisfaction from the public about the Neo-Luddites' increasingly enfeebled efforts to regenerate the environment. As a result, they had been asked to leave government. A new environmental agency would redouble the Government's efforts as it continued to *take the countryside back*.

Poor old Nicola, thought Fred. But the events of the last day or so worried him. First the riot, then he'd been attacked, then Pope escapes and now further proof of the Republic splintering and getting more violent.

The beeping of his phone interrupted him. He thought it must be Garqi by now but no, it was Sherry.

"Hello sweetness, what can I do for you I wonder?"

Sherry laughed and mentioned something unrepeatable but it wasn't long before she got on to the subject of her husband.

"Now listen to me for a minute, Frederick, and stop mucking about. There's plenty of time for that later."

"What, *mucking*?"

"Just listen," she said, loving the young man's every move. "Now. It's about Terry. He is really shaken up today, crazier and more paranoid than ever. I mean granted, I've thought for a long time that he was growing weaker, becoming less of a man. But it's gone too far now. I really don't think he's fit to lead."

"Maybe you should come over and we could discuss this further."

"I can't leave now, Fred, he's just woken up. To be honest, I think you should just come over here as soon as you can."

"I'm on my way."

Fred thought back to Hair's voicemail. The President had sounded somewhat unhinged. But why had Garqi still not got in touch? It had been a few hours yet still he had not returned Fred's call. This was odd. Fred wanted to talk tactics. No doubt when he did see Garqi Hair would be on the agenda. Fred was about to leave when his cleaning lady turned up, a middle-aged woman of Paraguayan descent.

"Hello Maria."

"Ola Signor Fred," Maria responded with a smile.

I suppose I can detain myself a little while, thought Fred, approaching Maria and planting a kiss on her lips.

## 18

## WELCOME BACK!

THE RAIN HADN'T abated and Pontiff made it back to Hellevue, running, walking, running, walking. He hoped that the newspaper story had not been read by all in Hellevue and if it had, that his disguise would work.

Poor old Clyde, he thought. This raincoat's a fucken treat. And he really didnae want tae gi'me his hat and scarf! That said, Clyde's trousers were far too short and Pontiff's brown boots were entirely visible below his new creamy mustard chinos.

Trying to keep in check the lung apples that were spewing forth, and worried as to what future damage would occur to his health, Pontiff composed himself as he set foot on his street. He pulled up the scarf to cover his mouth, pulled the hat down right over his eyes, and the jacket collars up. From afar, there appeared to be some sort of protest in the courtyard outside his 'L' shaped block of flats. He saw some of his neighbours with banners, the husband who had been detained by the Blackguard one of them. He thought he could see that his flat had been vandalised. Then again, the Blackguard had already ripped the door off.

But as he approached his domicile he could see for certain that it had been daubed with less than flattering comments. Ah good, thought Pontiff as he surveyed the volley of invective, my story's common knowledge.

Call yourself a hero? You fuckin traitor

Fuck off yor not welcom round ere you Scotch barsted!

You don't say, thought Pontiff. The large crowd were baying for his blood. His neighbours hated him, that much was clear. There were chants of L-U-K. That again, thought Pontiff. What is that? And what are they doing outside my house, and, fuckinell what's Huwi doing there screamen blue bloody murder?

Huwi Tenango, the diminutive man with the extravagant name, was the manager of The Forest Arms. He looked older than he was, but that was the pub trade, an industry that aged its workers with timeless effect. He was about thirty with a beard of faded evergreen. A Valleys boy. Huwi had started to drink in the pub a couple of weeks after Pontiff. He had been a Monorail driver at the time and between shifts he would pop in the pub as Hellevue was the last stop. He liked it so much he decided to move to the district. Apparently his missus was nonplussed with the arrangement. It was likely she suspected he fancied Clem, who worked there at the time.

Huwi had always been an affable chap, seemed reasonably intelligent, but had an inquisitive, childlike nature that at times spilled into over-excitement. Pontiff hadn't fully made up his mind about him but he didn't fully trust him. It wasn't that he was disloyal just that he seemed a walking liability. When the pub's owner decided he wanted to spend less time in the boozer he asked Clem to take over as manager. She declined as the juggling of motherhood, artistic pursuits and her band *Acid Circus* – a unique blend of folk, blues and the mode de jour, organic trance – had had to take precedence.

"I was just yer at the right time," Huwi said.

He had a wealth of bar experience and never seemed to get too riled by having to listen to pissed people's garbage and drivel, normally because he was party to the drivel himself. But he did crave experiences more fulfilling, more exciting than dishing out pints and the odd cocktail. And to be fair to him, he'd given it a good go. He'd campaigned for the rights of blind drivers. He'd even joined Militant Martin's campaign against the lawnmower, the gardener's oppressor. It had been on TV. The punters could always tell the state of Huwi's repair by virtue of a scar on his forehead. At healthy times the scar was an unobtrusive pink. As unsteadiness increased, the scar started to pulsate a rather garish purple. Today the scar was purple.

177

Pontiff was about to slope off when he heard a dissenting voice. A maddened John Rer had appeared from the other end of the street. He started shouting at the group, protesting Pontiff's innocence. He made his way into the middle of the crowd, enraged and drunk. Oh don't John, thought Pontiff. Please don't. As Rer's anger grew, so did the crowds'. Pontiff watched in agony as Rer was jeered and when racist abuse was followed by slaps and punches to his head, Rer was wrestled to the ground by a gang of men, his voice snuffed out as the crowd bayed like animals. Eventually, they filed back and all that remained was Rer's lifeless body.

"Death to the *Hellevue Hero*! Death to those that harbour him!" shouted Huwi.

Pontiff felt he, again, was responsible, and as he drowned in the most disgusting of traumas, felt also shame that in the name of self-preservation he had done nothing to prevent his friend's death. Then anger followed, anger that Garqi's lies had not only put his life at risk but had killed his friend. And for what? Feeling ever closer to his own demise and desperate to run from the scene, Pontiff settled for a brisk walk. What would he do if the Rev or Godfrey weren't home?

One strange thought needled into Pontiff's brain, though. This was all rather bold from the mob. They didn't seem concerned at all by the potential of their *own* arrest. But then Pontiff had not seen the Black-guard during the latter part of his journey back to Hellevue.

As he continued his walk through the district, Pontiff noticed that on the surface at least, Hellevue looked like it had re-established its identity. People had come out the woodwork, the storm from the Government suitably weathered. It was like a mass hibernation had been called off.

And then. A throwback scene. Pontiff was stunned as he saw congregating in the streets the artists, the fashionistas, assorted militants, musicians, Intelligentists – he recognised a few faces, and speakers espousing anti-government rhetoric. And there was that L-U-K thing again, printed on a series of banners and t-shirts. Was this more text message idiocy, a misappropriation of luck?

As Pontiff walked through the crowd, drinking in the atmosphere, there were a few who looked to be thoroughly enjoying themselves.

But for all this apparent joy, Pontiff noticed that for a greater number there was tension. The genuine happiness that had always been etched on faces at occasions like this, the gay abandon that had been such a welcome distraction from the misery of everyday life, seemed to have somewhat abandoned most of the people. Probably unsurprising given people were being murdered for their minimal rations, he thought, or abducted by the Blackguard.

But that wasn't it.

Some of the less-enamoured were being directed, herded even, required to sign a register of some sort, answer some questions. NIPSD cards were being taken from them as well.

"So we can co-ordinate efforts in the future, comrade."

There was a short burst of violence as a young man refused to hand over his card. His girlfriend was pushed to the floor.

Pontiff saw small groups of men carrying weapons at various junctures through the street. In something of a daze, he meandered along, watching the diversity of groups in action, catching snippets of differing opinion.

"I was one of the first researchers at the BBC to be kicked out by Garqi, arrested for terrorism after my *Citizen's Account* showed I had accessed a banned website. I said it was for research but that didn't wash. Well now I'm out of custody, I'm gonna show them what terrorism really is."

"I'm not saying everything the LibComs've done is wrong," said a skinhead man with a dog on a string. "Getting rid of the Royals was spot-on."

Pontiff laughed at that. Like any self-respecting Scotsman he had always been ideologically opposed to that bunch of buck-toothed, polo-playing thieves of social resources too. The maniacal glee with which the Royals had been booted out of Buckingham Place had certainly had its merits as a spectacle.

Some folk that probably hadn't enjoyed that pageant were the two nice-looking people Pontiff overheard just yards from the Marxist. They were listening to another speaker, a young woman.

"Comrades, our country has been hijacked!"

The man in a sweater looked to his wife.

"I wish they wouldn't use that 'c' word. Too many leftist connotations."

"Well we can worry about that later," said his wife. "I don't like siding with these people either but is the lesser of two evils and more importantly, the best we've got at the moment."

*These people?* What did that mean? Did they mean *KT?* Pontiff saw no explicit mention of the zine nor could he see the Rev or Godfrey anywhere. Pontiff hoped that did not mean they had been detained. He remembered the first time he'd gone to the Rev's, also in need of refuge. If he got refuge this time Pontiff felt he may well start thinking that everything *was* happening for a reason – that it was time to join Christ's flock.

As he walked past The Forest Arms he could feel a thirst gathering at the back of his throat. It didn't seem like such a refuge now that he'd seen Huwi. It was a shame because a better local you could not ask for. It was a classic public house of the times, a burned-out, exposed brick room adorned with battered sofas, assorted comfy and wooden chairs, cushions, and wooden tables dotted here and there. The bar occupied the middle section with galleys down either side leading to the toilets. In the left galley, the larger space, there was a small raised stage where the fireplace used to be and a little space in front to dance. Homemade cider, warm ale and English wine were squelched from perched casks. They had finally done a reverse-Dylan and de-electrified and every inch was covered by candles, lending a romantic ambience.

The cost of installing SwipeScanners for the NIPSD programme had put many people out of business throughout the land. But the choice was simple. Install the new technology or have your license revoked; one of those tremendous voluntary-compulsory measures governments are so good at. Of course, by the time the scheme was due to arrive in Hellevue, the district had appeared to fall off the government radar and so, like most of the district, it was old-fashioned doors at The Forest Arms. It's where Pontiff had stumbled across on his first night in London, about six months previously, just before Christmas.

After his divorce, the threat of violence from the shylocks and the cuts in academic funding, Pontiff needed a change of scene, to leave Scotland. Thankfully an opportunity had arisen and so after spending the last of his money on the Monorail journey to London, Pontiff arrived ready to start a new life. From the moment he'd come south of the border just about everything had gone wrong.

Having arrived in London, he had gone straight to the university only to be told the lecturing job and indeed the entire course had been axed as part of a change in governmental policy. He was, however, reassured that he would still be put up temporarily in the academics' block of flats, located near Hellevue, before he was moved on to social housing. Wanting to acquaint himself with his new area, Pontiff had gone for a stroll and popped into a pub (The Forest Arms) for a quick pint. And then another. And another. And soon he found himself in a round with a Reverend, a fascinating man, largish, possessing of grey cropped hair, glasses and infinite chins. The RevKev was a DJ – when electricity allowed – and he and Pontiff shared a love of Slowgrind-Psych. In his youth, the Rev had put on nights all over the capital. Pontiff had done the same back in Scotland and the two clicked immediately.

When later Pontiff returned to the block of flats to get his NIPSD card updated with electronic access to his new home, there was no-one in the office. It was 5:45 pm. It was supposed to be open until 6. He waited half an hour. No-one showed. As always, anything involving housing, NIPSD access and social services was the usual fucking farce. If the shoe was on the other foot you'd be fined and hung, drawn and quartered probably, thought Pontiff.

Furious, he left, had an altercation with some local thug, got back to the boozer, told the Rev of his predicament, who in turn agreed to put him up, and from there his new life had truly begun. A few weeks later Pontiff got his own place and when money allowed, drank in The Forest Arms, where he got to know Clem. With her and the Rev vouching for him, Pontiff was slowly inculcated in the plans for the future, led by Godfrey.

Godfrey and the Rev had been friends for years, having met through Ruth, a university friend of the Rev's. Ruth later became Godfrey's wife, the couple married by the Rev. Like Godfrey, Ruth was a writer though she had given it up before her death to concentrate on her literary agency. The three had all lived in Hellevue for a very long time. Over this very long time, this little band had a creeping sense that no-one else seemed to share the same grievances about the evermore encroaching deductions of liberty, and three years previous, the zine had been born. Tragically, Ruth – *Pensivia* – had died not long after the LibComs had come to power, hit by a bus just before the ban on private ownership, just before they retired buses.

Pontiff approached the Rev's rather humble home at the end of a narrow street's cul-de-sac. At the front of the house was a small garden – within which the secret parish church could be found – and as Pontiff walked through he could smell a fire coming from the back yard. Though the rain had stopped it was hardly what you'd call barbecue weather but with electricity not guaranteed, you had to get it however you could.

He put his hand up to the window and looked underneath it into the gloom. Nothing. He tried the door. It was locked. He started a surreptitious knock, a light, insistent tap. Unsure why he was trying to avoid attention, he loudened his efforts, all to no avail.

Pontiff walked down the side of the house towards the smell of the fire and knocked on the gate. As he did, a shaft of light beamed out of the window through which he'd just been looking. The back door opened and there was his old pal, the RevKev, the Rotund Reverend Kevin, the priest with the belly. As ever, he was dressed all in black – black jeans, black shoes, black shirt ("so it's not a total disgrace") – and the requisite white dog collar. Luck seemed to be abating its personal mission of destruction, thought Pontiff. Maybe the worm was turning.

The stout features of the RevKev had never been so comforting. Pontiff watched as the man of God grabbed some potatoes and returned to the back door. Pontiff made his way back to the gate and when he heard the door close, tried to intercept his old friend.

"Rev!" came the hoarse whisper-shout. "Re-ev! Rev ya bass!"

"Pontiff?"

"Aye man, open the gate!"

The bolt went and the door opened. Pontiff could see the Reverend was approaching what Leonard Cohen so beautifully cites as being *past all concern*.

"Fuck me, am I glad tae see you!"

"Pontiff, is that you? I barely recognised you!"

"That's the idea."

"Come'ere!" exclaimed the Rev, crushing Pontiff with a hug of alcoholic strength and exuberance.

"Jesus Chri- Sorry, Rev. It's jus you'll fucken kill me wi'at gut."

"I can't believe you're here. We were just talking about you."

"It's often bad news when people dae that," said Pontiff as the Rev released him.

"Indeed," responded the Rev with a laugh. "It certainly is in this district. I thought you were dead."

Pontiff laughed and took off the scarf covering the bottom of his face.

"Aye, well thass a fair assumption these days, eh? Nah. Nearly, but no quite. I'm still here. Just."

The Rev took in Pontiff's less than dapper physical appearance.

"No kidding. You're looking fairly smashed in." The Rev smiled. "Nice trousers."

"Aye."

The Rev motioned with his head for Pontiff to come in through the gate and placed the potatoes in the fire, maintaining a shambling elegance.

"You want a drink?"

"Like you wouldn't believe mate."

## 19
# WHILE YOU WERE AWAY...

"SO WHERE THE fuck did you get to?" shouted the Rev, slapping Pontiff's arm. "Happily Godfrey was fairly sanguine about the dangers of confiding in a person who then vanishes."

"Well Rev, God kept smiten me. I been dae-en a wee bitta bird at Shrink Clink."

The Rev nodded. He smiled. "Well that's what I hoped."

"Oh thanks very much!"

"No, no. You misunderstand. I was worried it could have been worse."

It was worse, thought Pontiff, but didn't feel he particularly wanted to go into the ins and outs of it all. But he did explain the quick turn-around. From freedom (of sorts) in the morning, to being banged up by lunch.

"An so that was it. Hud no choice. Thought I'd try tae be on ma best behaviour, jump through the hoops and hopefully get out as soon as possible. It'll be a walk in the park, I told masel."

"People get stabbed in the park."

"Aye," said Pontiff, with a smile, then softer, smile disappearing, "Aye. An thanks for so warmen a sentiment."

"Just recounting what I read in the papers."

"Aye, well, you dinnae want tae believe everyhen you read in the papers, eh?"

"Well quite."

"You know Rev I never fucken said-"

"I know you didn't," smiled the Rev.

He squeezed Pontiff's shoulder.

"I know you didn't."

"I saw the poster," said Pontiff. "When did she disappear?"

The Rev submerged his lips in his mouth momentarily before he breathed in, the sound of anxious air.

"Clem went missing about two weeks ago. Ben was ill, and when we went to visit them one day, they were both gone."

"Is it related tae **KT**?"

"We don't know. We don't think so. Needless to say Godfrey is in a state about her disappearance."

"Aye, I can imagine."

"But come on, let's get inside."

"I see the wee rag is huvven some affect though," said Pontiff as he ducked his head through the Rev's low back door.

"Yes Pont," said the Rev in evermore concerned humour. "A lot's been going on."

"Aye, I huv tae say, all the people in the street, no all of em looked too happy."

The Rev nodded.

"What exactly is this fucken LUK?" asked Pontiff.

The Rev took off his glasses, rubbed his eyes.

"Liberty for the United Kingdom."

Liberty for the United Kingdom. Liberty for the United Kingdom? Where had Pontiff heard that before?

"Isn't that-?"

"-the closing words of *Ockham*'s articles."

"So-"

"Let's go downstairs and I'll tell you all about it."

Pontiff walked through the kitchen, through another door and into a windowless room. Though Pontiff had been in here many times, he bumped into tables, creaked on boards and stumbled over the group of cushions that had once been his bed.

"Hold on!" shouted the Rev, appearing with a candle.

Now Pontiff made out the hatch. He lifted it, extended the ladder, and dropped down. The Rev followed, surprisingly gracefully. The cellar, roughly 2 by 3 metres with a low wooden ceiling, was lit by more candlelight. There was a small round table with two coffee cups on it and tucked under it were two wooden chairs built for children and an upturned box full of bibles. In the corner lay two cushions of faded azure. A dampness clung in the air.

"I must say, Rev, I expected a bad reception. But fuckinell, you should-" A tapping from the wall interrupted Pontiff. "Fuck is that?" he asked, suddenly apprehensive.

"I'll show you."

The Rev smoothed his hand over the wall, found the correct spot, and shoved. A gap appeared, and in squeezed a white-haired and bearded man with kind eyes sporting brown corduroy suit trousers, a purple smoking jacket, a black shirt and a red corduroy hat.

"Well fuck me, look what the cat dragged in."

"No Pont, that *is* the cat," corrected the Rev.

"Dear boys," came the hushed greeting from the newcomer.

"The legendary Godfrey Golightly," said Pontiff. "Awright *Enigma*."

"Legendary?" responded the old man, raising his eyebrows in amusement. "One can only disappoint when given so grand a title. But anyway, good day, Pontiff. Nice to see you again. Interesting morning I would imagine?"

He shook Pontiff's hand.

"Aye, I've hud better."

The white haired man laughed, eyes twinkling and darting. He took in Pontiff's appearance. Aye, thought the Scot, the trousers were a bad idea.

Godfrey exuded warmth and knowledge, somewhere between sixty -five and seventy, about 5"8, similar build to Pontiff, substantial looking, as though echoing the size of his brain. This was he, the editor of the most subversive, terrorist organisation in the country. In his purple velvet smoking jacket and general raggedy appearance, Godfrey looked your quintessential Osama.

And he was quite a character.

When Pontiff had first met him he had discovered the old man was still amenable to the odd dabbling in hallucinogens. There had been countless times after a session smoking, dissecting the political landscape and drinking vast quantities of brandy that Godfrey would withdraw to his room, gather up his pipe and tobacco, scratch his beard and saunter off in his red gown, frayed and worn by years of thinking. Over time he'd come to prefer *partaking*, as he called it, on his own. Found it more worthwhile, more enlightening. *For the thoughts, dear boy, the thoughts.*

"Well dear boy, it's good to see you back. Detained, I presume, before you could help us out with the drop?"

Pontiff nodded.

"And now you're out, this happens, eh?"

"Aye, it never rains but it pours."

Godfrey laughed.

"Yes. Anyway, do excuse my entrance. I feared it might be somebody else, but no doubt we'll get to that in a moment."

An empty brandy bottle rolled out from behind the secret door.

"Worken hard, I see," said Pontiff.

"Working very hard, dear boy," responded Godfrey with a smile.

"Whilst taking spiritual guidance from me," interjected the Rev, handing Godfrey a new bottle of brandy and a cup.

"I have no need for spiritual guidance, Reverend, just this," Godfrey said, raising the bottle, "what I always turn to when my mind is thirsty. Why don't we sit?"

The Rev and Godfrey took the two available chairs while Pontiff perched on the box of bibles. Godfrey poured three brandies and passed them round. "Ah, that's better," said Godfrey before turning to Pontiff. "It's not a pretty position you're in, is it dear boy? How has it all happened, I wonder? And why?"

"Fuck knows. I seem to have been selected by Garqi to play this little role. I donno why it's me."

"Mmm. Well, it is *most* intriguing. One can only assume that after the fiasco of the inauguration and the violent infiltration of Hellevue, the Government is trying a different tack. But, be that as it may, your name is rather compromised round here now."

"Tell me about it. You should see ma flat."

Pontiff told them what he'd seen, what had happened to John.

"Well," said Godfrey, "vigilantism does not normally require much prompting. Particularly as you're practically a foreigner. And I'm not at all surprised Huwi was there. I'm sorry about your friend though. I feared this would happen."

"So today must have been some welcome home to Hellevue," said the Rev. "Did you know anything about the story before you arrived back?"

"Well actually Rev, I got back a few nights ago. But I-"

"Why didn't you come and find us then?" asked Godfrey, the merest hint of distrust in his voice.

"Oh mate, I wanted tae. Especially after I saw the poster about Clem. But then I saw a load of Blackguard and huvven jus witnessed a rather gruesome murder I'd had about enough for one day. I thought I'd come an see you first thing in the mornen. Yesterday mornen."

"Why didn't you?" asked Godfrey.

"I hud an appointment at the jobcentre I couldnae afford tae miss. An then on the way I see the story. After ma interview I went straight tae *The Rumour*, tae find out what was goen on. In return for my compliance they offered me the chance of a better life an an award for ma civic mindedness."

"What did you say to that?" asked the Rev.

"D'you need t'ask? Just look at ma face. I escaped this mornen. I came here to clear mine and Clem's names."

Pontiff took a swig of his brandy and looked at the two older men digesting this information with non-committal expressions.

"Please tell me you believe me."

"Of course we do Pontiff," responded Godfrey, smiling.

"You've no idea how relieved I am tae hear that."

"Oh I can imagine. But of course we believe you. The story's patently absurd. Another family took Clem's old place within a day of her disappearance. The timing would be all wrong for you to be involved."

Godfrey paused, collected his thoughts. "I just can't believe Ben's gone." He looked at both Pontiff and the Rev, the latter putting a consoling hand on his knee.

"Well," said Pontiff, rubbing his bald head, swigging some more brandy. "Duren ma cosy wee chat with Garqi and Mormon, they intimated Ben wasnae dead."

"Really?" asked the Rev after a pause.

"Aye," said Pontiff, taking another swig. "I've came back tae Helle-vue so we can find them both."

Godfrey nodded through the gathering tears in his eyes, readied himself to speak. The Rev squeezed his shoulder. "Well, that is good news, dear boy," said Godfrey, wiping his eyes. He put his hand on the Rev's. "And it's good you're here, Pontiff. But let us be under no illusions. It will be difficult to find them. Even if we were family, their whereabouts would unlikely be discharged to us by the authorities. In any case, dear boy," he said, turning to Pontiff, "it will be very tricky for any of us to do anything. The LUK have announced plans to fortify our boundaries. The people that live in the wastelands surrounding Hellevue are to be relocated and LUK operatives are to move in to provide a permanent border force. No longer will we be able to come and go as we please."

"Aye, so tell us about this fucken LUK. Who are they? Is *Ockham* involved? Do you know who he or she is now?"

The Rev shook his head. "We don't know if *Ockham*'s involved. And we certainly don't know his or her true identity."

The Rev didn't look at Godfrey as he made this point but continued to give a quick précis of the recent past.

"*KT* in Hellevue came out about six weeks ago and a few days after it began to circulate we saw flyers for a meeting for a new group."

"The LUK?" asked Pontiff.

"Well, what would become the LUK. At that time they were known as *Respect The People*. But naturally Godfrey and I popped along. We wanted to see who we had inspired. Clem came as well. And Huwi."

"Huwi?"

The Rev looked sideways at Godfrey, pain and sheepishness present in equal measures. Godfrey raised his eyebrows and smiled.

"Yes," said Godfrey. "But we'll come to that in a moment. At this meeting one of the speakers was Arnie Shaw. Something of a loose cannon, very clearly defined ideas about right and wrong, known for being drunk and violent. He'd just been kicked out of the Blackguard and now he wanted to fight the hijacking of the British people. When he came across a copy of *KT* and became acquainted with one of the vendors he believed he had found the vehicle to energise the masses. He actually ended up doing a couple of districts – Hellevue and a few neighbouring areas – during the drop. But the more we listened, the more dangerous he seemed. You certainly wouldn't want to cross him."

"An so he's the leader of this LUK, is he?" asked Pontiff.

Godfrey shook his head. "No, dear boy. Do you remember Graham Calloway?"

"Aye. Why, what's he got tae dae wi'it?"

"He's the man."

"You're fucken kidden me!" shouted Pontiff, breaking into a trademark hacking laugh. "As in the ex-LibCom, Calloway? The lappen cat gadgie?"

Godfrey nodded.

"After his assets were frozen," said the Rev, picking up the mantle, "he went off radar, before he holed up in Hellevue. He'd diverted some funds during his government days to a few of his old friends here and when he met Shaw through mutual acquaintances they started to develop a plan. Someone asked him about that infamous TV appearance at that first meeting, actually. He said something along the lines of his cat impersonation representing the struggle of ordinary people, that getting food was akin to lapping at an half empty saucer of milk. He claimed he hadn't been sacked by the LibComs but had left over a policy disagreement."

"Naturally," said Pontiff.

"Anyway, while Godfrey and I held these two in rather low esteem and declined to attend another meeting, Huwi was rather taken with them."

"Yes," agreed Godfrey. "And then a couple of weeks later, about a month ago, I was sat at home with the Reverend here, one afternoon, when we were interrupted by these fellows, Shaw and Calloway. Imagine our surprise."

He gave a shake of his head, a wry smile appearing on his face. The Rev looked decidedly uncomfortable.

"They told us that they knew we were the zine chiefs," continued Godfrey, "and they wanted to discuss something with us. Naturally we denied what they asserted but it soon became apparent we had been found out. We asked them how on earth they knew it was us. Shaw told us that at the second meeting they announced they were changing their name-"

"To the LUK," said Pontiff.

Godfrey nodded. "And Huwi, realising the new name had been inspired by words from **KARMATARMAK** pipes up to say not only that he knows the zine but that he's in it."

"Fuckinell!" said Pontiff. "When did he join?"

"I let it slip one night that I was in it and invited him in," said the Rev with low eyes. "By the morning's sobriety it was too late."

"Jesus," whispered Pontiff.

"Mmm well, yes," Godfrey patted the Rev on the shoulder. "Anyway, our dear little Welsh friend told Shaw and Calloway that he could take them to the men behind the zine."

"Bet you loved that!"

"Oh..." said Godfrey, shaking his head, smiling and raising his eyebrows. "Anyway, Calloway was waxing lyrical about the name, how it combines art with revolution, you know, the usual lefty guff. I found him to be a bit obsequious, a bit sycophantic, at first. I wasn't sure why they chose that name considering theirs is a republican movement. Probably something to do with tradition I expect. Anyway, suffice to say, I said, *'look, dear boy, take the name but don't count on me to get involved.'* Godfrey paused before adding gravely, "but he told us we already were."

"And it's my fault," said the Rev. "If I had never recruited Huwi and his big mouth, our anonymity would still be protected."

"Well, Kev, it's all in the past now," responded Godfrey.

"Aye," said Pontiff. "Dinnae drag the past intae it. It was hard enough the first fucken time round."

"What's done is done," asserted Godfrey again. "And anyway, we'd still be living here under that mob regardless."

Evidently Calloway and Shaw had whipped up quite a level of support, keen to bring together the 'single-issue' groups of Hellevue, to create a unified force for rebellion in an area where art and politics mixed (as they always did in a nation's dark times). And as with the forming of all resistance groups there had been a degree of internecine warfare. But eventually those inclined to sedition realised that co-

191

operation and unity was the only way to get things done. Calloway and his hired gun, his Rottweiler, Shaw, had then begun to marshal people under the LUK banner.

"And now," continued Godfrey, "we're talking ex-journalists, artists, teachers, binmen, the unemployed, disenchanted military personnel, former government workers who have not been given long-promised perks of the ruling class, those that just like a scrap-"

"It's *that* group that worries me," said the Rev.

"Finally," said Godfrey, "they say everyone is united by a common goal."

"Where've we heard that before?" mused Pontiff.

"Quite. Anyway, having gone quiet during Republic Day and the siege, they're back. And revolution is nigh."

"And if there's any gainsayers now, they're put in their place sharpish," explained the Rev. "If your group isn't approved by the Central Committee of the LUK the modus operandi is being called in to meet high-ranking LUK Operatives and being told in no uncertain terms that your operation is not permitted. You are then informed you *are* free to join the LUK and *might* be able to espouse some of your beliefs though any literature or public events would require approval from the Central Committee."

"Yes indeed," agreed Godfrey. "An offshoot of *The Intelligentists*, for example, dubbed *The Movement for Extreme Intellectualisation*, wanted to re-introduce the academic tradition and string up the idiots. Alas a few of the *idiots* they had in mind were high-ranking LUK and so they were strung up themselves."

He refilled everyone's glasses.

"Huwi will say that times have changed, that the country has been hijacked. And I agree with that. But so now has our process been hijacked by those thugs that call themselves the LUK. The swelling of their influence is creating more problems for the people of Hellevue."

The Rev crossed himself, took his glasses off, rubbed his eyes.

"And you can't say they're not organised," he said. "They've embarked on a Mafia-like collation of money and goods. They've cornered the blackmarket of the district. Independent stalls and shops are now fronts for the LUK."

The Rev looked at Pontiff, fear in his eyes.

"After we'd done the drop in the surrounding areas, we wanted it to stop. The wrong people were emerging. We didn't want the drop in the Central District to go ahead but the LUK insisted. We knew there would be reprisals and if this lot were our hope, we'd rather not bother. All we can hope is that throughout the country different people will rise up."

"The Blackguard started pulling out en masse yesterday afternoon," added Godfrey. "And by the evening the LUK had reclaimed the streets. Last night there was a streetgig – attendance compulsory. From tonight, there is to be a curfew and anyone not present at the designated hour will have to answer accordingly. All in the name of unity. Now it is Calloway and his cronies who say 'the rules of the game are changing' and emote on 'the specifics of our age.' And as our personal freedoms, albeit much diminished, make way for his take on 'collective security,' you have to wonder as to his true intentions as well." He paused. "And I'm sorry to say, Pontiff, your name was rather vilified last night. There were banners making indiscreet reference to the type of treatment you could expect should you return. And of course when they went to visit you at your flat and you weren't there, it seemed clear that you had returned to safety. Outside Hellevue. Back with your media chums."

"Well I was wi'em. But *chums* would be a stretch."

"Well we're all running out of friends," said the Rev. "The LUK have commandeered **KT** as well."

He stopped.

"And put Huwi in charge."

Pontiff leant back in his chair, exhaled deeply, rubbed the back of his head.

"Yes," said Godfrey with a nervous laugh and another raise of the eyebrows. "So you see, dear boy, things are hardly a bed of roses for us either. But we three will stick together. We can certainly guarantee you a safe house. For what it's worth."

"Thanks man. I really appreciate that."

The Rev passed the bottle and Pontiff took another couple of hefty gulps while Godfrey rolled a joint. As the gathered engulfed themselves in a haze of purple, Pontiff slumped back onto a cushion on the floor. LUK, eh? What to make of it all? Pontiff felt inclined to give them a chance – surely something was better than nothing. Though there was the small matter of them wanting to kill him.

Aye. Who says life's predictable, he thought. I piss off for a wee bitta realignment an the whole fucken world changes. But after everything he'd been put through, revolution, or at least a fightback, was something Pontiff felt he had to take part in. And find Clem. Where was she? Fuck. So much uncertainty. No wonder some of the *Misaligned* didn't want to be released.

"Jesus, I jus thought," he said, breaking the noiseless bonhomie. "Another day and I'd've been in limbo, unable to cross into Hellevue's newly fortified borders."

Godfrey nodded. "Yes, dear boy, you're quite right." He sighed. "How much easier life was when the whole country was just living on a diet of whiskeysquash and Garqi's mindrot soap opera. If the bastard hadn't made it pay-per-view halfway through the series maybe the revolution wouldn't be about to happen!"

The Rev laughed, took another swig and a toke.

"Oh we got it all in Shrink Clink," said Pontiff, accepting the joint and bottle from the Rev.

"Is it true they do *pretty-making* in there?" Godfrey asked.

"Aye. *A pretty face is a happy soul.* Aye."

"Why didn't it work out for you, mate?"

"You can fuck off Rev! Nah, I was deemed attractive enough in m'own right."

That gave Pontiff pause for thought. Some journey to rehabilitation it had turned out to be.

"And so presumably, dear boy, you were released to take part in their little story about *hearts and minds* in Hellevue?"

"Aye," Pontiff responded. "I guess so."

Sensing this wasn't the moment to delve further, Godfrey changed the subject. "The old Rev's had a bitta bother with the powers that be as well, you know."

"What? That cannae be right," said Pontiff, leaning into the priest and giving his belly a rub. "God's looken after you, is he no?"

"Well I sincerely hope he is," said the Rev. "I'll be mightily pissed off if I'm wrong about the afterlife and this is all we've got." He paused for a glug of brandy. "No. What Godfrey means is they finally caught up with me. I received a letter recently in which I was informed my local NIPSD department knew I was a *Disruptive Dogmatic* and that I would be required to take courses to be taught how to escape the trappings of fantasy and whimsy."

One of the early *Cow* proclamations had been that scientists had discovered faith came from the same part of the brain as OCD and was to be treated as a mental illness. Though all religious leaders had been forced to renounce their Godly mission some time ago, not all had been formally de-collared.

"If I wanted to keep my rations..."

The Rev suddenly laughed.

"Just the other week my Personal Tutor told me I was going to function based on reason and that ultimately this would improve my life and the lives of those around me. He said my beliefs were relics of a bygone age, another impediment to our future, and that they were no longer relevant in our modern society. Yes, they've been telling me all sorts of great things. You know, that if God gave us free will, which entails let-ting us do whatever the fuck we want, their words not mine I should add, why does He periodically come back to punish us, while letting the weak be subjugated to evil action?"

"Well dear boy that does make Him a bit of a maniac, doesn't it?" said Godfrey, smiling at Pontiff.

"What did you say tae that?"

"I told them that they were small-minded imbeciles and that the notion of free will had all but vanished with their own demi-God, Terry Hair."

"Yes, well, dear boy," said Godfrey, "they are very similar, yours and theirs. You have to ask what type of God sets up a religion in which the only route to salvation is the torture, mutilation, humiliation and death of His only son. I mean, yes, I'm aware that that saves us. But why? Why does he set it up so we have to be saved like this? Why can't he just say 'Right, you're saved. Clean slate for everyone.' No, he has to go through the gore. He is a maniac, after all. Psychotic and blood-thirsty. It's all so unnecessary. To be honest, I find the Lord of the Rings or Harry Potter as believable as the bible."

"Oh fuck off Godfrey" said the Rev, "and pass me that bottle."

Godfrey obliged.

"It's true though, isn't it Pontiff?"

"Dinnae get me involved!"

"Oh we all you know what you think, dear boy. But look, the Bible is a satire itself, lambasting and punishing people for worshipping gods that don't exist. Yes, you talk of spiritual guidance, Reverend, well I am far more inclined to believe the Roman, Greek or Hindu multi-deity belief systems. To me they explain the complexity – and tribulations – of life much better. All powerful God cannot be, not unless he is a rather nasty piece of work."

Another hacking smoke-ridden laugh was induced in Pontiff.

"Oh fuckinell man, leave him alone, and let the man o the cloth wet his whistle, eh?"

He turned to the Reverend.

"You cannae escape this shite, can ya?"

"No you can't," he replied. "Sat here listening to Gandalf's half-witted attempts at cod-philosophy isn't all that different to attending my fucking *Disruptive Dogmatic Easing* classes. I tell you what Godfrey, if you are sick of the revolution why don't you swap sides and apply for a job down at the Public Harmony Unit? A cunt like you would fit right in."

More hacking from Pontiff.

"And you should join Battered Lungs Anonymous."

"Aye, aye," smiled Pontiff through chokes, pausing for another gulp of brandy. He was feeling much better. It had been a while since he'd had a normal conversation. *A normal laugh.*

All of a sudden, there was an eruption of rather unusual sounds, a beeping and buzzing from a bygone age.

"How can a priest afford a phone these days?" asked Pontiff.

"Faith," said the Reverend as he tapped the buttons. "Goodness me, listen to this. I've just received one of those Life Suggestion Texts. *BE GRATEFUL TO YOUR PARENTS – THEY'RE TRYING.* Trying to do what exactly? They're dead."

"It's a sign, Reverend," said Godfrey. "They're letting you know that all's well at His right hand and they are preparing your throne in the pure whiteness of heavenly eternity."

The Rev paused. Then nodded.

"Well, let's hope so. I'm counting on it. Anyway, who's hungry?"

There were murmurings of affirmation all around.

"Right, back in a sec."

With that, the Rev shimmied up the hatch.

"I'll help you," said Godfrey before he too displayed surprising agility in his clambering. "I left another bottle up there somewhere."

They'd been up there just a few moments when there was a loud rapping on the front door. Pontiff could feel his heart throbbing in his chest as he blew out the candle in the cellar. He tried to listen, at first only hearing his heart and breath.

Eventually his ears tuned in. Through the floorboards, Pontiff could just about make out what was going on. There was some low rumbling of chatter, then an intensity of volume. Huwi was here. Pontiff heard Godfrey laugh.

"I suggest you don' laugh!" screamed Huwi. "We've an assignment for ou!"

"Oh yes, dear boy?"

"You're gonna get in touch with *Ockham*. I'm guessin you've no'yerd from our anonymous compadre?"

"I'm to get in touch with *Ockham*... on your say-so?"

Pontiff could hear Godfrey's disdainful mirth.

"Look, I can only prrrotect ou for so long Godfrey!" spat Huwi. "Meanwhile Clem's probably languishin in some governmental, guantanomental, gulag! Am I the only one that cares about her?"

"Listen to me you young idiot. I know you are all awash fighting the machine. But just remember when you joined, OK? Just remember where you fit in with all this, and how long the two of us have known Clem. Remember a little bit of respect."

"Well things fit differently now dorn they? It's me you should be rrrespectin. Especially after it was your mate who's led to her capture, that Scottish bastard!"

So much for Celtic solidarity, thought Pontiff.

"Has e been yer?"

"No of course not," responded the Rev. "I expect he's still in custody. The same place he's been since he disappeared."

"Oh dorn be so naïve! You invite him to join us and then he leaves. He's got information on all of us. Once he got what he needed he was off. We'll be next if we're not careful. If he does turn up yer, you better let us know. E could go undercover and try and catch us!"

What was the matter with this prick, thought Pontiff. When had anybody ever gone undercover after printing their picture in a fucken newspaper?

"Well Huwi," said the Rev. "It seems you are consumed with conspiracy at the moment."

"Conspirrracy? Rrreverrrend, I'm fightin for what I believe in! Unlike some people round yer! You lot prefer disparrragin from the touchline rrather than gettin dirty!"

"After last night Huwi," interjected Godfrey, "I think we'll all be getting dirty by simple virtue of being attached to that mob running riot."

"Mob rrrunnin rrriot?" Huwi shouted. "Shaw and Calloway have united Hellevoo. This district will be the focal point in rrreclaimin the country!"

"Well that all sounds wonderful, dear boy. But I do just have one question. Where were they the other night when the Blackguard came in, when people were getting arrested? Or yesterday, when the PSU were snatching babies? Your precious LUK didn't fight then, did they?"

"Well maybe you should have thought of that before you rrreleased **KT**."

"Huwi, I tried to stop you lot distributing it for precisely this reason!"

"Bollocks! Anyway, we ad the bigger picture in mind. We needed to get ready for the rrright moment. If we'd fought then, we'd've lost! It was painful but we ad to do it that way. We weren't rrready to fight them but we are now. Like you always told me, 'Action without due thought is dangerous.' I didn't see you do anything anyway."

"What makes you think you're ready now?"

"You saw the crowds last night."

"Yes. Anyone caught inside when the orations were being delivered got to understand the meaning of rules pretty quickly, didn't they?"

"We ad to round people up! We needed to show defiance after the assault on Hellevoo! How else are we gonna bring about change without strong leadership?"

"Strong leadership Huwi?" exclaimed Godfrey. "They're a bunch of violent thugs. Calloway just wants revenge for being booted out the LibComs. He's not driven by ideology. He's driven by power-lust."

"Don't be simplistic."

"Don't be simplistic? For f-" Godfrey composed himself. "OK, look. Let's assume what you say is correct, that you can all agree who the enemy is now-"

"If the PSU or Blackguard, or whoever come tomorrow, we'll send em packin!"

"Well that's fine in the short-term, Huwi, and let's say that the first goal is reached, that of the destruction of the LibComs. Might not the splinter effect take over after that? In fact, will you even last until that goal is reached? There are so many conflicting ideas within the organisation that one unified vision on the future of the country is all but impossible. Not that that matters anyway. I think the country's probably ungovernable now."

"And why is that, eh? The situation has gone far enough."

"Maybe I was wrong to demand revolution. I fear what further measures you revolutionaries might introduce. Everyone is becoming radicalised and intolerant. And that includes you, Huwi."

"But I thought the problem was no-one wanted to do anything Godfrey! You want the LibComs deposed but you won't do anything except write a foo fuckin academic words! We can't afford to ignore the Government any longer! Thass the point. We have to rrrally together. If we want our freedom-"

"Freedom," responded Godfrey, "is a word bandied about by all-comers to the political debate, but what does that word mean these days? Measures to protect freedoms achieve anything but. Like getting out the bath, a towel only dries for so long before it makes you wet again. I wonder. Does *anyone* have the people's best interests at heart these days?"

Pontiff wondered if there had *ever* been a time leaders had people's best interests at heart.

"Huwi, I ask you, does anyone in Hellevue really believe the LUK are different from the LibComs?"

"Ah, this is fuckin rrridickalus, iznit?" said Huwi. "You two've got your'eads in the sand! It's convenient for'ou to imply peepul think that. I've no yerd a single word to that effect!"

"Well no," responded the Rev. "No-one dares say it out loud, do they?"

"Huwi," rejoined Godfrey, "this area was a great place to live simply by the virtue that there seemed to have been a collective if unwritten code to disregard governmental decrees. Now we've got that band of opportunists and intimidators seeking to gain power under some banner of rebellion."

"But that's what you wanted!"

On that, Pontiff was in agreement with Huwi.

"*They* are not what I wanted, what the area or the country needs, and certainly not the type of people I wanted to inspire. And to be honest, what would you know anyway? You don't even live in Hellevue now. Has your rabble even got a plan for governance? For that is the oft-forgotten essential of groups hell-bent on taking power."

"Rrright, that's it. I'm leavin. But we expect you to have contacted *Ockham* by tomorrrow."

"Don't hold your breath, dear boy."

"You betterrr'ad do."

"I am astounded you are adopting this attitude, Huwi," continued Godfrey. "Good day."

"Off you go then Huwi," said the Rev. "Nice to see you."

"I mean it!" and with that, the door slammed.

Just then, Pontiff appeared out the hatch. "What? No good byes?"

"No, just bad blood," said the Rev as his phone beeped again.

*"TOO MUCH THOUGHT LEADS TO NUMBNESS OF EMOTION."*

"Pontiff should come with me," said Godfrey, brain firing. "There's more room at mine and with some of the LUK coming here for their religious instruction, it'll be safer. I am sure I will be visited, but probably less frequently."

"As long as ma presence is kept under wraps, I'll be happy. Dinnae want tae be all sign language about masel."

"What do you mean?" asked the Rev.

"Well there's one glaren problem with sign language, isn't there? Everyone can overhear what you're sayen."

"Assuming they can spell properly," added Godfrey.

"Can deaf people be dyslexic?" asked the Rev.

"Yes of course," said Godfrey. "Why couldn't they be?"

"Cos it's made up?" offered Pontiff.

"Oh?" said the Rev.

"Look, lemme say, I've got nothen against dyslexics right, but apparently they have this disease that precludes them from spellen properly. Wellass fine. But if you're no good at maths or spatial awareness, there's no condition that labels that, is there? You're just shite at maths and spatial awareness. Well, if that's the case, then these people, these dyslexics, are merely hopeless at spellen and should not be accorded a special status. You got a free computer when I was at uni if you were dyslexic for fuck's sake! I didn't even get a free calculator. A fucken abacus woulda sufficed, ken? I told em, 'I cannae rewire a plug, what condition is that?'"

"Well that's learnable isn't it?"

"Aye, awright, but my point is that it all boils down to people no taken responsibility for their own deficiencies. We can't all be good at everythen. Just accept you're shite when it comes to words."

## 20

# MACHINATIONS

AT THIS TIME, a man very much not affected by dyslexia, indeed a man endowed with a near perfect academic and intellectual brain, with no disease, deficiency, condition or otherwise was just leaving his flat in a new car. Though refreshed after his tryst with Maria, Fred had re-signed himself to having to spend the rest of the day and maybe even early evening massaging a needy President's mood. But in the last couple of moments he had been told of a truly extraordinary develop-ment.

On his arrival at the Palace he was greeted by Sherry. The usual protocol was a snog and a ball grab but today she was concerned with the grazings on his face. Shards of glass had cut him following the explosion of his previous car's windscreen the previous night. When Fred informed Sherry of the happenings in the country, her response was almost psychotic in its affection.

"OK, Sherry, I'm fine. You better take me to the President."

Hair was in a state of serious alarm as Fred entered alone for the post lunch *tête-à-tête*, which increasingly resembled *couer-a-couer*. Here in the deposed Monarch's afternoon tea-room-of-choice was Hair, hoovering up lines, smoking cigarettes, perturbed by the dream he'd had the night before. A combination of pills, powders and potions had finally allowed him a night in which he could actually nod off. But it had also given the leader quite an array of visions and notions that had left him more than a little spooked.

"They're coming for me Fred. I see them, I see them."

He lunged at his confidante.

"You won't desert me, will you Fred? Oh please, PLEEEASE!"

Jesus, these people are fucking lunatics, thought Fred, as Hair grabbed him by his suit collar.

The President buried his head into Fred's chest and started to sob.

"Slow down, President. Whoa. Sssh, sssh. I'm not gonna leave you."

"They're coming," Hair forced out between more sobs, muffled by Fred's ever-wettening chest.

"Who is President?"

"I don't know, I, I can't make out their faces, but... they're advancing." He pulled away from Fred, his wide-eyed nervousness lingering in the air, red blotches on his cheek. "They're coming out of the dark, about to expose themselves, their hands start to rise, they have, I don't know what they have in their hands, but I force myself to wake because I know what's going to happen."

"And what's that President?"

"Murder!"

Fred stifled a laugh. Fuck me, he thinks he's Julius Caesar now.

"It's just a nightmare, President, everything's fine."

But that didn't sate Hair.

"You're the only one I trust now. Not Sherry, not those others. It's just me and you, Fred."

Again he pulled himself into his right-hand man, grabbing at Fred's cheeks. Fred saw genuine fear in the leader's eyes. Suddenly Hair leapt forward and kissed him on the lips. Fred pushed Hair away and the President collapsed to the floor. On his knees with his head down, again the sobbing commenced. Fred, for the first time in a long time, didn't know what to do. He mouthed 'fuck,' pulled a startled face.

"Now *you* hate me!" the President wailed. "Everyone hates me!"

Fred returned to his leader's side. "I don't hate you, President. It's just, well, it's just that we're...friends. Not..." He motioned sideways with his head.

"I'm sorry Fred, I'm just feeling scared. I'm so alone. You've no idea what it's like to lead, to give your all for the people and get nothing in return! If only they could see what I'm trying to do for them!"

Hair's eyes were bugged, and then in a whisper, "But my dream, it's real, I know it is."

He again collapsed into Fred and started to rock, comforted by his confidante's cradling arms.

This was an inopportune moment for Sherry to come in. On seeing her husband prostrate in Fred's arms, she rolled her eyes. Another pathetic eruption of unbridled weakness. It was all getting a little tiresome.

"Now, President," Fred said soothingly, "I think I may have some news that will cheer you."

Hair stayed cradled. Fred proceeded in the silence.

"A moment or so ago, I was given some rather startling information." Fred paused. "Incredibly one of the terrorists of **KARMATARMAK** has literally fallen into our lap."

Hair straightened immediately, sniffing away snot and wiping his eyes, suddenly alert like a child for a lolly after a nasty fall.

"Really," he sniffled.

"Ooh that's good news, isn't it?" said Sherry.

"Yes indeed," agreed Fred. "The PHU brought him in today. A routine check of some properties outside Hellevue proved to be most productive. A young gentleman with a beard of faded evergreen was reported to be in a very bad mood, disturbing the peace, kicking over recycling bins. When Blackguard accosted him, he verbally abused them. They demanded to search him and his home, and found writings he had clearly been working on."

Excitedly, "*Ockham*?"

"No sir, not *Ockham*."

Hair slumped.

"But it is certainly someone who might help us get close to him. See? This is what happens when we focus our attention elsewhere."

Fred didn't believe that for a moment. He was as astonished as anyone at this turn of events.

"We'll get that bastard yet!" said the suddenly defiant Hair.

"That's the spirit, President."

"So surely we need to head straight back into Hellevue! They're still scheming!"

"But sir, we found nothing in Hellevue. It's possible that the operation has moved to a different location. You know what these terrorists are like. Always seeking new safe havens. Hellevue might not be a breeding ground for revolution, in which case we don't want to alienate the people there."

In truth, Fred didn't know what was happening with **KARMATAR-MAK**. He would have to contact *Enigma*, ask for an update.

"Also, think about what happened to me. Think about what happened to Martin. The rest of the country needs reigning in."

But Hair was off. "Of that, there is no doubt," he was mumbling to himself, returning to his thousand yard stare. It was clear now this man wasn't running the show anymore. He was barely running his own show.

"Come on sir, this is just the fillip we need."

Fred led Hair through the Palace into a small room. There was a huge mirror through which Hair could watch events unfold next door. Fred left the President at his vantage point in the viewing booth to take up his own position in the adjacent interrogation room. Hair sat there, a hopeful smile diluted by confusion. Sherry seemed distant and he was feeling more than a little uncertain, his head not really a unified orb, shattered further by the mountain of powder in front of him.

Next door, a seated Fred surveyed the prisoner as he was bundled in and set down opposite him. There was a moment of silence. Fred's calm and measured manner was an attempt to be menacing and he was making a pretty good fist of it if the face of the terrorist was anything to go by. This was probably also due to the presence of six Blackguard.

Fred began by quoting some of the illegal words attributed to the prisoner, who remained impassive.

"Now. We know who you are. And *you* know that what you've been doing is illegal."

Fred circled with a Gestapo rhythm.

"However, we may afford you some leniency if you are willing to co-operate. We know you are small fry. But fried you will be nonetheless if you do not tell us what we want to know. Information we know you know."

He paused again.

"Who is *Ockham*?"

Of course, he knew that this man could not possibly know the true identity of *Ockham*. No-one but *Ockham* knew that.

"I suggest you co-oper-"

"I donnor," came the words in muffled Welsh tones.

Immediately the terrorist was kissed with a rifle butt just above his right ear, and went down in pain.

"*Don Coyote*," said Fred, mocking the name and smiling, "are you sure you cannot help us?"

"I donnor who *Ockham* is."

The guard once more used some gentle persuasion but as he made to attack again, Fred halted him with a raise of the hand.

"Oh come now *Mr Coyote*, you can do better than that. We have found some literature, albeit rather weakly constructed and emotively written."

Fred slapped a document on the table. He had never seen this writer before. He didn't think him very good.

"What you cunts need to knor," shouted the prisoner, scar on the head pulsating an increasing puce, "is there is an organisation startin to foment rrrevolution. Liberty for the United Kingdom. And we will destroy ou."

Fred stifled a laugh. This just gets better, he thought. They're using my words! He'd cooked that phrase up after a night on the drugs and birds.

"You may smile mate, but we mean it!"

"And **KARAMATARMAK** are involved are they?"

Fred was genuinely intrigued to know.

"Of course we fuckin are you idiot!"

At that, Fred went eccentric. He didn't take kindly to a man with less intelligence than he daring to berate him. The Blackguard didn't need a second invitation.

"Who is *Ockham*?" Fred shouted as they beat him. "Who is *Enigma*?"

Periodically they would stop to get a response but when the questions were not answered to a satisfactory level, great violence was meted out again. This was how it went until the questioned and questioners alike were pretty well exhausted.

Fred stepped back, told the Blackguard to stop.

He looked at the man's NIPSD card.

"Huwi Tenango, 36 Cordingley Road. Take him to the medical team."

Fred wasn't sure how he'd liked this violence stuff. Probably wouldn't do it again, but it was good to try these things. And you could never say never. He thought Hair probably would have enjoyed some visceral pleasure from the spectacle.

With this on his mind he was rather surprised when he entered the viewing room. Expecting to reap some praise –

"Hello Frederick," came the words in gruff tones. A sharp intake of breath. "Well done."

"Heath," responded Fred, half in surprise, half in greeting. He broke a smile. "Where's the President? I thought he was watching."

"He was, Frederick, (*suck-in*), he was."

"How long have you been here?"

Cliffe looked flustered, a bit sweaty. He straightened his tie. "I, er, (*suck-in*), just arrived, (*suck-in*). Clearly he wasn't talking."

"What? Oh that, him. Er, no that's right." Evidently Cliffe had not heard what Tenango had said. Fred instinctively felt that was a good thing. Too many things had started to slip from his grasp recently and he wanted to keep this information to himself until he was sure he knew what he wanted to do with it.

"Now, come, (*suck-in*), I wish to show you something."

Well, this *was* unusual.

As Fred followed Cliffe out of the door, Tenango's limp, somewhat drained and extraordinarily renditioned body was being dumped into a black hemp bag while copious amounts of blood were mopped-up by contract cleaners. The man in the bag had refused to give information on *Ockham* and had paid the ultimate price.

"Oh well," said Cliffe, "(*suck-in*) no need to go through the ball-ache of evidence gathering and the formality of charging at least!"

Cliffe making jokes? What did this all mean?

The two meandered along, not speaking, all the way to Hair's study. Cliffe knocked, and entered. And there sat Terry Hair, slumped, head first, two blades in his back, soaked in blood. Dead.

It was now that Cliffe broke the silence. He leant into Fred and spoke directly into his ear.

"Be under no illusions as to where your loyalty now lies (*suck-in*)."

Fred, not one prone to shock easily, was a little stunned. Of course, apart from this momentary jerk, nothing had changed for him. The notion of loyalty was lost on him. As long as all this didn't affect his ability to ring maximum enjoyment from life, he couldn't care less who was in charge. Cliffe's leadership probably wouldn't entail a dramatic shift from Hairism, his reaction to the rendition showing he wasn't so different after all. But Hair – and Fred – had clearly underestimated Cliffe's desire for power.

Fred stopped for one last look at the ghastly corpse of Hair. He hadn't looked the healthiest in recent times. He shouldn't have tried to keep up with me, he thought, but my, how prescient a dream our Terry had had. He was more switched on than anyone realised. Not that he could do anything about it when it came to the crunch. Ah well, *c'est la vie*, thought Fred. Or *mort*, in the case of our Terry.

"Walk with me," said Cliffe, sucking the life out of the atmosphere with his earnest-man routine. He wanted to discuss his concerns. Unruliness was afoot apparently. He didn't know the half of it, and Fred wasn't about to fill him in.

"Fred, as you know, people are starting to mobilise against the Government in rural areas, (*suck-in*). In some cases, platoons of Blackguard have deserted (*suck-in*). The absence of long promised but never delivered special treatment has started to jar (*suck-in*). Why did that grinning idiot offer so much? (*suck-in*) I told him we couldn't afford it! (*suck-in*) Well, maybe the time has come for us to afford it (*suck-in*)."

Hang on to your hats, thought Fred, there's a new sheriff in town!

"That's it sir, give our boys a bit more."

"We need to shore up our powers (*suck-in*). We need to step up *government glamourising* (*suck-in*). We need to re-iterate what we are doing (*suck-in*), how we are improving the lives of the populace (*suck-in*), why the country needs us."

He isn't gonna last long with that tick. The public don't like weirdness, thought Fred. He started to focus on this curious mannerism and started to lose interest in the thrust of Cliffe's words.

The new leader droned on and on and then Fred realised something that surprised him. All this government stuff had lost its fizz. I suppose once you've tortured people to death, what else is left in this type of work?

"Fred?"

"What, er, yes, yes, of course, Heath. I have lot of *Cow* stuff ready to go."

"And Hellevue? (*suck-in*) Should we return?"

"Ooh no sir. I think what you suggest is spot on. Look after our own and try to be more inclusive, reach out. That's what *I* would do."

"Good," sharp intake of breath, a hand through scruffy hair and the most plastic of grins.

Fred studied Cliffe. Now that he had finally acted after years of thumb-twiddling and lack of conviction he may think himself to be on a bit of a roll and start hacking down all elements of Hair's team. Knowing who was responsible for the murder of the now ex-President probably made Fred more vulnerable. In truth, the brutal measures doled out to Hair had unnerved him. Would he be next for the cull? So far it seemed Cliffe had no plans to marginalise Fred despite the obvious distaste he had for him. Fred felt he would be safe for as long as he was useful.

"So, (*suck-in*) at least we're off to a good start."

"Er..."

"The terrorist (*suck-in*)."

"Oh yes," Fred nodded. "Yes. We shall report it immediately that we have captured a terrorist who is helping us with our inquiries."

"Good (*suck-in*). It marks a certain type of immorality to mobilise against the Government (*suck-in*), a Government that clearly knows best!"

"I suggest upping dry days," said Fred. "To avoid an escalation of this seeping immorality."

"Good stuff, Fred (*suck-in*). I shall see you in due course then."

"Oh indeed Heath."

Fred watched Cliffe walk off. This all certainly represented a new and exciting chapter. Fred would have to watch himself now. Maybe a change of pace and scene was required. Maybe now was the time to extricate himself from this era in his life, hasten his plans whilst he was still able to dictate terms.

He also needed to ensure his aunt and mother wouldn't come. Fred had already had to stop his young cousins coming to stay so that he wouldn't have to give them work experience. He would explain to his aunt he was too busy with the new leader but would *PROMISE* they could come later. He knew how they operated. If he didn't give them that, they'd probably just pitch up uninvited.

After leaving Cliffe, Fred headed back to his flat. As he drove the deserted streets of the magnificently grand River Drive, his carphone did its jingle.

"Ah. Oli. Busy day, was it?"

Garqi laughed. "Eh. You know how eet eez."

"Great job on the security by the way. Really top notch."

Again Garqi chuckled. "I know. All my effort for nutheen. Ah well, dee next story come tomorrow. We see what appen den, ow your man Pope react."

"Did you hold the awards ceremony for him?"

"Yes. Well Piers did eet. I was busy. Today was very, very good business for MediaCorp International, Freddi dear, a major development."

"Oh yes? And what's that?"

Garqi did his trademark quattro-tut. "No no no, Freddi dear. All in good time. I must keep to myself until dee correct moment."

"Oh come on Oli. What is it?"

"Freddi dear, I cannot say now. But rest assured, eet eez big. But don't worry, dee door eez always open for a talented boy like you. I don't forget you gave me a foot in dee door in dis country. But very very interesteen communication. International. Dat's all I will say."

"Alright, alright. I suppose you know about Terry?"

"Yes. E meet stick end."

Fred swerved out the way of a fox.

"Yes. Eez good news for me. Wid grinneen idiot out dee way, dee timeen is perfect for MediaCorp International and our next step. Dis might bring my plans forward! But who you think did eet?"

"Well the Siamese brothers must have had something to do with it."

"Exacto. Dat's what I think."

"At Cliffe's behest, that is."

"Of course. But look, Freddi, LibComs are nearly finished. Bu-ut I av a role for you, just do not forget dat. Anyway, enough. Where is your boy?"

"Well he must be back in Hellevue," responded Fred. "But wherever he is, I expect what we publish won't make things particularly comfortable for him."

"No, no, true. But you know, I theenk your man ad a soft spot for dee murderer."

"You what?"

Garqi stayed silent.

"You don't mean.... What? Pope actually *knew* Romain?!"

"Eet appears so."

"Wow. I was closer than I knew with that aspect of the story!"

"Indeed. But look, Freddi dear, I must go. Wendi has my dinner ready. Ciao."

As Garqi hung up the phone, Fred swam through new torrents of confusion in his brain. Pope knew Romain? Wow, I hadn't thought of that, hadn't conceived it as a possibility. He pondered visiting Romain straight away, to see what she knew of the *Hellevue Hero*, but he had things to sort out. Garqi was right. Fred knew that Cliffe had taken over a government that was waning in popularity. What could the new leader do to alter this? Very little, probably. In fact, there was a good chance he'd make it worse. But what was Fred to do? And what was Garqi planning? Did Fred want to be a part of that, whatever it was?

## 21

# JOINED-UP THOUGHT

HAVING WAITED FOR the cloak of night, Godfrey and Pontiff arrived at the former's flat just twenty minutes before the metaphorical lights-out of the new curfew.

Happily, the route between the homes of the Rev and Godfrey – the latter located in the outer parts of Hellevue to the west – did not yet have the LUK patrol that were again becoming commonplace elsewhere in the district. Godfrey did note though, that because this part of Hellevue was slightly more well-to-do, there had been a number of mutilating burglaries like the one Pontiff had seen at the Monorail station. It was vital to be as vigilant of these attacks as it was LUK operatives. Despite the promise from Hair that *nocturnal safety was a primary objective*, there were no operational street lamps and you didn't want to be caught outside at this time of night. Not these days. Not in this part of town. Another *primary objective* that had fallen short.

The other distinctive feature of this part of Hellevue was functioning SwipeScanners, and they functioned so well that you couldn't go in or out of buildings save with their usage. Godfrey passed his NIPSD card over the scanner, did the eyes-fingers manoeuvre and Pontiff bundled in quickly behind, avoiding using his card and alerting the Government to his whereabouts. After two flights of stairs, they arrived at the entrance to Godfrey's flat. They passed through an insubstantial vestibule and entered a small, circular room – circular for joined-up thought, Godfrey reasoned. Immediately to the left of the door was a cabinet and a wooden record player, to the right was a small television, while the chamber's circumference was gilded by brown sofa. The only breaks in the uniform rotundity were doors for the entrance, the kitchen, and one leading to the sleeping and washing quarters. A round wooden table stood in the middle of the room.

"Come in, come in, dear boy. I think we could both do with some refreshment after our walk."

"Aye."

"What would you like?"

"Whatever you're huvven."

"Well take a seat and I'll see what I've got."

Pontiff sat and Godfrey opened the cabinet.

"Ah. Brandy," he said, poking his head in. "It's all I've got I'm afraid," he said, reappearing. "I know you're a whisky man."

"I'll take what I'm given. I know you're housen me at considerable risk an I really appreciate it."

"Not at all, dear boy. Make yourself comfortable. I'll fetch some glasses and rustle something up."

As Godfrey prepared some sustenance, Pontiff lay supine on the circular sofa, relieved he could relax for a moment. He felt exhausted and closed his eyes but no sooner had he drifted off than Godfrey returned with two plates of scrambled egg and long-life biscuits. He handed these offerings to his grateful guest.

"It's not the best but about all I can manage in these times," said Godfrey, as he poured two clay cups of Brandy.

"Ah mate, sgreat," said Pontiff levering himself up from the chair.

After a few moments of quiet interrupted temporally by the scrape of cutlery on plate, Pontiff asked – "D'ya think the LUK are gonnae succeed?"

Godfrey exhaled deeply and took a swig of Brandy.

"To be honest I dread any outcome. I think I've given up on the idea of revolution really. Increasingly I find myself wanting to limit my participation in the barrel-roll of life, to be immune from the vagaries and oft-occasioned danger that so characterises modern Britannia. I just want to find Clem."

"You and me both," responded Pontiff.

"It's only the thought of her that keeps me going. And if you say Ben's alive, then there's double the hope."

Christ, thought Pontiff. Where do we even fucken start?

There was a long gap in conversation as the two ate. Godfrey seemed to lose his appetite halfway through and took his plate to the kitchen.

"You know, dear boy," he said as he returned to the sofa, "I never imagined I'd want to shoe-horn **KARMATARMAK** into incitement of the masses. At the outset I never viewed it as a vehicle for change. It was meant to be a forum for debate. We wrote for pleasure, and to ruffle a few feathers. As you know, the starting point wasn't entirely political. It was as much about the slide to mental flabbiness as anything else. I used to wonder whether one day people would be able to wait for someone and sit and ponder life, be comfortable in their own company, and not have the pang to send text after text or play games on a tiny screen. I wondered whether if people stopped using mobile phones, they would start speaking and writing properly again because the scope of their tableau was bigger than a hand-held bit of plastic. I longed for a society in which sentences were not punctuated so painfully ad nauseam with the likes of *hopefully*, *basically* or *obviously*, and I did wish everyone would stop saying dude and high-fiving."

"That the mobile phone has hastened the slide to mental flabbiness is a point with which I concur most vociferously," agreed Pontiff.

Godfrey gulped down his brandy, standing up as he refilled Pontiff's cup.

"Raise a glass to our liberal, compassionate Britain, the People's Republic of Absurdia. Hats off to el Presidente Hair. The country is finally a parody of itself."

He shook his head, smiling as he sat back down.

"God, I wonder what Ruth would make of all this?"

He paused.

"She'd probably find the whole thing hilarious. She had such a blackly comic streak. It's why I loved her so much."

He looked at Pontiff, eyes glistening.

"She always hated it when people said 'you might get hit by a bus tomorrow.' And then, well, you know. Knowing what she would have said got me through those days after I lost her. I even managed to find it amusing I wasn't permitted to tie flowers to the railing where she had stepped into the road. Health and Safety. Said I was obstructing the walkway."

"Christ. There's a unique distillation of horror and black comedy running through everything these days, isn't there?" said Pontiff, pausing to drink more brandy. "It reminds me of a story my grandfather told me. His brother was a great traveller. And he was travellen somewhere in Southeast Asia one time, out walken through forest and temple ruins when he realised he really needed a shit. So he bends down, takes his flip flops off, takes his keks off, and starts tae squeeze. An at that moment a snake comes up an bites him on the prostate."

"Ooh you fucker!"

"Aye. Granddad said probleez at that moment he had the power to jizz venom."

Godfrey puffed out a blast of Asthmatic mirth and topped up the two cups.

"Are you gonnae get in touch with *Ockham*?" asked Pontiff.

"No. I do not intend to do any of *their* bidding. They may find him first, you never know. And to be honest, his identity is not of my utmost concern. It's possible we've already seen him. Incredible if he's managed to keep himself hidden with all that's been transpiring."

Godfrey took a sip of brandy, let it linger on his tongue. "I just cannot grasp that Huwi feels so strongly the LUK are the answer. He's treading a dangerous path getting embroiled with that lot. He'd be safer if he still lived in Hellevue."

"Why did he move?"

"His girlfriend's pregnant and she didn't want him to set foot in the district let alone actually work here. She hates him working at the pub and is always on at him to look for something else."

"Fuckinell, I doubt she hud the LUK in mind, did she?"

"No. She suggested the Blackguard."

"Fuckin briwyant!" laughed Pontiff, again breaking into a hacking cough.

"Here, you need it," said Godfrey standing up to hand Pontiff another brandy. "The LUK, eh?" he said, again thrusting his cup skywards. "A group that want to return us to freedom! Ha! And I thought the PHU were bad."

Godfrey looked directly into Pontiff's eyes, fighting back a lump in his throat. "God, what have I started?"

"I dinnae think you started it, Godfrey. No them anyway."

"Well maybe not. But **KARMATARMAK** is finished. Well, as it was. I have no idea what it is now or what it is to be. Huwi, the LUK, they can have it. I know it's no longer mine. But they can think again if they think I'm writing for them."

Godfrey took a long glug of brandy.

"Oh dear boy, we used to have such fun with it!"

"Aye, well fun may be all we have left."

"How wistful, but how true," nodded the host. He had finished his cup again and was well into the *in vino veritas* zone.

"The endpoint of Draconianism may not necessarily have been the destination when Hair set sail but my, he got us there in the end, didn't he? And though I warned of it, I never really thought that what I wrote would become vital in the vain hope of upholding civil liberty. Of course phrases such as that gave up their meaning a long time ago. It *is* time for the country to react. But...with Calloway, the speed to further Draconianism seems remarkably accelerated." He looked back towards Pontiff, his mood deadened further. "Where did this land go wrong?"

Pontiff remained silent. He wasn't sure quite how to react. The idea of a revolution was something with which he agreed but on the evidence he'd seen coupled with the dejection of Godfrey he too felt the LUK were not the answer. Of course the fact that he was now a national celebrity muddied the waters further, added a certain piquancy.

"I dinnae think it's possible tae get the change you want."

Godfrey laughed. "Well no, quite, we never have before."

Pontiff nodded a smile. "May I?" he enquired, holding up the bottle.

"Please," responded Godfrey with a flourish of his hand. "That's what it's there for."

Pontiff filled the two cups and Godfrey took another sip.

"But you're quite right, dear boy. And previously, people felt no inclination to fight for what they believed in politically, did they? When it came to that, they were, to use a common parlance, *yardsed*, *phased out*, indifferent, didn't believe in anything. As a result, the absurdly malign nanny state has been, if not born, certainly perfected."

"Extremism is the price of voter apathy, eh?"

"Well quite. All people used to believe in was wishing cancer on referees and making rape threats on social media."

"Aye. You didnae wan'tae get on the wrong side of the debate, did you? Member what happened to The Rev's mate after he spoke out against gay marriage?"

Godfrey nodded.

Within hours of the comment, *FASCIST* had been spelled out in shit on the stained glass window.

"And now," continued Godfey, "this sense of perpetual outrage means it's no longer acceptable to just go about your business. Now it's gang warfare, the old Bushist philosophy of *you're either with us or against us*. You have to sign up for something for your own safety. I don't want to over-egg my already eggy displeasure, but I'm beginning to think humanity, en masse, is a repulsive slop of goo. Really the sooner we realise that humankind is on its last legs, the sooner we can start enjoying ourselves. I say let's go out with a bang and end this miserable experiment called the human race."

Pontiff was quite taken aback at this show of melancholic misanthropy. "And what about future generations?" he asked. "Should we not fight for them? Isn't that what you wrote in the last *KT*? I may no believe in the LUK either but after everythen I been through, I want tae do somethen. I need tae. Don't you? We cannae accept the LibComs, surely?"

"Well if humankind's not going to be here forever, what use is legacy?"

"But your words inspired," said Pontiff. "They inspired me, at least. An I suppose legacy aside, I'm more interested in maybe huvven a better life than this!"

"Maybe if I'd never written a lot of people wouldn't be in the predicament they are in now. Maybe if I hadn't written, I wouldn't have inspired Calloway and Shaw."

"But Godfrey, you wrote for the right reasons. An anyway, they were already plotten, weren't they? It's no your fault these so-called rebels are usen muscular control. They're operaten at the base level of humankind."

"Humankind? Funny term that, isn't it, dear boy? I can discern very little benevolence. More a desire to control and impose as though endowed with some sort of divine right. Tolerance is not to be tolerated, is it, demonstrates a breakdown in moral conviction. It seems imperative in the current clime to possess an opinion, impress it upon everyone else and convert, convert, convert. God, I don't know if I care anymore. I'll be dead soon and what will any of this mean then? What use will a single word I've written have? Even if the Government is overthrown, what then? We'll get the LUK in and just keep going round and round in circles."

Before Pontiff could respond –

"Why've we got all this save the environment crap anyway? We're not actually destroying the planet. All we're doing is creating an environment that is hostile to ourselves. This piece of rock was here before us and it'll be here after us." Long glug of brandy. "Top up?"

Pontiff nodded. But he didn't entirely appreciate where Godfrey was heading with all this.

"Aye, wellatt's certainly one way o'looken at things. But *Plasticitis* was a legitimate concern was it no? Think of Clem's son. Think of what you stood for at the start. The environmental agenda was something you got behind. Certainly Clem did, eh?"

At the mention of Clem, Godfrey calmed, smiled, "yes, you're quite right, dear boy."

He looked at Pontiff and smiled again, in acceptance and agreement. "Forgive me. You're right. You're right, of course."

Godfrey walked quietly to the cabinet where he retrieved another bottle of brandy. He opened it and filled both cups. "And we will find her. It's the only thing left."

In truth, it was the only thing stopping Godfrey putting himself forward for voluntary-euthanasia. He loved Clem like the daughter he never had, intoxicated from the first time he had seen her painting art on the streets of Hellevue. But Clem intoxicated everyone she met. Born in Kerala, south India, her father had been a farmer but committed suicide after falling behind on his microfinance loan. Still very young, her Christian mother had then taken her to Goa. To make a living her mother trained her up as a beach trapeze artist. Mother would set up a rope and Clem would walk across it, perform some tricks, and then go round and take money of the tourists. "It was cynical," said Clem. "But then so is budget travel." Clem often added how she wanted to stab tourists in the eye whenever they uttered variations on the *they're so poor but so happy* theme.

When Clem was ten her mother was murdered and she was put up for adoption. A British couple brought her back to England and gave her an Indian name – Rekha. Clem hated it and at the age of sixteen ran away and changed her name back to Clem. Not long after, she arrived in Hellevue and spent her early years in the district living in squats and putting on warehouse parties. By the time she met Godfrey she was pregnant with Ben.

"It pains me Ruth never will see her again," continued Godfrey. "They were so close. And they made quite a pair. Such fierce but compassionate women! Neither could abide liars or fools. Clem's one mistake was that ex of hers, Ben's father."

"Where is he now?" asked Pontiff.

"In jail, I think. I don't care. But we will find Clem."

Pontiff knew Godfrey said it more in hope than certainty, that if he didn't try and convince himself he would never believe it.

"Yes, if that ex of hers was still around he'd be the first to be rounded up for a PSU course. Did you see this thing in action yesterday?"

Pontiff shook his head. "Nah. I hudnae even heard of it til you said somethen tae Huwi."

"Well it seems it's the Government's latest wheeze. Do you remember Sharon Taylor?"

How could Pontiff forget? She was a rather large woman and lived on the ground floor of the first big block of flats on from Pontiff's. She had initially been given a third floor flat but couldn't deal with the stairs. She was permanently on a diet and would say "*I mustn't eat so much, I must eat better*" and then have a lolly and a bacon and egg roll for lunch. Or she would have crisps for breakfast and say "*but that's all I had!*" Over the last year her life had taken a turn for the empty after the ban on non-state-run publications had meant the end of her favourite celeb-gossip magazines. The Citizenry had been urged to live in a manner opposite to vicariousness. She'd had to have this word explained to her. In short, she was told, live your own bloody life.

Godfrey explained that walking through the district the day before he had seen a crowd gathering outside Sharon's flat. The PSU had arrived with a pregnancy testing kit, keen to enforce the option they possessed to be judge, jury and executioner.

"So there they are, dear boy, stood on a little patch of grass outside her flat. In full view of the gathered they remove the testing kit and tell Sharon to spend a penny. They wouldn't even let her hold the stick herself! Anyway, naturally Sharon refuses to wee on command and so she's force-fed water and prodded to induce urination."

Godfrey paused for a long glug of Brandy.

"Meanwhile her mother's fainted, come round and fainted again, screaming in between. The father, as you know, is a rather meek man, quite unprepared for a tussle, especially with armed and trained operatives. He could only stand by and say encouraging things like, *'Don't worry lass'* and *'It's alright.'* Anyway, after she's pissed on the government stick, they confirm to her that, yes, she's pregnant and a nearby Blackguard immediately updates her *Citizen's Account* on his laptop. *Citizen deemed unstable*, he typed."

"Jesus Christ! Hard not tae feel a bit unsteady if a small platoon of armed men pop round your house tae decide whether you have any right over the being growen inside you!"

"Especially when this squad of men have the right to physically remove *you* from your home as well," agreed Godfrey. "For that's what they concluded. After remaining at the Taylor household for a little over twenty-seven minutes. Easily inside the time target, apparently. Efficiency, speed of judgment, Hair's message writ large. They'll probably be on course for a bonus at the end of the month. Credit where credit's due, though. The thing's only been going a day."

"And so what happened to Sharon?"

"Well as she wailed and screamed they asked her who the father was. *'My ex,'* she squeezed out between full-body sobs, sobs that induced a certain wobble in her physique and seemed to induce a quickening of the senses in the Commanding Officer, let me tell you. *'And where is the ex now?'* he demanded. *'Was he to be involved in the raising of this baby? Though quite how you thought you could bring a baby into this world without us knowing about it is beyond me.'"*

"Jesus wept."

"And so did Sharon. *'No... I, sob, "don't love him anymore,'* she replied. They immediately tried to take her away but Sharon was having none of it and held on to the door frame of her house while four Blackguard tugged at her to get her loose. *'Mam, don't let them! Dad! Dad!'* she screamed. But what could they do? Eventually with an almighty heave they loosed her from the house, taking the door frame with her."

"Fuck me."

"Quite. And the Commanding Officer then told her *'You'll thank us one day.'* The other guards picked her up and plonked her into the van, again amid much screaming. Once they had their hands free they cleared us onlookers, warning we'd be charged with starting an impromptu streetgig. Then Sharon was whisked away. And for her own benefit too, lest she forget."

"Where did they take her?"

"They said anyone receiving this service convalesces in a *LifeManagement4Life* Institute where more trained experts can monitor them. The most interesting point is that the orphanages promised by the Government are not yet up and running. It'll be a termination, a decision probably taken after a quick phone call from the field to PSU HQ."

"Aye Godfrey, this truly is Liberal Compassionate Britannia, eh? Killen unborn babies in the name of civil harmony, forcibly removen the so-called *misaligned* from friends and family, then dumpen them in the Shrink Clink."

"Well quite, dear boy. This last **KARMATARMAK** was supposed to be the final push to get the country back, but I fear I will never see freedom in Britain again."

## 22

# COME AGAIN?

*"IT IS WITH a heavy heart that I appear before you today,* (suck-in)."

Is it fuck! thought Cliffe.

*"During the night at around half-past eleven,* (suck-in)..."

The Siamese brothers had told Cliffe that sounded like the sort of time leaders died...

*"our esteemed President, Terry Hair, had a coronary arrest* (suck-in). *Medics were called to Buckingham Palace but despite efforts to revive him* (suck-in), *he died a short time later."*

I wish he fuckin well haddadone! It would have made this a bloody sight easier!

*"After meeting with the Cabinet it has been decided that I will be the one to replace Mr Hair* (suck-in)"

About bloody time to!

*"and carry on the good work that he and all of us in the Liberal Compassionate Party have been doing and will continue to do* (suck-in). *Terry Hair was a great leader,* (suck-in)"

Why did they make me say that?

*"and will be greatly missed* (suck-in)."

Yeah, like a hole in the balls!

*"But the work must go on..."*

"Oh I don't want to hear *him* bang on about our collective res-ponsibilities yaddy yaddy yaddah," said Sherry as she muted the tele-vision and pulled Fred closer to her.

"Of that, there is no doubt," Fred responded.

"I wonder what Terry's last words were," he added.

"*Et tu, Sherry.*"

"What?" Fred sat bolt upright in bed.

"What?" said Sherry dismissive, nonchalant.

"How do you know that?"

Sherry smiled, raised an eyebrow.

"You were there?"

Sherry nodded.

Fred was incredulous.

"You did it?"

"Well I didn't actually, you know, *do it*," Sherry responded, miming a stabbing motion.

"But you ordered it?"

"It wasn't just me."

"Well no, but...." Fred's mind whirred. "What, you and Cliffe concocted this together?"

"Why is that so astonishing?"

"Why is that so astonishing? Fucking hell Sherry!"

Fred was sat on the side of the bed, running his hands through his hair. "I thought you two hated each other."

"Well, I mean, yes, he is a terrible bore, with no sense of humour but we were in agreement that a change at the top was necessary. And anyway, life's too short for all that." She giggled, pulling a mock *oh-no!* face. "No pun intended."

"Well, I didn't see that coming. Although apparently your husband did. He told me of some apparition he had before-"

"Oh it worked did it?" responded Sherry, lighting a cigarette. "How wonderful."

"What worked?"

"Our little early morning spook session. We sent a couple of guys in to make ghost-like noises and generally be a bit eerie."

Fred started laughing.

"What is it?" Sherry asked.

"He thought all that was a dream."

Sherry erupted into a cackle and Fred felt a tiny bit scared. Here were people more like him than he had imagined. This was not what he had expected. Jesus, he'd been with her all night and she'd not mentioned anything! She'd come round late last night because she said her bed was cold. Fred *had* planned a night off to assemble his thoughts but took pity on a poor widow. Black widow, more like. He zipped his fly and tried to get focussed for his morning work. What he'd do next would be crucial.

"Brilliant," beamed Sherry as she flicked through Garqi's papers, laughing at the names for the PSU. "Which do you prefer, *Abortion Squad* or *Termination Crew*?"

Normally Fred would laugh too but not today. In fact, it unnerved him even more.

"Mother given Social Behavioural Points after teenagers caught for *swearing and arguing in the shared public domain,*" said Sherry.

Fred didn't like the sound of all this. Nor did he particularly like the sound of *his* mother on his voicemail, something about it being vital that the bondage between a mother and her child wasn't broken. Fred had too much to work out to worry himself with her. Even the fact that the next *Hellevue Hero* instalment was out today didn't move him from his task at hand.

"Do you think one day in Hellevue is enough?" asked Sherry. "Says here the PSU has moved on to other parts of the capital."

"Er, Sherry, I don't mean to be rude but-"

"You're busy, aren't you darling? Of course. Apologies. Asking questions that are none of my business. I'll be off. Anyway, need to go and make sure the *Clunking Fist* makes good on his promise and isn't gonna kick me out of the Palace! See you later, my sweet."

She grabbed Fred's face and kissed him on the nose. Such violent affection.

Fred knew that the time to act was coming. Maybe that Tenango character was right and this LUK *were* ready. As Cliffe had said, some Blackguard had deserted already and Fred had seen first-hand that tribal areas were hardly the place to retire to. People in government were always the first to know it was on its last legs and with Cliffe in charge the LibComs probably wouldn't last long now. He hadn't been surprised by the message he'd received from Denise late last night. She said she had no desire to work for Cliffe – who did? – and was now in the process of relocating to Brighton. Said Fred should come and visit her. Decisive woman, thought Fred. Maybe he would pop down.

But he had to work this out properly. He had to be safe when the Government came crashing down. Escaping before the LibCom regime had fully collapsed would be vital to avoid being caught up in the aftermath and reprisals. Those in government would pay a heavy price, no doubt. And with his track record and level of involvement...

At least Garqi could provide him with some alternative, whatever that was. But that probably would mean staying in Blighty and Fred had decided. He was going to meddle then vanish; a final bit of fun he couldn't resist. Then, so his plan went, he would relocate to another country.

Not so simple.

Fred was starting to feel genuinely nervous. He didn't plan to stay much longer, that was for sure. But for the first time in his life he didn't have all the answers.

Like the vast majority of modern Britannians, Fred had never been abroad. Though the ban on travel had only happened at the start of the LibComs tenure, the spiralling costs involved – environmental taxes on oil being the main one – had put it out of reach for the average person for quite a few years. Now, Fred was eager to experience what his father had talked of so feverishly in his youth. That was one of his abiding memories. That was why he was his father's son.

But the timing would be all-important. With any luck, he'd be out of the way, in a foreign clime, by the time the extent of his involvement in some of the more unpleasant government activity was uncovered. Ideally, he wanted to flee to France. It was always more of a mess over there. He would just blend into the chaos, but to get there would be tricky.

He had heard tell of some resourceful folk organising seabound vessels headed for mainland Europe and Scandinavia. But there were hazards involved. Many died on these treacherous voyages in decrepit old boats, often manned by inexperienced crew just trying to make a quick buck and enjoy a bit of adventure. And if you *were* lucky enough to arrive, then you had to contend with the rigmarole of being an Asylum Seeker.

According to the folklore Fred had heard there was often a frosty reception on the mainland. Particularly in France. *Les Gendarmes* would come and greet the brave and fatigued few perching on some rocks before packing them off to a holding bay for the authorities to figure out how they were to be processed. There had been communications between the French and Britannian governments but with the *Entente Cordiale* consigned to the scrapheap in which yesteryear's iPhone also lay decaying, official policy was to give a Gallic shrug, mutter '*c'est la vie.*' If there had been a sure-fire way of repatriating these people to the People's Republic of Britannia, then the French would no doubt take such an opportunity. As it was, they had all these Brits on their hands now, looking for shelter, wanting handouts. The proviso was compulsory French lessons as soon as your lips had touched a baguette.

The good news for the French Government was that anti-immigrants had been busy, killing a few Brits-abroad on arrival. This was probably the best deterrent they had. And it did seem to have an impact. Some said that often when the next vessel arrived from the Britannic landmass some of the stranded who had had quite enough of their continental jolly would try to get back on the boats to return to Blighty. But this was Fred's only option. And he had a smattering of French in any case.

Fred hoped that the collective might of a people wronged was about to achieve critical mass. He also hoped fervently he would be out of the way by the time it did. He didn't particularly want to be smeared all over the pavement, peeled off the ground and sent to his mother in a little brown parcel. He recalled now how he had alluded to this very scenario when selling his idea to Hair all those moons ago.

*"Sir, for a long time we have been a country mostly concerned with getting the next iPhone, yacht or whatever – whether that's the underclass looting in Tottenham or the elite-class looting of the banking crisis. But the revolution will come **here**, in Britain, when the middle class – the doctors, the lawyers, the graphic designers – can't scramble up the ladder. When **they** can no longer aspire, that's when there'll be visits in the night by gangs with baseball bats. The looters were punished more severely*

*than the bankers because more people associated with the rich, or at least, aspired to be part of the '1%'. When that is no longer an option, and people stare down the social ladder and realise they have more in common with the materialism of the dole bludgers, then hang on to your hats!"*

Fred knew the revolution was underway but he felt he could speed up the rate at which the Government crumbled. Provide more ammo and let **KARMATARMAK** and this LUK do the work. With that, he set to work on a missive to *Enigma*. He had no idea whether it would get through but he thought it worth a go.

## 23

# LIBERTY

A RAY OF golden sunlight permeated the room and as Pontiff awoke there was a half second of normalcy, of restitution, of grace. And then the horror kicked in. The psychological warfare of the hangover and awful recollection at the plight of Clem, himself, *everybody*, sludged through his blood like salty syrup.

He and Godfrey had spent a number of consecutive hours, both light and dark, drinking the ruinous whiskeysquash. Pontiff had always fancied himself a good old-fashioned honest smoker-drinker but the old man could certainly put the brandies away. Pontiff was glad he'd declined the hallucinogens.

He had vague memories of his host retiring to bed talking of thoughts in liquid form before he, himself, had started to lose the power of sight and began to slip in and out of consciousness. Pontiff had periodically awoken on the sofa, contorted. The rotundity was not ideal for slumber. He was certainly not enjoying much joined-up thought.

And so this morn Pontiff felt a little rough, lying unmoved on his back with his eyes closed. As he rolled over he inadvertently arsed the remote control, prompting the telly into action. Coming-to with the scruffy mug of Heath Cliffe in his face, Pontiff didn't see any need to stop drinking now. Quite the contrary.

"Holy fucken shit!" exclaimed Pontiff. The Joker was dead! Christ alive.

*"The work we have done since the Equalisation of living arr-angements will continue* (suck-in). *The savings we still have*

228

*from the disbanding of the Royals will continue to be used to lift
more Citizens out of relative discomfort* (suck-in)*.*"

Pontiff had been less than enamoured with the Windsors but having seen the alternative all was forgiven. He flipped the television off,
no desire to watch further.

The news of The Joker's death buoyed him momentarily, but a
sense of morbidity sent a wave of nausea washing through him, only
contributing to the biliousness of his belly and the pulsating of his head.
Sitting up unsteadied him and he dry wretched, gurgled and slumped
backwards into the sofa, hoping closed eyes and renewed thoughts
would give him a few moment's diversion. He drained the remainder
of a cup of brandy into his gullet and felt the warmth mingle with his
acidic stomach juices. He then began to feel rather uneasy. He needed
some fresh air.

The buzzer jolted him, caused his heart to pound. With the febrile
atmosphere of Hellevue Pontiff feared this could be a lynch mob. He
waited. The buzzer went again. A longer blast this time. Pontiff's heart-
rate was again raised to an uncomfortable level. There was nothing for
it. He'd have to wake Godfrey.

Pontiff tried manfully to propel himself off the sofa. Eventually, he
summoned the strength to rise, and once up, he actually felt better.
Shit-faced was a setting to which he was most accustomed. He opened
the door to his host's room and saw the old duffer in what looked like
the throes of a nightmare.

Pontiff nudged him and stood back, as though distancing himself
from an imminent explosion. Nothing. He stepped forward, nudged
again, but harder, and Godfrey awoke with a start of such violence he
tumbled out of bed.

"Jesus, sorry mate. Can I help y'up?"

"Thank you."

"I'm sorry tae wake you but the buzzer keeps goen."

With that it went again.

"It's been like that for a minute or so now."

"Right you are dear boy. I'll go and have a look. You stay in here.
Stay in the bedroom. It might be the LUK Media Unit."

"The what?"

"I'll explain later. Just stay in here for now. They won't come in here."

As Godfrey sloped off Pontiff felt truly abysmal. He really didn't fancy his host's chances of sweet-talking whoever it was at the door. His friend's calm facade had cracked. Godfrey had always seemed younger than his years but as Pontiff watched his old friend's frail shape move, this no longer appeared to be the case.

And is this now my life? thought Pontiff. Am I to be a fugitive forever? Was this now the LUK coming to make good on their blood-thirsty promises? Fuck me. I feel like Anne Frank and Julian Assange's lovechild. I hope he asked first.

Thirty seconds went by and there was no sound. And then Pontiff heard something – laughing – followed by the distinct sound of the Rev's wide gait thundering up the stairs. Pontiff rubbed his bald head feverishly, a sudden shooting pain went through his right eye. How much longer could he take this?

He vacated Godfrey's bedroom and sat magnanimously on the sofa, both arms extended across the bows. Godfrey entered the flat first, the priest with the belly following behind. He flashed Pontiff a peace salute.

"Reverend you fucken bastard! You'll gi'me a fucken heart attack!"

The Rev tossed some tobacco onto the table.

"A peace offering."

Pontiff snatched up the hemp pouch.

"All's forgiven."

"I also brought this."

The Rev set a bag of food on the table and Pontiff flitted between hunger and nausea as he emptied it.

"It's hardly plentiful," said the Rev. "Food rations have diminished further. We're all going to have to be very careful with what we eat, and when."

Pontiff took the long-life biscuits, the assortment of on-the-turn veg, the porridge oats and the dried river fish flakes to the kitchen, and put them in the cupboard. He then ripped a hunk off the old bread and mashed a lump of cheese into it. No point keeping that. With infrequent power, no fridges or freezers meant a perishables first policy. He handed the rest of the bread and cheese to the Rev.

"No thanks, Pont. I've eaten. Godfrey?"

Godfrey said nothing. He looked pained.

Pontiff hoped rolling a cigarette and lighting some candles might locate some calm. This became impossible when the Reverend handed him the day's paper.

*The Daily Rumour* had published a follow-up story on the murdering mother.

Pontiff began to read.

### "I ADMIT IT, I'M GUILTY"

*"I'd do anything to change what happened. In fact, I'm just so grateful to the Hellevue Hero for making me realise my awful mistake."*

Oh God, Huwi was probably right, Clem probably *was* in some sort of governmental, guantanomental gulag. But it wasn't only Clem's safety he feared for. The campaign to honour him was gathering apace. He turned to page two.

*"It is true that the Hellevue Hero did not attend his Awards Ceremony, held in his absence. But, dear Citizens, this hero is humble. His shyness and reticence for public accolade is a mark of the man. He is motivated only by doing the best for his community and country. He thanks you for your kind words and messages of support but for now he needs some respite. Rest assured we are in touch with him and when he wants to make his appearance, we will present him to you. Patience, Citizens, is a virtue."*

"You're all over the telly this morning as well," said the Rev.

"Fuckinell."

"Yeah."

Pontiff rubbed his face.

"Ah well, at least The Joker's death might take the heat offof ma story for a wee while."

"Yeah I just heard!" exclaimed the Rev.

Godfrey walked into the kitchen in something of a daze.

"I'll tell ya somethen Reverend, if God huz got a plan for us all, he's a sadistic bastard."

"I've heard that said. But we cannot know the mysteries of heaven."

"Aye well it's no the mysteries of heaven I'm concerned about. It's the mysteries of earth that trouble me."

From the look of the Rev's face Pontiff wasn't alone in that sentiment. Shaw had paid him a visit after Pontiff had left the day before. Helpfully, Huwi had informed the LUK that the Rev was Pontiff's best friend. Despite being challenged robustly, the Rev denied any contact.

"But Garqi's certainly done a number on you, eh?"

"Aye." Pontiff rubbed his head again, hoping for phrenological answers. "How we gonnae find her, Rev? Eh? An I cannae read any more about her boy. How can we know what tae think?"

That theme was occupying Godfrey's drug-addled mind as well. He felt jumbled in his mental dyspepsia, his attempts at philosophical musings and analytical contemplation were not having their usual desired effect. He came back into the lounge and began to pace the limited space in the middle of the round sofa.

"This is life, remember," he whispered to himself, "this is life. Inherently wonderful, inherently surprising, inherently deflating, inherently frightening, all of these things all the time, commonplace feeding the absurd back to the mundane and up to the exceptional."

"This ain't looken too pretty for any of us," said Pontiff as he and the Rev watched their friend circle like a stroke-victim cat. "Christ, what a mornen."

"I don't think the shape of the room helps."

"Aye," said Pontiff turning his eyes from Godfrey to the Rev. "Er, he was mentionen somethen about the Splenkstra taken hold or somethen?"

"Oh my goodness," responded the Rev. He crossed himself, and rubbed his eyes. "This happens from time to time when he partakes too much. Was he talking about translating words into liquid form?"

"Aye, aye. He said he was looken for answers yet kept finden himself translaten every word intae liquid form in his mind, aye."

"Don't worry. He'll stop in a minute."

And at that, Godfrey sat down.

"Did you mention something about Hair, dear boy?"

"Aye, he's carked it."

"I have no idea whether that's a good thing or not."

"Aye."

"Also," said the Rev, gravely, "there are reports that some **KT**ers have been arrested."

"Standard, dear boy. I would expect nothing less. Doubt there's anything in it. Just trying to flush us out, give us the hurry up."

"Maybe," continued the Rev. "But I saw Huwi's girlfriend on the way here."

"Oh yes?"

"Yeah, she was having a bit of trouble with the LUK's new social guidelines."

The new rules not only restricted movement for those in Hellevue. Friends and family from other districts wanting to visit had to be vouched for by a Hellevue Citizen before completing registration with the LUK border patrol. This morning as the Rev had gone to procure some grocery items, near The Forest Arms, near the north border of Hellevue, he'd spotted Huwi's girlfriend, frantic, being denied entry.

"She was shouting her mouth off about Huwi, shouting 'where is he? What have you done with him? You trashed our house!' He didn't go home last night apparently." The Rev paused, shook his head. "They were being very rough with her. I can't believe the brutality of these people. She's showing for crying out loud! I went over, calmed the situation down. But I couldn't vouch for her to come in. I didn't want to risk it. She's hardly the most together of women. I escorted to her parents' home, gave her some money. I promised I'd find Huwi and let her know. I feel dreadful."

Again Pontiff thought how timely his re-entry to Hellevue had been.

"She'll be alright, dear boy. She's got her parents."

"Well I doubt the LUK would have taken Huwi, that's all I'm saying," concluded the Rev. "What would be the motive?"

Godfrey went into the bedroom and returned with a rather battered-looking laptop.

"Do you mind if I pinch a fag, dear boy?"

"Not at all," responded Pontiff who then watched Godfrey roll a cigarette in one hand with strikingly swift dexterity. With the other, he turned on his machine to peruse the five minutes he allowed himself every morning. He did this as a matter of habit, looking at the LibCom website, Terry Hair's personal website and whatever Garqi was reporting to fuel ideas for his latest piece.

Also as a matter of habit he checked the array of email addresses he used for **KARMATARMAK**. Though very few people used the internet there was still, Godfrey was sure, an agency that combed the ether for seditious activity.

After a moment or two, "My God. Dear boys, *Ockham* has reopened lines of communication."

The RevKev blew out his cheeks.

"LUK'll be pleased," said Pontiff, sitting up.

The content of this latest missive was a little curious to say the least.

First, *Ockham* was delighted that the name for the resistance was the LUK. He said he knew *Enigma* would choose something like that, something that alluded to the traditions of the past.

Godfrey looked up.

"He thinks I'm in charge. Why on earth would he think that? Surely if he lives in Hellevue he'd know-"

Curiouser and curiouser.

But the thing that really caught Godfrey's eye, made the smoke catch in the back of his throat, was *Ockham's* claim that government agents had abducted, tortured and murdered a friend of free thinkers, a writer for **KARMATARMAK**.

The Rev gulped.

"You don't think Huw-"

"Or-" Godfrey couldn't finish that thought. A grotesque, sinking feeling told him it meant Clem.

As Godfrey read on though, his brain started to warm up, the after-surge of the drugs and drink started to wear off and a steadiness of mind that deserted him more frequently these days was re-enabled. There were myriad questions.

First of all, how on earth did *Ockham* know all this? By what means had he uncovered it? Surely these were suppositions. Or it was it merely agitprop, a bit of embellishment to embolden the nation, a further call to arms? Godfrey thought that must be the case for a moment. After all, *Ockham* hadn't revealed the identity of the writer. That called in to doubt the veracity of what he had written. But why lie about something so sensitive, so provocative? *Ockham* had always been so balanced and educated a writer, hence *Ockham's Razor*. Yet the tone of the piece was hardly in keeping with the ethos of the column. Something didn't sit right. In truth, very few things were sitting right in the mind of Godfrey. There was no explicit mention of where the abduction took place. Perhaps most crucially, if it was Clem, how did he know she wrote for **KARMATARMAK**? And if that was the case, surely that little titbit would have been part of the *Hellevue Hero* tabloid story.

"Now you do see what I'm saying?" said the Rev.

"Yes, dear boy, I think I do."

When the Rev had first mentioned Huwi's trashed house, Godfrey had thought it could have been a jealous lover but that seemed implausible. Huwi wasn't one to stray. Not unless his newfound power with the LUK had gone to his head and he was surrounded with revolutionary groupies.

"But let's not forget, dear boys, we accept articles from a lot of different people. It could be anyone really, given the numbers that were taken in during the raid."

Selfishly Godfrey was relieved if that was the case. No occasional contributor knew the identity of the **KARMATARMAK** hierarchy.

"In the past we have," agreed the Rev. "But this one was written almost exclusively by us, wasn't it? It must be Huwi. I expect Blackguard probably found articles he'd been working on in his house."

"Yes Kev, I expect you're right. If that has happened, that, dear boys, is distinctly bad news for us. If he's spilled the beans, which isn't all that unlikely let's be honest, then it won't be long until the Blackguard make a return."

But if it *was* true, and Huwi *was* dead...

"I think I need a drink," said Godfrey.

There was general concurrence.

"But how can *Ockham* possibly know about the LUK yet not know it was Calloway who has corralled the masses into revolutionary action?" continued Godfrey. "Clearly he does not live in Hellevue."

Pontiff looked at this deflated old codger, mentally battered from years of partaking but still possessing of some semblance of erudition yet.

"Of course, if it is true, who does that make *Ockham*?" asked the Rev.

"Exactly, dear boy! How on earth could he know all of this? Surely he must work for the Government, or at least have links. Unless he has been doing fearless undercover work? Maybe," continued Godfrey, in morbidly fascinated tones, "he was even present when it happened?"

"Godfrey, please!" snapped the Rev. "If it is true then..." He crossed himself. "God rest his soul."

"Well yes, OK, apologies, dear boy. But can we trust it? I just don't know what to make of it."

Neither did Pontiff. But if it was true he hardly felt bad for Huwi.

"Could it be a trap?" continued Godfrey. "Have my mails been hacked into?"

"Aye, mebee," said Pontiff. "But that doesnae mean you can't ask tae meet him."

"Or her," interjected the Rev.

"Or her," agreed Pontiff. "Either way I think protocol's gottae gan out the window a wee bit, eh? The course of events is hardly followen a pattern, is it? Unless, it's been ordained by some higher being, eh Reverend?"

"But where would I meet him? Or her?" asked Godfrey. "If *Ockham* lives outside Hellevue, how will he... or she, get in? Also I'm not entirely sure I want to be giving away my identity what with my survival largely depending on keeping that as far from the public domain as possible. What if it is a trap?"

"Meet em in Hellevue. I'd like tae see someone try and infiltrate this district. Even if they did, even if they knew it was you, what could they do?"

"No, I'm not going to do that. But I will respond. There's just a chance this person, whoever it is, might be able to give some info on Clem. If he – or she – responds to that, then I'll meet. But we must box clever."

There was a long blast on the buzzer.

"Oh fuck," muttered Godfrey, startling Pontiff and the Rev with the departure in his vernacular.

"That *will* be the LUK Media Unit this time I fear, dear boys."

There was another, long buzz, followed by two sharp stabs.

"Right Pontiff, get in the cupboard in my room. At all costs do not come out. Whatever happens. Rev, it is best you leave. I'll let you out when I let them in."

The two stood there, marvelling at the return to form of Godfrey's mental faculties.

"Please dear boys, hurry," said Godfrey, closing down his computer.

The idea of creating a buzz about your work had not been lost on Calloway. What he and the LUK needed to do now was spread the word about the rebellion and tackle the government spin machine. And that meant a new phase in LUK control. The creation of a Media Unit.

While the vast majority of the populace had come to follow a more 'natural' mode of existence, camcorders, video equipment, editing software and the like had gathered dust. Much of it was now out of order as the vast majority of electrical goods had been built to break down within three years so you had to buy another one. Yet buried deep in people's closets the LUK had found plenty of propitious devices. All this hitherto dormant equipment – which many folk had forgotten about or been too scared to use except for home videos or little films – had now been gathered, given a bit of a wipe and put to use for seditious ends.

Of course, getting use out of these archaic technological lumps required electricity and so having forced the denizens of Hellevue to hand over what gadgets they still owned, the Media Unit were now back out traversing the district, going house-to-house, using an hour's worth of electricity at each home they went to, charging equipment and editing footage. If they came round to use your supply and there wasn't at least an hour available to them they were not best pleased.

Naturally, in the films they were putting together the sense of community in Hellevue was highlighted, that the district was full of happy Citizens sharing rations, helping each other, living a decent life, the LUK at the heart of it all. Juxtaposed to this was footage of unnecessary heavy-handedness from the Blackguard. Training videos were being made as well, designed to inspire others to join the fight. From here, these images and videos would be sent to the state media. Whether they were played or not – and it was likely they would not – the Government would at least know of them. There had also been talk of posting some videos on the internet but that wasn't believed to be crucial as the audience would be so small.

Pontiff heard them come in, heard them plug in their equipment. From what he could make out the two electricity droogs had been joined by Shaw. As Pontiff expected, it didn't take long for Shaw to enquire about the *Hellevue Hero*.

"The dear chap would have to be out of his mind to come back to Hellevue. Anyway I would wage my house on the fact he's still in custody."

"Vat's a big wager," responded Shaw. "What about *Ockham*? In touch wiv him yet?"

"It's all but impossible, I'm afraid. The old passwords don't work anymore. I tried but I've heard nothing back."

"OK. And what about Huwi. You know anyfing about his whereabouts?"

Godfrey responded to the negative.

"No? Oh well. I fought you might but never mind. It just means you're gonna have to retake control of ve zine. We want a new one ready in a week. Rev can write summing an'all. An get ve rest of ve crew on board too."

"If I may ask, what use is **KARMATARMAK** now? Surely it has achieved what you wanted?"

"And what you wanted as well, surely?" Shaw retorted.

He paused, waiting for a response. "Also, I dunno if you know but President Grinning Prick has died."

Pontiff heard a corroborative mumble.

"And as a result he will be needing a funeral. Now, vat will happen in two days' time. And so we have decided to bring our plans forward and operations will begin in earnest on vat day. So we need to make sure vat vese fings are recorded so's we can spread our message far and wide, to unify wiv ve tribal areas, to report ve reclaimin of British land for British people. And vat is why you will be writing all about it."

It was probably laughing in Shaw's face that earned Godfrey a kicking. And it was probably because they didn't believe Godfrey portrayed the necessary commitment to his tasks that Shaw felt it unwise to leave the old dear in situ. He was going to go with them and do his work like a good boy. And with that, they were off, Godfrey in tow. As they left, Pontiff looked out the window.

Jesus fucking Christ! he thought as he looked at the man with Godfrey. Him? The very man with whom Pontiff had had a run-in on his first night in Hellevue was the gadgie Huwi hailed as a saviour? Godfrey looked briefly to the window and with that gaze a horrifying thought hit Pontiff. Would Godfrey return?

## 24
## IN MEMORIAM

TODAY MARKED A memorial of sorts for the one-time saviour of the land, Terry Hair. Fred knew Cliffe would rather spend his time massaging Asbestos into his eyes but he had to make an appearance for the sake of propriety. As did Fred, whose breakfast was digesting, but not quite as pleasantly as it normally did.

Fred had begun to hope he would be left out in the cold by Cliffe. If he was marginalised he could spend more time plotting his escape. Yet the rubber-faced tree seemed reliant on his advice. Though he didn't like Fred – Fred knew that amongst Cliffe and the Siamese he was referred to as the *Punjabi Homo* – the new leader certainly respected his intellect, political tactics and decision making. And so at Cliffe's behest Fred had been working almost exclusively on *Cow* announcements over the last two days, putting out reports of a new start for the LibComs, admitting that there had been the odd mistake. Crushingly dull.

During this time Fred had managed to look a bit more into sea travel and had decided that going incognito with a change of identity was the way forward. As soon as he had procured a handful of new NIPSD cards with different identities he would be off.

Strangely, Fred had sought no female companionship over the last few days. He wanted to get his head straight. He had had one conversation with Sherry at the Palace. She had refused to move out and had commandeered a wing. She was drinking heavily and dabbling in young girls.

"Widowhood seems to be suiting you."

"Oh yes," said Sherry with one of her trademark giggles. "You wouldn't believe the freedom."

"I can imagine."

"I've been practicing my miserable face for The Joker's funeral but as I'll be under a black veil I might allow myself the odd grin here and there."

This behaviour from Sherry no longer concerned him. The thing that most concerned Fred was the absence of response from *Enigma*. He was starting to think the message hadn't got through. Was the poor fucker even still alive? Maybe I should have told him the name of the writer, thought Fred. But he had decided against that. He wanted to tease *Enigma* in. He felt that would lead to greater action.

Fred grabbed a beer and started to mull over what would happen next, indeed what was happening now. If I'm scheming and so is Garqi, well what then? But what on earth has Garqi got up his sleeve? Fred had had no contact with the Italian in the last few days either, yet was sure that the development of which Garqi had spoken would be making progress. I wonder if they're making progress in Hel-

Fred's laptop pulsed. *Enigma*. Well here we go.

**Dear Boy, so wonderful to hear from you. Time is short and we all of us need as much of that as possible to ensure we are making the correct decisions.**

**I am uncertain about many things you write. But this is what I have understood from your missive.**

**The fact that you know about the LUK yet are not aware of the details of its inception gives me to believe that you do not live in Hellevue. If you did, you would know that the LUK was not started by me. THE LUK have hijacked KARMATARMAK. I do not back them.**

Fred wasn't sure whether to believe this. He suspected *Enigma* might be protecting himself.

**At first I was not entirely convinced that what you were saying was true. Why did you not say who it was? Here I am prepared to stick my neck out. I am certain it is Don Coyote who is gone. And if that is the case, here is what I think of you. You are either a government operative or a state journalist.**

**Either way, if what you say is true, you have links to the upper echelons of the LibComs and therefore I can appreciate you do**

**not want to reveal yourself. But if that is the case I have an unusual request on an entirely different matter.**

Fred had underestimated *Enigma*. He expected a man enraptured by the hurricane of governmental deposition. Instead, Fred had been systematically picked apart.

But what was this separate matter?

**It relates to the newspaper story involving Clementine Romain. She is an old friend and I am concerned for her safety. There is not even the remotest chance she is responsible for the death of her son nor would she have let him die. To be honest, I don't know whether to believe the reports that her son is dead. If you do have ways of finding out, of where she is, how she is, please let me know what you can.**

**I would like to tell you so much about life in Hellevue but these are dangerous times and I cannot afford to divulge too much to someone of whose identity I cannot be sure.**

**I await your response.**

I don't fucking believe this, thought Fred. Again he had that feeling that events were getting ahead of him. First, Sherry kills Terry and now this? And then another thought cannonballed into him. If this Clementine Romain is known by *Enigma* and also by the Hellevue Hero, do Pope and *Enigma* know each other?

Fred's intrigue in the Hellevue Hero was suddenly reignited. As yet, there had been no further stories. Both he and Garqi were far too pre-occupied. Fred was tempted to respond and ask *Enigma* whether he did know this Pope. But he thought better of it. He needed time to formalise a proper response. But if *Enigma* didn't support the LUK, and more specifically, didn't start it, what was going on over there? Jesus, I really must get out, thought Fred. There were too many things happening he didn't know about.

For now, Fred had the other issue at hand.

\*\*\*

The summer rains were lashing down as Fred arrived at the rather quaint choice for the ceremony, an old cricket pitch in the north of the capital. It was a wooded area once known as Hampstead Heath. Ever since the LibComs had taken a leaf out of Pol Pot's book and banned the practicing of religion, folk had had to get creative (or very secretive) with the type of funeral they had. Sherry had said her deceased amour would appreciate something uniquely English despite the fact he had set about tearing down most of the traditions of the land in favour of modernisation.

There was hardly anyone present, and those that were, were huddled under a makeshift marquee cover. Even the master of cere- monies (an elderly LibCom functionary) seemed bored. It was all a bit yesterday's news. Dead politician? What difference did it make? Esp- ecially when most in attendance were thinking good riddance. That's gratitude for you, thought Fred. Get people into power and yet they still can't wait to bury you. Dirty business, politics, but politicians probably get what they deserve.

Incredibly he didn't view himself as one.

Fred noticed that those present were quite keen not to appear too upset. Even those that had supported Hair. They didn't want to incur the displeasure of their new leader, who paid brief, cool tribute. It was to be expected, all this, thought Fred. When people sense a shift in power they quickly realign themselves to ensure they are in a good position when the change happens. Having got into this position, they weren't going to go and blow it with a bit of misdirected loyalty. Staying on-message was essential to political survival. Sherry, flanked by two female companions, claimed she was too emotionally tangled to say anything but she just couldn't be bothered. She just wanted to get back to the Palace and put all this Terry business behind her.

As the funeral was winding down, and a few people were taking surreptitious glances at their watches, sudden unprecedented action lifted the gathered from their narcoleptic milieu.

Ratatatatatatat! Ratatatatatat! Ratatatatata!

And then more gunshots rang out. A handful of government oper- atives went down. A bullet whistled past Fred's ear. It was like coming under siege at a 1980's IRA funeral.

Ducking down, Fred looked towards the pavilion where a gaggle of men dressed in camogear were reloading. He then looked down the small hill on which this part of the heath stood. Scores of Blackguard were powering up it, returning fire. In the middle of all this, in the cross-fire, the funeral brigade were almost all exclusively face down in the mud and screaming.

At the pavilion, some of the gunmen went down as more bullets whistled through the air from Blackguard guns.

Ratatatata! Ratatatatataat!

The remaining assailants began retreating into the woods, returning fire at intervals. Blackguard followed them in, firing, eliminating more of the attackers. Fred saw Cliffe and the Siamese brothers being bundled into a white car while Hair's body lay on a mound of sodden dirt, unburied, his casket tipped over by the fleeing mourners, more of which were being mowed down. One of Sherry's girls took a hit in the leg. Fred took cover down a ditch in some nettles and watched as Blackguard pursued the assailants further into the undergrowth. More Blackguard and PHU reinforcements arrived and as the attackers retreated further, they were picked off one by one. Fred mused it might have made sense to keep a few alive to gather some Intel.

But now Fred knew that if he stayed involved in government activity his life was at risk. He had never dreamed it would get this far. This was another reminder that the era in which he was master of proceedings was over. He would now be scrabbling around in the dirt trying to survive just the same as everyone else.

Nursing a few stings and caked in dirt, Fred emerged from his cover and saw Cliffe's white car about-turn and screech across the grass, churning it up as it went. Having searched the bodies of the attackers Blackguard had found that all had been carrying cards. They were handed to Cliffe, who seemed suddenly panicked. He dropped them from his grasp and returned to his car. Off it went, further spraying those that remained with bits of blood and mud.

Fred, rather sodden, ambled over to the gathered platoon of Blackguard and looked at the cards himself. The Government had had their first taste of direct conflict from the LUK. Tenango had been right. As Fred looked at the cards he found it strange and intriguing that while Tenango had been rabidly pro-LUK *Enigma* was decidedly reticent.

And then a strikingly dry and dapper looking Garqi showed himself, dressed in a white suit increasingly spattered with bits of mud. He was holding a tiny device, chuckling to himself. He looked up to see Fred walking towards him.

"Oh Freddi dear, you look awful."

"Where have you been, Oli?"

Garqi pointed to the sky behind him but stayed his gaze on his device. In the commotion Fred had failed to hear the *NewsZeit!* Chopper.

Garqi laughed.

"Dis eez perfect," he said, showing Fred some of the rushes of the day so far. Fred was in awe of the device, filled with covetousness. "Oh Freddi dear. Today I make amazeen television. We broadcast foo-neral live!"

"Wow, that's-"

"Also. We've receive some videos from dis LUK. We gonna broadcast dem shortly."

Fred was struggling to take all this in.

"An in dee next few days Piers will be printeen photographs in dee papers illustrateen dat great areas of dee country are in defiance of government rule."

Fred knew Garqi wouldn't be doing any of this sterling destabilising work unless he had his other plans in place. Fred wondered if Mormon knew everything, if he was in on it too. He remembered that Mormon had been in trouble in the past for faking war photographs but apparently he was pretty sure these were the real deal. Not that it mattered either way. But Fred didn't like the feeling of being side-stepped even if Garqi had given him an oblique offer of a new job.

## 25
# WHEN IS IT?

PONTIFF WAS FEELING better today. As though he'd woken up for the first time in, well, how long had it been? Days? A week? Maybe not that long, but these last hours had been hell.

The feature of this amorphous, unspecified time had been a descent into serious disrepair. He had had bouts of unconsciousness, fever, swollen joints as though from a bite, so painful he couldn't walk, a feeling as though limbs were broken, a hacking, phlegm-filled cough. He feared he had contracted *Plasticitis* and was preoccupied with notions of his own death. But for now, the aching and the coughing seemed to have subsided. This was most definitely a lucid moment. But what day was it?

The recent period of duress had also been characterised by solitude, and Pontiff's need to escape the madness this induced was becoming particularly pressing.

In the kitchen he opened the cupboard to see what meagre delights he could eat. He removed the bread he found. He knocked on it, a hollow tone communicating inedibility. It was dispatched to the bin. He noticed the long-life biscuits left only their wrapper and looking further, surveyed only a squidgy cucumber and a few tomatoes in the latter stages of putrefaction. A cold repast of decomposing fruit didn't really grab him. The remnants of a cold veg stew sat on the camping stove. The smell made Pontiff wretch. He had a vague recollection of making it. The last thing he'd remembered eating was some long-life cake. The whiskeysquash bottle was empty.

And then he thought of Clem. Fuck, I need tae get outside.

Hungry, alone, a prisoner, all booze drunk, all tobacco smoked, unable to turn on the lights for fear of discovery, Pontiff had decided that regardless of the reception he would receive, probable violence, maybe worse, he couldn't stay in Godfrey's flat for the rest of his life. He worried for the old man's safety, especially given his mental state when he had been taken. He wondered whether Godfrey would come back, whether he was still alive. He was, after all, an increasingly frail man who may have decided to voice his antipathy to Shaw and his gang.

Pontiff decided he would visit the Rev, try and procure some alcohol and tobacco, and go from there. He had looked in Godfrey's wardrobe, waded through the incredible range of mad psychedelic clobber, none of it suitable. Clyde's raincoat was too heavy – especially if Pontiff was going to have to wear a scarf and hat to disguise himself – so he needed an alternative item. He found an old waterproof jacket in his host's cupboard, put Clyde's hat and scarf on and was about to attempt an exit – though having not swiped in at the communal door, he wasn't entirely sure how he'd achieve that – when the door to the circular room opened and in walked Godfrey. He looked awful.

"Jesus man, y'awright?"

"Not massively, dear boy, no."

He put his bag down.

"Here. I brought some food."

Pontiff was suddenly ravenous though the sight and humour of his host disallowed the appetite somewhat.

"Why on earth are you dressed like that, dear boy?" questioned Godfrey, face cracking a smile.

"I was gan out. I dinnae ken where you were. Thought about gan tae see the Rev. It was this or nothen."

Godfrey's smile collapsed.

"The Rev's been rather ill. I was going to see him myself later."

Godfrey sat down, puffed out his cheeks.

"What a few days."

He turned to smile at Pontiff.

"How have you been, dear boy?"

"Well I been dae-en mental somersaults ever since I ran out of alcohol and baccy. But never mind that. What's happened tae you?"

"I've been locked in a room at LUK HQ, written almost an entire **KARMATARMAK** and while I was at it went about tidying up the LUK manifesto. The Rev was also supposed to be commandeered into action but as he was ill, the whole thing fell to me. In another room, a band of Neanderthal footsoldiers doodled campaign posters about Clem in which death for the Hellevue Hero was promised, along with anyone protecting him."

"Oh lovely," said Pontiff.

Godfrey nodded.

"But they've stopped going on about Huwi now. After I was taken off the other day we all swung by the pub. Huwi hadn't showed again. In fact, no-one's seen him for the last few days."

"So I guess that means he's the one *Ockham* was talking about."

"Well probably," said Godfrey, as he opened a bottle of apple brandy. He poured himself and Pontiff a glass. It was as far removed from smooth as you could find but it was a case of needs must. "It's hard to know for certain," he continued. "But I have managed to write to *Ockham*."

Godfrey told Pontiff what he had written, how he had been worried to ask about Clem in case it was a trap and she was then implicated by association. That would do her no favours in custody.

"But what choice did I have? It was worth a go, to say that I was a concerned friend. I also asked for information on Ben."

"What did you say about Hellevue?"

"Not a lot. I certainly didn't mention Clem was involved in **KT**. *Ockham* could be anyone."

Godfrey took another sip of brandy and leant back on the circular sofa, pressing the glass to his head. "Mind you, things are definitely changing. Garqi's been playing LUK videos."

"Jesus! Why?" asked Pontiff.

"Mmm, strange for the news to report something that challenges the hegemony of the Government's power, eh?"

Godfrey sat forward to pour another drink. He studied Pontiff's appearance again.

"Are you sure it's a good idea to go out there, dear boy? It isn't only your safety that's compromised if you're recognised."

"I know that Godfrey. But how long am I supposed to live like this?"

"Oh let's have some food."

Godfrey grimaced as he got up to go to the kitchen, still bruised from the other day, quite unaccustomed to receiving a kicking for breakfast.

\*\*\*

As Pontiff set off, garbed to the hilt (having been offered a pair of blue jean flares, he'd stuck with Clyde's chinos) the monsoon had abated temporarily. There was a crisp cleanliness in the air, the rain having removed some of the humidity. It was a glorious sunny day. Not ideal hat-and-scarf weather.

"Just remember what I said," said Godfrey. "And be back here within three hours. Here's some cash if you want some booze. I suggest you get it round here. This part of the district isn't quite so rabid. Good luck."

Over food, Godfrey had told Pontiff of the LUK attack on Hair's funeral but news of the morning's proceedings had clearly not got back to this particular part of Hellevue. As Pontiff walked the streets near Godfrey's flat he was greeted by fellow Britons standing around, laughing, playing football, drinking homemade scrumpy. Pontiff bought some and marvelled at, and resented in, equal measure these folk doing their best to thoroughly ignore the day's events. They may not even have known that Hair had died, let alone that it was his funeral, much less that the resistance had attacked.

This might be the part of town for me, thought Pontiff.

As he got further towards the hub of LUK territory a different atmosphere became apparent. It was like there was a deadline for some future action. The people looked mobilised, but in an enforced way, a pallor covering their faces. The reason for this remarkable yet sombre work ethic became apparent soon enough.

Pontiff looked in horror as he passed The Dissention Wall. There were names of people who had deserted the LUK. Their heads were on sticks. Citizens accused of being government sympathizers or those believed to have colluded with the Government had also met their demise. There had been interrogations of families of known Black-guard, some of them killed too. Sharon Taylor's neighbour was there. Or rather his head was. As was John Rer's. This probably goes some way towards explaining the pallor, thought Pontiff, and was all the evidence he needed the LUK were not the answer, nor that an after-noon constitutional might have the restorative effect he had hoped for. He saw posters all over the place – some less than flattering ones about himself. And a poster of Calloway with a cigar and two hot young women.

### "TODAY HELLEVUE, TOMORROW WESTMINSTER!"

As Pontiff shuffled on with increasing trepidation he noticed the long queue at the checkpoint gate, many being turned away. He dec-ided he'd seen quite enough but knew by now Godfrey would have left the flat and gone to see the Rev. Pontiff had promised he would not follow suit. He concluded that a game of street football with the some-what carefree folk near Godfrey's flat was the way to go. He melted into the crowd and tried to meander his way back from whence he had come. It was as effective as wading against the tide at a festival. From the other direction there was a sudden surge of people, cheering, fists pumping in the air, and Pontiff found himself in the middle, jostled from side to side, chants of "L-U-K!" filling the air.

The street was now teeming with LUK operatives and plenty of folk who seemed to support them wholeheartedly – that, or they'd seen the Dissention Wall. There was mass praising of the resistance, victories against the Blackguard being detailed. All Citizens were being urged to fight. Aside from sabotaging Hair's funeral the LUK had ambushed, robbed and captured military personnel in the surrounding areas of Hellevue. Pontiff was sickened as he saw three bodies in ripped Black-guard uniform being dragged through the street, spat on, kicked, punched. Fearing he was next and sensing he was about to vomit, Pontiff managed to extricate himself from the malevolent pack fever, finding refuge down a nearby alley.

But it wasn't long before his day got worse.

He had removed his hat and scarf, and was bent double, thick mucus hanging from his mouth when he became aware of a presence.

"You alright vare son?"

Pontiff straightened, turned towards the voice. Overwhelming nausea stymied his sight. A phlegmy bubble noise was all he could summon. Through his liquid vision he began to make out who was before him. On either side were Guevara clones, and there, in the middle, was a man he remembered. Pontiff felt he'd handled himself pretty well the night they'd met. Score draw would have been the neutrals' verdict. He didn't fancy his chances this time. Pontiff took in the physical appearance, the camo cap, the stubble, the missing front tooth, the feral eyes, the squat torso and lamented his decision to leave the relative security of Godfrey's abode.

"We know each uvver, don't we?" said the man with a smile, exposing more absent denture. He remembered this foreigner being pretty handy.

"Aye," said Pontiff straightening.

"I don't fink we've been introduced vo'. I'm Arnie Shaw." Shaw stuck out his hand. "You're Pontiff, innit?"

Pontiff nodded, holding his elbow.

Shaw snapped his teeth together, bulged his jaw.

"I fort it was you when I read ve papers."

"Aye," said Pontiff, wiping his mouth with the back of his wrist.

Shaw pointed his nose upwards, smelled the air.

If he says somethen about loven the smell of victory in the afternoon...

"There's a lot people don't like wotchoo did," said Shaw, snapping his head back earthwards.

I am never gonnae live this fucker down, thought Pontiff.

"Yeah, that barman in particular. E's got a real soft spot for vat Clem, innit? Wants to end your life." Shaw laughed. And then he started to shake his head. "What are we gonna do wiv you, eh? There's people screamin for your blood. I'm sure it would give everyone a lift if we paraded you about a bit."

So this is how it ends, is it? Down an alley with a toothless thug before huvven ma carcass thrown to the masses. Ah well. Seems fitten.

"Before we get to vat vo', I am intrigued as to when you arrived back."

Shaw rubbed his right fist with his left hand.

"It is naughty of you not to have made yourself known. Where have you been hidin? We know you weren't at your 'ouse. Have you seen it?"

Pontiff nodded.

Shaw made a gesture with his hand, and two cigarettes were presented by one of the Guevara clones. Shaw lit them both and handed one to Pontiff. Pontiff nodded, wiped some more sick off his lips.

"Well?" said Shaw again.

There was a long pause.

Shaw stared at Pontiff, smoked.

"I been back a few days. Sleepen rough. I came back tae Hellevue cos it was the only way to put things right. Tae clear ma name."

Shaw nodded. "And you haven't tried to get in touch wiv your old pals?"

"Nah. I mean I thought about it, sure, but nah."

Shaw pulsed his lips in and out. He turned to his two henchman, smiling a toothless grin.

"So what do we do? You have made it difficult for yourself, avvenchoo? That said, your story is very useful. Adds to ve indignation of ve Hellevue massive. Gives em sut'ing to focus their ate on. Yeah," he paused, "I am glad I've bumped into you thisartanoon."

Shaw allowed Pontiff a little stewing time.

"You know," continued Shaw, walking towards Pontiff, putting a hand on his arm, "I always said to Huwi, Calloway, and a few of ve uvvers, 'maybe he did it, maybe he didn't.'"

Shaw continued to circle Pontiff who smoked on like a Frenchman, sucking in the final tokes of stoicism.

"But don't worry," said Shaw suddenly, grabbing Pontiff by the shoulders, grinning broadly, "I'm ere to help ya." Shaw leant in, raised an eyebrow, ferociously chewed gum. "And I fink you," he said with a jab in Pontiff's chest, face getting closer, "could elp us as well. Yeah," said Shaw, walking back to his henchmen, "wiv your, shall we say, chequered past, I fink you should offer your services to ve community, don'choo? Presumably you don't want to have to swan around in vat preposterous get-up too much longer. State of vose fuckin trousers."

"You're very persuasive."

Shaw smiled. Aye, thought Pontiff, and if persuasion doesn't work violence usually does.

"Jus wha-"

"I'm glad you ask, I'm glad you ask, Pontiff. It's important for people to show willing. Particularly vose vat have let vemselves down such as yourself. Now, lemme ask you sut'ing. Have you grasped what we're tryna do ere?"

"I've grasped the idea that you cannae instigate change by being nicey-nice."

"Are you saying I'm not nice?" laughed Shaw. "Oh no," he said as he put his hand to his heart, "you hurt my feelings." He rubbed his stubble. "You know what Pontiff, I like you. You're a man who bucks ve system. I like vat. And d'you know what? Talkin to you today has given me a little idea. A little plan on how to use you."

Oh for fucken fuck's sake, what is this? thought Pontiff. Why am I flavour of the fucken month?

"Briwyant," he responded.

"Good. Cos I want to give you ve opportunity... to put right some wrongs." There was a pause. "How does vat sound to ya?"

Before Pontiff could speak-

"I see you're lost for words. Let me explain."

It was some plan.

Pontiff was to get in touch with *The Rumour*, agree to meet Garqi and Mormon again, say he would accept their accolades as long as it was done on live TV. Then the LUK wanted Pontiff to attack the Government with his acceptance speech before the LUK stormed the building.

"That sounds great. Um, the thing is Arnie, can I call y'Arnie?"

Shaw made a magnanimous hand gesture.

"The thing is, I fear I may well be sent tae prison with that little ruse and I've been in once, and escaped another time, so-"

Shaw was mock apologetic. He put both hands up.

"I've said ve wrong fing. I do apologise. I mean obviously I'm a bit insulted vat you doubt our capabilities. I mean it almost sounds to *me*... thatchoo don't want to be a part of all vis."

Pause. He chewed his gum.

"And vat can't be right, can it?" Shaw smiled, gumstrands on the canines. "If you help us, we'll help you. Your name will be cleansed round ere. You could have your life back."

Aye thought Pontiff, and owe you a debt forever more. Ah life, it's no what I hud in mind.

Of course without LUK support he would be out at the mercy of the masses. Had he made the right choice coming back to Hellevue? He was no closer to finding Clem.

"An so after I've made my little speech, you boys will be rescuen me, is that correct?"

Shaw nodded.

"If I may ask, jus how are you gonnae be on hand tae, you know, pounce?"

Shaw turned to his two aides and nodded, smiling. "He's good, innit?" he said, tapping his forehead. "Always finking." He turned back to Pontiff. His smile collapsed. "Look. We are entering a crucial phrase. Today, we've caused untold disruption at Hair's funeral. Annat's just ve start. More and more Blackguard are defecting to us. So yes, when we are ready, you will collect your little award and we'll be on hand. But ve most important fing," said Shaw, pointing his left index finger skywards, "is we are seeing more and more assistance from regular people and vat is creating a sense of enormous optimism and strength."

"Do they huv any choice?"

One of the henchmen stepped forward and slapped Pontiff.

"Do not show insolence to the leader!"

"Alright, alright, easy," laughed Shaw. "Ve fing is Pontiff, people are choosing to fight because vey know ve future is not Liberal Compassionate."

"Well it certainly isn't with you boys."

They didn't take kindly to that. Pontiff was no stranger to intimidation and wasn't unduly alarmed by being placed against a wall with his midriff exposed to some repetitive striking from the de facto deputy leader of Hellevue.

"Look Pontiff, I can see you're a bit emotional at ve moment but I'd advise you not to say anyfing you're gonna regret. Nowrovcourse, you don't have to give me your answer now. I'm gonna give you a little bit of time to fink about it. But, what I will say is, if you want to stay round ere, you will work for us. We can't protect you unless you do."

As he lay on the ground Pontiff spied his still burning cigarette. He picked it up, returned it to his bouche and staggered to his feet.

"Remember, we have ve power to change perceptions. If you join us, not only will your life be easier and safer, you'll also be makin ve revolution stronger. Ven you really would be a hero. If, on ve uvver-and, you do not come on board, well... good luck livin on ve streets out here. You'll be hunted down like ve traitor you are."

Pontiff remained silent.

"You were in ve streets earlier. You saw ve joy because of our attack on Hair's funeral." Shaw wiped something from his nose, looked at it. "If you don't join us, you can forget about living in vis manor, you can forget about living anywhere we have links. Now enjoy tonight, Mr Pope, and it will be some night. Think we'll be havin a bitta fun wiv our Prisoners of War."

Shaw smiled, rubbed his hands, before he serioused himself again.

"Tomorrow, we want your final answer. I won't detain you any longer. I wouldn't take a man's last night from im, I know what it's like. Just remember. You won't be able to show your face round'ere if you make ve wrong choice. And once you've made your choice, vat's it. You best get in touch wiv me tomorrow so vat we can come to a mutually beneficial arrangement. Vat's ve last time I'm gonna make this generous offer. Now fuck off."

Pleasant to the last, thought Pontiff. Of course, the only *fucking off* to be done was by Shaw and his aides, and Pontiff stared after them as they departed.

Pontiff had fallen foul of the rules of the land but held fast to the idea that falling foul of the LUK would be worse. Calloway, Shaw, their motivation was the same as Hair's. All political leaders had that same vainglorious streak, to be the saviour. There was little to choose between any of them, thought Pontiff. It was all rather teetering on the brink of Carry On Revolution, Carry On Up Your Cromwell. Aye, if it wasn't all so fucken serious. Pontiff had no desire to go back to *Life-Management4Life*. Or somewhere worse. He'd probably be in there indefinitely this time. The LUK could certainly afford him protection from the Government – in the short term anyway – and any time he didn't spend in government custody was time well spent.

# 26

# LIBERTY FOR THE UNITED KINGDOM

HAVING GONE HOME for a shower Fred arrived at Buckingham Palace late in the afternoon to find a frantic Cliffe flanked by the Siamese brothers. He was having some sort of tantrum, sporting his usual weathered look, that of a man who'd either just had a fight or was about to get into one. The big bags under his eyes looked like they would ooze with pus if pricked with a pin. All those years he could have been leader and now when he had finally managed to get the job events seemed to be conspiring against him. He wanted to cry. Which didn't surprise Fred. Cliffe had always struck him as a whinger and whiner. If Hair threw his toys out of the pram from time-to-time, Cliffe was the temper-tantrum wimp, melding ditherinesss with cold-blooded calculation. All these supremos really are, thought Fred, are kids with money and old people's fat.

"Look at this!" shouted Cliffe, incredulous as he watched Garqi's channels broadcasting LUK videos and footage of the attack at Hair's funeral. There had been news of other skirmishes and ambushes, and defeats for the Blackguard as well, all played out in gory detail by MediaCorp International's Britannic Broadcasting Corporation.

"How did we not know about the LUK? (*suck-in*) Fred? (*suck-in*) Did you know anything?"

"Nothing Heath, no."

"Didn't I say we never should have left Hellevue? (*suck-in*)"

Fred said nothing.

"Right (*suck-in*), we are going to cut off all rations to Hellevue and the surrounding areas (*suck-in*). Let's see how long their revolution continues with no food! (*suck-in*) What we save (*suck-in*) we'll give to government employees and military personnel (*suck-in*). That should keep them on our side. (*suck-in*) The Monorails will also be cut off to and from Hellevue (*suck-in*) and surrounding areas (*suck-in*). In the rest of the city (*suck-in*), we will introduce a curfew but in Hellevue (suck-in), we will create a siege, starve them, (*suck-in)* then strike and destroy these little shits who dare to fuck with us (*the largest, sharpest intake of breath, massive bottom lip suck-in*)."

"We'll take them down piece-by-piece, President," said the elder Siamese.

"Have you not listened to a word I've said, you imbecile (*suck-in*)! We're gonna take them out in one fell swoop! (*suck-in*) Make yourself useful and get Garqi on the phone."

"Do you know anything, Fred?"

"About what, Heath?"

"About why Garqi's doing this! (*suck-in*)"

Fred shook his head.

But he knew that what was happening at MediaCorp International marked a wider shift in loyalties. Fred sensed there were some in the employ of the Government who were starting to think that maybe all this wasn't such a good idea after all. The unnerving thing for everyone was that it still wasn't clear which way all this would go. But rest assured, thought Fred, once they knew who was going to come out on top, they would give that party their full backing.

It was also a worry that any Citizens watching may feel emboldened to believe the Government could not only be directly challenged, but defeated. What had happened today suggested the toppling of the Government may be imminent.

Will I be able to get out in time? thought Fred.

"Secretary says he's still busy, Heath," said the elder Siamese.

"Fucker's ignoring my calls! (*suck-in*)"

Cliffe knew he probably wouldn't be able to get Garqi to stop showing images of the revolution, but if he shut off Hellevue's power, in fact if he shut off the whole country's power, that would curtail the good news being spread about the resistance! Cliffe felt sure he was onto a winner with that.

The Siamese shuffled but it was Fred who spoke.

"That might put you in a rather tricky position, Heath. If you cut off the whole country that will only turn them away from you. You might be seen as tyrannical."

Cliffe nodded.

"Also, is it not best to address directly the people of Hellevue, counter what has been reported? Speak to them, show them who you are."

"Er, yes (*suck-in*), maybe. Do you think I should?"

"Undoubtedly."

Fred licked his mental lips in anticipation.

"Let me arrange it."

The Siamese were uneasy.

"Look. I'll talk to him," reassured Fred. "You know what Oli's like. He just wants to provide the best possible service to his viewers. I'll get him to send a pro-Government interviewer."

"What?!" exclaimed Cliffe. "(*huge suck-in*) You mean there are some that are not?"

"What I mean is someone who is especially a Cliffe-ite. It was a slip of the tongue, Heath."

Porridgemouth Siamese went to speak but Cliffe held up his hand.

"I'm doing it (*suck-in*)."

Why is Cliffe trusting me so much? thought Fred. He must be desperate. And frightened.

Who isn't? Fred asked himself.

\*\*\*

Pontiff buzzed again.

"Oh come on old man, you got tae be in this time."

He held his elbow, the throb and crisping blood on his skin causing him to wince. He buzzed again. Finally, he saw a shape moving gingerly behind the glass. The door opened and Pontiff was met with a haggard looking Godfrey.

"Ah it's you, dear boy, come in." He paused. "You look terrible."

"Aye, well I could say the same thing about you mate."

"Touché," smiled Godfrey.

"How was your day, then?" said Pontiff as they trudged upstairs.

"Not great. The Rev is still rather ill. We've got him some medication. Let's hope that does the trick."

He turned as he scaled the stairs.

"You?"

"Oh I've hud a lovely day. Eventful tae say the least. Turns out I'm now involved in another fantastic little scheme."

"Oh yes?"

"Aye, but let's huv a drink first, eh, and I'll tell y'all about it."

Aided by some whiskeysquash Pontiff told Godfrey about his contretemps with Shaw, and that afterwards he'd headed back home. With Godfrey not yet back, Pontiff had been forced to seek refuge in a nearby park. Here he'd bumped into a group of his old neighbours, keen to express their distaste for him. Remarkably, at that very moment, Shaw was refreshing himself with a little trundle through the same park, and intervened. It was at this stage Pontiff was persuaded to sign up to Shaw's plans.

"But that's not all," said Pontiff. "Being a generous gadgie he told me I should come and stay wi'him at LUK HQ."

"What did you say to that?"

"Well, I said I'd bumped intae an old friend, and that I'd be stayen there."

"I see. And that would be me, would it?"

"Aye. But dinnae worry. He doesnae think I've been here long. I was gonnae come back and ask your opinion but events took over and rather forced my hand."

"Well yes," replied Godfrey, pensively, "I can understand that."

"Of course Shaw did ask me how I knew you. An so the good news is you've get a new writen partner."

"So what's the next stage, dear boy?"

"Well apparently I'm tae get in touch with Mormon a couple of days after Cliffe's inauguration to organise another ceremony. For now, I'm gonnae stay here until I'm sure I'm no gonnae be lynched on the streets of Hellevue. I want tae be absolutely certain that Shaw, that patronising thug, has made it safe for me."

Pontiff laughed.

"At least, for now. Long term safety is highly unlikely."

With that, he took another hearty swig of whiskeysquash.

"At least I got booze."

Pontiff reached into his left pocket.

"Here's your change. Aye, I think I might get back intae the old routine for a wee while – stayen in an drinken. It's got tae be the safest option."

"Well yes. But we are getting closer and closer to the end game, dear boy. Garqi has been broadcasting more LUK videos today and Cliffe is due, well," Godfrey looked at his watch, "about now, actually, to address the nation."

"I love a bitta car-crash telly," said Pontiff.

They turned on the television to see Cliffe begin by pooh-poohing claims the resistance were making significant inroads and that he had become a lame duck.

*"But President, we have all seen the footage. Government veh-icles and machinery being turned over, prisoners taken. The Government is on its last legs, is it not?"*

Cliffe laughed uneasily before smiling a constipated grin.

*"I am indeed surprised (suck-in), as I'm sure are your viewers (suck-in), that you have played video (suck-in) that is quite clearly fabricated (suck-in) and is rather flabby propaganda. I am here to set the record straight."*

*"So are you saying that there wasn't an attack on Hair's funeral today?"*

*"Look (suck-in), what we must-"*

*"Was there an attack? Is it not the case you nearly lost your life?"*

*"Look (suck-in). What happened was a minor skirmish which the Blackguard dealt with very easily (suck-in)."*

*"A key feature of these LUK films is the heavy-handedness employed by the Blackguard and PHU. Can you comment on that?"*

*"I won't talk about a hypothetical situation."*

*"I'm talking about specific events."*

*"You are talking about a situation that is not corroborated by The Cow (suck-in). As I have already stated (suck-in), I will not talk about hypothetical events."*

*"Yes but I'm asking about..."*

*"Look (suck-in), one thing I will say is that it is vital that those determined to disrupt and cause terror (suck-in), are brought to book."*

*"But in some cases we have seen innocent Citizens being murdered."*

*"They are not inno-"*

*"You tell the security services to shoot to kill. And indiscriminately as well, I might add."*

*"We do not tell our security services to shoot to kill (suck-in). We tell them to immediately incapacitate."*

*"And that means shooting them in the head."*

*"Yes, in this instance."*

*"So you do have a shoot to kill policy."*

*"Look, I'm getting on with the business of running the country."*

"And a fine job you're doing too!" shouted Godfrey.

*"In a time when resources are stretched,"* continued Cliffe, *"(suck-in) the Liberal Compassionate Party is providing more services for the country than ever before."*

"Oh God, here come the statistics," said Pontiff.

In the makeshift TV studio at the Palace Fred was thinking much the same. He had never questioned Cliffe's sincerity just his competence for the top job. Hair had been successful initially because he'd come across as competent and Fred concluded you could probably be as dishonest as you liked as long as you were competent. Politics was all about perception, especially when the difference of substance on offer was so slim. Veneer was more important than the rotten wood that lay beneath.

Cliffe was staggering on...

*"Thirty new schools this year, a 2.9% increase in doctor surgery intake (suck-in), more rations for all the Citizenry-"*

*"Hang on. I thought you were going to announce you were cutting rations to Hellevue."*

*"What? I-"*

Cliffe looked towards Fred.

That wasn't supposed to be released yet!

"Oh, this just gets better!" roared Godfrey.

*"It is imperative (suck-in)," said Cliffe, trying to regain control, "that people are conscious of their own responsibility in ensuring their resources can reach the whole family (suck-in). And let me say now (suck-in), I know how people feel with the rations (suck-in). I had a very normal upbringing. But Citizens are wasting food each week (suck-in). And in an era when resources are stretched-"*

*"President, nobody quibbles with the idea that resources are stretched. The argument is that what little we have in the way of food, electricity and other commodities is finding its way into the grubby guts of the ruling elite in far greater quantities than the rest of the populace. People are starving. And this is one of the defining reasons for the resistance movement."*

Cliffe's fists began shaking.

*"The resistance are making no significant inroads into our lives (suck-in). The Government has absolute control (suck-in) and we're getting on with the business of running the country! There are pockets of turmoil, yes (suck-in), and as sections of the Citizenry become more inclined to revolt, more inclined to seditious activities (suck-in), our measures must become, for want of a better word, more extreme (suck-in)."*

*"Really? Wow. You heard it here. Extreme measures for the populace. So you plan to put more people into extremis?"*

*"These people are putting themselves in extremis! What we must ensure (suck-in) is that they don't put others into difficulty. To do this (suck-in), I am announcing today that conscription will become compulsory in the next few days (suck-in)."*

"Fuck me," said Pontiff. "That's fighten talk, no jus your usual bureaucratic chaff."

Fred also was rather taken aback at this revelation. How on earth does he propose we do that?

263

"President, if the LUK do not pose a significant threat, why are you introducing conscription?"

"Conscription is a precaution (suck-in). And in government, it is all about ensuring you have the necessary contingencies in place (suck-in)"

"So the LUK are growing in stature then? Or at least, you are concerned that they have the potential to do so."

"We are taking the decisions that are ensuring the safety of this country (suck-in)."

"Why don't you just invade Hellevue and end it once and for all? Surely that would be the best thing to do. Is this not just further evidence of the legendary dithering for which you are so well-known?"

With that, Cliffe rose, ripped off his mike and walked off. And then walked back. He'd exited at the wrong side. There was a bit of kerfuffle and Godfrey's television ceased.

"Conscription, eh?" said Pontiff. "There's gonnae be a big fucken scrap."

"Indeed. I fear that death is on the horizon."

Pontiff laughed, drunk. "Aye, I think you're right. Wonder what it'll be like when we do die."

"A bloody mess, probably," responded Godfrey.

## 27

# ESCALATION

THE THREE DAYS since The Joker's funeral had been unbearably tense for many in government, including Fred. Tomorrow was the *Clunking Fist's* Inauguration yet it could hardly be said the new leader was feeling entirely upbeat about the thought.

After the disastrous interview Cliffe had wanted to speak to Garqi directly but having made the journey to MediaCorp International HQ, he was astounded by what he found. He knew Garqi had manoeuvred himself well but he didn't expect a military presence outside the media man's vast skyscraper, nor did he expect to be refused entry. Maddeningly for Cliffe they couldn't verify his identity. He also saw many mid-to-low ranking LibComs coming and going, now seemingly working alongside Garqi. Cliffe realised he needed more men on his side, and fast. Indeed, the situation had become so critical in his mind that conscription had started forthwith. Operatives were told to not waste time on forms and checks and the like. Just get people signed up and armed. As a consequence the screening process was not as thorough or sophisticated as it might have been.

What Cliffe had most wanted in the run-up to his big day was a message of control and competence from the Government coming through the media. What he got was Balaclava-clad men appearing with ferocious regularity on the nation's television screens, detailing victories of skirmishes, telling stories of how they had come by their weaponry. Conscription had handed out arms to all comers, including those of private militias. So now there were revolutionaries being armed by the Government, using this weaponry to engage the very same Blackguard that had armed them. There had been attacks by dissidents all over the country, Blackguard had been ambushed and in many cases relieved of their military machinery. And despite the black-out in Hellevue the LUK had managed to send in more footage of rations being shared in Hellevue and a Citizenry ready for conflict. To top it off, the Neo-Luddites had come out the woodwork, new leader Nicola Clegg saying it had been a disaster entering into coalition. Now the Neo-Luddites had new political partners. Standing in front of a *Bankers For Justice* banner, Clegg proclaimed –

*"I never thought I'd be standing side by side with the bankers but there you go. Just shows what a mess we're in and I'm prepared to work alongside whoever in the national interest."*

An incandescent Cliffe had finally received a phone call from Garqi who apologised for what had happened at the MediaCorp building entrance. He also promised to sack the interviewer.

*"I sorry Eath. Misunderstandeen. We sort out now. I not know he'd do dat. I give him specific instructions to be nice, to be pro-Cliffe."*

With regards to what else Garqi had broadcast –

*"Eet eez in your best interest, believe me, dat we show dis footage and dese videos. Eet does not look good eef we are seen to be suppresseen what eez common knowledge. Eef we expose eet for what eet eez, Eath, more people will support you. We will expose them as two-bit terrorists."*

Cliffe had waited a long time for his moment in the sun, thought Fred, but it was clear he was losing his short-lived grip on the country. He may have felt an inalienable right to lead but his years of dithering behind the scenes had served only to eat into his time as leader. Now, in a panic, he was causing himself more problems. The whole country was armed, and mainly by him.

This thought sobered Fred as he sat alone in his flat this evening. Finally his new NIPSD cards had arrived. He flicked through his array of new ID's, sucking down beers, smoking ravenously, dipping into his extensive narcotic supplies. He was having many doubts. Was trying to flee the right thing? Should he join Garqi? No. No. Fred had had very little contact with Garqi over the last few days. And whatever happened, he wanted out of the country. If he stayed, in whatever capacity, he felt sure he would meet his end.

He daydreamed of quaint, traditional English villages, real cricket-and-ale type places with streams and little shops, village greens. He slapped himself-to. No chance. Not now.

His phone jolted him. Mother. Fred let it ring out and listened to the message. It was frantic.

*"Oh Fred! It's chaos here! Everyone's fighting. Your Auntie's dead! I've no money. I'm coming to London on foot!"*

Fred had thought he'd be out of the way before she showed up but really, what difference did it make? He could still leave whenever he wanted. In fact, if she was here, at least that would assuage the little bit of guilt sifting through his pores. At least he could leave her some-where comfortable to stay though how long anyone's predicament could be regarded as comfortable was anyone's guess. Fred thought of *Enigma* and the blackout in Hellevue. Anything but comfortable, prob-ably. Fred thought about responding but wanted neither to confirm nor deny anything. And with the electricity down in the district there was probably no point anyway.

***

Pontiff and Godfrey were sat on the round sofa with a melted candle on its last legs their only company. There were only a handful left. The sparseness of the room flickered back at Pontiff from the walls, their shadows the only signs of life. They had been in here ever since the last wave of violence. It didn't matter that the LUK had pronounced Pontiff innocent. Nobody was safe in Hellevue now. In fact, Pontiff's position had probably worsened due to his perceived affiliation with a mob that had waned in popularity.

The major issue was that Hellevue's food stocks were lowering. With rations cut off and no electricity, chaos had ensued. Throughout Hellevue, as supplies lowered, tension heightened. There had been murders, attacks, raids into neighbouring districts for food, raids from neighbouring districts, muggings on the streets. Nobody could feel safe even in their own home. Morale was teetering.

Calloway himself had been out in the streets trying to calm tension. *"We must be defiant! The LibCom dictators are testing us! Soon it will be our time! Surely we can all agree who the true enemy is!"*

But people were no longer inclined to believe him. The routes in to provide supplies were decreasing despite the presence of ex-military personnel. With so many factions taking root people were openly wondering whether the LUK in its current guise was what the country needed. Pontiff had overheard a conversation to that effect when he had gone to procure some whiskeysquash.

*"Those associated with Calloway are gonna be rounded up and given the Ceausescu treatment."*

With all the unrest in Hellevue Calloway and other high-ranking associates had visited some of the rural autonomous zones south of the capital to seek affiliation between them and the cityborne LUK. But these rural folk had long since been independent and were none too impressed with urbanites swanning in with video equipment, advising them that it was in the best interests of the country for them to make anti-Government films.

*"You London people. So wrapped up in your little bubble. We're very happy without you out here in the boonies."*

A few LUK had been killed and Calloway had just about escaped with his life. And he had just about managed to stay alive in Hellevue too, not easy given the widespread resentment he faced.

Of course, this apparent breakdown in the LUK was not what Cliffe was seeing. From his vantage point they looked strong and to be growing in strength all the time. Privately at least, he feared greatly for his position. Little did he know that while outwardly the LUK were projecting their seemingly unstoppable pursuit of power, gaining in popularity and strength, behind the scenes all was not unified. Cliffe was, from his perspective, tragically unaware that the community spirit increasingly being seen on footage in the national media was somewhat fabricated and that the attacks being reported all over the capital were happening without sanction from the LUK.

As the candle flickered, Pontiff and Godfrey passed a whiskey-squash bottle between them. Stacked high in the corner of the room were copies of the LUK manifesto. In the absence of electricity, Pontiff and Godfrey had not been asked to write any more rousing revolutionary rhetoric. Instead they had been asked to circulate what Godfrey had already penned. With Shaw and Calloway not presenting themselves, Pontiff and Godfrey had aborted their assignment in the interests of personal safety.

Godfrey cursed the black out. He had hoped *Ockham* would respond with news of Clem. Though Shaw had asked him to write a piece about Clem in the latest LUK literature, Godfrey had managed to absent it. He didn't want his beloved Clem used as a prop for that bunch of hoodlums. Now he was flitting between insanity and absolute conviction that Clem would be found. At the very least he wanted to clear her name.

"Dear boy," Godfrey said, interrupting the gloom. "I fear there is a maniac in my brain pretending to be me."

Pontiff had grown accustomed to this type of observation in the last few days and didn't move from his slumped position. Godfrey leaned forward to top up his glass yet found only an empty bottle.

"I've always believed the only tangible things in life are mental and physical health," he said. "Well, one down, one to go."

"Well maybe," Pontiff responded with his eyes closed, "but a lot feeds intae given you that health. What about the soul? The spirit?"

"Surely mental and physical health give you the soul."

"Nah. The mind and body are not constituent parts of the soul. It transcends that. A sick man can still have a free soul."

"Well, dear boy, if that is the case, then good, because I feel like a sick man." Godfrey paused. "I just want to see the sea and forget. Cornwall perhaps. Yes, take Clem and Ben to Cornwall."

Both jumped at the knock at the door.

"Go away!" shouted Godfrey.

"It's the Rev," came the reply.

"Dear boy, I'm sorry. Come in," said Godfrey, staggering to his feet, kicking the table and extinguishing the candle in the process. The Rev entered and Godfrey hugged his old friend.

"We were hardly expecting you. I was going to stop by tomorrow. Are you feeling better?"

"Well my illness has subsided if that's what you mean," said the Rev, taking off his glasses and rubbing his eyes.

"Rev," greeted Pontiff. "Enjoyen the mayhem?"

"Oh, indeed. Here, I brought you this."

The Rev handed Godfrey a bottle who in turn poured everyone a generous whiskeysquash.

"War is in the offing, dear boys," said Godfrey, mentally pert after a swig of alcohol. "And there will be many more than just two sides."

## 28
# THE BIG DAY

EXHAUSTED, FRED WAS trying to ready himself for the day's events. He had barely slept, unaccustomed to dealing with anxiety and the effects of over-indulgence in narcotics. Normally his constitution was magnificently robust. Today he could barely focus on anything. He had looked over his laptop to see if there had been any correspondence from *Enigma*. As expected, nothing. He looked through his clothes again, uncertain what to take. He checked and rechecked the location of his NIPSD cards.

Get a grip, he told himself.

He reached into his drawer for some powder to fortify his ailing courage when the buzzer announced the arrival of a visitor. Sherry. She blew a kiss at the camera. Fred was motionless. A buzz again. Reluctantly, he let her in.

"Hello my sweet," said Sherry as she entered. She kissed Fred, took off her thin summer jacket and dumped it on the sofa. "All ready for the bash?"

Fred nodded.

"Oh dear darling," said Sherry as she plonked herself onto Fred's lap. "Are you OK? Has Cliffe been asking you to work through the night?"

"Something like that."

"Oh dear, Freddy darling. Don't worry. He's not going to last."

My God, thought Fred, what did she have in store for Cliffe?

He lost concern for that when it became evident what Sherry had in store for him.

Sherry stood up, let her black dress drop to the floor.

One more time isn't going to hurt, he thought, though he was rather fatigued. But even if his libido was not quite pumping on all cylinders, he wanted to make sure everything seemed as it should be.

After the act, Fred's head was a little clearer. It always was after this type of thing, though the woman with whom he had just communed was one of the people of whom Fred was most scared. It certainly made no sense to tell Sherry of his plans. It had been fun but now he wanted to move on. And not just in amorous matters. He was sure Sherry would want in on his effort to leave Britannia but he didn't want her in tow. She was hardly the subtlest of women.

Fred needed to shower and as his were considerably longer than the four minutes allotted the average person, he nestled in there for a while to refresh his thoughts.

Sherry, reclothing, fancied powdering her nose, and started rifling through the desk. Opening up the third drawer, she found what she was looking for, though there wasn't as much as usual.

She also came across a Zondyke Plethora ash and sauna set.

"Oh, he's not doing that, is he?" she worried to herself.

She placed the tubing on the desk, in the process doing away with the screensaver on Fred's laptop, nudging the machine back into life. Being curious, Sherry thought she'd take a little look.

There, in front of her, was a whole raft of *Ockham* articles. She started paging through them.

"My my, this is interesting," she said aloud. "Wonder what this can all mean?"

Must be for analysis, she reasoned.

On further investigation, she found correspondence with *Herr Enigma*.

Surely a trap, clever boy that he is.

But as she searched further the truth became illuminated. *Ockham* articles had been written on this very machine!

Well I never, she thought.

Delving further she uncovered correspondence with Garqi, notes on Pontiff, the whole *Hellevue Hero* concoction, and finally, a section on Clementine Romain, the child killer.

From custody, a Blackguard had written –

**Prisoner 350125 had to have her arms twisted (haha!) but we got the confession. She is now officially guilty. Oops, I mean she'll enter a guilty plea for 'the trial.' The sexy little thing!**

Sherry was taking this in when the computer pulsed, alerting her to a new message, freshly delivered.

**We need to meet. I'll be in Hitler's, just inside Hellevue, tonight. Eight. Bring news of Clem. Enigma.**

Well, well, well. Is this newspaper Clem? wondered Sherry.

She was aroused by the magnitude of Fred's scheming and being a mischievous sort, thought she'd have a little bit of fun. First, she copied the Blackguard message, then pasted, and finally hit send.

Let's see what *Enigma* makes of that!

Then, she found a bit of paper and inscribed in lipstick:

*"See you at Dribbly's Inauguration.*

*Don't work too hard, Cruella x"*

Sherry pressed the paper on her rouged lips, made an indent and made her exit.

Fred had stayed in the shower a while and was relieved to see Sherry had gone. Then he realised if he didn't hurry up he would be late. He threw on some clothes and was about to head out when he spied Sherry's note. As he retrieved it his laptop whirred into life. Fred stared hard at the screen. And then he began to experience a sensation most alien. Outright fear.

Oh my God. Oh holy shit. What had she read? What has she sent?

Fred saw that *Ockham* files had been accessed. He read the exchange of messages. He saw that Sherry had not prefaced what she had written at all! Fred paused. Hang on, he thought. I thought there was no electricity in Hellevue. Has *Enigma* moved? But how's he going to react to all this? And did Sherry know everything now?

Fred looked down at his laptop and berated himself for failing to turn the bloody thing off. Undiluted panic gripped him. He couldn't think straight. Where was Sherry? He had to talk to her. He rang her but the call went unanswered. She was making her way to her flat in Knightsbridge with one of the pall bearers from her late husband's funeral.

Fred looked at his latest effort for Life Suggestion. It felt prescient.

### *LIFE'S HURDLES ARE A CONFESSION FROM EXISTENCE THAT YOU ARE STILL ALIVE.*

Fred tried to think. Was he now in quite considerable danger? Would Sherry tell Cliffe? They had killed Hair together after all. Was this her plan all along? Had she played him? Would she fuck him over now too? Surely not, he thought. Fred felt that Sherry, like him, had no particular allegiance to anybody, least of all Cliffe and the LibComs, despite the denouement to her deceased husband's life, but especially because of what she'd just said concerning the new leader. Fred felt fairly sure if there was anyone Sherry felt anything for, it was him.

So, what to do? He hadn't counted on his own carelessness hastening his need to act. As if on cue, Fred received a message.

**"Naughty boy. You have been busy x"**

Shit! What do I make of that? Is she just playing? Is this a joke?

But Fred hadn't got the joke. He'd got the fear. Was her ignoring his call a polite way of telling him he was done for? Or was she just trying to shit him up a bit? For sport? He had to think quickly. If he didn't go to the inauguration suspicion would be aroused but if Sherry did mention anything, Fred was sure he would feel what it was like to be on the wrong side of a mode of governance he had helped create. What to do? His plans to vacate the country would have to be dramatically moved forward.

Fred grabbed a beer and turned on the TV. Final preparations were being made for Cliffe's inauguration, the timing of which was significantly later than the leader would have liked, according to the presenter. Cliffe pushed that to one side, plastic smile churning, breathing-in tick working on overdrive.

*"Ah, well, ah (suck-in), Terry Hair only died (suck-in), ah, a week ago, (suck-in, massive smile)."*

He continued by saying that yes, he was clear, in an ideal world, the whole thing would have happened much sooner, instantaneously ideally. But the business of running the country and the security of its Citizens had had to come first. Now though, Cliffe was sure everything was in place for a smooth ceremony. And with that he walked off.

Of course, MediaCorp were talking up the potential of the LUK, showing footage of terrorists attacking Hair's funeral. In the background Cliffe could be seen watching this footage, his face turning a hot cardinal as he remonstrated with the producer. Reading his lips, they seemed to say – *This is not what was agreed!*

Happily, Porridgemouth Siamese had a simple but effective caveat. *"Yes, but we killed them all."*

And that, he was sure, sent out the right message. It certainly sent a message to Fred.

It was getting late but there was one thing Fred hadn't yet considered. Maybe a meeting with *Enigma* wasn't a bad idea. Fred had always been intrigued to discover the identity of a man he had been in contact all these years yet never seen. Finally the moment to meet seemed opportune, if not vital. Could *Enigma* help him? Could he use the resistance as a means of escape?

What am I thinking? thought Fred. Hellevue's the last place I need to go! Especially after what Sherry had sent *Enigma*. Maybe now represents the best time to leave. Numerous platoons of Blackguard, PHU and what military personnel still loyal to the country had been called up to the inauguration. Even from *LifeManagement4Life* Institutes all but a few been called up as well. A smattering of troops remained at all government checkpoints but many facilities in the capital had been reduced to a minimal presence. Fred knew he would be able to whistle through these checkpoints on his way out of the city.

But no. Finally his brain settled.

For now he would play the percentages, assume Sherry would say nothing, and go to the inauguration. After that would be time to move. Travel tonight under cloak of darkness. He would drive as far as was safe in his government-issue vehicle and then try and make it on foot. He knew that out in the rural areas, in the autonomous zones, there was no telling what would happen to him, but this was all there was for it.

Into his father's briefcase he put:

a change of clothes, his laptop, some money, his array of NIPSD cards, two revolvers, his narcotics stash, whisky and a series of disguises.

Facial prosthetics was a skill Fred had learnt at university during his film-making days and appearances for Footlights. Now it was entirely possible those skills would save his life.

"Be with me father," he said out loud.

The final thing to do before waving good-bye to the easy life was to write a note to his mother. He had not actually spoken to her in months. Fred felt remorseful as he pinned a note to the door.

*Mother, I'm going away for a while. Help yourself to whatever you need. Treat this as your home. I have changed the Swipe-Scanner access to recognise your NIPSD card. Take care. Love, Fred x*

\*\*\*

"You gonnae gan?" Pontiff asked the Rev and Godfrey, turning away from the window.

The Rev shook his head. Godfrey didn't answer. He was still pre-occupied with the cruelty of the electricity only coming back on for three minutes. He had no idea whether *Ockham* had responded or not.

Pontiff looked back outside.

"I bet at one stage Calloway intended presence on this fucken protest march to be compulsory for all in Hellevue, ken?"

No response.

"There's actually a pretty good turnout," continued Pontiff.

Godfrey was still frantic, sat on the round sofa, periodically pressing the power button on his laptop to see if there was any electricity.

"But if he does live outside of Hellevue, he won't come will he?"

Fuck me, thought Pontiff. We can't have this til the end of days. He opened the window to hear what was going on.

A small garrison of LUK would stay behind to guard Hellevue, led by Shaw. Calloway knew that even if the protest was successful, the aftermath would be tricky. Before they set off he addressed the gathered while Godfrey and the Rev joined Pontiff at the window.

"Some of you will lose your life. But think of the greater good my brothers and sisters!"

"He'll probably lose his life soon enough," said Godfrey.

"Indeed. I dread to think what he'll come back to," responded the Rev.

"By inference, dear boy, I wonder what on earth we'll be subjected to in Hellevue this afternoon. What do you reckon Pont-"

But as they turned to where their ally had been standing, they saw only the thinnest of air and a swinging front door.

Pontiff couldn't sit inside and listen to these two old men any more. The Rev was too large a unit to be of any use out there. And much as Pontiff loved Godfrey, he couldn't sit cooped up with the old gadgie and his hallucinogenic witterings. It was time for action! Pontiff reached for Godfrey's hip flask and took a long glug.

I'm sure the old man won't mind me taken a stiffener for battle, he thought, pausing momentarily at the main door to Godfrey's block of flats, glad that the blackout allowed him the freedom to decide his own movements, no longer in need of his host to swipe him out. Pontiff knew they would have tried to stop him but how else were they going to find Clem? He hadn't been able to help Susan but maybe there was still a chance for Clem. With that, he burst through the door to join the back of the procession.

It wasn't long before it ran into trouble. As the marchers made their way through an area controlled by a rival faction, Pontiff found himself alongside some stragglers at the back, peaceful middle-class protesters. Jesus, what the fuck are they doing in Hellevue? he thought. Out of a derelict pub came a group of ten toothless types who, person by person, introduced themselves to the jumper-wearing flag wavers.

"Oh come on people," said one of the Hellevue-ites as he went down under a flurry of hits, "we're not French!"

"Nah mate!" shouted Pontiff, as he laid one of the attackers out. "This is more like the Shankhill Road, only wi' less spitten."

As others from the procession rallied round Pontiff extricated himself from the crowd. Fleetingly, he realised he could escape. But what had happened in the preceding moments reminded him that every ten metres would be a battle for territory with whoever he came across.

Christ, we're like fucken wild animals. We've no hope.

A Monorail train trundled by. Empty. Normally this kind of thing brought people out in their droves. Then again, it wasn't a Royal death.

No-one cares, thought Pontiff. We think we're fighten for the future of Britain? Ha! Nobody outside of this wee radius gi'es a flyen fuck! Not for the first time Pontiff thought London may have inflated ideas of its own importance.

As he turned to continue his solitary trek to Westminster a swirling wind whipped up discarded pages from the day's newspaper. Backed by this prevailing gust, the slightly strange, beaming face of Cliffe's mug swooped, careened and sandwiched the aching face of Pontiff. SLAP! It stuck like glue, wrapping itself round his head, a kiss from the new President.

\*\*\*

Fred had arrived at a far more serene mental place by the time he arrived at *Cow* HQ. He parked his car and made the rest of the journey to the Palace on foot, accompanied by a handful of Blackguard.

There were moderate if muted crowds in St James Park, likewise Green Park, the law on no loitering temporarily cessated. Incredibly, thought Fred, there were some that defied common consensus to come out to support their government, scattered also down the Mall. Maybe they hadn't seen the news or heard what was happening and were still caught in the old fashioned view that they were safer if they came to show their support for their leader. There was a line of Blackguard all the way down the Mall as well, mingled in the crowd, and more on various rooftops. It was surreally tranquil.

Cliffe had longed for this special day like a young girl dreams of her future marriage to the Prince and he had no intention of being made to look a fool at his own do. His plan had been to populate the city with all the might he could muster.

Ultimately, however, he had been dissuaded from removing troops from outlying areas, regions in which the Blackguard were achieving parity at best. Some parts of the country had been lost already, and losing more areas outside London would render holding the capital rather meaningless.

No special provision for transport had been made this day. Cliffe had seen what had happened to Hair with the minimal crowds and the empty Monorail trains despite much trumpeting beforehand about the laying-on of more, and though he had enjoyed seeing his rival squirm and appear to have little popular support he did not want the same fate to befall him. Also, he didn't want to give a free ride to those that opposed him. If they were to come and disrupt then they could bloody well pay for the privilege. He had considered closing the Monorail down altogether but felt that that a behind closed doors inauguration would illustrate a fear he possessed but did not want to exhibit.

As Fred arrived at Buckingham Palace he could see Cliffe on the stage in the grand driveway, talking through procedure with the day's officials, checking and re-checking security arrangements, smiling his strange plastic smile. It was worryingly quiet and Cliffe's keen nose could smell something untoward in the air. His arse was going, the lot.

There also were the Siamese twins fussing over their leader. Fred gave them a little wave. He was perfectly happy to be relegated to first reserve. He wanted to be off the team altogether.

The pleasing hush-like hiss that greets splendid summer days was gradually being disturbed by the sound of helicopters. None belonged to the People's Republic of Britannia. All were the property of Media-Corp International, ready to record the day's events. Clearly Fred had arrived just in time as the event stewards were beckoning forth the gathered Citizenry. And in they came. Quite a number. Once Cliffe was satisfied the crowd were where he wanted them – more than the Grinning Idiot had had! – he began, the mike coming into life a good few seconds after he had started to say how he would carry on the government's good work yet also that he represented a change for the people of Britannia, a change that would take the country forward and... Fred switched off. He wished the mike had been as well.

So, having spouted off about his hopes and plans, the whole thing seemed to be going off without a hitch for Cliffe. He was welcomed forward to sit on the throne Hair had purloined from Westminster Abbey, there to be inaugurated as the second President of the People's Republic of Britannia.

"Just say President (*suck-in*). Leave out the 'second' bit."

As Cliffe stepped forward, and waved at his supporters, chanting began. At first it was hard to make out exactly what was being said, but huge numbers of people had arrived at the back of the crowd. Cliffe halted proceedings. He wanted to ensure these new supporters were going to get the opportunity to see him coronated.

But as they approached, the cries loudened, and they weren't as favourable as Cliffe had imagined.

*"Fight, fight fight, fight for your right!*
*Fight fight fight, fight with all your might!*
*Fight fight fight, we'll fight you all night!*
*Fight fight fight, we're gonna beat you alright!"*

Bellowing this catchy if unoriginal chant got the mob going, though as it went on it seemed there were a few too many words to remember. Often people would forget if they were on line two or three. At times, it sounded like they were listening and singing along to music through headphones without knowing the words. They got the sounds right but there was a sort of general consonantal inaccuracy.

There were other chants as well. 'L-U-K, L-U-K,' and 'What do we want? Liberty! When do we want it? Now!' et cetera.

Cliffe had known he would not get away without something happening today. But the timing was excruciating. So close to the promised moment! But at least his men were ready. And though he was never quite the orator of his predecessor, out came the megaphone.

"Right," he nodded, and sucked-in.

Some of his supporters cringed, just hoping it wouldn't be a complete embarrassment in the oratory stakes. Whatever happened with the violence-and-what-have-you was neither here nor there. Just don't look like a twat while you order it was the collective fingers-crossed wish.

"We've been, ah (*suck-in*), expecting you," Cliffe intoned over the megaphone. "If you persist with your, ah (*suck-in*), illegal antics (*suck-in*), you will leave us no choice but to detain you for questioning (*suck-in*), or worse (*suck-in*). I remind you it is not in your self-interest to carry on with this protest (*suck-in*)."

As the protest advanced, Cliffe ploughed on. He was firing out statistics about improvement of quality of life, facts and figures and agendas and moral compasses and mandates for change, truly incredible stuff, thought Fred.

The elder Siamese brother tugged Cliffe's arm.

"Er, President, I think we need to, er-"

"Yes thank you, aide," Cliff responded.

He turned to the Head of the Blackguard and was about to speak when a huge explosion set the stage rocking. It had come from Constitutional Hill, three hundred metres to the left of Cliffe.

"Right! (*suck-in*) It's time we wake these people up to themselves!"

"My, sir, you sound like Ter-"

"Don't ever mention that name in my presence!" snapped Cliffe. He turned to look into the sun, imagining he was a captain on his ship surveying Cadiz. "We will crush this rebellion."

As Calloway's band marched closer, Cliffe gave one final warning.

"You are not helping us help you (*suck-in*). If you persist we have no choice but to take action (*suck-in*). This is for your own safety!"

Suddenly, a rocket whistled over Cliffe, careering into the entrance of the Palace. More explosions went off, bombs in vehicles were being detonated. Mass ranks appeared from Vauxhall Bridge to the southeast, down Birdcage Walk, just ahead of Buckingham Gate. Fires were raging, Blackguard cascaded off rooftops as they came under fire.

Then more crowds started to pile in, filling the ground near Buckingham Palace, and certainly not all bearing the colours of the LUK. Pontiff entered the fray on Birdcage Walk having come over Westminster Bridge. He noticed Calloway was conspicuous by his absence from the front of the march.

The LUK had been joined by other groups from within and outside the capital. There was Bankers For Justice, the Neo-Luddites, Cameroon's Tea Toff Party – a new conservative grouping led by a man with very few real beliefs. He was grappling with a floppy-haired blonde fellow over use of a megaphone.

He'll probably be in charge next, thought Pontiff.

There were ambulances powered by vegetable oil, tanks, a smattering of weaponry, certainly more than just the odd big banner that normally categorises these efforts. It was a protest march in the umbrella sense of the phrase but those involved were looking to come up with something more than mere dissatisfaction.

"Right (*suck-in*), here we go!"

With a wave of his arm, Cliffe ordered the fightback. A hail of bullets was unleashed. He then called for the water cannons, his face contorting with glee as protesters were sent spiralling through the air. If water was a precious commodity, political power was even more so. Pontiff narrowly evaded the aquatic attack and sneaked down Buckingham Gate on the south side of the Palace. His movement was timely as Cliffe ordered another shower of bullets. Blackguard from their various vantage points rained down a hail. A few of the innocent pro-Cliffe crew may have copped a bit as well but never mind, thought Cliffe. The end justifies the means. In fact, in the melee it was hard to make out who was on whose side. Screams rang out. There were fist fights between those both pro- and anti- LibComs, people being knifed.

Then Cliffe grabbed a gun himself.

"TAKE THAT YOU FUCKERS!" he shouted, as he mowed down wave after wave of LUK. The Resistance were being beaten! After the archery onslaught of gun fire, Cliffe ordered the PHU and Blackguard ground force go in for the metaphorical kill.

Christ I hope Garqi's getting all this, thought Fred, who had taken a position of safety behind the stage.

He needn't have worried. Garqi was circling in of the helicopters above, though after one had been shot down, his mothership beat a retreat to a safer airspace.

But old Cliffeyboy is actually giving a rather good account of himself, thought Fred. Finally the man's got an outlet for all that pent up anger!

Despite fighting back vigilantly, bullets whistling all over, LUK going down, Blackguard going down, it soon became apparent to Calloway that all that could be achieved, had been achieved, and a tactical retreat was ordered. Men, women and children had been lost, their screams drowned out as the PHU surge led to more deaths. Others were cut off from their allies, split by the Blackguard, and kettled. Pontiff found himself in a quieter section, and looking back on the horror of the battlezone he saw that though many LUK had retreated, many were being arrested, beaten and shot.

Enoch, you got your rivers of blood, but we are unBritish in a way you had not imagined possible.

"Hey! It's the *Hellevue Hero*!" someone shouted. "Hey everybody look! He's blessed us with his presence!"

Pontiff was oblivious to the crowd nodding and talking in recognition. He couldn't hear the words for the mounting din that surrounded him now. But he was suddenly aware of a jostling for position near him, everyone wanting to touch him. He was in a group of government supporters. The crowd started to chant.

"Hell-vue He-ro! Helle-vue He-ro!"

The noise built and more Citizens surged in from the back.

Suddenly, swamped, Pontiff found himself hoisted onto the backs of the crowd and was surfed to the front and onto the stage on which stood a sweating, panting Cliffe. The crowd were still chanting his name, evidently thrilled by the presence of a celebrity.

Cliffe, still holding his gun, turned to the crowd and Emperor-like, raised his hand for them to stop. Pontiff eased himself up from his prostrate position and stood. Slowly the noise began to dissipate save for the odd bit of distant gunfire as the LUK were beaten back.

"Friends (*suck-in*), Britannians (*suck-in*), Citizens (*suck-in*), this was supposed to be a happy day (*suck-in*). And it still can be (*suck-in*). Before I officially become your new president (*suck-in*), let us applaud a truly modern man (*suck-in*), a Britannian of whom we can all be proud (*suck-in*). The Hellevue Hero! (*suck-in*). Please (*suck-in*), step forward!"

Fred, standing at the edge of the stage was dumbfounded. My God, Pope! He was also amazed at the dexterity at which Cliffe had weaved the hero's presence into the proceedings. For his part, Pontiff had certainly not expected to be in this position and was unsure what he would do. He stepped forward.

"On a day of horrific violence from Citizens in this country who care not for our great nation (*suck-in*), it is indeed heart-warming to see a man who has done so much to try and change the terror heartlands (*suck-in*), and has come here to stand shoulder-to-shoulder with true Britannians (*suck-in*). Take a bow, son."

Cheers and whistles erupted again as Pontiff bent down, momentarily catching Fred's gaze. As Pontiff returned to a standing position, Cliffe handed him the microphone.

"Please (*suck-in*), address us."

Pontiff took the device. The crowd silenced.

Everything happens for a reason, eh?

Pontiff looked out at the crowd. To start, he thought he'd have a bit of fun, get them on his side. He put his right hand behind his right ear and leant forward towards the crowd. Cheers erupted. Pontiff then stepped back, slowly raised his hands together, palms up, demanding more noise. He got it. He kept raising and raising and then slowly made circular motions until the backs of his hands were facing each other. He then whipped them apart like a conductor. The sound stopped immediately. Pontiff waited a second before he repeated the manoeuvre. The sound went up, then he hushed them again.

"Thank you Westminster!"

As cheers erupted once more, Pontiff reached for the hip flask, had a good glug. An idea struck him. He felt imbued with energy, the whiskey renewing him. He felt his head clear, an epiphany descend.

Dinnae fight the trajectory into which life propels you. If I'm goen down, I'm goen down in a blaze of glory.

But he realised he didn't have long. He had to work out the most economical way to disseminate the most information.

"Now," he began, "I've been described as a hero."

Here, Pontiff adopted mock humility.

"I am no hero. True heroes are few and far between these days. Yes indeed."

He began to walk the stage, stopping next to Cliffe.

"Thanks to this man," he motioned to the LibCom leader, paused for a swig from the hip flask, allowing Cliffe to prepare for a compliment. "Thanks to this man, the nation is engaged in the celebration of idiocy!"

Silence.

"Well clap then!" shouted Pontiff, applauding, motioning to the crowd to join in.

Cliffe didn't know what to make of this all, but clapped anyway. Fred. Fred could not quite believe the majesty of what he was seeing. This man Pope had certainly lived up to the billing he'd had in his mind. Blackguard were shuffling.

Pontiff whipped his free arm through the air to get the crowd to stop.

"But that aside, you want tae hear about me? I'll tell you. Signor Oli Garqi. Now there's a hero. Concocted quite a story did he no? You've all read how Clementine Romain let her son die because she did not give him medication?"

There were murmurings of agreement. Pontiff nodded.

"Now, I don't know if the wee man is really dead or no, but what you've been readen is lies! Clementine Romain is innocent. She is a fantastic mother. She and her son were abducted by government forces. They arrested her for a murder based on a testimony from me which I never gave. I never even spoke tae the press! I was in fucken custody at the time!"

Stunned gasps rippled through the crowd.

"Aye, I know."

People started shouting, Blackguard started mobilising.

"And it was all at the behest of him!" shouted Pontiff, pointing at Cliffe.

Fred saw Cliffe's protruded, constipated lips giving way to the nervous simper.

"Gathered fools," continued Pontiff, "I give you the wonderful President, and his Liberal Compassionates!"

The President began shaking his head in disbelief.

"No, no!" he shouted. "(*suck-in*) What is the meaning of this outrage?"

Fred was experiencing undiluted glee at this spectacle.

My, this Pope's oeuvre is rather agitative! I like his style! Of course, it's a little shady on the detail and it's thanks to me, but still!

As Blackguard made their way towards Pontiff, he took another glug.

"I've seen rapes in Life Camp, I've been subjected tae-"

That was all he had time for.

Presently, Pontiff found himself grabbed round the neck with his arms strapped behind him, given a truncheon in the ribs, knees in the back and a boot in the head as he went down. He was dragged through the crowd and bundled into the back of an adjacent meat wagon. Whatever happened to him next, Pontiff had at least managed some disruption, put the record straight. And that was impressive given the weight of forces stacked against him.

Meanwhile Cliffe did his best to move on from this episode as quickly as possible. Surrounded by bodies and blood in an area of the capital reduced to the unliveable, and sweating profusely, he finally reached his destiny. He was President. He had wanted to move into Buckingham Palace after the inauguration but the earlier rocket had probably rendered the gaff temporarily unusable. For now he would have to content himself with Number Ten. As would Fred. Like all LibComs, he was called into an emergency cabinet meeting.

For Fred, the day's happenings had cemented two things in his mind. First, that leaving would be rather dangerous and second, how much he liked this Pope, how much he admired him, how much he wanted to meet him. Fred was beginning to see this Pope as some kind of kindred spirit, a soulmate even, and this had led to another alien sensation – a sense of loyalty to a man he'd never met. Well I suppose I am responsible for all this! he laughed.

But after everything he'd put the man through, Fred wanted to set him free, maybe even escape with him. Fred admitted to himself that traveling alone into the tribal areas consumed him with fear and the strength of the Scot had amazed him. In fact, he thought Pope's survivability might be something that could save them both.

And Garqi had been implicated. How would that sit with the Italian mogul? Would he have continued with the live broadcast as Pope made his revelations?

## 29
# THERE'S ALWAYS SOME FANATIC

THOUGHTFULLY THEY'D PERMITTED Pontiff a TV in his cell so he was able to watch part of the latest news bulletin. Incredibly there was a momentary flash of what looked like the new President himself opening fire on the crowds.

Also, there seemed to be a fair amount of discrepancy over what the truth of the day was.

*"The President tried to reason with violent protesters who were hell-bent on creating carnage,"* said a LibCom spokesman.

*"Happily the protest was quashed and Cliffe was sworn in to the delight of the crowd."*

While a reporter from a blood-soaked Buckingham Palace argued –

*"There is a prevailing sense that more Citizens will join the struggle for revolution as the injustices of the country bite still further. The failure of Cliffe is evident. He is like a lone man in his castle. The LUK will come again."*

*"Not at all,"* rejoined the spokesman. *"It's just that there's always some fanatic or other trying to ruin it for everyone else."*

That'll be me, thought Pontiff.

And then, there he was.

*"Here is a man,"* continued the LibCom spokesman as footage of Pontiff's escapades played out, *"who was previously a decent Citizen yet is now given over to the forces of alcoholism and terrorism. We have detained him not only for public harmony, but also for his own safety. By his own admission he's been in*

*custody before and see how he drinks while he talks? Again, the importance of Life Administration is demonstrated. Dry days must be adhered to otherwise you will end up like this tragic case. It is this ill we need to cure and only we, the Liberal Compassionates, can do this."*

Then Pontiff watched the new President outside Number Ten, looking somewhat flummoxed and fatigued.

*"As we have seen today, (suck-in), there is an element in our society that seeks division (suck-in). I cite Robert Pope as the most recent example of an individual whose sole purpose was to denigrate the country (suck-in), our wonderful health service (suck-in), and who sought to make political capital by twisting an already tragic occurrence (suck-in), that of the death of a young child. (suck-in) We must fight together to ensure these people, these criminals, do not take a foothold in our society (suck-in). We will not tolerate disharmony and we will not tolerate sedition or wanton destruction of the peace (suck-in). And we will not tolerate a lack of tolerance (suck-in). Hellevue is the terror heartlands (suck-in). And it must exist no more (suck-in). Thank you."*

Pontiff began to think of his friends when his ears were filled with the dulcet tones of the editor of *The Daily Rumour*, Piers Mormon.

As Pontiff looked back to the TV, he spied the smug Chirac-esque face of the owner sat next to him in the plush surroundings of Media-Corp HQ. Mormon spoke first.

*"In light of today's outburst made by a former friend of this newspaper, I feel it important to set the record straight. The assertion that we would fabricate a story at the Government's request is unfathomable."*

Garqi nodded in agreement.

*"Eet was a brilliant piece of investigative journalism dat Mr Pope elped create. Eet was a piece that Mr Mormon, as editor, ad a duty to run. Maybe I sack eem eef e don't publish eet!"*

Garqi laughed. Mormon laughed. Pontiff sat stony-faced.

*"But seriously,"* continued Garqi, *"eet eez indeed regrettable dat a man previously eld in such igh esteem by dis publication*

*would act in dis way. But certainly Mr Pope ad shown signs of veereen from what we would define as an acceptable path. Iz long eld problem wid drink has, unfortunately, rendered im borderline schizophrenic and, at best, severely bi-polar. What we saw today was dee ranteens of a mad man, addled by booze, a brain destroyed by dat new deadly drug, Zondyke Plethora. We av testimonies from iz neighbours about episodes of violence. E eez clearly a tormented man."*

Well that last part's true, thought Pontiff.

Mormon picked up the baton.

*"Maybe he accuses us of manufacturing this story because of his guilt at shopping a member from his own working class. I don't know. I can only speculate as reasoning seems a distant dream for him. As much as we showed empathy and understanding he, unfortunately, seems beyond repair. I can only hope that some time in the care of the right authorities will help him overcome his problems. He's been going off the rails for a while now. A bit of time to think and reflect might be good for him."*

*"Exactly right,"* agreed Garqi, who looked gravely at the camera. *"Robert, I'm appealeen to you directly, sort yourself out. Ow can we, your friends, elp you unless you elp yourself?"*

Pontiff shook his head, not in disbelief. It was too late for that. Unfortunately he could believe whole-heartedly what he was seeing.

What next? he thought, puffing out his cheeks. His heart beat shallowly and erratically. He'd been publicly denounced, discredited, ridiculed even, and general consensus was now undoubtedly that he was a crackpot. And you couldn't loose a pissed maniac in society. He'd get lynched. His situation could only be worse if he'd been branded a paedophile. Ah well, a warrior knows the potential consequences, as his grandfather had said to him. Yet still, pretty bewildered he felt, in no small amount of physical pain and no closer to Clem as he tried to bed down for a few hours kip. This was all so horribly familiar.

\*\*\*

"Behold the condemned man," said the first Blackguard, opening Pontiff's cell.

"Tough old fucker," said the other. "Stupid trousers, mind."

"Oi! Hellevue Hero. Up. You got a visitor."

"Did you see him today?" said a third. "Dear oh dear."

"Doesn't he realise the country's changed for the better?"

"I think he's just a malcontent, to be honest."

"I think he's just a fucking idiot to be honest."

"OK, that'll do guards," came a feminine, chocolatey voice.

With reticence, Pontiff allowed his head to turn.

"Oh would you look at that," he said.

Dr Zini nodded, her mouth closed and thin-lipped. They snapped open in an instant. "Hello Robert," she said, moving a mass of grey hair that obscured the black leather eye patch.

Not for the first time, Pontiff was recuffed before the guards left them alone. "I'm sure you'll appreciate my security provisions. I hear you've been causing yourself problems."

"Good news travels fast, eh?"

"Well I saw your little performance earlier actually. Most impressive. Not only do you assault my staff at Life Camp but you attack media people and then try to start a riot at the coronation of our President."

"In fairness, I think the riot was in full swing already."

"Nonetheless, it's quite a malevolent conspiracy theory you presented out there, isn't it? Government meddling, lies. It's pretty incendiary stuff. And rape, Robert? I thought you understood."

Pontiff's gaze wandered around the cell before he looked directly into the doctor's green eye. "How is she?"

"Who?" responded Zini.

Pontiff stayed his eyes on Zini, gave a knowing look.

"Oh Susan you mean. Why she's fine, better than ever. She's been released."

"Really?" said Pontiff, hope permeating his tone.

Thank God it was going well for someone.

"Yes, she hit it off rather well with her next *IJP* – love at first sight you might say. They certainly didn't mind performing for us. Yes they got engaged and were released together."

Why am I even surprised? thought Pontiff.

"Yes, it's proof our medicine works. In the main," added Zini, looking pointedly at him. "That is what I will argue in any case. My reputation is on the line but I'm going to try to convince them to let me take you back into my care so I can carry on my work with you. You are clearly still misaligned."

Pontiff thought he'd rather take his chances in proper prison.

"I'm fond of you, Robert. You could be in here for a long time."

Pontiff nodded.

"Robert, I..." Zini composed herself, smiled at Pontiff. "I think of you sometimes. And I think you do of me."

Aye. In my worst nightmares.

"I think somewhere in your troubled mind, today was all about trying to engineer a return to see me again. I fast-tracked you too quickly to the exit. You weren't ready."

She collapsed her smile.

"And I'm sorry. For now though, I am duty-bound to give you at least caution for today's events."

"A caution? I think it may have gone beyond that. An anyway, a caution from a doctor?"

"That's right Mr Pope. It's in line with new government direct-"

"Jesus Christ."

"Robert, kindly stop interrupting me. You wouldn't want me to make a more severe diagnosis, would you?"

"I dinnae think it'll make much difference."

"Think on what I say. I'll come back tomorrow."

"Super."

Zini got up to leave, turning before she did.

"There are reports of violence from within Hellevue."

She paused.

"Lots of deaths apparently."

# 30
## *HITLER'S*

IN A DIMLY lit all-night Schnitzel bar named *Hitler's*, Godfrey waited, nervous. He was sat at a small round table, wearing his trademark red corduroy hat, consuming brandies, feet getting incessantly caught in the tablecloth of deep burgundy that went all the way to the floor.

*Hitler's* was a little-known hangout, the type of place frequented by those very much in the know and the arbiters of taste, a dwelling for the intelligentsia. Godfrey had spent a lot of time here in his early twenties in his quest for adventure, excitement, decent conversation and the opposite sex. There had always been exceptional food and music, candles on all the tables, waiters in penguin suits. Though the menu had suffered somewhat in recent times, the atmosphere remained nonetheless.

*Ockham* was now late. In truth, Godfrey didn't expect him to show. Nobody would choose to come to Hellevue and Godfrey lamented not suggesting a venue outside the district. And he would have done had he known earlier how easy it would now be to leave Hellevue.

Government reports were correct. The atmosphere in Hellevue was charged. Since Calloway's band had returned skirmishes had being taking place all day in the district. The area was covered in bodies, fires were smouldering, people were out in the street, some were looting, others were drinking whiskeysquash, others were alienating themselves from themselves with Zondyke Plethora.

Earlier, after Calloway's band had departed Hellevue, and Godfrey and the Rev had tried in vain to find Pontiff, they had bought some coffees from a street vendor. Rediscovering some serenity after the violent exultations of the march preamble, they were pondering what to do with the day when the atmosphere in Hellevue just offered to change. After finishing their coffees they were making their way to The Forest Arms when a rocket was fired into the street from the end terrace house. The coffee vendor was killed and carnage ensued, multitudinous groups clashing with each other in pitched battle on the streets. Looting and smash and grab raids took place, murders occurred, horrible beatings begat more grotesque violence. LUK depots were overrun, LUK operatives killed, weaponry and money stolen. LUK HQ had windows broken and Godfrey was certain he had seen Shaw lobbing a Molotov into the building. After three hours of brutal savagery the various factions withdrew to regroup.

As the district rested, news of the massacre at Cliffe's inauguration started to filter through and soon after, the surviving members of the protest march returned sporting a look similar to those that had survived the Hellevue bloodbath. Trudging through the district the returning protesters could see it had been laid to waste. Arriving at the shell of LUK HQ, Calloway spoke briefly with Shaw before he turned to address the small crowd. Godfrey and the Rev had made their way as well, desperate to see if Pontiff was among the returners' number.

Incredibly, despite the mammoth loss of life both in Hellevue and Westminster, a moral victory was declared by Calloway.

"That showed those fucking bastards!" shouted Calloway, fists clenched and pumping.

Touché, thought Godfrey, as he watched Calloway in this violently ecstatic mood. He noted that the LUK supremo seemed to be experiencing the specifics of being a leader in these times. Intense paranoia, pressure, distrust, a sense that his mighty kingdom was crumbling, but still clinging to the last vestiges of megalomania.

"The final days of the Government are approaching!"

"Not just for them," whispered the Rev with a nudge.

Shaw wore a pensive expression.

"Admittedly, there have been a few deaths but we expected that!" shouted Calloway.

A few deaths? thought Godfrey. Almighty massacre more like.

Then Calloway spotted him.

"I see your mate didn't wait for the cavalry and went for it anyway. Bloody marvellous! We heard him over the tannoy as we retreated."

"Yeah," shouted one of the gathered, "The Hellevue Hero mounted the stage and gave old Cliffe and the crowd a right mouthful! Stupid bastard didn't give us an opportunity to rescue him though."

"He'll have lost his life like all those others," said someone else.

"Gave his life you mean!" cried Calloway. "He dedicated himself to our cause! But we're not finished yet. This is just the start. It's clear we're fighting not only for the country but also Hellevue."

As Godfrey tried to digest what had been said, Calloway addressed him again.

"You, like everyone Godfrey, and you Reverend, have got a few more little things we need you to do for us."

Godfrey feared that there would be no end to these little things.

"For now," continued Calloway, "there is planning to be done!"

He needed to ensure his tilt at supreme overlord didn't stall, his chances of survival diminishing by the hour.

So on a night the very many groups of Hellevue were pondering their next move, Godfrey and the recently arrived Rev were pondering theirs. Brief mention of Pontiff and the inevitable gloom that followed meant their table had fallen silent. As they sat in this silence, they were alerted to some comings and goings by the door. It was Shaw and Calloway.

"Fuck are they doing here?" said Godfrey, stomach fluttering through the vast quantity of brandy. He wanted to remain incognito but he cut a rather prominent, forlorn figure, clothed in bygone style. However, the LUK hierarchy were far too preoccupied. There were two other men with them.

Then a curious scene began to unfold.

At the bar, a bearded man in glasses was looking over at two other men on the table adjacent to Godfrey and the Rev. The bearded man at the bar raised his glass. One of the seated then motioned to one of the Penguin suits. The waiter advanced, a man of thirty years, black hair slicked back with a centre parting, gelled Poirot-style, no discernible chin.

"You see that gentleman at the bar, Penguin."

Penguin turned, turned back, and nodded. "Yee-es."

"We request his presence. We have a message for him."

"Oh yes?"

"*Voices echo through my mind like a cathedral for centuries now*."

Penguin nodded, and about-turned. The Rev and Godfrey saw him approach the bearded man.

Presently the waiter returned with two drinks. As he placed them on the table, he spoke.

"Never go to bed on a full mindhead."

One of the men nodded.

"Tell him *Constantinople*. And get him a drink."

This was not at all strange. This kind of thing happened all the time in here. It was not the done thing to just approach someone at a table. You had to wait for a Penguin. That was the protocol and, in the current climate, ensured some security too.

The Penguin returned. But upon his return this time his demeanour let slip a slight testiness, minor exasperation.

"Sir, the gentleman thanks you for his drink and has another message."

"Go on."

"*Rangoon*."

"Tell him *Sucre*."

"Very good sir," and the Penguin disappeared again.

When he returned, it was with the bearded man. Relief for the Penguin.

Arriving at the table, he pulled a chair out for the new arrival, who in turn popped a £100 note into his hand. Penguin nodded, the man sat, calmly pulled his chair into the table and began a conversation in hushed tones. The Rev and Godfrey thought it prudent to look away. Best not to engender disfavour with an unwanted intrusion. As he did look away, however, Godfrey noticed that one of the original table dwellers was passing enormous knives under the burgundy cloth and into the hands of the other two. It wasn't uncommon to carry protection of some variety, but to distribute them in a setting like this? Godfrey struggled to maintain his balance. He slumped suddenly and slid off his chair, began muttering and jerking.

"Godfrey, are you alright?" asked the Rev, worried his great friend was having some sort of fit.

Nothing.

"Godfrey!"

There was nodding, a drawled apology. From the floor Godfrey cracked a smile through worried eyes.

"Perhaps we should get out of here," whispered the priest. "I'm suddenly feeling a little exposed."

As he helped Godfrey back onto his seat, the Rev saw that the three men had left their table, and were approaching Calloway and Shaw and their two companions. As they arrived the Rev watched Shaw stepping away. Calloway stood up, panicked.

"What have you done?" screamed Calloway at Shaw. "Why? No! Don't!"

"My God," said Godfrey, opening one eye, "the fucker's betrayed him!"

Godfrey and the Rev watched as Calloway was restrained by the two men he had sat with. He let out a series of petrified screams.

"We are the Church of The Undeniable Faith," said one, "you have chosen to commune with infidels! For this, you must die!"

With that, the three knived men grabbed Calloway, pulled his hair tort like he was being electrocuted, and severed his head. While CUF operatives sealed the exits Shaw, who had not watched Calloway's ordeal, turned to see his former friend's head rolling around the floor. Immediately he vomited, mixing noxious yellow liquid with the deep red of Calloway's spilt claret. A film crew captured it all.

The RevKev stood up and heaved Godfrey onto him, putting his left arm round his shoulders.

"Right, come on!"

Nothing. Nothing from Godfrey at all.

The Rev felt a nerve start to jangle. The sound of rain was intensifying but the old man's faculties were deadening. How long did they have?

"Godfrey!"

Suddenly, the old man jerked into life and jumped to his feet.

"Dear 'oy," he said, swaying. He started to nod profusely.

Oh for fuck's sake, he's totally lost the plot!

As this transpired, the Penguin glided over.

"Perhaps sirs would like to leave the back way?"

The Rev, struggling under the strain of his great friend an ally, nodded, and Penguin came to his aid to shoulder the burden.

"Right, old man. You feel up to getting home?"

Godfrey nodded before slumping onto Penguin's shoulders.

"Come on," said the Rev, "we'll go to mine. It's closest."

"Fine fine, dear boy, fine."

Godfrey reached into his coat, pulled out a hip flask, and after one final slurp of brandy, recalibrated his internal mapping capabilities for their trudge. He stuck out his right hand as though catching the wind, and turned.

"Let's go."

Before they could, though, the nice young knife-wielding maniacs of the CUF surrounded them. Godfrey held one hand up to his left eye.

"Ah, brothers," he drawled, and crossed himself.

The Rev nodded skyward, relieved the old boy had enough about him to do that. Happily, the man who had kindly removed Calloway's head recognised the Rev.

"Ah, Brother Payne. Allow us to-"

A window smashed, a bottle popped, flames erupted.

"Die you medieval scum!" came a cry from outside.

In came another Molotov.

"Atheist Fundamentalists!" someone shouted while the Rev and Godfrey crawled through the gathering smoke and flame.

The Penguin, the embodiment of calm, remained standing.

"Sirs? The back way?"

"Yes, we'll get out the back way!" shouted one of the CUF operatives.

Godfrey suffered a coughing fit as he watched the first CUF head outside and all around came squalling screams and gunshots in the burning wreck of *Hitler's*.

"Die Infidels!" shouted the knife-wielding CUF operative, now having located some guns.

"Thank Christ for the cavalry, Rev!" wheezed Godfrey.

The flames had nearly destroyed the main seating area of *Hitler's*. As the Rev and Godfrey made their way to the back door they watched Shaw exit before they were again met by the polite young CUF boy. He had come back for them.

"Come brothers, let me help you!"

Rain fell heavily in the side street, and all was a throng of destruction and carnage. Hellevue's free-swim version of violence had kicked off again.

Having been hauled out of the burning wreck, Godfrey was rather keen to get back to his own flat, his circular room, and some brandy.

But their saviours wouldn't have that.

"It is not safe for you brothers. You must come with us."

Fuckinell, thought Godfrey. I don't think I can take much more of this.

Outside the Rev looked for the Penguin. He wanted to slip him some notes but he was nowhere to be seen. He wanted to go back inside for him.

"It's too dangerous Brother, we must leave now!"

A new spurt of flame had engulfed the venue.

"Brothers! We must leave! Come on!"

With reluctance, the Rev bundled away from the burning wreck. As they reached the end of the street, the Rev whispered to Godfrey, "Not so dismissive of the church now, are we, eh?"

The old man laughed.

"What denomination are they, dear boy?"

"I have no idea. I think this could be out of the frying pan, into the fire."

"Quite. It's a good job you're so popular, Kev!"

"Yes and thank God, and I do mean that literally, that you crossed yourself."

"A show of solidarity, dear boy!"

"Survival more like."

As they sloped through the rain, slowed by Godfrey's incapacity and the warding off of the odd ambush, the Rev remembered this CUF. Like many groups in Hellevue, they had been affiliated to a larger organisation but had splintered after some disagreement about the correct name for their little band. Certain members of the group had wanted to call it the CUT, the *Undeniable Truth*, but others, more moderate ones, felt a gentler epithet would be more beneficial in the long run.

"We don't want to ram it down people's throats," argued one.

"Don't we?" said another.

## 31
# ON THE EDGE OF A CLIFFE

TO CAP WHAT was proving to be a busy night for all, Cliffe had sparked into action. He'd thoroughly enjoyed opening fire on the rebellion and was now going to finish them off. And having decided to go for the jugular he wanted to be on hand to witness the destruction. He also wanted his cabinet to experience the spectacle and demanded their presence on the front line.

For the love of God, thought Fred. He fancies himself a king heading into war. Heath V. When am I gonna be able to leave?

As Cliffe prepared to sort out this LUK problem once and for all he sent Garqi a message.

*Get down to Hellevue!*

Having mobilised the Blackguard, the PHU, the police, the PSU and military personnel, Cliffe had assembled the lot outside the terror district. The LUK, and the rest of Hellevue for that matter, were now in for some fireworks. For Cliffe, an attack in the middle of the night was exciting. No way was he going to allow another counter-offensive from the resistance. Hellevue was surrounded and bloodshed was about to ensue.

Fred felt jittery.

He'd made the journey to Hellevue in a tank with the elder Siamese and as he popped his head out on the outskirts of the district the first thing he saw were rows of heads on sticks. Jesus, they've gone medieval! And surveying the fires and general exhaustion Fred couldn't believe that agreeing to *Enigma's* request to contribute to another **KARMA-TARMAK** had resulted in this.

300

Fred's phone vibrated. Mother.

**Arrived in city. No money for Monorail. Walking. What's your address again? Mum x**

He also saw he had a message from Sherry.

**Hellevue Hero spot on – now that would be a story!!! Maybe someone else was to blame? I told you he was unpredictable. Looks like he's landed you in the shit! x**

"Here!" shouted Cliffe. "Take this!"

"Oh. Thank you Heath," said Fred as the President handed him a pump-action shotgun, certain now that Sherry had not said anything. At least not to Cliffe. But then the President had such tunnel vision, nothing was going to distract him.

An arm signal from Cliffe initiated a burst of machine gun fire from atop a row of tanks. A handful of Hellevue residents went down. Grenades were lobbed in afterwards. There was brief retaliatory fire but the threat was soon snuffed out.

An old woman appeared from a house near to where Cliffe stood.

"I'm glad you're finally doing something about immigration," she said. "There's a lot of foreigners in there causing unholy chaos. Not enough places at the local school for my kids."

"You fucking bigot!" shouted Cliffe as he mowed her down. "We don't even have immigration now!"

After the initial successes on the Hellevue border, Cliffe was about to order his men to invade when he had his attention turned to a pinkening and orange-ing of the heavens. Luminescent tracers started winging their way through the sky, explosions thundered, fires erupted on the horizon.

"These fuckers are better armed than we thought! Shoot for the skies! Let's put these dissidents to sleep!"

With gunfire, bullets and bombs whistling all around him it suddenly dawned on Cliffe that explosions were going off in Hellevue as well, and when he saw planes swooping in and firing indiscriminately, he had to re-evaluate. The dissidents were firing at the planes as well! What was this then? Who were in these planes? And what were they doing in Britannia at two o'clock in the morning? Save the odd helicopter, no-one, nobody, *nothing*, had been airborne for years. One of

301

*NewsZeit!*'s mediacopters went down. Immediately, two more appeared.

"Where does he get his resources from?" Cliffe shouted.

But Garqi was the least of his worries.

Houses were being blown to bits next to him, tanks were being overturned, Blackguard lay bleeding. It was all getting a bit too much for the new President. Nothing had gone right for him since he had become supreme leader of the People's Republic of Britannia but now he could sense his dreams unravelling. Just when he thought it couldn't get any worse. It was time for a tactical retreat, to think again. Next stop, Downing Street and some respite.

Fred had taken momentary refuge under a partly incinerated tank and as the planes circled away, seemingly to restart their aerial run, Fred made a dash for it. He doubted he could run the full way back to Westminster but all he could think was that in his car was everything he needed for his getaway – the NIPSD cards, his laptop – vital nobody found that! If that was totalled, so was he. At least he had an extra weapon now. That would help both him and Pontiff.

He thought he was making good progress until a van going at breakneck speed screeched past him. The door slid open, two sets of black-clad arms reached out, and Fred was hauled in. In the van were Cliffe, the Siamese, and a gaggle of Blackguard. A couple seemed a few limbs short of human.

"We need another meeting, Fred (*suck-in*). Who the fuck are these flying people?"

Not another meeting, thought Fred. This twat arranges meetings to arrange meetings. No wonder he doesn't know what his favourite biscuit is. But at least death, or bodily compromise, had temporarily been averted.

His phone buzzed. Oh God! It was mother again. She needed directions and wanted to know *what are all the explosions darling*?

\*\*\*

In the moments just before this, the Rev and Godfrey were in their shared room at their new temporary residence. It was in a poorer part of Hellevue and many shared the house that constituted CUF HQ. Sat with a coffee at a small round table, Godfrey was rediscovering some equanimity. It was quite probably the rotundity that was helping him.

"Reverend, dear boy, sorry for my performance earlier. I was dead to the world."

"Much like our dear friend, Calloway."

Godfrey laughed.

"Yes, still, I suppose that's what you can expect if you court extremism. What an unholy alliance of religious zealots and dogmatic-atheists the LUK is."

"Perhaps 'was' would be more accurate."

"Yes, you're probably right dear boy. It's all to be expected I suppose. Calloway tried to be all things to all men, mainly being a self-publicist and-"

"And now he is no more."

"Mmm, indeed. Misunderstood the zeitgeist, I think."

Godfrey lounged back in his seat which squeaked every time he moved. "If we were being generous we could say Calloway maintained a philosophical approach that allowed, indeed celebrated, ambiguity. Perhaps he was aware that life is far too complex to assign great over-arching truths, that you cannot subscribe to anything with absolute certainty, and that that is particularly true in matters of religion and politics."

Godfrey paused to sip the last bit of his coffee. He placed the mug down, and wiped his mouth.

"If we're being realistic, we can just say he courted allies at any lengths and had no guiding principal save the pursuit of power."

"A bit like Shaw," responded the Rev.

"Well quite. Although I think self-preservation became his guiding principal. I suppose you can't blame him for that. I wonder where he is."

"Off courting his next allies, I expect."

Godfrey exhaled, pensively, contemplating his surrounds.

"God I need some booze, Rev. My mind and soul are thirsty."

"I'll doubt we'll get any here."

Godfrey let out another long sigh.

"No. Another one of those OCD rules. Abstention leads to a clean soul."

The Rev smiled.

"Maybe you'd be better off with the Atheist Fundamentalists then?"

"Dear boy, as you well know, I am not an atheist. And if I was an atheist I'd be a lot more easy-going than that lot. What was it they used to say? *God probably doesn't exist. Now stop worrying and enjoy your life.* Did they stop worrying and enjoy their life? No, they went on a bloody crusade!"

"So why don't you pop over and hang out with the Philosophical Agnostics. I know you share their principals and their *but it's all unknowable* rubbish."

"Total understanding is impossible."

"Bollocks. They're just scared to stick their neck out."

"Unsurprising given how hazardous that is in the People's Republic of Britannia."

At that, an ear-splitting explosion went off in the street outside. And then another.

The Rev looked out the window to see a man in a tank eviscerated. A one-sided Battle of Britain was taking place and some of the CUF boys were out on the street firing their machine guns skywards. A few went down as another bomb crashed into the street. The incessant incomings jolted the house, knocking open a cupboard door. Out rolled Shaw's head.

"Ah," said Godfrey. "That's where he got to."

## 32

# THE BUNKER

HAVING GONE TO Number Ten to find it no longer existed, Cliffe's van had headed to the damaged yet still moderately useable Buckingham Palace. With news that many more mid-to-high-ranking LibComs had been terminated in the Hellevue firefight, things were looking bleak.

Accompanied by six Blackguard, down to the war bunker went Fred, the two Siamese and the leader. It was grandly sized with enough air, supplies and facilities to last a long stay. That unnerved Fred. In fact, his anxiety was growing by the second. He no longer knew where he would be safest. The Palace seemed like a crazy idea. Whether he went out into the wilds of the tribal lands or not, Fred felt seating himself ten metres from Cliffe was a sure-fire way to be seating ten metres closer to his own demise.

The blitz showed no signs of stopping. Reports were coming in of many casualties. Hospitals and ambulances understaffed and under-equipped at the best of times were now completely over-stretched. Cities on the south coast had been hit and the capital had been razed in parts. Word came that Tower Bridge was capsized. Even St Paul's had taken a bit of a hammering, the dome now a hole. Fred was convinced that was a sign things were only going to get worse.

Concerned that superstition was taking root in his brain, Fred pootled off to powder his nose.

As Fred disappeared to the toilet, the rest congregated around Cliffe. He felt exposed. All around him were eyes, waiting for a decision. He hadn't realised that a leader had to make all the decisions, quickly, and get them right and that some might disagree. That almost seemed unreasonable. Did he have the courage of his own convictions?

"Who are they?" he cried. "(*suck-in*) What does all this mean?"

From the toilet, Fred heard no-one answer. Ask Garqi, he thought. And – I need to extricate myself from this little gathering.

Cliffe looked exhausted. If only it was an economic crisis I had to deal with, he thought wistfully. Then again... But Cliffe felt he had to address the nation. The elder Siamese advised a restoration of electricity to Hellevue. Cliffe agreed.

It aint gonna make the blindest bit of difference, thought Fred. We've subjected them to terrible slaughter. What are they thinking? Pin it all on the invaders?

Cliffe picked up the phone to Garqi. Surely the Italian would take *this* call.

But at that moment Garqi was busy with something else. Portsmouth, Dover and Brighton were being liberated. That was what they were being told anyway. It was from Brighton the TV cameras reported first. Cliffe put down the phone and watched the footage.

A crowd stood on the beach, a pissed rabble that had stumbled out of the all-night boozers. There were injuries and dead bodies and craters where bombs had landed. The gathered were transfixed by the fleet of boats in the harbour. A dark-skinned smiling gentleman alighted the first vessel, dropped jauntily onto the shingle, and spoke.

*"Greetings. How are you this fine evening?"*

Nothing.

The man looked at his watch and tittered.

*"Maybe is morning? But please, my name is Asif and we are not here to hurt the Britannic people."*

*"Bit fuckin late for that mate!"* shouted someone from higher up the beach.

Asif didn't engage the questioner.

*"With our new prospect of wealth, we have come to liberate you!"*

A rather inebriated woman asked a pertinent question.

*"Where are you from?"*

*"We are from Demoqristan."*

*"Where?"*

*"Demoqristan."*

The woman looked puzzled, but someone nearby gave her a brief précis. According to the annals of history, Demoqristan was a country that had felt the benefits of Western Interventionism some time before.

The liberator-in-chief pointed and smiled.

*"He clever. Yes. He right. We have come to return the favour, to set you people free... And, inshallah, crack open a new market."*

*"A new market! What?"*

*"We have discovered a new energy source in the Middle-East. And-"*

*"The where?"*

*"Friends, Britons, countrymen, we know that very few of you know anything of us, that the world has, how you say, relocalised. But we have to come to change that.*

*"In the graves of long dried-up black gold, we have found new fossil. We have come to release you from the shackles of New Democracy. Our Intelligence told us of the massacre at the inauguration of that terrible ugly man, Heath Cliffe. We know you do not like him. We don't either!"*

"How dare he!" shouted Cliffe.

Fred cracked a smile and it was all he could do not to crease uncontrollably. Haha! It's finally happened, he thought. Blighty breached for the first time since Billy the Conq. And all based on Intelligence! Intelligence? That's had a chequered past in the business of liberation. And this is what Garqi meant by foreign investment! The snake! Fred knew he had links to other countries, but bloody hell, a new energy source? That's the last thing that region needs.

Cliffe flashed a disdainful look.

"Sorry Heath," said Fred. "I think it's just a bit of hysteria."

Asif was continuing.....

*"We have come to restore a universal value to the people of these islands! Consumerism!"*

Cliffe watched on in stunned silence, the suck-in going berserk, fists shaking, eye socket pus-bags growing.

"Right (*suck-in*). I want Blackguard to start arming all Citizens in areas in the south and down to the coast (*suck-in*). Irrespective of their political persuasion up to this point (*suck-in*). It is surely in all our interests to repel an invasion!"

"Yes, but sir," said Porridgemouth, "it's not clear that everyone will view it that way. Think of conscription. Some areas down there are independent. We might make things worse for ourselves."

"Make it worse! (*suck-in*) How could it be worse?"

"Jehovah, Jehovah," mumbled Fred.

"We will dispatch all forces towards the South bar a garrison stronghold for London (*suck-in*) just in case the LUK, or anyone else for that matter (*suck-in*) sees this as an opportune time to seize power."

"That makes sense sir," said the elder Siamese.

Obsequious fuck, thought Fred. But this is it. This is the control hub of the country. Us four. Good fucking God. I need to get out of here forthwith.

Fred returned his attention to the television. Through the crowd, the liberator-in-chief had made his way into a pub. The cameras followed him in. Asif ordered a pint of local ale and to celebrate a rather successful mission to date, lit a cigar. Little did he know how officious the people of Britannia had become, even in the face of invasion.

*"You're gonna have to go outside with that thing. Health and Safety."*

*"I sorry. I not know all rules."*

The liberator chuckled, picked up his drink and made for the smokers huddled outside under a wilting umbrella.

*"And leave that in here. No glass outside, either."*

As Asif made his way outside he was approached by an irate Home County-ite.

*"Listen sir, this invasion is repulsive, grotesque, rude beyond words! While I may be vehemently opposed to the Government, the outrage and indignity of a bunch of foreigners swanning in and liberating us is far more revolting. We can do that ourselves, thank you very much, and in our own good time. So piss off!"*

*"Oh come on mate,"* said one of the regulars, *"these Demoqri-stanis can't make it any worse can they?"*

*"That standpoint is not only incredibly naive but totally unacceptable!"*

As a skirmish started, the reporter took to the camera.

*"As you can see the situation is far from clear. How many groups are there? It's hard to tell. Government groups, Demoqristanis, myriad resistance groups. What a mess it is. There are so many factions in operation that it seems there may no longer be universal loyalty to the idea of one country."*

"Fucking Garqi!" screamed Cliffe. "(*suck-in*) We never should've let that stinking Iti in this country! (*suck-in*) That grinning idiot Hair lets him bankroll us and now we're being fucking hijacked!"

A phone buzzed. A Blackguard answered it.

"Er, yes, of course."

The guard placed the phone on the desk.

"Er, Mr President, it's Signor Garqi."

Cliffe sucked-in, battle face on, picked up the phone.

"Oli... What?... Yes, no (*suck-in*)... I'm fine... In the bunker (*suck-in*)... the bunker!... It's the safest pl-...You've what?! (*suck-in*)... Now?... (*suck-in*)... Oh fuckinell! (*suck-in*)... Hello? Hello!"

Cliffe slammed down the phone.

"Fucker's trying to catch me out! (*suck-in*). Apparently there's a film crew upstairs (*suck-in*). Sherry let them in (*suck-in*). Didn't even know that bitch was still here!"

Despite his rage, Cliffe's natural instincts – firm hand on the tiller and all – was to downplay this whole Demoqristan development.

"I'll go on TV and tell the country not to worry," said Cliffe, an anxiety-laden wobble cascading through his face.

"Heath," said Fred, "realistically, once people have had their roofs bombed-in and relatives are lying limbless on the sofa, defiance is more the order of the day."

Before Cliffe could respond, his favourite interviewer was back on the nation's screens.

*"I'm sorry that last report had to be cut short. We had a minor technical issue. But we now have a major announcement for*

*you. We are going live to Buckingham Palace to hear from the President himself!"*

"Go on sir, quick!" said Fred.

Looking jowly and dishevelled Cliffe shimmied up the ladder of the bunker. A Blackguard opened a hatch at the top. Fred was the first one out after the President.

For once, Cliffe didn't simply bark out a pre-prepared statement, but spoke from his not inconsiderable gut. The nation's few remaining television sets blazed with his message.

*"We are a nation under attack* (suck-in) *and we need to unite against a common enemy. As yet, we do not know who they are* (suck-in) *or why they come."*

There was some whispering off stage from a Siamese.

*"Er, I mean, yes* (suck-in, strange plastic smile*), we do, er the, er* (suck-in), *"Demoqristanis, er, are.... Anyway* (suck-in) *I urge all Citizens* (suck-in) *to put aside their differences and fight to defend the sovereignty of this great nation* (suck-in). *Rebellion forces are holding the country to ransom if they refuse to corroborate with governmental forces!* (suck-in).

*"As a goodwill gesture* (suck-in), *the siege of Hellevue will cease immediately and electricity will be restored* (suck-in). *Essential services will resume in all areas* (suck-in). *In return* (suck-in), *I am calling on the LUK and all affiliate terrorist organisations* (suck-in) *to cease their activity with immediate effect. I believe it is the duty of all Britannic Citizens* (suck-in) *to join forces and repel these invaders. We are ignoring our obligation to each other* (suck-in) *if we do not fight as one."*

It might have been as well not to refer to his opponents as terrorists, thought Fred. Didn't really create amenable feelings. But that was the man's style. He wasn't about to go all touchy-feely now.

*"I can categorically say, we not lose this fight for freedom* (suck-in). *They say they will run our affairs. I say, that will not happen* (sharp suck-in). *No matter how far these invaders push us, we will win. We must pull together* (suck-in). *In return* (suck-in), *I promise free and fair elections as soon as conditions allow."*

Fred could sense Cliffe was starting to sense his very own Churchill moment. He'd clearly forgotten what happened to Winnie after he beat the Nazis. And anyway, first he had to win the battle.

*"For now (suck-in), I'm getting on with the business of running the country. (suck-in) Thank you."*

"That was excellent sir," said Porridgemouth, amid a general atmosphere of back-slapping and self-congratulation. "And there have been a number of responses already."

"Really?" asked Cliffe, allowing a shade of positivity in his tone.

"This arrived while we were on air," said Porridegmouth, opening a thin brown package.

"Hold on!" shouted the older Siamese. "It might be a bomb!"

"Oh don't be so wet," Porridgemouth retorted.

There was a disc inside and Cliffe and his entourage gathered round a computer. After a moment's loading, a rather poorly lit room came into vision. A man in his late fifties sat on a chair and spoke.

*"I am Pastor Ian Parsley, leader of The CUF. We have considerable support and are ready to help in the leadership of this land."*

"Who the fuck are the CUF?" asked Cliffe as the video faded to footage from a bar, presumably in Hellevue. It was heart-warming – the decapitation of Calloway replete with images of two old men in the background, looking worse for wear.

"And Calloway was the fucking LUK leader?" screamed Cliffe.

Fred was equally shocked. Clegg with the bankers, Calloway with the literary terrorists. He remembered Calloway saying he'd return to frontline politics the day he was marched out of Hair's office. All this time, thought Fred. Bloody hell.

"But they want to help us?" Cliffe asked Porridgemouth.

Finally, thought the President, things are turning my way.

"To be honest President," responded Porridgemouth, "we haven't got the first idea. It seems there are any number of different factions operating in and around the slum and they all seem to believe they have a bargaining chip with which to play."

"What do you mean?"

"In return for support against the invasion they request a stake in the power and running of the country. We have at least six other such discs here. And actually, a lot of them aren't confined to Hellevue. Probably explains how they've been able to make these films so quickly."

"Who do you suggest we work alongside?"

"Well, the problem is sir, because there is now no one overarching leader to deal with, any number of two-bit operators are putting themselves forward as representative not only of Hellevue but many other districts. There is only thing of which we feel certain. The LUK is no more. I'd suggest letting the district implode. They can't be trusted to fight alongside us I wouldn't have thought."

"But this CUF is willing to talk to the Government?"

"Yes sir. But remember, this CUF also decapitated its last allies so I wouldn't be inviting them round for tea just yet. And in other parts of the country there will be some without electricity who probably don't even know we've been invaded."

"Maybe not," said the President, "*(suck-in)* but this is further progress! The LUK down and parts of Hellevue wanting to join us!"

"Indeed," said the elder Siamese, "and maybe those factions still fighting against us will follow after your speech."

Jesus, it's like being cooped up with Gadaffi and sons, thought Fred. You're going down!

But he sensed this was his moment. As Cliffe and the Siamese and other assorted sycophants began to scheme – God help us if this lot are the ones to defend us – Fred sloped off, unnoticed. There was just one more thing he wanted to do before he made his escape.

## 33
# NO TURNING BACK

PONTIFF COULDN'T SLEEP. He'd heard distant rumblings of artillery, the odd flash lighting up the corridor outside his cell. He'd been convinced bombs were being dropped. He'd shouted out to the guards to ask what was going on but had been told to keep quiet. He surmised outright fighting must have commenced between Hellevue and the Government.

Now it was deathly silent. The bombs, if they had been, had stopped. Pontiff wasn't sure if any other prisoners were being held here as he'd been unconscious on his arrival. But with Hellevue probably a battleground at the moment, Pontiff felt it likely a huge number of Blackguard had been dispatched there.

Pontiff lay back on his thin mattress, perched on a stone slab. His stomach lurched as he thought of Godfrey and the RevKev. And again, more violently, when he thought of Clem. He had failed to find her and would now not have the chance. A lifetime in custody awaits, he thought. Should I have stayed with the LUK? Should I have read *Best Practice Going Forward*? After all, it did spell out the dangers to a *Recent Realigned* about becoming a resident once again, possibly even permanently. Possibly so, thought Pontiff. Should I have made a run for it after escaping from *The Rumour*? Should I have-

Bzzzzzzzzzzzz.

Pontiff turned his head slowly to the cell door. He lay still for a moment and then the NIPSD scanner beeped. He sat upright, stood up, looked at the device. It was flashing. Barefoot, Pontiff walked to the cell door.

*"Application to exit Correctional Facility... Environmental Footprint being calculated... Patience, Citizen, is a virtue."*

What? That message only appeared after you'd swiped your NIPSD card. Pontiff's had been taken off him soon after he had arrived.

*"Individual Carbon Footprint: 1.8. Thank you Citizen. You are helping in the drive towards a cleaner, more efficient country."*

The door clunked and began to slide back. Holy fucken shit! The NIPSD Engine Room must be goen haywire after the onslaught! Pontiff stepped out of his cell, nervous possibility cascading through him. But what next?

To escape, he would still have to navigate armed guards. How many, he didn't know. And then what? He looked around, turned right out of his cell and began walking down the corridor. Pontiff hadn't seen the full dimensions of the barracks but the place was tiny. There were only a handful of cells. Pontiff counted four including his, all empty. As he walked down to the end of the corridor there were a few doors that looked like locked offices. He turned the corner. It was another dead-end but there were two more cells on either side. After a quick glance Pontiff surmised they were empty too. He turned back to retrace his steps, to put his boots on, to think of a plan of attack, when he heard –

"Fuck off, alright!"

Pontiff knew that voice, that greeting. He spun around in an instant, slipping on the floor. He tripped over and crashed onto the ground just yards from a pair of female feet.

"Ah ya fucker!" he shouted as he looked at his now bleeding toe. He looked up and could see the flash of dark brown eyes through the gloom. "Jesus Christ Clem! What you dae-en here?"

"I might ask you the same thing. Alright you fucking bearded Switzerland!"

Pontiff staggered up, swaying slightly.

"Give us a hug then," said Clem, pulling Pontiff into her medium-sized frame. She was 5"6 and dressed in an oversized all-in-one white linen suit. "When did you get back on the fuckin radar?" she asked, pulling away quite roughly. "I'd practically written you off! Great performance at Cliffe's inauguration, by the way. Brightened up my day."

"Cheers."

"So, how you been?" smiled Clem.

"Ah, y'know. Ups and downs. You?"

"Oh I've been treated marvellously."

Clem paused, scrutinised Pontiff's appearance.

"What the fuck trousers are you wearing?"

"Don't ask. But fuck me Clem, I'm so fucken relieved tae find you."
He hugged her again. "But what *are* you dae-en here? An why you got
the Life Camp uniform on?"

"Er, maybe cos I *been there*?"

"Don't do that upward inflection thing, Clem."

"Ha! I only do it cos I know *it will annoy you?*"

Pontiff smiled. "Aye, I fucken *know you do?*"

"Anyway," said Clem, slapping Pontiff's arm, "what about you? As
you recognise my attire can I assume your time has been punctuated
by a spell at Shrink Clink too?"

"Aye, *LifeManagement4Life 1872*, aye."

"No way! That's where I was! Where I refused to sign the confession."

"Confession?"

"Yes Pontiff. For the manslaughter of my son."

"Jesus Clem, I..."

"Pontiff. Ben's not dead. Don't ask me how I know, I just... After I
refused to jump through their hoops I was brought here. That was just
over a week ago."

She paused, looked around.

"And now we're both here."

"Aye, what are the chances?"

"So what's your escape plan?"

"Fuck knows. Huvnae got one."

"Well let's get your boots on and we'll work it out."

\*\*\*

Fred knew he had crossed so many different people it was inevitable it
would all catch up with him soon. The medieval lust for gruesome punishment he'd seen in Hellevue meant he feared greatly for his health.

He had straddled so many borders between black and white that anyone from either (or any) side would have good cause to end his experiment with life.

He had walked back to *Cow* HQ and soon discovered the barracks at which Pope was being held.

That, and that another inmate was there.

This is fucking extraordinary, he thought. You'd think they would have kept them apart. Joined-up governance failed again.

Post-haste, he headed to the west of the city in his car. After a few minutes his phone started ringing. It was *Cow* HQ.

Fuck that, thought Fred. I'm not going back.

But no sooner had it rung off than it started again. Then his car phone, then his government pager. A message appeared.

**"Needed back at HQ to verb Cow ops. Dispatch has been sent to your flat and will pick you up from there."**

No it bloody won't, thought Fred.

Then another beep. This time it was Garqi.

**"Where are you? It won't be long before the people of this country have their desire for ownership and the latest craze reignited. The end is nigh for the LibComs. You want in? It's not too late for you to join, you know. These Demoqristanis could use you…"**

Fred was tempted but he had had quite enough excitement. All he wanted was to get to Pope and help the man whose position was as tricky as his own. He also wanted to help *Enigma*, tell him where his Clem was. Bit of decency at the death. It was a calculated risk. Fred knew that *Enigma* would have his hands full in Hellevue and wouldn't be able to get to the destination quickly. Fred didn't fancy a meeting. In any case, he didn't know whether *Enigma* would even be able to read it, but Fred wanted to sign off nonetheless.

**Enigma –**

**Apologies I could not meet you earlier. As you suggested, my life is tricky. Getting into Hellevue would have been impossible. This is my final act as Ockham. You won't hear from me again so I wish you good luck. And may our hopes to bring down the disgrace that is the LibComs come true. Quite how such buffoons like Hair and Cliffe got this far is beyond me. Maybe the Demoqristanis can facilitate our dreams in the short term.**

**Clementine Romain is in Barracks 342, near Maida Vale. Adieu.**

\*\*\*

At first they thought Fred had gone to the toilet for a really long shit. They had now concluded he had left the building. But why?

The continuing reticence of Fred to answer his phone or respond to his messages had unnerved Cliffe. Though he had always resented Fred for usurping his position at the LibCom Roundtable, he needed the man's brains. He knew his own survival probably depended on the presence of the *Punjabi Homo*. Reports were coming in that the Demoqristanis' marauding through southern England was proving to be rather successful. Areas of the South Downs had already been taken. Apparently the invaders-slash-liberators had been met by pockets of resistance but they had been hopelessly outgunned. As the assault on Britannic land was becoming increasingly serious, it was becoming increasingly obvious that the military was not going to be able to prevent further inroads. The Demoqristanis were making an inexorable march towards London. Garqi was hardly helping with the reportage on the television. They're gonna walk this invasion, thought Cliffe.

And that is why he needed Fred's input.

A car had been dispatched to fetch Fred at home, as a matter of some urgency. The squad had been told to enter if necessary. Wake him, whatever. Just bring him back to Cabinet at Buckingham Palace!

"Er, sir," said Porridgemouth, interrupting Cliffe at his desk back down in the bunker. "We have news on Fred."

"Is he here?"

"Er, no."

Porridgemouth shifted on his feet.

"Well what is it?"

"When the platoon arrived at Fred's flat, they found an old, very confused woman at the door trying to enter."

"So?"

"She asked if they knew where her son was."

"Ye-es?"

"She said she had some strange correspondence from him. This was it."

Porridgemouth handed Cliffe the phone. Cliffe's eyes scanned over it.

"What th... Fred is... *buffoons like Hair and Cliffe... Demoqristanis can facilitate our dreams in the short term!*"

Cliffe dropped the phone. He was apoplectic. Fred was *Ockham*!

"Put it out across all government channels that Fred is a deserter to be taken dead or alive. And don't let it get anywhere near Garqi!"

Maybe he knows too, thought Cliffe.

"Also, send a dispatch to Barracks 342. Bring in this Clementine Romain!"

Cliffe needed a walk to digest all this. Again he blamed Hair and raged at the folly of the deceased ex-leader.

He left the bunker and went for a wander around the Palace. As he did so another thought struck him. Fred had killed a **KARMATARMAK** colleague.

Dazed, Cliffe walked into the room that hosted cabinet meetings. There was a pissed Sherry, swigging at some vodka.

"What the fuck are you doing here?" demanded Cliffe.

"Considering my options, Heath, taking stock. Be a dear and pour mummy another drink, would you?"

"*(suck-in)* Get it yourself."

Sherry got up. "Call yourself a gentleman."

"No *(suck-in)*."

"No wonder you never married," Sherry responded as she sat back down with some fruit juice, a glass and another bottle of Vodka. She sighed as she lounged, took a good long sip. "Ooh I am rather excited about the imminent arrival of the foreigners. I think the leader's rather good looking and I'm sure he'll make a better fist of leadership than you! I have decided that the position of First Lady is one that suits me rather well. I have a proposal for the Demoqristan leader when he arrives."

"You salty old slag! *(suck-in)* What do you think he'll make of you?"

"Well I'm probably bolder than the girls he's met back home that's for sure! I can welcome him to the country with open arms."

"Open legs more like."

"Just cos you didn't get any of my action."

As Cliffe glared at Sherry with a mixture of lust and disgust there was a light tap at the door. Porridgemouth walked in.

"Er, sir, sorry to disturb. We've taken Fred's mother into custody, arrested her as a potential accomplice. As for Fred himself, he left *Cow* HQ thirty minutes ago. We have alerted all stations, barracks and checkpoints to detain him."

"Right." Cliffe turned to Sherry. "*(suck-in)* I'll deal with you later!"

As Cliffe and Porridgemouth walked off, Sherry reached for her phone.

\*\*\*

Fred's mind was whirring.

He was shovelling drugs and booze into his system knowing the next few hours were going to be crucial not only in terms of his own survival and Pontiff's, but also Cliffe's and his ability to retain *his* crown. That thought comforted Fred. Cliffe had so much on his plate at Westminster that cerebrations on absconding government ministers would probably wait.

He'll be surrounded by sycophants, trying to deal with invasion, he won't worry about me.

Of course there was the outside chance that if Fred didn't answer his phone they might try and track him down. Fred had been seen at *The Cow* offices and wondered how long it would be until his computer was checked to see what he had last looked at. He worried there would be a dispatch waiting for him at the barracks to take him back to Buckingham Palace.

He didn't realise the situation was far more critical than that.

Fred was satisfied he had left no evidence, and it had been long enough now that Sherry had clearly said nothing. But after he'd rescued Pope, would they get out of the city? And negotiate that, what about the tribal areas? What about tomorrow?

Almost on cue, his phone buzzed into life again. It was Sherry.

He could do without that, he thought, and let the phone ring out.

319

Fred's neck pulsed as he arrived at the barracks. It was a small, two storey facility. Fred knew it was primarily used as a holding bay before prisoners were transferred. He left his briefcase, laptop and few belongings locked in his car and took with him his gun and the goody bag he'd prepared for Pope. His neck throbbed again.

*"I am in blood*
*Stepp'd in so far that, should I wade no more,*
*Returning were as tedious as go o'er."*

Fred swiped in and walked through the doors.

Directly ahead of him, ten metres away, was a raised desk. Two Blackguard were sat behind it, evidently playing a game of some sort. On either side of the desk were four steps leading up to the entrance hatches. To the left of the desk, Fred's right, was a lift. Also on Fred's right, just adjacent to the front door as he came in, was the stairwell which led to offices upstairs. Behind the raised desk was an open-plan office and to the right of the desk, Fred's left, was the corridor to the cells. One of the many government intercoms was blaring.

*"Be vigilant. NIPSD is having problems. There are reports of mass breakouts from correctional facilities and Life Camps. Be vigilant."*

One of the guards noticed Fred as he approached, and nudged the other.

"Mr McVelly," said the former, jumping up. "Good evening." He paused. "You're out late, sir."

"Good evening guards," Fred responded with a smile. "Yes, well, an anti-terrorist's work is never done. But I'm not staying long. On that note, I am sure you know about the change of plan regarding Pope."

The two Blackguard looked at each other. They didn't seem like the sharpest tools in the box.

"C'mon guards," said Fred. "Get the cuffs and take me to him. Then I'll take him to the President."

"Yes sir," said the guard on Fred's left, the guard closest to the corridor to the cells.

He plodded down the steps. It was all painfully slow.

"Quicker!" shouted Fred.

"Sorry sir."

At the bottom of the steps he turned to his colleague at the desk.

"Go in that back office and get the cuffs, Nige. I thought I'd left em in this tray down here."

"OK Dave," said Nige.

*"Following invasion, all Blackguard bar small garrison stronghold to be dispatched south to meet Demoqristanis. Situation critical."*

"Ooh, that's exciting Dave," said Nige from the backroom.

"Nigel!" screamed Fred. "Hurry the fuck up!"

"Yes sir. Sorry s-"

*"All units, all units. This is a security announcement. Repeat, this is a security announcement. Detain Fred McVelly, Head of Cow Ops, immediately. Repeat, detain McVelly immediately. Detain McVelly immediately."*

Dave looked at Fred and shrugged apologetically. Fred's mind began to corrugate. Sherry. That fucking bitch!

Nige returned from the office holding the cuffs. He looked to Dave for guidance.

"Er, sir, looks like we have orders, erm, to detain you?" stammered Dave, stumbling as he ascended the steps to the desk.

*"All units, all units. This is a security announcement. Repeat, this is a security announcement. Detain Fred McVelly, Head of Cow Ops, immediately. Repeat, detain McVelly immediately. If he resists, use force."*

Again Dave and Nigel looked at each other. Dave shrugged, and nodded.

"Er, sorry sir," said Nigel, uncertainty issuing from his larynx, "but looks like we do have to detain you after all?"

"OK, OK. Let's just calm down." said Fred, his neck-pulse returning. "NIPSD is clearly on the blink. You heard what that thing said earlier. It must be a NIPSD error or the Demoqristanis fucking with everything."

"But sir," said Nige, "we-"

Dave nodded.

"That makes sense, Nige."

"Of course it makes sense," said Fred. "Now look, we haven't got time to fuck around. It is urgent this prisoner is transported now. We are taking him to President Cliffe. Do you want to ring the leader and tell him why his meeting is gonna be delayed?"

Nothing.

"No, I didn't think so."

The guards remained impassive.

"Well come on then!" screamed Fred.

From round the corner Pontiff and Clem were hearing everything. They'd already tried to escape, thinking that if cell doors had been released maybe an alternative exit would also be open. Alas no. They'd searched in vain for weapons. Again, nothing. They'd thought about staying put and devising a plan to escape when the guards returned but then they heard this little scene unfold.

President Cliffe, eh? thought Pontiff. He and Clem exchanged a look. This just gets more preposterous by the second.

"OK, sir," said Nige. "If you'd like to foll-"

"All units, all units, detain McVelly, repeat, detain McVelly immediately. He is the terrorist, Ockham. Repeat, he is the terrorist Ockham. If arrest not possible, take him down. Activation Code 29/L. Cow authorised. Detain or neutralise McVelly! This is not an error. Activation Code 29/L. Neutralise McVelly!"

"Oh for f-" said Fred, swinging his head to one side, his arms lolling against his legs.

As Nige looked again to Dave for guidance he spied Pontiff and Clem.

"How did they get out?"

With that, Fred was back in the land of the sentient, his head erect again.

"See!" he shouted. "Clearly NIPSD is on the blink otherwise these two wouldn't be standing here! Doors are opening, misinformation is spewing out the speakers and frankly you two are displaying gross incompetence."

"So you're not Ockham?" asked Nigel.

"Of course I'm not fucking Ockham!" shouted Fred.

"Maybe he is Nige," said Clem from round the corner. "You can never be too careful."

"Shut up! No-one asked you!" shouted Dave, looking to his right.

"Ah come on guards," said Pontiff, "that's no way tae talk tae a lady, is it?"

"He said shut it!" shouted Nige.

*"All units, all units, detain McVelly, repeat detain McVelly immediately. He is the terrorist, Ockham. Repeat, he is the terrorist Ockham."*

"Jesus Christ!" shouted Nigel. "What do we do? What the fuck do we do now, Dave?"

"Yeah Dave, what next?" asked Clem.

"I said shut it!" shouted Dave, pulling his gun out and pointing it at Clem.

"Let's just all calm down, eh?" said Fred.

"You be quiet too!" shouted Nige, pulling his gun on Fred. "Sir. Sorry sir."

"Dave, tell Nigel to put his gun down," said Fred, matter-of-factly. *"If arrest not possible, take McVelly down. He is a traitor. Activation Code 29/L. Cow authorised. Detain or neutralise McVelly! This is not an error. Activation Code 29/L. Neutralise McVelly!"*

"Dave?" said Nige, turning momentarily to his senior officer.

Dave was keeping Pontiff and Clem in his sights but in that brief moment the two Blackguard heard an ominous click from by the door. Both turned to point their guns at Fred who stood in front of them, his gun trained on them.

"Now look, we're all getting a little excitable," said Fred. "I am here at the President's request and he has asked me to bring the Hellevue Hero to him."

Fred bent down, ensuring one eye and his gun were always trained on the two guards. He opened the bag by his feet.

"What are you doing?" shouted Nigel. "Don't make me shoot!"

"Just relax," responded Fred. "It's just some presents from the President." He eased out a bottle of whiskeysquash and a large pouch of tobacco. "See."

Fred set them down, looking at Pontiff and Clem as though presenting an offering to tame a wild animal. He gave Pontiff a nod, and placing the whiskeysquash on top of the pouch, slid the bundle over. It stopped about three or four metres short of the corner behind which Pontiff and Clem stood.

For a moment no-one moved.

Finally Pontiff broke the silence.

"Right. Now. Guards, as I see it, that's a gift from the President, an therefore it's my Britannic or human or some fucken right to have it. Are you gonnae promise me you'll not shoot while I pick it up?"

"It will look very bad for you if you don't let him, believe me," said Fred.

Dave and Nige again shared a look. Dave scratched his head, closed his eyes.

"Right, I'm comen out," said Pontiff, "unarmed. I'll even put my hands in the air, how about that?"

As Pontiff approached the whiskeysquash and tobacco, he said, "I'll have tae put ma hands down now as I'm picken this up, OK?"

Pontiff coughed as he reached down to pick up the gifts. A spot of blood splatted on the floor. Fred was again impressed by the sheer stamina of the man not to be broken.

"Oh aye, jus what I fucken needed. Tell the President thank you," said Pontiff.

"Well you can thank him yourself shortly," said Fred, catching sight of Clem for the first time. So you're her, he thought, the one *Enigma* loves. In the midst of concocting the Hellevue Hero plan Fred had never seen with his own eyes this Clementine Romain. She was undoubtedly beautiful.

*"All units, all units, detain McVelly, repeat, detain McVelly immediately. He is the terrorist, Ockham. If arrest not possible, take him down."*

"Oh turn that fucking thing off!" shouted Fred, unleashing a round into the transmitter.

"Right, you... you shouldn't have done that!" shouted Nigel.

"Mr McVelly, you need to calm down," said Dave, keeping his firearm pointed at Fred.

Clem nudged Pontiff.

"I feel bad I got arrested if these two fuckwits are representative of the standard of Blackguard," she said.

"What did she say?" asked Dave.

"Just that I'm enjoying the show," responded Clem. "How you gettin on, Nige?"

But Nige didn't answer. He was staring at Fred, gun-barrel straight.

Ravenous for a drink, Pontiff opened the whiskeysquash bottle and gulped from it. Clem opened the pouch and after removing a clump of tobacco was rummaging for some rolling papers when she felt something rather unexpected. At first she didn't believe what her hand made out but as she squeezed it to her palm she knew what it was; the cold metal of a tiny pistol. She removed it, saying nothing, and hid it in her Life Camp uniform.

"Here," she whispered to Pontiff, handing him the tobacco and the papers. "Make me one, would you?"

"Look, Guards," said Fred, "I have told you. There are problems with NIPSD. That Activation Code is clearly false. I should reprimand you for not having a full list of all the codes. If we lose our minds now we will not be able to repel the invasion."

Pontiff took another swig from the whiskeysquash and rolled the cigarettes.

"You get the matches?" he asked.

"Will you two keep quiet!" shouted Dave, taking his aim away from Fred.

Instinctively, Nige followed suit and with their backs turned, Clem watched Fred ingest a mouthful of pills and snort from a wrap.

"Oh fuck it. Here we go!" he shouted.

BANG!

Down went Nigel, rolling down the three steps on his side of the raised desk. Dave clambered over to his left, down the steps to Nige's body.

"Nige!" he screamed.

"Come on Pont, let's go!" shouted Clem as she leapt forward clutching the pistol. "I'll cover you."

"What the fuck, Clem! Where dyou get that fucken thing!"

"Come on Pontiff," shouted Fred with one hand on the door. "I don't want to hang around any longer than I have-"

Bffffzzzz!

The wall next to Fred's eye exploded as a shot rang out, and he darted into the stairwell to his had hit him in the shoulder.

"Get behind this corner Clem right. Clem fired a shot but unsighted by the desk it whistled over Dave and the bleeding, whimpering Nigel lying prostrate on the floor. Fred!" shouted Pontiff, feeling exposed as the only combatant with no weapon.

"Everything you said today," called out Fred, staying concealed in the far corner up the stairwell, "it's all true!"

"Eh?"

"I said, everything you-"

BANG!

A shot rang out from Dave's gun, the bullet eradicating the lobe of Pontiff's right ear.

"Jesus fucken shit!" shouted Pontiff, clutching his ear. He turned to the far side of the desk to see Dave duck back down. Blood covered Pontiff's hands. He held a piece of cartilage between his fingers.

From behind the stairwell, a shot flew out of Fred's gun forcing Dave to clamber up the steps on the left side of the desk to take cover. Nige tried to move but went down again as another shot rang out from Fred. Dave popped his head up from behind the parapet and fired two shots at Fred who again took evasive action in the stairwell.

"Nige! Nige!" shouted Dave but there was no response.

Pontiff was suddenly aware of movement next to him. "No!" he whispered, reaching out a hand, but Clem easily evaded his grip.

With stealth she ran airlessly and silently towards the desk before vaulting over it and somersaulting through the air. Dave was holding Nige's weakened body when he detected Clem's flying presence above him. He turned to shoot but Clem was too fast for him, shooting his hand as she landed. Blood, fingers and the gun flew out of Dave's hand.

"You fucking bitch!" he shouted and came towards Clem, who shot again, this time into his leg.

"Aaaaaagh!"

Dave went down in front of the desk, minus a hand and a kneecap.

"Jesus Christ Clem," said Pontiff standing up on the other side of the desk, blood pissing out of his ear.

"How you getting on there?" Fred shouted.

"Ah, jus great, ken," replied Pontiff, slipping back into his laceless boots that had come loose.

"Shall we depart then?" called Fred.

"Let's fucking go!" shouted Clem.

Fred was swiping his NIPSD card on the SwipeScanner as Pontiff grabbed the tobacco and the whiskeysquash. Was this *Ockham* or not?

From the back office another transmitter crackled into action.

*"Turn yourself in, son. It's no use."*

It was a woman.

*"They know what you've done. They know what you've been planning. If you come in now and see your old mum, they'll drop the charges of murder of the* **KARMATARMAK** *terrorist Don Coyote. Fred, darling, I love you and I'm so proud but come in now. It's over."*

*Don Coyote*, thought Pontiff? Where had he-? My God. It was true. Huwi was dead.

Pontiff thought again of the horror of John Rer's death. It was hard to feel sadness at the passing of a man like Huwi.

*"All units, all units, that is Ockham's mother. Repeat, that is the terrorist Ockham's mother. McVelly is Ockham. Neutralise or bring in, neutralise or bring in."*

Fred felt murmurings from his heart as it fluttered before exploding into its beat. Fuck is she doing on there?

Clem turned to Fred who had still not managed to get his card to work the SwipeScanner, still digesting how his mother had come to make that announcement. And then it twigged. He looked at his phone. There it was. The crushing truth. He hadn't sent the message to *Enigma*. He'd sent it to his mother. He also saw the message from Sherry. She'd been trying to warn him.

"Who's *Don Coyote*?" asked Clem.

"Huwi," said Pontiff, thinking of *Enigma*, thinking of how he would react to the news that it was *Ockham*, the old man's favourite writer, who was responsible for Huwi's death.

Clem also grappled with this revelation. Pontiff had given her a history of the last few weeks while they had searched for an exit and she was well aware of what Huwi had done, and intended to do, especially to Pontiff, that it was all out of some misguided devotion to her. Though she'd never liked Huwi and had berated the Rev for getting him involved in **KARMATARMAK** it was hard to think he was dead at the hands of this besuited man here in the barracks. Was this really *Ockham*?

"You killed Huwi?" she asked.

"Oh surely you don't believe that, do you?" responded Fred. "You don't wanna believe my mother, she's insane."

He turned back to the SwipeScanner, not having a good feeling about where all this was heading.

Neither did Pontiff. He wanted to escape. But with this guy? He motioned Clem over to him to take refuge behind the corner again.

"Oh fuck it!" shouted Fred when the SwipeScanner refused to work. He ingested some more powder from his pocket.

"Look Clem," whispered Pontiff, "this gadgie doesnae look too together. I don't know who he is but I dinnae think goen wi'him is good for us."

Clem agreed but as she peered back to look at, well, who? – *Ockham*? McVelly? – she inadvertently kicked the whiskeysquash bottle towards the desk.

Fred jumped at the sound, turning towards it.

"Look, are we getting out of here, or what?" he said.

"You must be out your mind if you think we're goen with you," responded Pontiff from behind the corner.

"Oh for fuck's sake! Because I killed some fucking Welsh barman? Christ, so what if I did? You think Huwi's special? No-one's special! I was beginning to think you were, Pontiff. Don't make me change my mind."

"Are you really *Ockham*?" shouted Clem.

"Of course I fucking am! But you don't know the half of it. You've done remarkably well, Pontiff."

He turned back to the door, gun pointing at it.

"Well, I must depart, either with you or not. And...."

Fred spun round, dropped his gun down.

"Hang on. What do you mean, *Huwi*? Did you know him or something? Fucking hell! I mean I knew you two knew each other. Garqi told me. How Pontiff had the hots for the child murderer."

Fred snorted from a wrap, put a handful of pills in his mouth and took a swig from hip flask.

Pontiff looked at Clem.

"Just shoot the fuck," he said. "An then we'll get out."

"No. I want to hear what he says. Don't worry, Pont, I know what I'm doing."

She smiled.

"So you've got the hots for me, have you?"

"Just fucken concentrate, Clem."

"But you both knew him?" continued Fred. "Are you in **KARMATAR-MAK** too, Ms Romain? *Enigma* didn't say. And you Pontiff, are you? Are we all literary comrades?"

Fred started laughing. He wasn't surprised at this latest revelation. He reached into his pocket for another wrap. How had things got so beyond his control?

"I couldn't believe it when *Enigma* asked after you, Ms Romain. You young lady, you. And I thought, why? And then today, you, Mr Pope, I see you defending the child murderer. My, this is lovely. So romantic. And here I was thinking we were the same Pontiff, you and I. I thought you did it all for a laugh. Based on what I've seen, the disregard for the dry days, the scant regard for authority!"

Pontiff didn't know what to make of this. Clem's brown eyes blazed with an angry pain.

"But you are a strong man," said Fred, vacating the stairwell. "Like me."

He wandered over to the bodies of Nige and Dave, kicking at both. Dave moaned but Fred didn't seem to notice.

"When I first came upon your existence, Pontiff" – Fred paused to shovel some more powder up his nose – "I thought you were an isolated alcoholic. And I was right."

Fred smiled at the truth of that thought. "But I certainly found it most unexpected that someone who had been through so much would still be battling so hard," he continued, waving his gun as he spoke. "You didn't just cede to our offer of the easy life. I never imagined you had so much substance. I only found that out as you played along with my little game." Fred paused. "You know I never normally smoke, but tonight..."

He lit up a cigarette.

"Little game? What do you-?"

"I liked the fact you understood the absurdity I created. You never let it defeat you. I admire that." Fred drank again from his hip flask. "They'll be here soon you know. We have to resolve this one way and another. I suggest you come with me."

"What dae you mean *little game*?" asked Pontiff again, the juices of anger and anxiety cocktailing in his guts.

"Oh come on, you're quicker than that. *The Hellevue Hero* thing was my idea. When it was brought to my attention that young Ms Romain was failing as a mother the story practically wrote itself."

Pontiff couldn't believe it. Had this man had a plan for him all along like some demented deity? He was the architect of Pontiff's misery?

Dave was moaning more loudly.

"But why do all this if you're in **KT**?" shouted Clem.

"Have you learned nothing about me? I live for fun! How the fuck was I allowed to do all it, eh?"

Fred continued to traverse the entrance hall.

"How the fuck could I get to the top and practically run this country? I was testing the theory that we are run by nodding, dribbling muppets with bulbous noses, coiffed hair, and suspenders underneath their suits, and they are! The great tragedy is that the only people who want to run this country, any country, are social perverts."

"From where I'm standing, you look a social pervert," said Clem, noting that the maniac was looking rather less dapper than before.

"You're probably right!" exploded Fred, taking another glug from his hip flask.

Pontiff and Clem did likewise from their bottle.

"Anyway," continued Fred with an ungainly effort to maintain his balance, "the whole country's a perverted mess now. If it wasn't before. We are about to be run by foreigners. Your lot are fighting each other, others are fighting the Demoqristanis. This is our best chance to leave. You will be as lost and repressed under these foreign troops as you were under me!"

"Ma lot?" said Pontiff. "I'm no affiliated tae anything. Jus tryna stay alive."

Fred laughed.

"That makes two of us! That's why I've come to respect you, Pontiff. You've done remarkably well. You both have. I want to get you out of all this. But we're running out of time. So come on. I'm trying to bloody rescue you. I want to go abroad. I want you to come with me. We're the same after all!"

"You're no like the usual politician, thasfoshir," responded Pontiff, still behind the corner. "But mate, we aint the same."

"Listen to me you yardsed cunt," said Clem, measuredly. "Where is my son? You took him from me. Now you're gonna tell me how I'm gonna get him back."

"No no no. Hang on a moment. I didn't take your son. It just gave me an idea. I merely picked up the baton. Or as they say in politics and football, I picked it up and ran with it. Anyway, it all seemed to fit in nicely with the PSU. What doesn't kill you, makes you stronger."

Fred paused.

"I should have used that for a *Cow* announcement."

He laughed. He found it hilarious, painfully so.

"God people are idiots! It's incredible what they will swallow!"

"Where is my son?"

"I haven't got the first fucking idea."

"I know you know," said Clem, again in self-possessed tones.

"Oh you know I know, do you? But you know what you don't know?"

Fred paused to laugh at his Rumsfeldian English.

"She fucked a lot of you, that Dr Zini. I used to watch footage of them all at Life Camp. Made for great viewing while I was entertaining. I would have fucked her an'all I have to say. There must have been worse ways to get your escape, eh Pontiff? And Ms Romain, she didn't half want to taste your brown sugar! I saw the way she stroked you during your entrance interview!"

Fred laughed uncontrollably again, staggering with an acid-swirl. He started mumbling, hitting his hand towards his head and continuing his howl-like laugh.

Jesus fuck, thought Pontiff, he's gan tae meltdown.

"They've got it wrong! The fools, the fools!" shouted Fred, making aeroplane hands like a young boy. He began to run around the entrance hall. "Double agent. Double agent! Ha! I work for no-one! Pontiff, you actually had the offer of the good life. And you chose this? Unbelievable. I thought it's because you had morals. Now I realise you just have no sense."

He might be right, thought Pontiff.

BANG!

A shot flew out of Fred's gun.

BANG!

And another. He was shooting in any direction.

BANG! BANG!

Two shots flew out of Clem's gun. The first whistled over Fred's head, the other caught him just on the top of the shoulder.

"Aaagh, you fucking Bearded Switzerland!"

"Fucker's stealin my lines!" shouted Clem as she shot again.

BANG!

This time an arm shot.

"Aaagh. Fucking stop doing that!" Fred shouted, collapsing to the floor. He raised his hand to shoot. Put it down again. Used the other hand. Click, nothing. He fumbled in his pockets for more rounds.

Clem went to finish off the job. Click.

"Fuck!"

She darted back behind the corner.

Pontiff made a run for the desk, taking in Fred's feral and distant look, the dribble on the chin. He had taken off his suit jacket and was making a rudimentary tourniquet. Frantically Pontiff searched for a weapon. He wanted a gun. He saw the whiskeysquash bottle on the floor but then saw Fred, satisfied with his self-nursing, starting to reload. Pontiff ducked behind the desk.

"It is certainly a shame I shall have to kill you both too if you won't come with me. I did not enjoy killing your Huwi."

He eased himself up off the floor.

"We could have gone to France together. We're soulmates, Pontiff, as I've told you. The only two that understand this sham. Ms Romain can come if she wants as well. We could share her. But look, Pontiff, Ms Romain, there is an easy way and a hard way to do this. But you know, if I was going to revert to type, I would have to say..."

Fred adopted an official tone, "You are enemies of the state. You have absconded from a government facility and are now resisting arrest. You are a threat to the greater shared public domain. It is my duty to incapacitate you in accordance with protocol dealing with any interface with a terrorist. A head shot is the only way to neut-"

Fred slipped in blood, a gun shot rang out, and the gun slid from his grasp and across the floor. He started to laugh again. And then he vomited.

Pontiff reached down to the floor where he saw the bottle. He picked it up. He looked over the desk slowly, and seeing that Fred was somewhat incapacitated, rose and walked over to him.

Pontiff stood directly above Fred. Puke hung from the suited man on the floor. Pontiff's neck was covered in blood. More had congealed around his ear.

"Go on," said Fred. "It makes no difference now. I'm finished. You're fin-"

Pontiff thrashed the bottle into Fred's face. It crumpled, his nose giving way. Pontiff then picked up a large chunk of broken glass and plunged it into Fred's neck. The spray of blood flooded Pontiff's gaping mouth as he ripped the shard out and plunged again repeatedly. When he had not the strength to carry on, he slumped to the floor. Relief.

Relief lasted about a second as Pontiff heard an ominous click behind him. He turned, covered in blood, to see Dave pointing a gun at him. Dave didn't quite have the strength to pull it but he was getting closer. So this was it. For fuck's-

Thmmmpppdd!

Dave fell to the floor revealing a gleeful looking Clem holding her pistol by its butt. "I think we should leave," she said.

She picked up Fred's pistol and fired a couple of rounds into the SwipeScanner. It buzzed, the door opened.

"Let's go."

Pontiff nodded, stunned. He looked round at the three bodies on the floor. He couldn't move.

"Come on!" shouted Clem, putting a hand in his armpit.

"I'm comen, Clem."

Pontiff staggered up. "What about our NIPSD cards?" he asked. "And shouldn't you change out your all-in-one?"

"We haven't got time for that. Just grab their guns."

Pontiff relieved the two Blackguard of their weaponry and picked up another couple of magazines. He removed Nigel's trousers and shirt and picked up Fred's jacket. He then exchanged footwear with Fred noticing they were the same make and size. With the soul of his new boot, Pontiff sunk the shard of glass deeper into Fred's neck.

"Clem," he called, pulling down his trousers. "Put these on. They might fit you. And these," he added, handing her Nigel's shirt and the suit jacket. Pontiff pulled on Nigel's trousers and they stepped outside.

Rain fell in torrents. They could hear Blackguard vans screaming through the night, sirens blaring in the distance. They knew they would be stopped if they drove off in Fred's car but spying Fred's laptop Pontiff smashed the window and pulled it out. He gave it to Clem who protected it from the downpour under the suit jacket. They walked off, in the rain, a glow on the horizon southwards.

# 34
# ROUND THE TWIST

*"IT HAS BEEN discovered that Head of Cow Operations, Frederick McVelly, was a double agent and part of the resistance movement.*

*"When McVelly absconded from a cabinet meeting late last night, Blackguard visited his flat where they discovered McVelly's mother on his doorstep. He had inadvertently sent her a message intended for the head of the terror group, Herr Enigma. By signing off as 'Ockham' he confirmed his own guilt.*

*"As Ockham, McVelly was alerting Enigma to the whereabouts of the murdering mother of Hellevue, Clementine Romain. Ockham, the key writer for the terror group, was none other than McVelly himself."*

"Why the fucking hell is this being reported?" shouted Cliffe from his sleeping bag.

He struggled up from the floor in the King's old bedroom. "(*suckin*) Who authorised this?"

The two Milipedes – also in sleeping bags – said nothing.

*"It has also been revealed that another member of the resistance was brought in to government custody as a result of operations in Hellevue. This man, Huwi Tenango, known as Don Coyote, was brutally murdered by McVelly in an act of self-preservation. It appears that last night McVelly tried to rescue the Hellevue Hero from custody. It is believed he is also part of the resistance. In the firefight McVelly was killed whilst the Hellevue Hero escaped with a woman, believed to be Clementine*

335

*Romain, the murdering mother of Hellevue. Their whereabouts
are unknown. One Blackguard died, another is critically ill."*

An announcement that Fred was a deserter, terrorist and pervert
was not what Cliffe had wanted.

"This makes us look weak!" he cried.

"I thought it was a good day to bury bad news," said a young aide.

"Jesus shit! I hardly call that burying! (*suck-in*) And I expressly told
you this should go nowhere near Garqi! (*suck-in*) In any case (*suck-in*), it sends the wrong message. We're trying to be inclusive! (*suck-in*)
We are not tracking down terrorists to kill them (*suck-in*), we're trying
to unite the country to fight the fucking Demoqristanis! (*suck-in*)"
Cliffe stormed off to the bathroom. "How can people be so incompetent
at a time like this?"

One of the brothers called him back.

"Er, sir. Garqi's on the news now."

"What's that fucker doing now?"

*"Eef, a year ago, you ad told dee man on dee street what would
be appeneen today, e wouldn't av believed you. In all honesty, e
would have laughed eet off as a joke. Laughed at you, probably.
Told you not to be so ridickoolus. Baat, be dat as it may, eet eez
appeneen. Ere we are. In truth, dee seismic events of last night
and today befit dee seismic events of dee last year. In fact, wid
all dat az appened in dis past year, opinion eez divided.*

*"Eet seems many people don't know whedder dey think what
eez transpireen eez a good thing or not. Dee announcement of
elections, suntheen I tried ard to get Cliffe to agree to, can now
only be viewed as desperate and opportunistic."*

Cliffe let out an agonised wail.

*"Cliffe's been caught wid his pants down and dat's where dey
will stay."*

Garqi started to walk towards Buckingham Palace, the camera
zooming out to reveal Demoqristani troops waiting patiently
for their cue.

*"Today we ask, are dee Government still relevant? In fact, does
a government even exist? President Cliffe eez asleep in dare
leaving a country at war wid eetself. I urge all Britannians to*

*vote for peace and welcome our liberators. I am throwing my full backeen behind dem and urge the country to do dee same."*

Back inside in the Palace –

"Where the fuck are our protection? (*suck-in*) What happened to the Blackguard?"

The young aide handed Cliffe a copy of the day's paper and a note from Garqi.

*"Read it and weep, bitches! Oli x"*

"We're fucked sir," said the elder Milipede. "The tabloids do tend to hold sway, don't they?" He carried on flicking through *The Rumour*. "There's a statement from Garqi here in which he says that once he realised how evil the Government was he relinquished his post."

Porridgemouth stood at the window. "I think you should have a look at this. We're surrounded."

Cliffe came to the window accompanied by a nervous stench emanating from his posterior.

"Fucking bitch!" he exclaimed as he saw Sherry run out of the main gate and hug Garqi. "(*suck-in*) She must be pissed and full of her meds."

\*\*\*

Godfrey and the RevKev awoke, amazed to still be alive.

"Must be divine intervention this place didn't get hit," said the Rev as he got up and pulled back the curtain. "Wow. Look at this."

With considerable effort Godfrey raised himself from his pit.

"Good grief, dear boy. Welcome to Dresden, eh?"

There was a knock at the door.

"Ye-es," called Godfrey.

One of their rescuers, a young man, popped his head round the door. "Just to let you know, breakfast's ready."

Godfrey and the Rev both nodded.

"Oh and electricity came back on half an hour ago and your mate's on telly. He's escaped."

"What?" shouted Godfrey. "When?"

"Last night apparently."

Godfrey made his way into the small den-cum-kitchen area as quickly as he could move his war-torn seventy year old body. His compromised mental threads were starting to reknit. The Rev followed close behind, and they soon discovered that the Hellevue Hero had an accomplice.

"That fucking extraordinary bastard!" shouted Godfrey, soon also digesting the revelation that *Ockham* was a government advisor. The Head of *The Cow*, no less!

Though McVelly's car had been found with an array of fake NIPSD cards his government-issue laptop was neither at his flat nor in his car. It was believed that the *Hellevue Hero* and the child murderer had the laptop, probably stolen to protect themselves. The identity of other members, like the editor, *Herr Enigma*, remained unknown.

As the Rev and Godfrey discussed what to do next, the machine-gun fire of events that characterised the morning soon delivered again.

"Je-"

"Careful" said the Rev.

"-umping Jack Flash!" shouted Godfrey at the TV.

The room descended into silence at the incredible events unfolding on the screen.

The leader of the Demoqristani forces was addressing Britannia from a rather grand location.

*"Good afternoon Britain! And how are we this fine day? The liberation is proving to be successful and you shall soon be free! I stand before you today, here Buckington Palais."*

There was an interruption.

The Demoqristani leader turned away from the stage and received some counsel from a familiar face.

*"I apology. Buckingham Palace."*

"Piers fucking Mormon!" shouted a CUF operative. "What the fuck's he doing there?"

"And there's Sherry!"

"No surprise there."

The Demoqristani leader continued.

*"We have captured Cliffe, those weird young political geek brothers and anyone else we found in there. But honestly, they*

*were in charge? How you say, Blimey! Your President Cliffe was
trying to escape into some hole, the little weasel, but we have
him now!"*

He paused and looked around.

*"I admit there is some superficial damage to this great palace.
We sorry for that,"* he said, accompanied by a nervous titter.

Bloody hell, thought Godfrey, this is all getting a bit bloody much
now. I mean really, a foreigner in the holy of holies?

*"But please, let me explain some of my reasoning, my moti-
vation, to come to your country and help you. I have always
held love for this great country. I always wanted to own Premier
League football team. I love tea. I love Monty Pyton. I could not
bear the thought of the British people being in bondage any
longer. I am liberal man. I had to act. And then we see him
massacring you. We come straight away!*

*"However, not only we come to save you but also the world. We
have knowledge that your evil dictator Heath Cliffe had plans to
renew Britannic Empire. Resources are low here, no? I see the
destitution you live in. We know your Mr Cliffe was putting
more money into military to launch strikes on neighbouring
countries to secure resources. It was the duty of a liberal,
civilised, developed country such as Demoqristan to act for the
good of the British people and the good of the world.*

*"Also, it was, **IS**, my express wish, that civil war be avoided.
Because I feared your great land was descending to that, I took
the decision that I did.*

*"But look, I fair man. Later, we have a debate, me and Cliffe. We
then have a vote. A phone-in perhaps."*

He laughed.

*"You decide! We'll put big screens up."*

He paused, turned to look at Garqi, who gave the thumbs up.

*"Ah good, that already started. Til later my beautiful Britann-
ians!"*

"Shall we go and survey the land, dear boy?" said Godfrey.

"I expect it's dangerous out there," responded the Rev.

"I expect it is. Booze, that's what we need."

"You're not wrong."

"Are you sure you pair of old codgers know what you're doing?" asked one of the CUF members assigned to protect them.

"Yeah," said another. "You won't last five minutes out there."

"Well, dear boys, we'll take our chances. But thanks for putting us up. You are in my mind if we are given the vote. Adieu."

Outside everything was detritus and destruction, undiluted chaos. Self-preservation ruled. There was a scurrying amid the rubble, armed kids, a total breakdown in order. Hellevue was very definitely under the control of no group in particular.

"Thank Goodness I am of the age at which I am nearly ready for the exit, dear boy. It'll certainly be interesting when the liberators get to this part of town!"

After a leisurely stroll through the carnage, they arrived at Godfrey's flat. Or rather, the space it used to occupy.

"Ah, good. I see mad radicals or Demoqristani bombers have put paid to that." He turned to the Rev. "Pub?"

"Certainly."

The Rev looked skywards and crossed himself.

During the night, The Forest Arms had become a haven from the pogrom, Brits rediscovering the blitz spirit in booze. As many were now homeless the pub had become a refuge and Godfrey and the Rev joined in, a soak in liquor the only answer to their ills. The general mood had exceeded hope and fear and landed at post-historical resignation.

It was approaching something like the old days, thought Godfrey, the Citizens here not affiliated to one group or other. There had been some fights, but generally people just wanted to drink and be numb. Zondyke Plethora helped in that regard and Godfrey, unable to locate his much-loved hallucinogens, decided to give it a test drive.

"Easy on that stuff," said the Rev. "We'll need our wits about us out there."

Suitably stiffened, they bought some milk bottles filled with wine and made for the door. Expecting the worst they swigged repeatedly at the wine, and wandered.

\*\*\*

Clem was still sleeping under the large dank pink blanket she had found. They had spent the night under it, cuddled up together in the doorway of a cycle repair shop having eschewed the homeless village of old and thinned hemp sacks. As Pontiff felt the fine graze of drizzle on his face he felt Patagonian bleak. His soggy clothes were embossed in permanent dirt and he could discern a sort of eggy, filthy smell. Not as obnoxious as sulphur, more like stale popcorn mixed with cold tea farts. He ached.

Pontiff was now almost entirely inclined to subscribe to his sister's philosophy. If he hadn't gone to Cliffe's inauguration and been arrested there was a good chance Clem would still be in custody and he would be no closer to knowing her whereabouts. Of course, there was still the issue of finding Ben. And the fact that he was a one-eared murderer.

He looked around for what supplies they had left. Having broken into a government alcohol shop the night before, they had helped themselves to hemp sachets of tobacco, rolling paper, a gallon container of beer, and a few edible items. In Fred's briefcase they had found some dried beef, potato crisps and a few bits of fruit. Pontiff was also delighted at the presence of another bottle of whiskeysquash. It was a bit rough, more burning than warming, but it was still good. Not as good as Rer's best, but good. He took a breakfast gulp.

Pontiff thought of what they had discussed the night before – their experiences of Life Camp, their similar impressions of Dr Zini and the Ratman, and what Clem had gone through in custody. Given a confession to sign she had demanded to see her son's body. When this was refused, she refused to sign. She was convinced Ben was alive, especially when she was told she could expect to be enrolled on some PSU courses. The two of them had worked out that while Pontiff was in solitary Clem had arrived at the same *LifeManagement4Life* facility.

They had also discovered on Fred's laptop extensive details of how he had masterminded the LibComs' rise to power and dictated their law making. There were journal extracts illustrating Garqi's role. They didn't know how they would use it, but they were sure it would be vital currency.

Reading **KARMATARMAK** files and articles written by *Ockham* was fine, interesting, amusing even, until the gravity of a young man fooling the whole country permeated their brains, and worse, that this young man had created such hell for both of them.

They accessed records of correspondence with Garqi, located footage of Pontiff's trip to *Rumour* HQ. Clem was rather impressed with his performance.

They also read Fred's early ideas for the *Hellevue Hero* news story he had sent to Garqi.

> **"Now that Miss Romain is in custody we can then commence the next stage of proceedings. I have just the man for you – a drunk, a Misaligned, a no hoper who we can manipulate."**

The *Pope at Life Camp!* folder had more written files and video.

*Violence for Popey!* contained scenes from Pontiff's final days at *LifeManagement4Life*, the beatings, the few hits he landed on Blackguard.

But it was *Dirty, Naughty People!* – the footage of his tryst with Zini, the exercise he thought had ensured his freedom – that reacquainted Pontiff with that familiar nausea sweeping through his soul. This was when it all got too much and he could investigate no longer. He hadn't cried for years. The last time had been when he realised his marriage was irreconcilable and that was a good while before they'd actually called it a day.

More positively, Clem had discovered the hospital at which Ben had been treated. It was unclear if he was still there now but at least they had a starting point. Now to find the Rev and Godfrey as well.

With all this on his mind Pontiff became aware of some movement next to him. Clem was stirring. And then he saw she was shaking, giving off silent sobs.

"Fuck me, y'awright?" he asked, putting his hand on the wall to steady himself. He crouched down next to her. Clem, unable to vocalise, slumped into him, crying openly. Pontiff manoeuvred an arm around her. He thought of Susan. Christ, was she truly OK? Married with an *IJP*? He hugged Clem closer, and thought of what she had told him – that she never once cried in custody. She hadn't cried the night before either. It had been her doing the comforting. For a few moments Clem's body jerked silently before the atmosphere was altered with an enormous eruption from Pontiff's gut. The belch shook them both.

"Fuck," drawled Pontiff. "Sorry."

A new jerking started in Clem. Laughter.

She pulled back from Pontiff, looked up at him, wiping remnant moisture from beneath her smudged eyes.

"And here I was thinking you were the perfect gent."

"Aye, sorry."

"And you've wiped your scabby, fucked ear all over my shoulder!"

Pontiff put his hand there.

"Nah. It's dry," he said, and took another gulp of whiskey.

"Do you need any more?" asked Clem, pulling away from Pontiff with a grin, hitting him on the arm.

"Dinnae worry about me sweetheart. I can go wi'e best of em."

"Gimme some then."

Clem swigged and handed the bottle back to Pontiff. She breathed in deeply, wiped her mouth with the back of her hand.

"God that's rough!"

"Aye. But it works."

Pontiff turned to Clem.

"You alright?" he asked.

She nodded and smiled.

He kissed her forehead.

"So, how do you want tae play this, Clem? Shall we go an find your wee boy?"

"Absolutely. The place is south of the river."

"So-?"

"So let's go and have a look at what's going on. We've got guns. We'll be fine."

Pontiff nodded.

"Right."

He leapt up with surprising agility and gracefully avoided landing on his injured toe.

"Do you need a hand getten up?" he asked Clem.

"Ah. Mr Chivalry's back. Even when pissed with a broken foot. But just worry about yourself, baldie. I'm not a fuckin invalid."

"Awright," said Pontiff with a smile.

He then watched Clem struggle to rise from under the damp blanket.

"Er, kind sir?" she said.

"Oh so now the lady wants ma help, eh?"

He helped her up and they held each other's gaze for a moment.

"Right," said Clem suddenly, putting a hand through her hair, and looking around to see what they should take with them. "Shall we?"

And so, freezing and damp, they strolled the streets again.

"Fuck me, all this ramblen. I feel like I'm part of the Kendal Mint Cake crew," said Pontiff, hacking into a cough. "Ma mucus tastes salty an'all."

"Come on old man," laughed Clem, linking her arm through Pontiff's.

As they walked they saw bodies lying everywhere and fires reduced to fizzing steam masses by the incessant rain.

And then they came across one still-burning fire, and a hardy woman selling tea.

"I've no lost ma faith in this country yet!" exclaimed Pontiff.

They paid the woman well for her troubles from Fred's wallet.

"Last night," said the woman, who didn't seem to recognise Pontiff nor make comment on his ear, "there was loads of fighting, looting, the usual. But now the Demoqristanis have total control of this area. They came here through this morning, capturing, killing or dispersing the resistance."

As they chatted, news filtered through that Cliffe had been captured. This didn't ruffle any of them greatly not did it seem to trouble the other brave souls out on the street. Yesterday there may have been elation. Now there were other things to worry about. The only surprising thing was that it had happened so fast.

"What do you want tae happen?" Pontiff asked the woman.

She closed her eyes, gave a weary shake of the head.

As Pontiff and Clem continued their walk they saw Demoqristani troops for the first time. Fittingly, they were congregated outside a *Life-Management4Life* Institute. "We are closing down all machinery of LibCom iron-fist rule!" shouted the army translator.

And then they set about liberating the social prisoners inside, prisoners that looked perfectly happy to be in there. Pontiff and Clem looked on as the *Misaligneds* were told to – *GO AND ENJOY YOUR FREEDOM NOW*. Freedom seemed a frightening prospect for some.

"You can imagine how unsettling it is," said Clem. "One minute you're being instructed on the reasoning behind National Alphabetisation, and the next you're being shoved around by someone with a limited grasp of English who you've just seen bayonette your favourite teacher."

"Aye. Especially when most of them have never seen a foreigner before."

"You are free, ugly or beautiful, this is your land again!" shouted a Demoqristani.

Pontiff and Clem watched as the stunned interred were ordered out into the dazzling early morning light of the new dawn.

"They look fairly underequipped for re-assimilation, wouldn't you say, Pont? Shock coupled with anxiety."

Having been released back into the wild, the *Misaligneds* of *Life-Management4Life* were awaking to a new country. The Government that had created the safety net some of them had so needed had disappeared. They were baffled and petrified in equal measures.

Then, incredibly, they saw Sharon Taylor.

"Wow, she's looking slim and hot!" said Clem.

"She must've hud *Pretty-Making*."

Pontiff recalled Godfrey's description of her vehement opposition to incarceration, but now, bizarrely enough, she seemed to believe what they had told her at the time, that she would thank them for it one day. And she was remonstrating with the liberating Demoqristanis to this effect. They wanted to try the guards and Life Technicians for acts against humanity. She wanted to thank the very same people for getting her life back on track.

After the troop had been led out, and the Life Technicians had been arrested for said crimes against humanity, some of the liberators went to douse the camp in petrol. They wanted to destroy the place of the *Misaligneds'* oppression and torture before their very eyes, make a symbolic gesture to demonstrate it was over.

One of the recently liberated spoke up.

"Erm, excuse me, I don't mean to talk out of turn, but I think what you are about to do is a bit unnecessary." He paused to light another cigarette from the burning embers of the one he had just smoked. "Surely you can put this place to good use. It's a bit of a waste to just destroy it, don't you think?"

A couple of the liberators looked at each other.

"That's not a bad idea actually," said the translator.

Huge numbers of homeless people were being created on an almost minute by minute basis. With bombs, civil war, housejacking by partisans of various persuasions and public transport a non-event, where would they all go? So literally minutes after being released, freed, liberated, the troop were led back into Life Camp.

"They'll probably have a better time of it than most us out here in the real world," said Clem. "Supplies, shelter."

"Look at that one," responded Pontiff. "He looks delighted, like he's goen home. What must these liberators think of us, eh?"

Sifting through the mood of mass uncertainty, Clem and Pontiff heard of the debate planned for later that afternoon. Huge crowds were making their way down to the Houses of Parliament to watch it unfold live while others watched in awe as huge screens were erected. The change was coming fast.

\*\*\*

Godfrey and the RevKev had rediscovered a touch of vim and had made it all the way to the banks of the Thames.

As the old boys perambulated the destroyed streets of the capital, the former was feeling surprisingly refreshed and clear-headed. They stopped to buy a paper, the special commemorative edition Cliffe had read just hours before.

### DEMISE OF A DICTATOR

There were the requisite unflattering images of Cliffe, and descriptions of his short-lived, ill-fated leadership.

"They got that out quick," said the Rev. "We haven't even had the debate yet!"

"I just wonder whether Garqi and Mormon weren't in on the whole deposition-liberation shindig," mused Godfrey, as the two wandered through the huge crowds. "I expect Garqi, in his Italian way, slimed his way into some deal. As for Mormon, well he just follows wherever his master takes him, doesn't he? I wouldn't be surprised if they head up some sort of consultancy-cum-ad-agency to spread the good news of Demoqristan, the official press cache to the new leaders, the spin advisors, on hand to help explain the need for these liberators to stick around for a little while in order to ensure an orderly transition of power."

Blackguard were conspicuous by their absence amid the multitude of screens, bunting and union jacks. There was a decent smattering of people. Just outside the Palace of Westminster, in Brian Haw's Commemorative Garden – named thus to prove the Government wasn't anti-protesting – Asif stood on a stage, his beaming smile a definite winner.

The Rev and Godfrey were stood thirty or so metres from the stage when Cliffe, looking haggard and scared and being booed like a pantomime villain, was led out onto the scaffold.

"OK, OK!" shouted Asif, smiling. "Thank you so much for coming. So good to see so many new friends in the crowd! As promise, here is debate. As I am gentleman, and we are in home of gentleman, Great Britain, I let that fuckwit Cliffe go first. Please, ugly man, tell us a story."

"I have only a few things to say (*suck-in*). Dear Britannians (*suck-in*), I implore you to see that these liberators are not here to liberate (*suck-in*). Rather, they have come to incarcerate (*suck-in*), incarcerate you again in the old ways (*suck-in*)."

"OK Heath, thank you. Very good."

Asif clapped, briefly and camply. He then laughed.

"Incarcerate? Ha. I not know all words but I know dis one. But I tell you, Great Britain, after a period of reindustrialisation in the Middle East, we are now ready to give our gift to the world. We know what everyone wants and needs. This liberation is to restore a universal human value – Consumerism!"

"No thank you," said Godfrey to a young woman selling commemorative candles.

"A basic human desire, what everyone in the world, irrespective of culture, creed and tradition believes in!" continued Asif.

"Citizens, do not be so blind!" shouted Cliffe. "(*suck-in*) How can the Demoqristanis demand the world adheres to their philosophy on the correct mode of existence? (*suck-in*)"

"That's a bit rich coming from a British leader!" rejoined Asif.

"They want to sell you useless goods that will return you to the era of illness and disease! (*suck-in*) You will be slaves (*suck-in*), diseased slaves! (*suck-in*) All they want is your money!"

"Ha! This Cliffe is both ugly and a hypocrite!"

"Well he is a politician," said the Rev.

"In our pursuit of the LibCom hierarchy," continued Asif, "we have visited a string of governmental grace-and-favour abodes and discovered unbridled luxury, gadgets galore and details of second homes in the countryside. These 'Liberal Compassionates' *(Hair finger spasm)* were so keen on the virtue of you, the common man, living in austerity, because they wanted everything for themselves! They urged you to live modestly yet watched footage of you on their plasma tellies! We will give plasma tellies back to you!"

Cliffe shook his head in wobbly rage.

"Do you not remember the great piles of junkmail that promised incredible offers on holidays, two-for-one pizzas and loans? (*suck-in*) It is incredible we ever allowed so catastrophic and useless a system (*suck-in*), and believed it a necessary offshoot of civilised society! (*suck-in*) We ended that waste, waste that led to millions dying of *Plasticitis* (*suck-in*), and that is precisely what this invader wants to bring back! (*suck-in*) All this energy is unnatural!"

"How can it be unnatural?" demanded Asif. "It's created on earth! You're the unnatural one. Let's have show of hands."

The voting was unclear.

"OK, I win," said Asif. "Ugly, you lose!"

\*\*\*

Pontiff – partially disguised under a hood and Clem – wearing Fred's suit jacket and a scarf taken from a smashed-in shop window – had missed the debate as they walked down to Westminster. Now they found themselves in the Haw Commemorative Garden just in time for the Demoqristanis' coup de grace. Back onto the stage came Cliffe. Incredibly, it was snowing as he was led out onto the gallows, Cliffe shouting something about this being evidence of climate change.

"Do not let them destroy all our good work! If you would only see what I, we (*sharp intake of breath, bottom lip vacuumed-in*) were trying to do for you. You ingrates!"

Did Cliffe deserve what was about to happen to him? It was hard to tell. As the noose was fitted round his neck, a slew of charges were read out. And so having been captured earlier that day Cliffe was now to feel some LibCom efficiency of justice.

Yesterday inaugurated, today hanged.

Tough racket, politics, thought Pontiff.

Some of the onlookers seemed to think it quite fitting that the man who had been partly responsible for the reduction in trials by jury would receive no trial and only a loose interpretation of treason.

"For cavalier riding roughshod over the Britannic peoples."

"No!" screamed Cliffe.

"Be brave Heath, ya bass!" shouted Pontiff.

As Cliffe's neck was throttled by the noose and cracked, some of the crowd cheered. Some filmed it on mobile phones as the henchman from Arabia looked on.

Others in the crowd found it all a bit bloody much actually.

"Someone needs to tell these people that's not what we do here."

"They'll have us wearing veils next."

"I'm sure these cultural differences will iron themselves out."

"OK," said Asif. "Let's hear from the crowd."

"Will there be an end to the NIPSD programme?"

"Are we to be non-alphabetised?"

"Can I buy a new phone?"

"Will the Monarchy be restored?"

"The answers to all these questions will be revealed in due course."

"So that'll be a no then," said Godfrey.

"By pitching up over here, do you not think you are responsible for the mess we are now in?" shouted a man in the crowd. "With beatings and beheadings rife I think most people, regardless of their political bent, are less than impressed by your invasion."

"Who said that? It is not invasion! It is liberation. Anyway, you had bloody march about it at which thousands were killed or captured. You must have wanted us to intervene!"

"This has gotta be the first instance of change coming about by a protest march," said the RevKev, as the man in the crowd was led away.

"Well quite. And even so, a carte blanche to invade?" responded Godfrey. "It's never as straightforward as these liberators think, is it?"

"First the football team, now the Government."

Mormon, the token English coach in the team, sidled up to the Liberator-in-Chief to answer the next round of questions on his new boss's behalf.

"Is it true that farmers have been attacked by Demoqristani troops in tribalised areas for refusing to trade their goods?"

"There are many who jealously guard their crops at the expense of other's lives," responded Mormon. "These people have a responsibility to feed the rest of the land. Unity is our goal."

"Well these liberators better start getting food on people's tables otherwise the situation will only get worse. It's such a mess."

"Yeah," voiced another in the crowd, "but it's our mess. And that seems to be the growing consensus, doesn't it? How long are these occupiers planning on staying?"

"Growing consensus?" shouted Asif over Mormon's attempts to respond. "We've only been here a day! Give us some time. How you say, bloody hell, please! I think we achieved quite a lot so far, actually! Our avowed hope is that we can hand back areas to British control. It's going to be a hell of a task bringing unity back to this once sceptered isle. But as Piss say, unity is our goal. Elections will take place as soon as is..."

He looked at Mormon.

"Practicable," said the advisor.

"Prasti- what?"

"Practicable."

"Practicing?"

"Practicable."

"Ah, yes practicable. This difficult word (*nervous titter*). But it's not all doom and gloom, though. For starters, we going end ban on big gatherings. But streetgig no return willy-nilly." He motioned at Mormon to explain the fine detail. "Piss."

"It's Piers."

"Piers! Ha! Sorry (*another nervous titter*)."

Mormon nodded and turned back to the crowd.

"What Asif means is that tonight there will be a nationwide Freedom Streetgig."

"Oh Christ," said Godfrey. "No doubt the practicalities of that will be Arabian henchmen poking us in the ribs and slapping us if we don't laugh."

"Yes," agreed the Rev. "Like many countries before us, we too will find out that liberation does not mean more freedom."

Garqi lurked in the background, barking orders to photographers and journalists. Once the constellation was in order the Demoqristani leader returned to the lectern.

"Finally, I want to address all breakaway and resistance groups. You must cease your violence and open lines of communication with us. It is together that we can rebuild this great country for the wonderful people that live here."

"Ah," said Clem, in another part of the crowd nearby, "this is good news. Just like our politicians he butters us up while taking the piss out of our intelligence."

"We will not be re-introducing parliamentary politics straightaway," continued Asif. "A period of stability is required. We are aware that splinter groups throughout the land are vowing they will continue to be engaged in guerrilla warfare, but the simple truth is that they all remain as illegal as they were under the Government of the Liberal Compassionate party. What we welcome is frank and open dialogue and no violence. If parties want to be considered for the parliamentary process, they have to demonstrate to us their total commitment to non-violence. If you do not co-operate, we will be forced to take appropriate action. OK, that is all. Thank you!"

"Aye," agreed Pontiff. "If you close your eyes and ignore the accent, it could be anyone up there."

"All new regimes start with bright hopes," said Godfrey as the crowds started to disperse, "a sweeping away of the old notions that had left things stagnant, stuck in their ways. But in time this optimism wanes as a new order is implemented and becomes immovable. The refreshing cool gust of change becomes like the trail of a fart locked in a biscuit tin. The fresh ideas become their own frustrating inevitability, and so the cycle starts again as we crave change. Eventually these revolutionaries become authoritarians in need of deposition. And who do we put in their place?"

"Another bunch of half-wits probably," said Clem.

Godfrey turned in an instant. A smile of undiluted joy and eyes filled with longing swept through his features. Months of worry were lifted.

"Clem, my dear girl, Clem!"

Godfrey squeezed Clem tight to him, tears cascading down his cheeks. The Rev removed his glasses and rubbed his eyes before he too bear-hugged Clem, lifting her up. Pontiff didn't miss out either, Godfrey wrestling him practically to the turf in jubilation.

"Where on earth is the rest of your ear, dear boy?"

\*\*\*

Despite the early flurry of snow, it was now a glorious summer evening, the sun burning brilliantly.

Pontiff, Clem, Godfrey and the RevKev had been halfway up the first run of the London Eye's circular voyage when it had suddenly ground to a halt and the lights had gone out. Not long before, as they had tried to make their way south to the hospital in which Clem believed Ben to be, they had been cordoned off by Demoqristani troops. Both sides of the river were heavily fortified by the liberators and to demonstrate that the average Briton was delighted with the day's festival, everyone in the area had been sent up the London Eye to celebrate. And so here the four were, sat in their carriage, swinging in the breeze.

Having looked through Fred's laptop, been told of the escape – and what happened to Pontiff's ear – Godfrey and the Rev were both up-to-speed. How to use this information had not been decided. For now, they were just glad to all be together, though locating Ben was still on everyone's minds.

They paraded the carriage, drinking, looking at what remained of the great pillars of British Democracy. Big Ben was a shell, smouldering and blackened and next to it stood the relic of a still burning Houses of Parliament. Westminster Palace had been partially usable but anti-immigrants had firebombed it to avert the very real and unedifying prospect of foreigners using it.

"Jesus," said Pontiff, looking at the wreckage on the other side of the Thames. "D'you think we're safe up here?" Another terrorist attack at any moment seemed a distinct possibility.

"My dear friends," said Godfrey, "here we sit on the precipice of change. Soon we will see the re-opening of borders and nations reac-quainting themselves with old foes, renewing old hostilities. It is a testament, is it not, to the great resourcefulness of humankind that everyone managed to find enemies closer to home, in accordance with the limitations of the times. Now we're going to be re-civilised, no doubt. The arms race and property development will resume once more! Bring on the renewal of the global interchange of weapons, bombs, ideologies and electrical goods! It is surely a vain hope to think the good burghers of Britain will not renew their desire for all things ephemeral. It *is* persuasive."

"Yep," said the Rev. "It won't be long til we revert to a polluting throb once more with the promise of consumerism and round the clock electricity."

"Well," continued Godfrey, "as winter approaches with its prover-bial cold snap, the Demoqristanis' reintroduction of energy and heating will undoubtedly be well received. But if we are to be restored to our previous existence, and we opt for, or rather, have opted for on our behalf, the resumption of widespread electricity usage, what price free-dom?"

"We may even find ourselves pining for these days!" laughed the Rev.

"It's like our very own Ground Zero," said Clem, looking over the river to the burning relics of British power. "Who's gonna liberate us next? The French?"

"Yes," said Godfrey smiling, "it is most likely the road to sedition will have to be travelled again. Of course, we'll never reach the end. Every corner takes us onto a new road as long and unforgiving as the last. We've been there before and we'll be there again. And just when we think we've reached the end, we'll turn onto it once more, its circularity sending us round the bend at every available opportunity."

He paused for a swig of wine, smiled to himself.

"But the cyclical nature of life is comforting. Reminds us that these things have a habit of sorting themselves out."

"So you're sayen dinnae worry?" Pontiff asked.

"Worry? I wouldn't dream of it, dear boy."

# THE END

## Acknowledgements

First, to Sky Branagan. As you once said, that I've enlisted a sort of quasi-editor who can't spell and whose grammar is appalling is satire in itself. But for your general vibe guidance and being a great sounding board, I doff my hat to you.

To me Ma. So much appreciation for housing me at a crucial moment (along with keeping me in booze and food at said crucial moment), and for the unwavering support.

To Josh, The Man With The Pan, my gratitude for designing a fantastic cover – despite my continually giving you misinformation.

To Wilma, for reading the novel in its entirety in an early draft, and to Driller, Scan, The Welsh Wizard, Whippet and Yassir for reading the various extracts I shoved in your general direction. To you all, thanks for your time, patience and constructive feedback.

To Business Dad. Thanks for always reminding me I'm doing the right thing.

To Wine Bastard. Vielen Dank for the trips to the outer cosmos that kept me on the straight and narrow.

And finally, I raise my glass to Sigmund Fraud, my publisher (and now friend), and a chance drunken conversation in a pub in North London.

# Acknowledgements

CPSIA information can be obtained
at www.ICGtesting.com
Printed in the USA
LVOW04s2000211016
509751LV00008B/514/P